DEMON SONG

Tor Paranormal Romance Books by
C. T. Adams and Cathy Clamp

THE SAZI
Hunter's Moon
Moon's Web
Captive Moon
Howling Moon
Moon's Fury
Timeless Moon
Cold Moon Rising
Serpent Moon

THE THRALL
Touch of Evil
Touch of Madness
Touch of Darkness

WRITING AS CAT ADAMS
Magic's Design
Blood Song
Siren Song
Demon Song

CAT ADAMS

DEMON SONG

A Tom Doherty Associates Book New York

This is a work of fiction. All of the characters, organizations, and events portrayed in this novel are either products of the author's imagination or are used fictitiously.

DEMON SONG

A Tor Book
Published by Tom Doherty Associates, LLC
175 Fifth Avenue
New York, NY 10010

www.tor-forge.com

Tor® is a registered trademark of Tom Doherty Associates, LLC.

Library of Congress Cataloging-in-Publication Data

Adams, Cat.
    Demon song / Cat Adams.—1st ed.
        p. cm.
    "A Tom Doherty Associates book."
    ISBN 978-0-7653-2496-2
    1. Bodyguards—Fiction.   2. Magicians—Fiction.   3. Demonology—
Fiction.   I. Title.
    PS3601.D3697D43 2011
    813'.6—dc22

                                                          2010036116

First Edition: March 2011

Printed in the United States of America

0   9   8   7   6   5   4   3   2   1

DEDICATION AND ACKNOWLEDGMENTS

As always, we dedicate this book to our favorite two men, Don Clamp and James Adams. We would also like to thank our terrific agent, Merrilee Heifetz, and our editor, Melissa Ann Singer. We'd also like to acknowledge Jennifer Escott and Melissa Frain, for all their hard work, as well as all the behind-the-scenes people at both Writers House and Tor Books, who make the creations of our imagination into reality. To the assistants, receptionists, art, promo, sales, accounting, and every other department we might not know exists—*thank you*. You guys *rock*!

Thanks also to our family, friends, and readers. You make this not only possible, but fun.

TO OUR READERS

Welcome back to the world of Celia Graves. We're very excited to bring you this new episode in her adventures. In some ways, this book marks a turning point in her life. While she will continue to be a professional bodyguard, her role in investigating problems, rather than just being swept away by them, will grow and shift. We hope you enjoy all the new people you'll meet in this book. They'll continue to be a big part of Celia's life. For better and worse.

DEMON SONG

1

You can't turn off intuition after you've spent years developing the sense, honing it to a razor's edge. I could feel *something* gathering among the seemingly innocent racks of clothing. The voices of my two best friends in the world faded into a background buzz, and I found myself shifting the way I was holding the shirts I'd planned to take to the dressing room so that I could use my hands if needed.

My eyes moved from person to person in rapid succession while my feet backed toward a wide aisle that could be easily navigated. The bored but patient father of a tween girl wasn't a threat. Neither was the mother with one child in a stroller and another held by the hand. Clerks moved among the holiday-festooned racks like ballerinas performing *The Nutcracker*; I tracked them briefly. The best salespeople are often empaths or psychics. They're attuned to those shoppers who want approval—codependents in the process. They weren't the cause of my alarm, either.

Or were they?

Nothing I could see accounted for the tingling of my skin.

It forced me to raise the bar and start checking the area over again, which made me noticeable.

"What's wrong, Celia?" Dawna had taken one look at my face and begun to spill panic from her pores. The whisper from her perfectly colored and edged lips held an edge of fear. Things didn't used to bother her as much, but she had been attacked recently and was still a little skittish.

She wasn't the only recent victim. The part of me that had been transformed by a vampire bite could feel her fear, taste it, smell it. While my reaction wasn't as strong as it might be closer to sunset, it still made my vision go into the sort of hyperfocus that makes vampires one of the apex predators in the world. Dawna wasn't going to be my victim, though. Not ever.

Then I spotted him. I shook my head slightly and transferred the hangers from my hand to Dawna's exotically tanned one, motioning her toward the dressing room. She obeyed instantly, grabbing a few additional random skirts before pulling the third member of our group, Emma Landingham, toward the sheltered hallway. Emma was obviously reluctant. Dawna was practically having to drag her away. It was unlike her—usually she was very practical about avoiding danger—and made me a wonder just what she was up to. Emma had obviously been trying to get up the nerve to tell or ask me something all day. But even when I'd asked her directly, she'd changed the subject and acted evasive.

Whatever her problem was, it would have to wait. Trouble was brewing.

I'd believed the teenage boy in the next department to be the older brother of the bouncing tween girl—just like he'd planned. But once I concentrated my vampire sight on him, I could see that his energy was all wrong. He wasn't a bored sibling. He was following them, just at the edge of their comfort zone . . . not so close as to be noticeable, but enough that he became invisible, part of a family unit.

Was he after the girl? I watched where he looked whenever eyes weren't on him. No, he had no interest in her, which relaxed me just a bit. His focus was on the jewelry counter. Instead of being cluttered and difficult to reach like in most department stores, this one offered a straight shot to an exterior door and, worse, was being restocked, so the display cases were open. The girls' clothing department was a short, straight walk down the aisle from jewelry, which made his choice simple.

I started scanning for store detectives but saw none. Was it shift change? Were they cutting back on personnel? That seemed stupid this close to Christmas. Maybe the boy knew something I didn't, because he started dissolving his act. His hand moved instinctively toward the pocket of his hoodie as he started looking for threats. Either he didn't see me or he didn't consider me worrisome. His mistake. The rectangular lump I spotted in his pocket was similar to the one under my jacket, but I was betting he didn't have a concealed-carry permit in his wallet. The weapon turned a simple, impulsive snatch and grab into armed robbery with possible injuries.

The problem was that I wasn't a police officer or an employee of the store. I was just a self-employed bodyguard who happened to be at the wrong place at the right time. Even under a broad definition of citizen's arrest, I couldn't detain

him, disarm him, or hurt him without risking arrest myself . . .
and the possible loss of my license.

But I also couldn't let him rob the store and possibly shoot
someone.

I hate my life sometimes.

I started toward him, hoping I would think of something
between misses' petites and jewelry. Without making my movements obvious, as I neared the shoe department I let my face
light up at a particularly sparkly dress sandal—which actually
was really cute—and headed for it. The shoes were directly
between the would-be robber and the slender young clerk
crouched behind the open display cases, oblivious to her pre-
dicament.

My entire focus was on the teenager as I increased my
speed. I might not be able to pull my gun or throw him to the
elegantly patterned tile with a flying tackle, but I could inter-
cept him and strongly suggest he find another way to occupy
his afternoon. His every movement seemed like frames of
stop-motion animation thanks to my supernatural sight, so I
didn't worry that he would pull his gun before I could react.
But I hadn't expected that when my vision slipped into vampire mode the rest of me would, too. In fact, it wasn't until I
stepped directly in front of him and put out a hand to stop him
that I realized my skin had taken on a pale green glow. A
glance into a nearby mirror showed me that my lips had pulled
back to reveal fangs.

The look on his face was priceless when he finally turned
his attention from the glittering gold and diamonds to see who
had bumped straight into his chest.

"Holy crap!" His eyes went wide and his face got nearly as pale as mine. He backpedaled so fast he stumbled against a display of boots and spilled to the ground, taking the whole carefully arranged stack of red and green boxes with him. The battered 9mm fell from his pocket and was lost among the boxes of size 8s.

Before he could react, I was crouched down next to him and reaching for his arm. With a smile on my face, as though I was helping him up, I pulled him close. The scent of his fear made me remember that I hadn't had a nutrition shake before we came to the mall. But I had to ignore that and concentrate on what I was doing. I'd love to say it was easy, but it wasn't. Bloodlust is nothing to be casual about. I found myself staring at his neck, watching the warm glow of energy trapped under supple skin. So much energy, and my stomach was so very empty. I shuddered and forcibly moved my eyes from his neck to his face.

His wide eyes took in my fangs and probably now red eyes before coming to rest on the .45 Colt nestled under my arm, revealed when my jacket swung open as I reached for him. Oh, and let's not forget the long line of drool dripping onto the plush carpeting. Mustn't forget the drool.

He struggled to pull away, but there's really no way to break a supernatural grip unless you also have superstrength. My voice became a hiss normally reserved for bad things in dark alleys: "I know what you're planning, and I'm sick and damned tired of guys like you making my clothes cost more so the store can recoup the losses from theft. You are going to get your lazy ass out of this mall right this second and find a legal way to make a living, or I swear on everything holy that I'll find you some cold, lonely night and make you regret it." I parted my lips so he could get a good look at what would be chasing him. No, I wouldn't really eat him or drain his blood. I don't plan to *ever* try human blood. It could be that one straw that breaks me. But I could scare him really well.

In fact, I already had. His blood had retreated so far from his face that he didn't even smell good anymore. His white lips opened, but only a squeak came out.

I raised my brows and leaned close enough to smell the scent of liquid courage on his breath. "Got it?"

He nodded, slowly at first and then in a rush of movement that gave him the appearance of a bobblehead doll. "Yeah. Got it."

Leaning back, I pulled him to his feet as I stood. "Good."

He didn't so much run out of the store as scrabble, using both hands and feet. The guard who had finally come to investigate the commotion noted the boy's guilty exit and raised a walkie-talkie to his lips. Whatever he said caused the security cameras to spin in the boy's direction and follow him out of the store.

I was so busy watching all this that I didn't notice the father of the tweenage girl shooting holy water at me until the stream hit me in the face. Sadly, I've come to expect being doused in holy water and having crosses shoved against my chest in the past few weeks. The fangs sort of give the impression *I'm* the threat, rather than the punk I'd just stopped. Fancy that.

"Hello! How rude was that?" Dawna had arrived and was at her touchy best. She tends to translate adrenaline into confrontation once she forces her way past her fear. She simultaneously pushed away the man's water gun and handed me a stack of tissues from her purse. "Do you see anyone on fire here? She just stopped a robbery. A little gratitude would be nice."

"A robbery? What robbery?" The man's eyes went wide, moving from the doorway where the kid in the hoodie was having his hands cuffed by the boys in blue to the guard using a hankie to pluck a semiauto pistol from among the boxes of boots. Finally, his gaze landed on me, the pale lady with red eyes and fangs—the good guy who was patting her face carefully to avoid smearing her makeup.

"Jeez, Dad." The girl at his side rolled her eyes and crossed slim arms over her chest. "It's broad daylight. How could she be a bat? And don't you watch the news or anything?" She turned to me. "You're Celia Graves, aren't you?"

Her father lowered his eyes to the floor and grabbed her elbow, guiding her away from me with a reddened face. At least he had the dignity to mutter a soft, "Thanks, sorry," as he walked past.

"Please don't leave the store, sir," the guard called after him. "We might need to talk to you later."

I was already pulling my wallet out of my purse. Before the guard even asked for it, I'd handed over my bodyguard license and carry permit. He raised brows a little at that and only then noticed the slight bulge under my arm. I obliged by discreetly opening my jacket. He wrote down my information on a pad before handing back the two documents and then dipped his head toward my arm. "Nice tailoring . . . and I appreciate the discretion. We'll call if we need a statement. Thanks for your help."

The shrug was automatic as I tucked my wallet back into the messy depths of butter-soft leather. "Discretion keeps people like you handing *back* the permits." It's why I pay big bucks for custom blazers. Nobody's supposed to notice the gun, and I keep it holstered until needed. It wasn't needed today. "Oh, and you might consider junking up the aisle next to jewelry. It's a pretty attractive target."

He nodded and started to walk at a brisk pace toward the exit, probably to turn over the gun to the cops.

I turned to where Emma was swearing under her breath, apparently realizing that she hadn't predicted the robbery attempt—a hard thing for a clairvoyant. But hey, not every event is worth a vision. I don't know why she stresses over it. "I'm going to need something to eat . . . and soon. I got a little twitchy just now. Let's hit the juice bar when we're done here."

The three of us have started using "twitchy" to signify that I wanted to chomp on someone's neck. It sounds a little less threatening to people on the street. "Here you go." Dawna, bless her heart, pulled a bottle of a meal replacement shake from inside her tiny purse, where it should never have been able to fit. But she always manages to find handbags that resemble TARDISes in their ability to hold more things than they should. Sadly, the drink was banana flavored. I loathe bananas.

"Thanks, but I'd rather wait for something not so . . ."

"Eww, banana. How can you stand those things?" Emma and I shared more than a few tastes, which I was discovering now that I was getting to know her better. We'd been friendly acquaintances for a while, but it wasn't until our shared friend Vicki Cooper was murdered recently that we'd gotten close.

"Maybe you'd prefer chocolate." The voice behind me froze me in my tracks and the appearance of a bottle of chocolate Ensure over my shoulder made me shudder. The man who owned the bland, helpful voice was neither bland nor helpful. People disappeared when he was around. Unfortunately, I owed him for saving my life. He managed to make sure I wasn't staked and beheaded after the bat attack and covered my butt later when I needed it.

I still didn't know why.

"Thanks, Jones." I kept my voice blandly pleasant. I didn't trust the man as far as I could throw him and had no plans to ingest anything that had ever been in his possession. But I took the bottle, over the wide-eyed objections of my friends, who were vigorously shaking their heads and mouthing the word "no" at me.

I wanted to prove a point. Smiling, I gave the bottle a little squeeze, just a little gentle pressure. Just as I expected, one side sprang a leak. What a shock. I turned to see Jones smiling at me. He's not much to look at—not handsome or ugly, neither tall nor short, he moves with easy grace that's not threatening. He's the kind of man who would easily disappear in a crowd. Literally. Not only did he have mind magic, but I'd actually seen him disappear—a trick only the strongest mages seem to be able to manage. I returned his smile and handed back the soggy bottle. "So, what'd you inject into in it, Jones? Would I keel over dead in a few minutes or just pass out in traffic and roll the car?"

Emma was glaring at him now. She didn't like him, even if her brother Kevin worked with him.

He put a hand over his heart and offered a hurt-puppy face. "You wound me, Graves. Can't you believe it's just a defective bottle?"

I let out a small chuckle. "That depends. If I pour it on a potted plant, will it sizzle like stir-fry?"

"Ooh," he said appreciatively. "No, but that's an interesting image. All this would do would make the plant damp." At my raised brows he added, "Well, honestly, plants don't really *sleep*, do they?"

Knockout drug. Okay. "So, why are you here, Jones? Or is this something you do for entertainment on the weekends—take time off of killing to wander around the mall offering women mickeys?"

He smiled and it made him actually stand out. He would probably clean up well. He noticed himself in the mirror behind me and turned the smile off like he was flicking a switch. "I shouldn't find you as entertaining as I do, you know. Dangerous for both of us. But you should already know why I'm here. Unless . . . Emma hasn't done as she promised."

Dawna and I turned as one to stare at Emma. "You're working with *Jones?* What the hell, Emma!"

She glared at him again, but he was nonplussed. Then she turned back and met my eyes. "I'm not working with him. And I didn't make any promises. I asked him for help. I wanted to ask you, Celia, but I . . . I was afraid."

Okay, that hurt. "I've worked really hard so you would never be afraid of me, guys."

Her slender arms crossed over her chest and her eyes went to the floor at my feet. "I know; I know. It's just . . ."

Jones let out an annoyed sound. "He's going to be dead before you finally get around to spitting it out, you know. We're already hours late and sneaking in is only going to get tougher after dark."

His words were soft but utterly serious. I turned my head and my friends did as well. "Who will?"

His hands were tucked in his pockets, casually. But his eyes . . . those eyes held anger, worry, and something dark and dangerous that I wouldn't want to cross. Ever. He raised his chin toward Emma and I felt my stomach tie in knots. "Her brother. Still want to shop?"

Oh, fuck a duck.

2

A pained sound from Emma forced me to turn her way. I almost wished I hadn't. How could I stare into her terrified face and still tell Jones no? Because I wanted to. I was angry beyond words at Kevin. He and his father had kidnapped me, trussed me up, and offered me up to a demented siren who wanted me dead. Yes, Emma's life had been at stake, and yes, they had had a plan to save us both. But I would have volunteered to help if they'd only *asked*. I was still hurt and insulted at their behavior, especially since I'd considered Kevin and Warren to be two of my closest friends.

Now I knew why Emma had been so hesitant all day. She'd rightly assume my first instinct would be to say no. Plus, Kevin's a werewolf as well as a black-ops commando. There isn't much he can't handle. I couldn't imagine what I could do that he couldn't do for himself. Still . . .

"What happened?"

Instead of answering, Jones turned and walked away. I was guessing he didn't want to discuss whatever it was in the middle of the store, which made sense. I followed at his heels and

Emma and Dawna followed me in turn. Our own little parade, without the floats.

The sun was right in our eyes as we opened the door. Damn. I'd thought it was earlier than that. Had we really been shopping long enough for sunset to approach without my noticing?

Jones walked straight to a nondescript gray sedan at the edge of the parking lot. I caught up to him so we didn't look like we were playing crack the whip. "Jingle Bells" was playing from loudspeakers outside the store. Cool ocean winds and my ever-present flock of seagulls made the whole situation totally surreal. Even Jones looked up to watch the white birds swooping and dancing in the air above our heads.

"You have a very weird life, Graves. Did the gulls follow you before the siren blood activated?"

I shook my head. "The most attention seagulls paid to me before was to poop on my car. Can you see why me sneaking up on *anything* is impossible? My freaking feathered entourage goes everywhere. Can't someone else help you with this?"

"I've already tried everyone else." Emma caught up to us; she sounded both frustrated and afraid. "I had a vision last night. One of the strongest since I saw the vampires attacking you in the alley. I didn't even know Amy had been captured, but Kevin went to get her out. She made it out safely, but they caught Kevin. Unfortunately, I didn't know where he was— who *they* were. I just saw bars and heard screaming. I asked Dad, but he couldn't find out anything. So . . . well, Jones was all I could think of."

"And I found him. But there's no chance of getting him out without your help."

My head shook of its own accord. "I find that hard to believe and it's even harder to believe that Kevin would want me involved."

Emma smacked me on the shoulder, so apparently she was no longer afraid of me. "Celia! If Kevin needs help, we have to help him. He'd do the same for us."

I didn't let my jaw drop in shock, even though the comment deserved it. I didn't even laugh sarcastically. Instead, I took a deep breath and let it out slow. *For you, Emma. He'd move the world for* you. *Not* us. I knew exactly where I stood with him—somewhere slightly lower than dirt.

I was still so angry with him, so hurt. Part of me wanted him to suffer. But another part, which I prayed every day was still the larger portion, wanted to rise above the pettiness and show Kevin and his father, Warren Landingham, what true friendship was. But it had only been three weeks since the night they'd betrayed me, and I wasn't sure I was ready to face them.

Jones was watching me with an odd expression. He leaned on the car door and crossed his arms over his chest. "I have to admit you've surprised me, Graves. I expected I'd have to hold you back, not convince you to help. Can you at least tell me where he is in the facility?"

I felt myself rear back in surprise and the looks Dawna and Emma gave me said they were clueless as well. "What facility? How am I supposed to know where he is?"

Jones raised his brows like he didn't believe me. Apparently he believed I was kidding and was about to announce that I'd take him straight to Kevin. But that wasn't going to happen. I stared at Jones while the sun continued to lower and my stomach growled. My gaze moved from his eyes to his neck. His body started to glow faintly and I felt my breathing growing shallow and my muscles tensing. He very carefully didn't move, but his center of gravity shifted just a bit, preparing.

"Okay, this is getting ridiculous!" Dawna finally exclaimed, exasperation plain in her voice. She grabbed my hand and shoved the yellow bottle into it. "You. Drink this before you go nuts. It's been nearly four hours since you ate and you exerted yourself with that robber. Hold your nose if you have to." She turned to Jones.

"You. Tell them why Kevin might die and what facility he's at. I'm going to go back inside the mall and get us *all* something to eat. Apparently it's going to be a long night—whether you plan to take me and Emma along with you or if we're just waiting by the phone." With that, she turned and started to jog back toward the mall entrance.

I shuddered and blinked and then grimaced at the bottle. She was right, of course, but I didn't have to like it. Jones was already starting to look yummy, and that would be counterproductive on a number of fronts. I twisted off the lid, held my nose, and literally poured the drink down my throat, successfully avoiding most of my taste buds. I managed not to choke or gag, which was a plus.

Jones sighed, then opened the back door of the car and pulled out a sealed four-pack of chocolate Ensure, still in shrink-wrap. He tossed it toward me, but I let the bottles hit the ground at my feet. I'd wait for Dawna. Her I trust.

Emma spoke, her voice filled with anger fueled by fear: "Where is my brother? You still haven't told me. You owe him your life, you know."

"Several times over," Jones agreed. "But I still find it difficult to believe Celia doesn't already know the details. I thought all you'd have to do is mention you 'saw' the capture and she'd be racing to his side."

"Believe it," said a new voice. I jumped. I couldn't help it. Even with my super new senses I hadn't heard our newest member approaching. Damn it. I hate it when real vampires join the party. I hissed and moved back as Edgar, an extraordinarily powerful vampire, simply appeared in the shadow of a nearby palm tree.

If you saw Edgar walking the streets of L.A., you'd assume he was an ordinary businessman on his way home from the office. As long as you didn't catch sight of the fangs peeking out from under his upper lip, you'd never have a clue he was the most dangerous person in a fifty mile radius. The fact that he was out in nearly broad daylight told me he was even more powerful than I'd realized, and I'd already put him at nearly the top of the list.

"She's not lying, John. I'd know."

Jones and Edgar were on a first name basis? Terrific. Why wasn't I surprised?

Jones hadn't even flinched when Edgar arrived, which meant he'd either invited him or could sense him. "She's his Vaso, Edgar. She *has* to know. She's blocking the connection or lying."

"Vaso." The word rang a bell, but it had been too long since lycanthrope cultural studies in college, so I turned to the resident expert, Emma. My questioning look made her nod and respond with lecturelike precision. "A werewolf often chooses a human partner, called a Vaso, to maintain its energy level. Excess energy is one of the leading causes of off-moon shifting and aggressive tendencies. In order for a werewolf to maintain a human appearance in normal society, the energy must be bled off periodically."

Okay, that made sense. "Meaning Kevin *has* a Vaso, since he worked in IT at the university for a couple of years and nobody but us ever caught on that he's a werewolf."

She nodded. "Kevin always hinted that you served that role."

That was news to me. He and I had never really talked about his condition. "Wouldn't I know? I mean, that's sort of personal, isn't it?"

Jones cut in. "Precisely, because the partnership isn't just a physical thing but a mental link. The human has to know where and when to find the wolf when he needs to have energy drained. So, you should know where he is."

"But it makes no sense that I'd be the Vaso. Even when we were speaking, we barely spoke, and I sure as hell didn't come running at his command." I'd considered him one of my closest friends, but we weren't close in the commonly understood sense. "Since when do you two chat? I thought Edgar was a hard target and you were hunting him."

The organization Kevin had worked for in the past, and had gone back to work for recently, was some sort of quasi-governmental agency that ran black ops and hunted supernatural criminals—*hard targets*.

Edgar shrugged. "We live in a world of shifting alliances. Now that you're out of play I figured helping get Landingham out will make him less likely to *actively* hunt me."

Jones nodded and reached into the car to pull out a file folder. "Hewitt here is one of the best there is at getting inside locked buildings and removing people. So he's useful even if he's no longer affiliated with the Company."

I was confident I didn't want to know the history of either statement, so I didn't reply or ask for details. But it was handy to know Edgar's last name. It made him feel, oddly, like less of a threat. Weird.

"Besides," he added, instantly quashing the whole idea of him being less than a threat, "I wasn't there when you killed either Lilith or Luther, Celia, And I'm *very* curious about just how tough you are."

In other words, did I do it alone or had it taken an army to kill two vamps, one more than a thousand years old? I didn't answer, just raised my brows. Luther I'd done myself, but a devout reverend had held Lilith at bay with a glowing cross while I tossed a magical knife at her. Edgar had never seen my knives and I wasn't about to share the details. Let him wonder. Just like he was letting me wonder how he had so much intelligence. That wasn't supposed to be possible for vampires. How was he sane and smart enough to trust in an operation? And how had he traveled to the parking lot while it was still daylight? It was nearly sunset, and he was keeping to the shadows, but still.

My sire had been powerful enough to be able to be awake in daylight, but he couldn't be out in it. Could Edgar? That was a very disturbing thought.

"If you're done having a 'who's tougher' lovefest, could we get on with saving my brother before he's dead?" Emma's voice was as sharp and angry as I'd ever heard it. Not that she had the right to be. We'd been shopping for the better part of three hours and she hadn't said a word. So now it was my fault? I raised my brows at her and she blushed.

Jones handed me the manila folder and I flipped it open. Emma was beside me instantly, her golden hair brushing my arm in contrast to my own pale blonde as she leaned in to read the documents inside.

There were stacks of paper paper-clipped together and I quickly realized that they were dossiers of people. The first was for Ronald Tarnique, father of two pretty dark-haired girls. I frowned as I read about his perfectly normal life. What was I missing? "Okay, so he was a corporate executive for one of the major charities, nice house, good income, happy family. So?"

Jones flipped to the final page of Tarnique's dossier. It was a court order sentencing Tarnique to life at the California State Paranormal Treatment Facility—aka "the zoo." It was the very facility I'd fought not to be sentenced to. It was located in the desert outside my hometown of Santa Maria de Luna; I'd watched TV exposés on the place that would curl your hair and heard rumors that would make you lose your lunch. According to the paper, Tarnique had gone on a rampage and slaughtered forty people at a school bake sale. I flipped back to the original police report, which had the man—as a werewolf—chewing kids' limbs off and then eating said limbs covered with cake frosting.

Emma grabbed the file from me and read the first few pages

again. "This doesn't sound right at all. Something doesn't add up. Lycanthropes can't put on acts this good. To raise a family, exist in the corporate world long enough to become a manager, participate in society, and then . . . *this*." She looked at Jones with haunted eyes. "What sent him over the edge?"

"Therein lies the question." He tapped a finger on the edge of the folder. "All of these cases didn't add up. Amy got suspicious. She told Kevin and said something was very wrong." Amy, Kevin's girlfriend, is also a werewolf. "She said the one thing all of these people had in common is that they'd recently visited the zoo. Tarnique had been interested in having his charity provide resources to the facility to better the lives of the prisoners."

He shifted another paper-clipped stack to the top so I could see the picture of a pretty woman with a Farrah Fawcett–style hairdo. "Tamara Cornith, also a lycanthrope, went on a similar rampage—right down to the bake sale—in the same week, two hundred miles to the south. She'd been to the zoo months before to see her husband's aunt, who was a guard. But they met in the parking lot, just long enough for the older woman to sign some papers. Cornith never even made it inside."

"What does this have to do with Kevin? Has he been frequenting bake sales?"

Jones shook his head and opened his mouth, but Edgar spoke up. He was now leaning against the fender of the sedan and watching us with interest. "No. Amy apparently got curious and decided to talk to the people in the file."

"She'd mentioned to me," Emma added, "that she was going

to try to get a visitor's pass to the zoo. She thought something was going on there and she wanted to see for herself."

"She got inside." Jones let out a noise that was both annoyed and frustrated. "And they decided to keep her. They locked her in a cage and Kevin called me to help get her out."

Emma's outrage was immediate. "They can't do that! They have to have a court order to put someone in prison. They can't just *keep them*."

"Are you sure?" Jones sounded amused. "Amy *is* a werewolf. Kevin thought they might have some sort of sniffer that alerts the staff. It would be a small matter to lock up a guest and ask for a sanctioning order to keep them. What judge would refuse if it was claimed someone went berserk inside the facility?"

"But they're already overcrowded. Why in the world would they want *more* residents?" As the words left my mouth I realized that, while it made no sense, it also made perfect sense. There were plenty of people in the world who'd be happy to lock me up in there, just because I have fangs.

"We're thinking there's more at work here than overzealous right-wingers or bureaucratic red tape. Something a little more . . . sinister." The way Jones said it made my stomach twist in knots.

Edgar smiled grimly. "Precisely. It would be a perfect place for a demonic being to set up camp. It's well known that the mentally unstable are more open to possession. Add magical ability to that, and . . ."

Oh, hell.

Most people don't like to think about prisons. Consciously,

everybody recognizes they're necessary, and so long as nothing bad happens inside they remain just outside our perception
of normality. But while the inmates were locked up, plenty of
people came and went from any institution every day—from
deliverypeople to friends and family . . . and of course, every
guard. I'd experienced for myself just how persuasive a greater
demon could be. Even knowing he was going to torture me,
toy with me until I went insane, then kill me hideously, I'd had
to fight not to walk willingly into his arms. Someone already
unstable would be toast.

"You said Amy got out. Is she okay?"

Jones took back the folder. It was pointless to read any more.
I knew what I needed to. "She's not . . . she's in a coma. She
has brain function, but she won't wake up. We don't know
what they did to her. Warren's got the top experts in the field
on it—including warrior priests who have already done at least
two exorcisms." He paused. "Kevin got her out, but they captured him."

"And you had to get Amy to safety." I understood. Anytime
people in our line of work go on missions, whether guarding
celebrities or getting people out of the line of fire, there's a
chance we won't make it out. We have to make choices and I
was actually glad Jones had made the same one I would have.
You get the wounded out and leave those capable of taking
care of themselves behind. It sucks, but then most things involving danger do. And as angry as I was with him right now, I
also knew Warren had more resources than most. He knows
everyone in academia who is involved with the paranormal,
and I knew from personal experience that every religious

leader in the world had begun to realize that California was becoming a hotbed of demonic activity. The militant arms of the Christian churches, along with Muslim, Jewish, and Hindu religious warriors, were all working together to confront a true hell on earth.

Warren would have no problem finding people to take care of Amy's soul.

I stared into Jones's eyes for a long moment while "O Come All Ye Faithful" played in the background, then nodded. I was terrified down to my toes, but I had to help. "Okay, I'm in. But if it's a demon stronghold, we can't risk going in without an army behind us."

"There's no way we can get one in time," Emma said. "Assuming anyone would believe us. Demons can influence people so subtly that the police and courts would be likely to say we're nuts, because nothing overt is going on."

"Exactly," agreed Jones. "We have one choice, which is to get in the same way we did last night. As far as I can tell, nobody figured out how we got in. We should have gone back out the same way, but there was no way to with Amy unconscious. She was dead weight."

That meant the route either was underground or involved climbing. Either Kevin or Edgar could easily carry her for hours unless it was an issue of dexterity. That meant I needed gear. "I'm not dressed for this. I say we go in after dark and after I've had a chance to get some tools and proper clothing. We won't do Kevin any good if we're not prepared for whatever they can throw at us."

"I've got everything we'll need. We're in a hurry." While I'm sure he believed that, he didn't know what I had available to me.

"No offense, but for something like this I want tools I'm familiar with. Besides"—I pointed at my feathered friends—"they aren't exactly native to the desert. Let's let them go to bed so they don't signal our arrival. Kevin's tough enough to last for another hour or two." I believed that absolutely and let the confidence show in my face and body. Jones let out another disapproving noise while Edgar shrugged. Emma looked at me for a long, silent moment and let out a deep breath before nodding.

"Fine. I'll take you to wherever your *tools* are." Jones opened his car door. "Get in."

That so wasn't happening. I smiled cynically. "Look, it's not that I don't trust you, but . . . well, I *don't* trust you. I'd rather you not know exactly where I keep my stuff. I'm sure you feel the same." Paranoia, thy name is Celia Graves. "Just tell me where and when to meet you."

His expression shifted from surprise to offense before settling into respect. "You've got GPS?"

At my nod, he leaned into his car, punched a few buttons on his Garmin, then wrote something on the back of an envelope he picked up from the floor. "Use these coordinates. Meet me there in two hours. Hewitt and I will go start scoping out the facility. We'll be ready to move in once you arrive."

Edgar spoke up then: "I haven't eaten yet, Jones. I doubt you want me to snack on a demonically possessed person." Ouch. I don't know exactly what the result of that would be, but *bad* seemed likely. "Of course, I'd need less if . . ." He left the statement unfinished but raised his brows at Jones.

No. He couldn't really be suggesting that Jones donate blood. I'd heard that magical blood had more kick, but Jones didn't seem the type to agree to that.

But he shook his head with only mild annoyance, not the outrage I'd expected. "Fine. But no more than a pint. I can't afford to be less than my best."

Eww. And they seemed so . . . casual about it. "Oh my god! You have *got* to be kidding. Have you done this before?"

Edgar seemed taken aback by my outburst. "Celia, vampires drink blood. It's what we live on. Whether it's Jones or a random drunk in an alley or one of your friends, I plan to eat tonight. You may have the luxury of being able to pick and choose your meals, but I don't. One of these days, you might not have the choice, either, so you might as well get used to the thought. Eventually you *will* become a full vampire, by accident or intent or simple biology. There's no way to avoid it."

With that and probably to prove his point, he grabbed Jones's arm. Jones didn't move a muscle as Edgar's lips peeled back to reveal delicate fangs. His eyes glowed red and Emma gasped. She backed behind me and even I wanted to turn away. But I couldn't escape those eyes and the need behind them. The vampire inside me struggled to reach the surface. It wanted to share in the feast, and when Edgar drove his teeth into the soft flesh my whole body shuddered. It took more effort that I'd imagined to hold my ground. Even closing my eyes didn't help, because soft slurping sounds made every nerve tingle, so I covered my ears. What I really needed were nose plugs, because the sweet copper that filled the air made me moan. I turned away then, just barely managing to avoid banging into Emma, and started to walk. I ran smack into Dawna, who was holding bags of succulent-smelling food that erased the copper from my nose. There was spaghetti for Emma, Chinese for herself, and when I opened my eyes I saw a tall cup with a straw that I was betting was mine.

Before she could react to my slamming into her or to Jones playing blood donor, I brought the straw to my lips and began to suck. Surprisingly, it was warm and thick and tasted equally of fruit and something I couldn't quite place. Whatever it was, it satisfied the hunger of both vampire and human.

I looked at Dawna questioningly while continuing to drink. She had given Emma one of the Styrofoam containers and Emma had a sick look on her face as she stared at the rich tomato sauce. Jones's blood was dripping onto the pavement. Jones didn't seem to mind; he reached for one of the containers of Chinese with his free hand and a calm expression. Dawna handed it to him at the farthest reach of her arm. The discomfort on her face was the same sort of expression she would use while watching a relative snacking on live crickets. And she had relatives who did.

"What's in this?" I finally got enough down to tear my lips from the straw. "It's really good."

"It's a mixed-berry smoothie with lots of au jus. I asked the guy at the Chinese place to cook my beef slightly and pour the bloody broth in there before adding the stir-fry spices. Glad you like it."

The look on my face as I regarded the cup made both men laugh. Edgar used the back of his arm to wipe blood from his lips before he said, "At least your friends have common sense,

Graves." His fangs weren't showing, and he seemed once again like a collected, albeit amused, businessman, instead of the evil bloodsucker we'd just seen. I refused to dignify the comment and went back to drinking my shake. "I think you'll find that eventually beef won't be enough. There's a reason why we instinctively seek out humans to feed from."

"I'm doing just fine." And I was. I was treating my vampirism like a food allergy. Adapt, but never give up your sense of self and humanity.

They were both still chuckling while they got in the car. Edgar took the wheel while Jones opened his food container and dug in as the twin holes in his wrist dripped down his arm. Crap. I so didn't want to work with these guys. Yeah, they're professionals, and powerful. But they seriously creeped me out.

"So what's the scoop?" Dawna was looking pretty green and hadn't touched her food. I could tell she was hanging on by teeth and toenails. It didn't surprise me that this bothered her, given that she'd been attacked just a couple of weeks ago. The question was, would she collapse later? I'd have to make sure Emma stayed with her.

"Are you okay? I'm sorry you had to see that."

"Me, too." A shudder overtook her. "I have the feeling I'll have a lot to talk about with the therapist this week."

I hoped I wouldn't be needing to join her in the session room by the time we got Kevin out.

3

Forty-five minutes later, I was in my third-floor office staring at the contents of my weapons safe. The safe is stark black bespelled steel. Running from floor to ceiling and taking up most of one wall, it doesn't really match the rest of the decor. My office is fairly feminine, with its peach walls, drapes pattered with cabbage roses, and dark wooden furniture. The safe is heavy enough that installing it required putting in several reinforcing beams underneath to hold the weight. Those beams had been a real pain in the tail to find because they had to fit the guidelines of the building's historic-landmark status. But without them, the safe would probably have wound up crashing down through the ceiling of the second-floor bathroom, which was primarily used by the lone attorney in our building—and his clients.

I'd already changed into clothes more suitable for covert operations—heavy black denim pants, a black turtleneck, and my favorite "Frankenstein" boots with the steel toe inserts. I could put my hair up under a stocking cap if needed, which left only my pale face standing out like a beacon. I could take care of that later.

First I strapped on my knives. Created by the former love of my life, Bruno DeLuca, they were major magical artifacts. Bruno is one of the most powerful mages around, and it had taken him five years to bespell the blades. I shuddered just thinking about it. I mean, seriously, he'd bled himself every day for five years to create the magic in those knives. I was pretty sure they'd also been blessed by Matteo, Bruno's warrior-priest brother. Which made them perfect for hunting demons.

It had been one of these knives that had killed Lilith. She was some kind of evil beyond a typical bat, because she'd been able to call a bitten priest while he was on holy ground. That takes some oomph. Killing her had turned the metal of the knife itself black. No amount of scrubbing or grinding could turn it silver again. I'd tried.

The knife's mate was still gleaming and bright. Not long ago, I'd been forced to gift it to the queen of the sirens—and it had hurt me terribly to do it. She'd given the blade back after she'd had to use it to kill a member of her own family. Emotional pain seemed to follow the knives, but they worked and that was the important thing.

I shook my head. I needed to focus and get moving. The shoulder holster was next, for something with a higher caliber than my regular Colt. I wanted stopping power for any demon I might run into in the prison, so I moved up to a .44 Magnum. Then I reached for a black vest, which was a magically resistant Kevlar creation of Isaac Levy, my tailor and weapons specialist. It had multiple pockets and loops for weapons. I grabbed a stack of magical spells encased in ceramic disks, things that even non-magic humans can effectively use.

I checked each spell, making sure the raised codes on the edges hadn't worn down. There's seldom time during battle to read labels, so the disks are distinguished by size and shape and by the symbols carved along the edges. I pocketed disks that could cause short-term blackouts and others that were "boomers" that emitted powerful sound and light.

I was still hoping that another mage I knew, John Creede, could put a full body-binding spell into a disk. There were a lot of occasions to use that one in my business.

The black hinged case housing my newest gadget caught my eye. It was a perimeter detector that could sense the demonic. After my first one disappeared on the job where I'd been effectively killed, I'd bought a new one—the deluxe model, with a blessed silver cross. Just like the warrior priests use. I tucked it into another pocket.

There was a knock on my office door. While it was after hours and the front doors were locked, our building houses several businesses that operate 24-7. Like Bubba, the bail bondsman down the hall from me, for example. The attorneys don't work nights, and since nobody else was in the building when I arrived I called out, "Come on in, Bubba!"

"Close," said a familiar voice as the door opened. "Bubba let me in." Speak of the devil. John Creede poked his head in the room. He looked good. I hadn't seen him for almost a month, since his partner in the security firm of Miller & Creede had tried to kill us. Miller had been killed in the attack and Creede had gone back to the business to try to salvage what he could of the multinational corporation he and Miller had spent a decade building. "Got a minute?"

"Just that." I shut the safe door as he walked in. The bolts snapped closed with an audible thunk and the light on the door turned red to show it was locked. "I have to get to a job."

"Perfect timing then." He was dressed in gray suit pants and a white shirt with the collar open to reveal curling hair the same sandy color as the waves tight against his head. His sleeves were rolled up to the elbows, as though he'd just come from a long boardroom session. In other words, yummy. He looked tan and trim and less stressed than the last time we'd seen each other. I was glad. As he walked closer I could feel the tingle of magic that always accompanied him. He didn't seem to be generating it on purpose, but it made my whole body react. Add to that the fact that his cologne made my knees weak and I couldn't help but stare at him, a deer caught in the headlights.

He smiled at my reaction to him. I shook my head and let out a deep breath to clear the cobwebs. "Do you have this effect on all the girls?"

"Most," he admitted with a tip of his head. "But it's stronger with you. Maybe that says something." Maybe. But that didn't mean it would go anywhere. I was so out of the dating game right now. Nothing but heartache—and I had more important things to worry about. I glanced at my watch and he noticed. "Right. I get it. You have places to be. Like I said, it's perfect timing . . . for this."

He pulled a small box from his pant pocket. It was about the same dimensions as my little seeker car, which I pulled out in response. "Already have one. But thanks for the offer. I would take a body-binding spell charm if you have that one ready."

He chuckled softly and it made my stomach lurch again. Damn it. "Haven't had time to work on the binding spell. But you don't have one of these. Trust me." Two steps closer and he was about as near as I could stand. Then he opened the box and my entire focus went to the contents, a tiny gold contraption, about the size of a bumblebee, with mesh-covered wings and huge mirrored eyes.

"Ooh! What is that?" I'd honestly never seen anything like it, which said something. I'm a total gadget geek and scour both the consumer electronics and military application shows for new toys. "Can I touch it?"

"Absolutely. I'm hoping you'll try it out for me. Right now I'm calling it 'Fly on the Wall,' but I'm sure marketing will come up with a better name if it holds up in the real world." He picked it out of the box and handed it to me, then pressed a button on the small metal contraption. "Take a look."

I was turning the fly around in my hands, but when he held up the box I realized the fly was transmitting high-definition images that could be viewed on the screen at the bottom of the box. One half of the screen was a close-up of my face, while the other displayed a view of the entire room.

"I'd heard that cameras were starting to do fly-eye images, but I've never seen one this small or with such sharp focus."

"Blame that on magic," he said with a grin that told me he was happy I was impressed. "But that's only half of it. Watch this." Taking a tiny bead about the size and color of a BB out of the case, he pressed it against a small plate on the back of the fly and all of a sudden I was holding a real-live horsefly. The feet moved and the head turned and it felt totally like a living bug in my fingers. The images on the screen moved when the head did, and I fully admit that I let out a little girly squeal of delight.

"How cool!"

"We're not done yet." Creede sounded like a kid with a new bike as he pulled up a small antenna and joystick combo from the side of the screen. The fly's wings began to vibrate against my hand. When I let go, it hovered above my palm. The joystick steered the fly around the room, and no matter how abrupt the insect's movements, the pictures on the screen stayed clear. "It records, too. Want to try it out on your job tonight? It's a prototype and you have such an . . . interesting life that I know you can give it a real workout."

I stared at the screen, totally engrossed. It would be perfect for this job. We could find out exactly where Kevin was in the prison without risking any of our hides. "Um, I'd like to, Creede. But honestly I'm not sure if I . . . that is, if it will survive the night. It's going to be a rough job. It's your only one and that wouldn't be fair." I glanced at him and saw that his whole expression had changed.

"Do you need backup?" He was dead serious and I appreciated the offer. He was a powerful mage and I'd seen him in a fight before.

"Probably." I nodded and sighed. "But it's not my party."

He'd been in the security game long enough that he understood what I meant. He directed the fly back to his hand and put it back in the box without a word. I couldn't help but admire his easy familiarity with it. I knew it wouldn't work that easy for me. After it was turned off and closed, he forced the container into my palm, making my whole arm tingle nicely. "Take it. It sounds like you'll need it, and I can make another if need be. In fact—" He reached inside his pocket and pulled out a small charm ball with a tiny glass window set into it. "Take this, too."

I turned it in my free hand curiously. "What is it?"

"This is a magical beacon. If you get into water hot enough you need out, crack the glass with a thumbnail or even your teeth and I'll show up to help. All of the M and C people have one. Actually," he said with a smile, "probably a dozen operatives will show up if you break that particular one. It's keyed to my personal magic. I have more than one employee who will drop everything to save the guy who signs their paychecks."

That made me laugh as I tucked it into a pant pocket. I wanted that one close to me. In fact, it might wind up inside my bra, which is seldom searched, even by the bad guys. And if I was being strip-searched, I wanted it where someone might break it by accident.

I squared my shoulders and looked once more into those flame-licked hazel eyes. "Thanks, Creede. Really. For everything." I meant it and it came through in my voice.

He growled and frowned, because I'd just broken the rules. Tough-guy bodyguards don't thank each other. It's considered gauche and . . . *soft*. His sudden discomfort made me smile and caused me to impulsively reach out and hug him. I didn't plan it; I swear.

The things the touch of his body did to mine were beyond description. Even the vest, stuffed with Kevlar and "toys," couldn't stop his magic from bringing my skin alive. Every nerve stood at attention, and goose bumps crawled across every inch of me. The scariest thing was that I absolutely knew he wasn't just reacting to my siren abilities. He had a charm to prevent himself from being magically influenced by me. A grunt from him told me the reaction wasn't one-sided. I started to pull away, but he would have none of it. His arms snaked around my body and held me tight against him, while his mouth moved to my ear and stopped just before making contact. I could feel his warm breath on my earlobe.

Now panic tore through me, because all my body wanted was for him to tear off my clothes and throw me to the floor. Bruno had made me feel like that sometimes, but this was different. It was superficial, lust without emotional depth. But that didn't make it any less real or wanted. I hadn't had sex in a long time and my body knew what it needed. "I have to go, Creede."

He didn't respond except to move his hands up my back, which made my stomach tighten and my fingers dig into his muscular shoulders. "I know." The words pushed into my ear softly, a mixed message. What did he know? That I had to get to the job or that I wanted to feel his fingers on my skin, his lips close over mine? Then I remembered he was a skilled telepath. Crap. While I hoped he was using discretion, he could easily know what I was thinking before I'd even processed the thoughts.

His lips began to move against my neck and his hands slid down to grip my hips possessively. My heart was thudding in my throat. Interesting that I was less afraid to hunt the demon than to have this man touch me.

"Yes, it is. Very interesting." My eyes widened at his words and at the feeling of his lips against my cheek. Delicate but powerful, the sensation strong enough to weaken my knees. His lips lingered there for what felt like an eternity while my brain swam, unable to think.

"You have to let me go, Creede." My voice was a whisper and I could hear the fear in it. Who exactly was I afraid of?

He returned the whisper, and while the words made me think he was amused, his tone was low and serious: "I'm not the one who has somewhere to be. This is yours, Celia. You can pull away if you want to. I won't stop you."

I couldn't see my watch because my fingers were gliding through his so-soft hair, pulling his lips closer so they were once more moving against my neck. Bad. I knew I was being bad. Kevin needed me. He could be dying while I was letting a handsome mage tease me breathless. Creede's hands were cupping my butt now. It felt so good. Then the hands paused and the whisper grew chiding. "Come on, Celia. Concentrate. I know you can get past this like you can get past your fears. There's a time and place."

The tone startled me, brought me out of my fog. My pulse slowed to near normal and I could think again. Now I knew what this was all about. Creede was a business first, pleasure second sort of guy. Just like me.

"And this isn't the time. Right? I'm too busy avoiding the job to do the job well." He'd been teasing me on purpose. Getting my mind shifted away from old worries and fears, onto a path toward new things. Including the task at hand. I took a deep breath and let it out slow. "Thanks, Creede." Another thanks earned me another growl in my ear. I kissed him lightly on the cheek and pulled back. "I think I've got it out of my system." Not the sex part, but the worry and fear. I felt calmer and he let a smile reach his eyes.

"Of course, you realize this isn't over. As you can see, I was enjoying myself."

I refused to look below his belt line. I had felt exactly how much he was enjoying himself. "Another time, in the far distant future."

"Maybe. Or sooner than you think." Now the old Creede was back, the ladies' man who was a consummate flirt. Damn, he was good. He turned on his heel and headed toward the door. "Make sure you give that a good tryout. I'll expect a written report when you get back from your job."

I rolled my eyes and crossed suddenly solid arms over my vest. "Like I have time in my day to write reports? Pfft. I'll call you." I was feeling back to my old self and I was grateful. I hadn't realized how much my nerves and memories had been getting to me.

He was in the doorway now and his eyes were sparkling merrily. "And I'll take your call, provided you agree to have dinner with me to give me the details." Was he asking me on a *date*? Maybe my face showed my shock, because his smile broadened into a grin. "I'll consider that a yes." He left and I could hear the creak of old boards under his shoes as he walked toward the staircase. "Like I said," he called out when he was halfway down the stairs, "sooner than you think, Graves."

His low chuckle made things inside me tighten again, but it made me smile, too. I'd been hurt a lot lately and Creede was a breath of fresh air—not too serious and not demanding. And there was respect there, both ways. Maybe that was exactly what I needed right now.

4

The fly worked just as well as it had in my office. Unfortunately.

The camera revealed sights that sickened me. Sedated humans crammed into cages lining the dungeonlike basement of the "treatment center." Cages. They seemed to be about the size for a Great Dane, made from steel bars as thick around as my wrist. There was no furniture, no toilet facilities. Just row upon row of cages filled with naked, comatose people curled into fetal positions. Even a Super Max prison had more amenities than this. "This is disgusting. We have to get them out of there."

Edgar lowered the night-vision goggles he was using. "You can't be serious." His whisper sounded equally amazed and horrified.

"Keep your mind on the mission, Graves." Jones's voice was an annoyed hiss in my ear. "I wouldn't have brought you if I'd thought this sort of thing would bother you."

"Well, it does," I snapped back quietly. "I wouldn't put a dog in a cage where it couldn't even sit up straight. What kind of life is that?"

He responded by pulling the fly's case out of my hand. "Give me that joystick." He started to move the fly and pushed my hand away when I tried to get it back.

"Damn it, Jones."

Jones stared at me, his eyes blazing with internal fire. "Look at the screen, Graves."

He was hovering the fly inside one of the cages. I didn't want to look. It made my stomach hurt to think of that person's life, or lack thereof. Jones made a disgusted sound, then repeated, tensely, "Look at the screen. Really look. No sores, no fleas, no dirt on this guy's skin. He's had a shower or bath sometime today. His underwear and shirt are snow-white. They look better than the ones in my dresser."

Okay. Now I was forcing myself to look and Jones was right. There was no urine or feces, and if the guy had been caged for very long, there would be. "Oh. But . . ."

"Now look at the electrodes on his forehead," Jones continued. "They're inducing dreams. See the smile? Part of the treatment here is to provide normalcy, to keep the person remembering interactions that aren't tainted with violence. Yes, he's in a cage. Get over it. These are superhuman creatures who are very likely insane. If they had enough room to move, they could bend the bars or they'd dislocate something trying."

Oh. Now I felt like a fool. I was probably blushing, given how hot my face felt, but at least in the dark nobody could see. Except for the vampire, of course. Oh, and the mage with the fire in his eyes. Damn.

"I've been inside, Graves. Many times. Don't get me wrong; there are parts of the facility you don't ever want to see. There are places that would make you lose your lunch. But this batch has a good set of keepers."

"Why can't the whole facility be like this?" Yes, now I was championing what I'd just complained about. Some people are never happy.

Jones shook his head. "You are a piece of work, Graves."

I was getting itchy from sand seeping into my clothes. "We need to find Kevin. This is taking too long. When are we going in?"

It was Edgar who responded. "When we're ready. When we're sure where we're going. There is no hiding once we're inside, Celia. The barrier will start to scream the minute we penetrate it, and then it's only a matter of time before they find us. This isn't a sneak in and sneak out mission. Only brute force will get us in and out again safely. People are probably going to die, and we'll be the ones killing them."

Whoa. That wasn't what I'd signed up for. "I'm already on a short leash, guys. One more trip to court and I'm this place's newest inmate. You guys might be able to crawl back under your respective rocks once he's out, but I need to work in this town again. Why *can't* we sneak in and out?"

That set them both back on their heels. "Look," I continued. "We have our fly. We can use it to figure out a way in. Can't Edgar bespell a guard so we can take his uniform?"

Jones now looked amused. "So with twenty-first-century technology and supernatural abilities, you want to stage a World War Two movie breakout?"

I shrugged as best I could; my shoulders were cramping inside the pipe. "If it works, why not?"

"Are you willing to use your siren abilities as well? Kevin told me you were horrified by what you did to Eirene's followers."

That stopped me cold, because Kevin was right. In the struggle to keep myself and Emma alive and keep the greater demon from being loosed, I'd mentally fought a siren queen for mental control of her men. Eventually, there was nothing left of their minds to follow either of us. It had eliminated them from the battle, but I'd sworn I'd never again manipulate a person. I swallowed hard and tried to think what others would do in my place. Bile rose into my throat and I forced it back down. "Can you manage it without me?"

"Sneak in, without using violence, and remove someone without alerting trained magical guards?" He let out a snort that might have been loud enough to hear if there was anyone close. "Not bloody likely."

So I could have a violent, bloody confrontation where I would probably have to kill someone or a quiet, sneaky rescue where I'd probably have to manipulate people into doing what I wanted and risk them becoming brain-dead. Great. Just great.

Maybe there was a third option. The fly was working fine, but it was slow. We were losing too much time while it searched. I concentrated, then whispered into the darkness, "Vicki? Ivy? Are you guys out there?"

The air cooled noticeably enough for even Jones to look around. "What the hell?"

I pulled a penlight from inside my vest and held it where nobody outside our little group would see it if it lit up. "Vicki, is that you?"

The bulb flicked on once. One blink meant yes. Two meant no. It was a crude method of communicating, but it worked. Ghosts stay on this plane of existence when they have unfinished business, finding their murderer or revealing information to a loved one. I wasn't sure exactly why Vicki had stayed behind, but so far she had been acting as a sort of resource when I needed eyes on the ground. Vicki wasn't the only ghost in my life; there was also Ivy, my little sister who'd died violently when we were children.

"Can you find Kevin inside here?"

One blink. Vicki had known Kevin as long as I had. Plus, she'd told me once, she'd seen him in animal form. That would be helpful if he wasn't human at the moment.

Jones sounded both confused and annoyed when he whispered, "What the hell are you doing, Graves? Who are you talking to?"

"Vicki Cooper. Remember her? My clairvoyant friend from Birchwoods?"

"Yeah. She's dead."

"Mostly, yes. Say hi, Vicki."

Edgar made an odd sound and handed me the night-vision contraption. There was an amused expression on his face. Strange to see a vampire with a smile. "Here, take a look."

As the goggles spun my way, I had to smile. I turned them around so Jones could see the lens, where, in tiny little print, a reversed *Hi! :)* appeared in frost.

I raised my brows and probably had a triumphant expression on my face. "Now it's time to play the game my way. Vick, can you find the fly attached to this joystick and take it to wherever

Kevin is? Maybe flick a light in the room or something if it's on an outside wall?"

One blink of the flashlight.

"Is Ivy here, too?"

Two rapid blinks. I don't know why that worried me, but it caused me to ask a stupid question about a ghost. "Is she okay?"

A series of rapid flashes didn't make any sense to me. Maybe I needed to learn Morse code. It might be that Vicki didn't understand the question or it was too complicated to answer. "Never mind. Not important right now. We'll talk tomorrow. For now, find Kevin. 'Kay?"

One blink. And then the temperature returned to normal.

Jones was shaking his head silently, disbelief plain on his face. It made me shrug and comment, "Hey, you're a mage, he's a vampire, and I'm vampire-siren-human. Why not ask a ghost to help free a werewolf?"

"Freaking unbelievable."

Jones, Edgar, and I huddled around the tiny screen. At first there was no change. The fly hovered in the air, waiting for instructions. Then a wind caught it and began to propel it down the hallway. The night erupted with howls from inmates who could either see or sense Vicki's presence. Guards, alerted, could find no cause. No sensors were tripped, no lights glared red, and a fly floating on a breeze was ignored.

Sights moved past too quickly to identify, though I glimpsed a couple of stairways and various doors that might or might not lead to the outside. But I knew the fly was storing the images for later viewing. I wasn't sure how big the hard drive was, but I was betting there was at least a gig or two of memory.

Finally the fly came to rest in a room and we got our first look at Kevin. He was stripped naked and chained to a table. He wasn't dead—his chest was moving—but his limp position and slack face told me he was unconscious. "Did he have those bruises and cuts when you went in?"

Jones shook his head grimly. "Those are all postcapture. Normally, they'd have healed by now." Normally, werewolves heal quickly, almost as fast as vampires. Something was keeping Kevin from healing himself.

The light began to flick on and off in the room and we all raised our eyes to the wall in front of us to see a corresponding flicker on the third floor, at the far end of the building. "Edgar, can you carry a person in flight?"

He gave me a small smirk. "I think there was a children's movie once that said it best. With the extra weight, I can't fly. But I can fall with style."

I couldn't help but chuckle. I'd seen the same movie. "Jones, can we do *any* magic once we're inside the barrier? Will my boomers or charms work in there?"

He thought for a long moment, tapping his index finger on the side of the fly remote. "The barrier's goal is to prevent any magical tampering with the security of the facility—any magic that's categorized as an attempt to effect an escape, for example. But there may be a chance to *enhance* the security system to our benefit."

Ahhh. "So if we made the barrier stronger in certain places—"

He completed the sentence with a smile. "Like in front of a breach to the wall for example . . . then yes, it might divert power from the rest of the barrier."

Suddenly the fly's control screen flashed red. Apparently the fly had a feature Creede hadn't mentioned. The word "Demon" was blinking in red at the bottom of the screen. A demonic presence had walked into the room. She had taken the form of a doctor's aide or nurse if the uniform was any indication and was carrying a skill saw. If I could pick the least likely place for a construction saw to exist, it would be an infirmary. She stared at the unconscious werewolf with undisguised glee and then plugged the saw into an outlet.

Fuck a duck. Our deadline had just moved up.

Jones apparently agreed. "We're going in. Now."

Edgar was already moving toward the hole under the wall and I followed with as much mobility as my trapped-for-too-long legs would muster. Thankfully, Vicki isn't just any random ghost. The lights went out in Kevin's room as we raced the length of the building, which was a good block long. Edgar had just started to float up the three floors to the darkened window when a metal chair crashed against the bars, shattering the glass and showering it down on me and Jones.

Of course that set off the alarms, but it was too late to stop the party. I was still carrying the fly remote and glanced down to see Vicki create a wind that whipped the cord out of the wall and repeatedly slammed the plug against the nurse's face. When I moved the fly so I could see Kevin, the nurse noticed it.

She plucked it out of the air and stared into the two fly eyes, which put her whole face on one side of the screen. While there was no sound pickup on the device—which I'd suggest to Creede as an improvement—there was no mistaking what she said: "Hello, Celia."

I dropped the remote as I felt a stabbing sensation in my chest. Not long ago, I'd had an exorcism done to sever my ties to a particular demon. It had left scars on my chest that looked like claw rips. At first I'd thought the scars were burning, but the feeling went deeper . . . like something had grabbed my heart and squeezed. Not good.

I'd known there was the possibility that the same greater demon might be behind this, but running into him so soon after my death and resurrection by doctors and priests was terrifying.

Part of me wanted to freeze and scream, but training and common sense overrode the impulse. Guards were running in our direction. By sheer instinct I pulled a boomer from a vest pocket and tossed it while I scooped up the remote. The boomer went off with an effect that was closer to a party popper than the deafening, blinding incapacitation that I'd become accustomed to. Damn. But it wasn't the only thing in my arsenal. I tossed a mudder. Full of concentrated water, it created a three-foot-square patch of thick mud. The guards stumbled and fell to their knees, the ground literally stolen out from under them.

As Edgar began to pry the bars away from the concrete window frame, Jones pulled the pin on a military grenade and threw it at the wall, simultaneously casting a spell that silenced the explosion.

The barrier reacted to the explosion by sealing the breach, taking power from everwhere else in the system. I could feel the pressure against my body lighten and I could move almost normally.

My next boomer worked perfectly and the guards were
down for the momentary count. I looked at the screen to see
the possessed nurse flying around the room. Let's hear it for
ghostly tornadoes. I needed to wake Kevin and get him ready
to go. Because none of us were going to be able to carry him
once he was on the ground—we were all going to be watching
our collective backs.

"Cover me, Jones!" I called, but because of the silence spell
no sound came out of my mouth. So I tried the siren trick I'd
learned on short notice while on the Isle of Serenity. I stared
at the back of his head as he pushed air around, making it
impossible for the guards to get off a shot at any of us. *Jones*, I
thought. He flinched and turned his head slightly. *I'm going to
try to contact Kevin. Keep them off me. I won't be able to see
them coming when I'm concentrating.*

He didn't respond either verbally or in my mind, but he
shifted position so he was directly between me and the guards.

It was very odd to have people moving and fighting in utter silence. Even the tornado upstairs was soundless. Unfortunately, that meant I couldn't contact Vicki. Because while
she was doing a great job keeping guards out of the room, she
was likewise preventing Edgar from getting in. Frustrated,
he was now on the ground, helping Jones keep the guards
off me.

I concentrated on Kevin. Beaten, battered, and unable to
protect himself. Yes, he was an ass, and yes, I was furious at
him. But that didn't mean I'd let some demon hag cut off his
limbs. *Kevin. C'mon, buddy. Hear me. Wake up.*

There was a smooth, blank wall of quiet inside his head.

This wasn't just from being knocked unconscious. This took drugs and lots of them. *Kevin. Wake up. Amy needs you.*

Thankfully a werewolf metabolism is an amazing thing. The more I called his name, the thinner the wall in his head got. I don't know how I could feel it, but I could.

Kev—ahhh! It was the scream that finally woke him. I tend to react unfavorably to bullet wounds. My whole body spun around when the bullet entered my shoulder and I found myself on the ground staring up at a lot more people than had been there when I'd started to contact Kevin. The pain was intense and caused a reaction I should have expected. The vamp inside totally came out and I leapt on my nearest enemy before I could stop myself.

But that tiny bit of me that was still human refused to slam fangs into the man's neck, despite the scent of blood that filled the air. . . . Instead, I grabbed the rifle and ripped it from his hands and used it like a club across his jaw. He went down like a rock and lay still. The glowing red eyes I'd glimpsed before he fell told me that the nurse wasn't the only possessed person here. I slid my blackened knife from its sheath and laid the flat of the blade on the man's chest. Even unconscious, he screamed—silently. Hopefully I had just sent the demon back to hell where it belonged.

Sound returned just then and my ears were assaulted by screams, shouts, sirens, and gunfire. Louder than all that was a howl of pure rage and pain from above. As I put the knife back in the sheath, I looked up to see Kevin at the window, his hair whipping from Vicki's storm. The guards looked up also and aimed their weapons in his direction.

No. They would not shoot him. That I could prevent. I leapt into the nearest guard just in time. The guard's shot went into the cinder block a foot away from Kevin.

We went down in a tangle of limbs that made my shoulder erupt into intense pain. I struggled to keep from screaming a second time. Edgar jumped on the guard directly to my left before he could pull the trigger. He perched on the man like a spider, holding down each limb, hissing, fangs bared. I turned away just as Edgar's head thrust downward and the man screamed.

A different movement caught my eye. Kevin had decided not to stick around long enough for anyone to get off another shot. He'd jumped from the window. A human might break his legs, hitting the ground from three stories up. But Kevin just landed in a crouch, his face contorted into a snarl of fury.

A hand grabbed my wrist and pulled. It was my bad arm, so I hissed in pain and reacted, my fist sizzling toward whoever was attached to the hand. Jones is nimble; I'll give him that. He shifted his head so that my fist sailed past his ear.

"Time to go." He raised his other hand and his eyes blazed with power.

Air pressed against my head until I thought it would explode, and then the world dissolved to white.

5

Y'know, vampire healing isn't your friend in a gun-fight." The voice, male and pure Jersey, brought me back to consciousness. My eyes popped open as I recognized the speaker. Gaetano, a medic who'd patched me up before, shook his head and cut deep into my shoulder with a scalpel. Thankfully I couldn't feel anything other than pressure, which probably meant I'd been treated with a combination of morphine and a sedative spell.

"You healed right over the bullet. If I don't get it out, it'll sting every time you move your arm."

"I'll take healing over the alternative, thanks." My tongue felt thick and unresponsive and it was impossible to keep my head straight. Good thing Gaetano was one of the good guys—or at least less bad than those who had shot me. Of course, I had been breaking out a prisoner, so maybe I was a bad guy and so was Gaetano. "By the way, are we the good guys or the bad guys?"

He smiled then and let out a snort. "Depends on the day, Graves. Today we were the good guys." I remembered the glowing eyes of the nurse, who'd smiled with a saw in her hands, and agreed with a shudder. Gaetano's hands pushed my shoulder down harder on the bed. The click of metal on metal said he'd probably reached the bullet. A weird sensation in my shoulder told me I was starting to metabolize the drugs. It was going to hurt soon, maybe before he finished. Maybe it would be better to concentrate on something else.

I was in a bed. The softness and the sheets gave it away. But whose bed, and when did I get there? Without moving my head, I looked around. I seemed to be in the basement of a house. A hot-water heater stood in a corner and I could see the back of a staircase beyond Gaetano's muscular arm. "Where are we?" The direct approach is often the best.

"Safe house." His voice held concentration. "Quit talking. It makes the drugs wear off. You're starting to flinch."

Yeah. "Should you give me more?"

His brown eyes flicked my way. Pretty. There was frustration mingled with amazement in his expression. "I've already given you enough to kill a full human, Graves. If you just relax and don't think, they'll work fine."

"Celia."

He stopped again. "What?"

"Celia, not Graves. I'm not a soldier."

Another snort and a shake of his head. "Then you're hanging out with the wrong people." He put bloodstained gloved fingers on my eyebrows. "Now relax and let me finish, okay?" He closed my eyes.

There was a warm, vibrating weight on my chest that moved when I did. My eyes opened slowly, enjoying the sensation of heat and movement. Orange and white fur was all I could see. Why was our office cat, Minnie the Mouser, in the safe house?

Then I realized she wasn't. I was in my office, lying on the couch. What the hell? I put a hand on the cat and gave her a stroke or two. She responded with extra purring. Then I gently lifted her up and put her on the floor. The purring stopped and she gave me an annoyed look with wide green eyes before walking into the nearest sunbeam on the carpet to begin bathing her face with one paw. I sat up and immediately regretted it. I'd been through a battle, and from the way my shoulder moved I was betting there was a bandage underneath my shirt, which was actually a button-down shirt and not a black turtleneck with a hole in the shoulder. Oh, crap. That meant my shirt had been off while Gaetano had been operating on me. Logical, and it shouldn't bother me. Except it did.

My vest, clothing, and wrist sheaths, with knives, were neatly stacked on my desk. My first thought was to check the safe. The lock was still red, but I wouldn't know if they'd used my palm to deactivate the magical part of the locking system until I looked inside. I was hoping not, but I wouldn't put much past Jones.

I spun on the couch and sat up. The sound of crinkling paper had me looking around and then groping in the pockets of my bloodstained jeans. I hoped they'd been dry when I'd

been laid on the couch. A folded slip of paper came out after a
second of tugging.

> I don't date soldiers or coworkers, but you're not
> either. Call me.
> Gaetano

A phone number followed, and not surprisingly, it was local. How else would he have been around to swoop in, medi-
cal kit in tow, twice in a month?

Feast or famine. That's nearly always how it worked with
me. For five years, I couldn't get a date on a bet. Now I'd at-
tracted a growing flock of men, milling like the birds that were
undoubtedly outside my office.

The problem was that everything I'd heard and experienced told me it was all frosting, no cake. Having a date who
is magically compelled to worship the ground you walk on
isn't quite the same to me as earning his respect and him liking me as a *person*. It didn't matter whether I could help it or
not. I didn't want to wind up like some of the starlets who
abound in Hollywood and complain nobody respects their
minds while on their way to the plastic surgeon to add a cup
size. Maybe I needed to get a whole bunch of those anti-siren
charms made up and hand them out to everyone I met.

I stood up and went to the desk, automatically checking
each and every pocket of my vest. The place where the bullet
had pierced the vest was obvious—the fabric covering the
strips of Kevlar was frayed and slightly charred. Jeez! Were
they using tracer rounds or something? I could fit my ring

finger into the hole. It felt like a .30-06 to me, except that a
hunting round would probably have gone right through me.
Maybe I would call Gaetano sometime, just to ask what he'd
pulled out of my shoulder.

Nothing was missing from the pockets except what I knew
I'd used in the fight. I didn't know whether that was good or
bad. Damn my paranoia anyway. I could think of a thousand
hideous spells that could be contained in seemingly innocuous
ceramic disks. I might think I was throwing a mudder and wind
up choking to death from a lack of oxygen around my head.

I sighed. Better safe than sorry. Part of my weapons safe has
a containment unit where I store unknown stuff until I can
take it to experts who can tell me what it is. All my disks would
have to go there.

I put my palm on the sensor of the lock mechanism, then
entered the code. There was a long pause. I've gotten used
to the pause. It used to open right up, but that was before the
vampire bite. The tech people got it to work for me after my
DNA altered by telling it I was pregnant. Nobody knows what's
going to happen at the nine-month mark. I needed to add a
note to my computer calendar to remind me of my "birthday"
so I could clean the safe out the day before. I'd hate to not be
able to get to my stuff just because I forgot. Finally it let out a
confirming beep and the reassuring *clunk* of the lock that
I'd been told could be heard everywhere in the building. I
opened the door. Everything looked just as I'd left it, which
made me feel better.

I'd stowed my now-unreliable tools and was just finishing
putting replacement charms in the vest pockets when there

was a light tap at the door. Minnie and I looked up at the same moment and her questioning *mew* coincided with my, "Yes?"

It was both creepy and endearingly cute.

"You okay in there?" Dawna poked in her head with Dottie right at her heels in an odd contrast of personalities and visuals. "We heard the safe open."

Dawna is our receptionist. She's my age, Vietnamese American, and was the epitome of high fashion in a cherry red skirt and blazer and sleek patent-leather heels. Dottie, on the other hand, is elderly, with a delightful lack of self-consciousness, a white-bread, walker-using American in vivid red velour sweats. Two halves of a whole or maybe just a vision of all of our futures. Dottie is our backup receptionist—brought on when Dawna suffered a mental collapse that put her in the mental ward for a little while. As far as I knew, she wasn't doing inpatient therapy anymore. Emma still was.

"I'm moving slow, but I'm moving. What time is it?" I was guessing it was around ten o'clock given the position of the sunbeam on the floor, but I could be wrong. "Hopefully I know what *day* it is. Anyone know when I got here?"

Dawna shrugged, but Dottie said, "According to the security log, three men and one woman entered at seven fifteen this morning."

I wondered immediately *which* three. Then I noticed that Dawna looked as startled as I felt. "We have a security log?" I asked.

"That shows the sex of the person who entered?" said Dawna. When she nodded, my eyes met Dawna's and we nodded.

"Sweet." It came out of our mouths at the same time, which made all three of us chuckle. I'd have to see what else the log showed.

"Oh, and it's ten twenty," Dawna added. "You have someone on the phone and someone in the waiting room. Should I tell them both to get lost or do you want one or the other?"

Did I want to see anyone? Actually I didn't feel all that bad. I should be hungry, but I wasn't. I briefly wondered what that meant—had Gaetano or Jones gotten some nutrition into me? I felt sore, but not to the point of turning down work. "Depends. Who's who?"

"Your old therapist, Gwen, is on the phone. She says it's important. Detective Alexander is downstairs. She's been waiting nearly an hour and says she'll wait all day if she has to."

Crap. Well, there could be worse people waiting I suppose. Like my mother, for example. But she was in jail. One of the many reasons I had a therapist.

"I told her you'd had a long night. Was it a *successful* night? I haven't been able to reach Emma." Dawna was being deliberately coy with Dottie right there. I understood, but it wasn't really necessary. Like Emma, Dottie was a clairvoyant. I seem to know a lot of them. Vicki had been, as well. I was betting Dottie already had seen what had happened. She'd told me that once she met me she started getting multiple images of my future—mostly of future dangers. Naturally. The death curse put on me as a child saw to that.

I nodded. "We got Kevin out and he was fine last time I saw him. I don't know more than that. But I'll bet you can't reach Emma because she's back in Birchwoods."

"Okay. Gwen first and then I'll see Alex. Everything else okay? Is there a reason you're both in the office today?"

Dottie beamed at me, total excitement in her eyes. "Dawna's teaching me how to do billing." Awesome! I'd worried that Dawna would take Dottie's hiring as a condemnation of her mental state. Looking at her now, I didn't think the smile on Dawna's face was fake, but I wouldn't know for sure until I could meet with her privately to dance around the subject.

"Great. I have several bills to go out this month." Because I damned well was going to send a bill to a certain monarch of Rusland for at least the cost of my friend Bubba's boat. Bubba had helped me out so that King Dahlmar could meet with my ever-so-great grandmother, the queen of the sirens. The boat was destroyed in a very ugly way (think big chunks of it sinking slowly into the ocean) and I owed him a new one. Not that he'd asked for it, but our relationship was a little more . . . tense than it had been.

I put my hands out and made little waving motions. "Okay, shoo. Give me five minutes to talk to Gwen. Get Alex some coffee or something."

"Already taken care of. Gwen's on two." Dawna shut the door. I waited until I heard Dottie's walker on the stairs before I sat at my desk. I would rather she didn't climb the stairs with her bad hips, but there's no stopping her. God knows I've tried. She just said, *I'm old enough to know my own mind, dear, and I'll deal with my own consequences.*

I stared at the desk and tried to think where I'd left off with Gwen the last time we'd spoken. She'd refused to take me back as a client, and that had hurt. Years ago, she'd helped me keep my sanity after my kidnapping and Ivy's death. Then Gwen had fallen ill and had to struggle with her own sense of mortality. She'd let her license lapse. For a while I'd been seeing Dr. Scott and Dr. Hubbard at the Birchwoods sanitarium, where Vicki had once lived. But now Dr. Scott had his own problems to face and Dr. Hubbard . . . well, she was nice enough, but she wasn't Gwen.

Why she was calling now? Perhaps she'd changed her mind and was willing to work with me again. I hoped she wasn't going to say that she was disappointed with me after my latest appearances in the tabloids. Disappointing her would be second only to making my gran cry on my scale of "worst days ever." Just the thought of harsh words from Gwen made my stomach hurt and a burning like bile rise in my throat.

You're allowed to expect good things, Celia. Just the memory of her quiet but forceful affirmations made the tension in my shoulders release a little. I took a deep breath and pressed the button.

"Hi, Gwen. Sorry to keep you waiting." I went for brisk and businesslike despite the fact that my hand was trembling. "What can I do for you?"

"Good morning, Celia." Her voice was calm and collected. Not angry or excited. That could mean anything. Damn. "I hope I didn't call at a bad time."

Hmm. Let's see . . . how to field that. *Bad* is such a relative thing. "No. Not at all. I do have someone waiting, but I have a few minutes."

"Great. I'm hoping you can stop by my office to talk. There are a few things I've just been told that affect you directly."

Her *office?* Yay! My shoulders dropped to nearly normal. "Sure. When were you thinking?" Lord knew when I could fit it in. I grabbed my flip calendar and started turning pages. Ouch. Not looking so good. I had meetings with potential clients every morning this week, plus jobs every afternoon and evening until Christmas. December is a busy time of year for bodyguards. There are holiday parties and benefits nearly every day where celebrities want to mingle and be seen—but not let certain fans, the ones who adore them far too much, get close. "I have an hour or so next Monday morning. Nine o'clock?"

There was a pregnant pause before Gwen sighed. "I was hoping it could be today. It's rather urgent."

Urgent? "What kind of *urgent?* I'm not doing too badly right this second." It was true, though I knew I was blithely ignoring most of the problems in my life, hoping that the holidays would be a blur of only mild discomfort. I'm not a holiday person despite Gran's best efforts. I save Christmas morning for her—fresh biscuits and coffee around the tree—but other than that, I leave the season to people who enjoy it. Like Dawna. And Emma. They're so into sugary goodwill it makes my teeth hurt.

There was a second, deeper sigh in my ear. "It's not about you, Celia, although I do want to hear about what's really going on with you." I *knew* she'd catch me. . . . "This is about a friend of yours. I'd rather not say any more on the phone. Do you have time to drop by today?"

A friend? There aren't many people in my life who fit that description, but the ones I have are important. "Um, sure. Do I need to set a time or should I just drop by?"

"You can drop by." She paused briefly, then said, "I'm working at Birchwoods." I started in surprise.

"What? Why?" There was probably a note of horror in my voice. I'd been kicked out of Birchwoods by Dr. Scott. I got why . . . he'd rightly objected to one of my siren cousins walking through security without a single person stopping her and then psychically manipulating him into giving her information about me. But . . . damn it!

Her voice sounded surprised when she spoke: "I thought you knew. I'm the new administrator. The announcement was in the papers last week. Of course, I can't do full sessions with patients until my license is renewed, but the center needed a new chief after Dr. Scott became a patient and I'm well qualified for that."

Ah. That would explain it. I've been avoiding the press lately nearly as carefully as a movie star involved in a scandal. "Sorry, I don't read the paper much. But congratulations!" I meant it. A new chief meant new rules and my being eighty-sixed from the facility could be swept away with the stroke of a pen.

I did know that Jeff Scott needed therapy. I'd suggested it to him myself, very sincerely. He'd been traumatized by a mental attack magical kidnappers had inflicted. From his description it had been the mental equivalent of rape. They'd tortured him because it was *fun*. I'd killed or disabled most of those responsible, but he couldn't seem to get past it. That I understood only too well. It becomes disabling and therapy is really the only way out of the maze in your own brain.

"Thank you. So I'll see you sometime today? I'll let the gate know to pass you through."

She might have to insist. The gate guard, Gerry, had once been a friendly acquaintance—before I'd saved a stadiumful of baseball fans by manipulating him and a bunch of cops. Then he turned into an anti-siren crusader. I still didn't know if it was by his own will or the result of another manipulation by Eirene.

I pressed the cutoff switch after our good-byes, the receiver still in my hand. I was feeling . . . odd. I was happy that I might be able to have Gwen as my therapist again one day but curious—and worried—about what she was going to tell me. Emma was an inpatient there at Birchwoods, but she'd seemed generally okay while shopping, outside of her concern for her brother. Dawna was in outpatient therapy and also seemed fine. Not knowing what was wrong made me want to jump in my car and head straight over. Except that Alex was still downstairs and I had an eleven o'clock meeting with a P.I. I'd hired about a mysterious heir Vicki had posthumously asked me to investigate.

I released the cutoff switch and pressed the intercom for the front desk. "Yes, dear?" I was getting used to being called that, as were the other tenants. Hard to argue about office propriety when confronted by watery blue eyes and a patient smile.

"Send Alex up, please."

"Of course, dear. But have you eaten yet?"

I sighed. No. Of course I hadn't. If I'd gotten here at seven fifteen and woke at ten fifteen then I was definitely due for a shake. Except that I really wasn't hungry and didn't know why. But I'd had it hit me without warning before—like at the mall. "Thanks for the reminder. Give me five minutes."

She hung up without another word. It'd probably be a good idea to take a look at my shoulder, too. It used to be that the only refrigerator in the building was in the lunchroom on the first floor. But since I need nourishment every four hours, I decided that having a fridge in my office would be a good idea. In part because of Dottie, we were also looking into an elevator for the building. It was officially a landmark building, so the elevator would probably have to be either a period art deco one or a freestanding external one that wouldn't alter the building's lines, with a window becoming a door. We'd had two tenant meetings on it without coming to an agreement.

Eventually I'd have to decide, providing the Will was deemed valid. Vicki had left the building to me. I hadn't told the guys yet—Bubba would be fine with the idea, but Ron, the attorney who has most of the first floor, would have a conniption fit. But hey, Ron was an ass. Vicki had even asked in her video Will if her ghost could watch when I told him.

After grabbing a chocolate nutrition shake from my mini-fridge and drinking down half, I walked to the bathroom. In the mirror, which was framed by bright pink, candy-stripe wallpaper, I looked a wreck. No wonder Dawna had asked if I was okay. My face was blood smeared and my hair was sticking out at all angles.

I used to have pale, translucent skin that burned easily. Now it was white enough to cause guys like the father in the mall to spritz me with holy water. It might be even more noticeable if not for my light blond hair. Dark hair would make me look three days dead. We'd been experimenting with makeup palettes to make me seem more . . . natural. The shopping trip had mostly been a success—nobody had gone screaming or running until I went vamp and got all glowy—so I was satisfied with the foundation and blush we'd settled on. I'd bought three sets of the colors. One for home, one for here, and one in my purse for emergency touch-ups.

The shirt I'd woken up in was a man's . . . and from the way it hung on me, the man was a linebacker. I sniffed at the collar to see if I could get a hint of who it had belonged to, but it just smelled of clean cotton and Downy fabric softener. Stripping it off, I was pleased to note that I was wearing a bra. Strange how the little things like modesty ease the mind. But there was blood on the bra as well as the gauze bandages, so it would have to go. Let's see . . . three hours. Would I have healed under the bandages? Would it be safe to shower? Hmm.

Naw. Probably best to give it another half day. Gaetano said he'd had to reopen the wound. I would take a sponge bath and wash my hair in the sink. Alex would understand. She's been through more than one messy raid.

In fifteen minutes I was clean, blow-dried, freshly painted, and dressed in my own clothes. The linen cabinet now doubled as a wardrobe, so I had client-worthy clothes available whenever needed. Another reason for our shopping trip. Pale colors offset with black or rich, intense colors like burgundy seem to suit the "new me," so I put on a pair of black jeans and a pale yellow sweater set with baby blue and pink embroidered roses. Not too bad, actually, with the light brown eyeliner and "peace rose" blush. Not stark, not threatening, and very not vampirey.

Since I wasn't sure whether Alex was here as Alex or as

Detective Heather Alexander I definitely wanted to appear non-threatening. Nothing to see here, Officer. Just a peace-loving citizen . . . not a prison-raiding, shopper-terrifying, fanged monster.

I drank the rest of the shake as I walked back into my office. It really tasted good after toothpaste—a chocolate cool mint shake. They should team up to market that flavor.

Alex was waiting for me in a client chair, reading the latest issue of *Bodyguard Quarterly*. They have trade journals for nearly everything now and it was a great place to find out about new gadgets. Crap! That reminded me. I didn't remember seeing the fly in my vest. Well, shit. I wasn't going to enjoy telling Creede I'd lost it. With any luck it was in my car.

"Morning, Alex. Sorry to keep you waiting. Want a soda?" She turned her head and took in my appearance with raised brows and general approval. I skirted around the coffee table just as she tossed the magazine the five feet backward to it. Good aim. It hit the top of the stack of magazines and stuck like an Olympic gymnast.

"Celia. Sure. I guess." She looked and sounded haggard but determined. It's hard to lose someone you love, especially to murder. Rumor had it that, like me, she'd thrown herself into her work to escape the pain and emptiness. I think I fared better. While she hid it well with makeup, I could tell from the fit of an outfit I'd seen her in before that she'd lost weight and had a few more wrinkles around her mouth. She took the drink I held out. "You're looking well."

I shrugged as I sat down in my office chair. "I'm trying some colors that don't make me look so . . . well, you know."

She nodded and then took a deep breath. I could tell that part of her wanted to be annoyed with me for not being a blubbering mess. I had been for a couple of weeks, but it had become a little easier because Vicki was still around in ghost form. We talked. Which reminded me, we needed to talk about Ivy. Damn. Alex said, "You've been avoiding my calls and I'm starting to get a lot of . . . pressure from above."

So. She was here as a cop. Playing innocent was only playing, but I do it well. I wasn't about to panic and throw myself on her mercy until absolutely necessary. "About what?"

"The department needs your help. Our guys on the street are getting edgy. They're demanding protection."

That stopped me cold. "Protection? From what?" She was silent for a long moment, obviously uncomfortable. Her fingers nibbled at her blazer trim before tucking into a pocket. Her foot began a light tapping on the floor that I'd seen before when she didn't want to tell Vicki something about an active case she'd foreseen the events of.

"They want siren charms. Two of the cops Eirene manipulated are having post-traumatic stress symptoms. The staff psychologist says the only thing that will help them even start to get over it is protection against future events." She gave me a disgusted look that had both frustration and fear in it. "I've been resisting putting you in this position, but I'm afraid they're going to hold it against me if I don't get you to donate hair or skin samples for anti-siren charms. You're the only siren they know and I'm the only one on staff who knows you."

Whoa. I honestly didn't know what to say to that. I understood the fear of being out of control—doing things against your will. Whether or not you realized it was manipulation until later was pretty irrelevant. But while I sympathized, I was also offended and worried. Because DNA samples can also be used effectively in spells that are a lot less benign, and there were more than a few cops who'd felt I should be hunted as a monster. And then there was the obvious implication. "In effect, they want an anti-*Celia* charm. Isn't that right? I presume your department witch told you there are two kinds. A true anti-siren charm would take a lot more magic and would have to be recharged periodically. Wouldn't what you're *really* asking for break something like a hundred years of precedent about discrimination against individual magic users? I don't plan to break the law, so it would be punishment before an event." Last night excepted, of course. And I wasn't even sure I'd broken any laws. Other than throwing myself into one guard to keep him from shooting Kevin, the worst I did was break through the magic barrier, and I'm not sure it's a crime to break *into* a prison. I wasn't the one who actually got Kevin out.

She sighed like she agreed with me but had to present the official viewpoint. "Except it's not just you. Once Queen Lopaka sent that letter to the governor saying that you were certified royalty and he made that press statement about how proud he was to have a royal who was a citizen of California . . . It's only a matter of time before there are official state visits or before other powerful magical visitors come to see you. That's going to put an extra strain on our department. How can we protect the citizens if visitors can run mentally roughshod over our people?"

Fuck a duck. Lopaka and the governor? Jeez, I really did

need to start reading the newspapers. I was surprised there weren't a dozen reporters sticking mics in my face when I went outside. "When did all that happen?"

Now *she* looked surprised. It softened the lines on her face and made her look more like the Alex I remembered. The semifriend. "Have you been living in a cave? The only reason the press isn't on your doorstop is you're not the flavor of the week this week. There are other people with siren blood in California—both male and female—but not all of them have the ability to manipulate minds. Right now, the press hasn't quite figured that out."

Ah. Now I got it. "And without charms, none of your guys are willing to tell the press about me for fear I'll retaliate. Is that it?" She had the decency to blush slightly. She covered it well, but I knew it bugged her. "Y'know, I can't see any wins for me in this situation, Alex. There's no way to know if a charm made with samples from me would be effective against other sirens, even if the department witch added extra oomph. If I give you DNA to make charms, then cops who already don't like me will go public or use them for God knows what. The press will hound me and I won't be able to do my job. What's my incentive?"

She shrugged slender shoulders and flipped her short blonde hair just as I heard a click. It sounded just like the little digital recorder I used for keeping notes. She was *taping* our conversation? Okay, that's a total violation of multiple laws. But all of a sudden she relaxed into her chair and let out a snort. Apparently with the taping done, she could now be open about her *own* opinion of the department decree. "Precisely. I tried to tell them you weren't stupid and would figure that out. But I said I would try. And I have. I'd do exactly what you did and refuse. It's ridiculous. Our own department witch couldn't give any opinion about the charm's effectiveness. She said we'd just have to try it and see. But she didn't like the idea, either. Too risky, she said."

"You know I could sue the department, and you, for taping this without permission?"

She nodded but didn't say anything out loud—probably thinking I'd been doing the same thing. I wasn't but should have been, damn it. "As a favor, I would appreciate a formal refusal . . . on the record." She put her hand back in her pocket. "Ready?"

I held up a hand. "Wait. Let's talk this out for a second." This might be a golden opportunity for some backroom dealing. I needed to tell someone official what was going on at the prison. Yes, Jones might take care of it, or his company might have been the *cause* of it. Tough to tell with shadowy government organizations. "I agree that the police should be immune to mental manipulation—even from me. That just makes sense. And I know people who would know what kind of charm would be effective against all sirens. What I'm leery about is giving the samples and how we can be absolutely positive that that's *all* they're used for. And frankly, I have a problem that you might be able to solve . . . or at least help solve. So, I'll make you a deal."

Her eyes narrowed, but she nodded. "I'm listening."

"The trick is that I can't tell you everything about my problem without involving other people who don't want to be involved."

A second nod. "Still listening. Not liking, but listening."

"First, let's put the device on the desk, where we can both see that I'm not about to make an 'open-mic gaffe.'"

The slim silver and black recorder was on the desk in moments. It was a tape unit, rather than digital. Not a big surprise. A lot of cops were back to using tapes after a recent case in Michigan where a digital recording had been altered by a simple spell. It had been good for the local economy. The tape-manufacturing plant at the edge of town that had closed in the nineties was back open and working three shifts to supply the sudden demand.

The tape wasn't moving, but just to be safe Alex took out the microcassette and set it on the desk next to the unit. I took a deep breath and let it out slow as she reached for the red and silver can in front of her and took a long drink.

"There's a demonic presence possessing guards and prisoners out at the zoo. I want the police to get some priests out there to cleanse the place before it spreads."

Apparently, this bore no relation to whatever she'd thought I was going to say. Her eyes went wide and she spewed a mouthful of cola across my desk. I managed to scoot back fast to keep the spray off of my shirt. I grabbed tissues and started to clean spit and soda off the polished wood—and the tape and tape recorder. Her coughing fit would have made me laugh in other circumstances. Not today. Finally Alex got control of herself and said, "Excuse me? Why do you think that?"

I leaned back in my chair, my head swimming. So many things I couldn't say. "That's the part I can't tell you about. What I *can* say is that it showed on a detector and I confirmed it visually." I held up my hands helplessly and stared into her wide green eyes. I knew I was asking for a lot. For a local police detective to question a state facility was bucking ten levels of protocol. Yes, I could call one of the warrior-priest organizations, but I'd be put on a list to *check it out*. A request from Alex would go to the top of the pile. "I'm afraid you'll have to trust me on this. You know I wouldn't ask unless I felt it was important."

She began to tap her fingers on the desk. I didn't realize she chewed her nails. I'd never noticed before. But they were down to bleeding on some fingers. She looked troubled. I needed to convince her, but how?

"Wait! Vicki was there, too. Would you do it if she confirmed it?"

Alex's whole face brightened. It was well established in law that ghosts couldn't lie.

Alex looked up. Her voice dropped to a reverent whisper. "Vick? You there, hon?"

There was no response. No chilling of the room, no breeze moving my hair. I was sorry but not surprised. "She was pretty tired. Did she visit you at all yesterday?"

Alex nodded. "She showed up right at dusk and listened while I ranted about my day. It's not . . . not like it used to be, but it's something. She left suddenly. I presume because you called?" There was a pain in her voice that I was powerless to remove. I didn't know why Vicki would choose being with me in a crisis over being with her hurt and lonely lover. The siren queens claim Vicki's my spirit guardian. I don't know about that. I do know our friendship was strong enough to survive the grave. That's enough in my book.

"She'll probably be back later today. You can ask her then, when I can't give her any hints. If it checks out, will you go?"

"That's your only condition? You'll give the samples if I do it?"

Now it was my turn to tap fingers. "I'd still like to check out what the charm needs to do . . . and *not* do. And I want guarantees there'll be precautions against the samples being misused. But by tomorrow we should both know. Deal?"

She nodded. "What I can do until I hear from Vicki is check the board and the incoming bulletins, see if there have been reports of anything strange out there. I can do that without alerting anyone. We're all supposed to look at those anyway, and I'm behind on them." She smoothed her skirt as she stood. "If what you say is true, I'll do whatever I have to do to get the priests out there, even if I have to drive one there myself." She picked up the cassette and put it back in the machine. Without asking if I was ready, she pushed the record button. She remembered just where she left off. "Your incentive is to do the right thing. For yourself, for the people of this city, and for all of us who protect them."

It was all true and, again, I didn't disagree with the concept. I paused an appropriate length of time before responding. "I want to talk to a mage I know to find out more about the process . . . and the *consequences*. Call me tomorrow about this same time and I'll have an answer for you. Deal?"

She reached across the desk with her right hand and also met my eyes in a way that wasn't for the tape. "Deal."

After a few more pleasantries to show she had taped the whole interview—as such—she left. I sat in my chair, thinking a thousand different thoughts.

6

By the time I went downstairs, to both stretch my legs and take the soggy, sticky tissues to the main trash can in the kitchen—which got emptied every day, unlike mine, which I dumped whenever I got around to it—the investigator had arrived. I'd only worked with Shawn Beall once before, but he'd done a good job and had only charged for his actual time. When you're a sole proprietor, money is the bottom line—regardless of the client's ability to pay. My goal was not to gouge Vicki's estate. I wanted the truth, whether it came cheap or expensive. But cheap was always better.

Shawn followed me back to my office and took the chair Alex had so recently vacated. Shawn is one of those guys you wouldn't really look at twice. He looks like a computer geek . . . and he is. But the small frame, unruly dark hair, and pop bottle glasses hide a sneaky, near-criminal mind and a surprisingly athletic body. He's got the wiry frame and agility of a long-distance runner along with the determination of a pit bull. The combination is the gold standard of a good investigator.

"So, what have you got for me?"

He pulled an envelope from an inner jacket pocket and

handed it over. "Wish I had more, but there's more dead ends than leads. Take a look. I'll answer any questions I can."

I slit the envelope and scanned the pages inside. The first page was a profile of one Michael Murphy, known as Mickey or Mick to family and friends. The photo was just as I remembered him at Vicki's Will reading. Carrot orange hair was neatly combed to the side and a scattering of freckles dotted his face below vivid green eyes. I remembered a cultured southern accent that got stronger the more befuddled he was. There had been plenty to be surprised about that day. The only person more shocked than her parents, best friend, and lover to learn that Vicki had left a quarter of her multimillion-dollar estate to a total stranger was the stranger himself.

I'd been tasked to find out *why* she'd done it.

I was still wrapping my head around the fact that she'd trusted her clairvoyant gift enough to write a Will that would inevitably be challenged. While it was no crime to give money to a total stranger, it was a little odd and might lend credence to her mother's allegation that Vicki wasn't in her right mind.

So, my goal was to prove there was a good and valid reason for my friend's act before the lawsuit went to court. Fortunately, the law firm Vicki had used was one of the best in the state, so I was pretty sure I'd have all the time I needed to search.

Mickey had a wife, Molly, and two daughters: Beverly, aged twelve, and Julie, who was eight. They lived in a comfortable home in Fool's Rush, Arkansas, where Mickey was a law clerk for the local county judge. Molly ran a diner she'd inherited from her parents, and the girls were above-average students. "Okay, so pretty normal people." I flipped the dozen pages. I didn't want to sit here and read while Shawn stared at me. "Give me the condensed version."

"Sure," he said with a nod. He settled back into the seat and interlocked his fingers over his stomach, his arms resting comfortably on the padded rests. "I checked all the obvious connections first. Vicki is English on her mother's side and, despite the surname, German on her father's. Cassandra Meadows can trace her lineage to the *Mayflower* and, trust me, a thousand fans have done so quite convincingly. Jason Cooper's grandfather emigrated from Germany after the First World War—the family surname was formerly Braun. Nobody really knows how or why the name was changed at Ellis Island, but it appears the government had something to do with it. I'll have to do more checking, but it looks like Franz Braun was a chemical scientist and our government wanted something he'd invented." That piqued my curiosity and I began to ask questions, but Shawn held up a hand bearing a rather heavy gold wedding ring to stop me. "That doesn't really matter right now, because Mickey Murphy's family comes from old Irish stock. Molly is apparently quite the amateur genealogist and was happy to show me the scrapbooks she's put together."

Since the investigation had been requested in front of Mr. Murphy, it seemed logical to have Shawn interview them openly. "Mickey's multi-great-grandfather came to this country to help the colonists fight England. He used his salary to bring his wife and kids over. No prior trips to either Germany or England and I can't find anything to indicate that the Murphys or DeVeres—Molly's family—ever mingled or crossed paths with the Coopers or Meadowses. Of course there could be something that I missed, since I'm not a specialist in such things. I hope it's okay that I subcontracted out part of the search to a company that specializes in lineage searches."

I like it when investigators don't try to reinvent the wheel. Find people who do the specific job, pay them, and get back to work. "No problem at all. Is the information in here to give to the attorney?"

He nodded. "At this point, I'm wondering how you want me to proceed. I could sit back and wait for the genealogy report, or look for something in the present time that directly ties Ms. Cooper to the Murphys. It could be as simple as them meeting at some point in the past that she didn't consciously remember. A flat tire he helped fix, a really good meal at Molly's diner, who knows? Finding that out would require lots of interviews and time on the road. And it might turn up nothing. Ultimately, how much money do you want to throw at this?"

Well, Vicki could be absentminded. It was the mark of clairvoyants that they could disappear into the future and totally forget what was happening in the present. So it might well be that simple. "Speaking of being on the road, the summer after college Vicki took a long trip to 'find herself.' She rented a car and drove from her mother's place in New York to her own home, California. I'd gotten the impression at the time that it was a fast trip, just a few days. But maybe it had taken longer. Maybe things happened that she just didn't remember, a hundred visions and a half decade later."

He tilted his head with an odd look and pulled a pad from his pocket. "First time I'm hearing that, and I spent a couple of hours talking to her parents." His pen tapped on the page.

"New York to California, huh? A lot of ground to cover in a couple of days. Do you remember anything she told you? You were best friends even then, right? Did she rave or rant about anything?"

"No, I just remember her mentioning what she called her *senior trip*. I'll work on it overnight. Maybe something will pop into my head."

He tapped the pen on the pad for a moment and then nodded. "Okay. But it could be the key to everything, so think really hard. We'll talk again tomorrow. Same time?"

I flipped the calendar a day and then checked my watch. It was nearly noon. My only morning appointment was at ten. "How about eleven? My afternoon's packed, and I might need driving time."

Shawn pulled out his BlackBerry and punched the screen a few times. "Done and done." He stood up and pointed the pen at me. "Think hard," he repeated. "This could be the difference between a short search and one that takes years."

I agreed. "I'll pull out all the stops. I promise." I desperately hoped I wasn't lying, but I feared I might be. I did know a couple people who might be able to help, but it was a long shot at best.

He let himself out while I gathered together my purse and car keys. Moments later I walked past the front desk, mulling over the dozen things I still needed to do today, like remember to look for the fly in my car. I held out a hand expectantly and, as always, Dawna responded by stuffing a stack of messages into it.

Muttering, "Thank you," as I reached for the doorknob, I was startled when Dottie's voice stopped me: "Sunscreen?"

Dawna added a reminder: "Umbrella?"

Crap. I'd forgotten to slather myself up before heading out-doors. Again. Guess I was still tired from the night's activities. . . .

"Thank you, ladies." Shaking my head, I started back up-stairs. My makeup had a 50 SPF built in, but I'd only put it on my face, not arms, hands, or neck. Yes, it was winter, but it's also California. So far I hadn't turned to ash in the sunlight like most vampires. But I burn like nobody's business. Just get-ting to my car, the morning after I was turned, left me with second-degree burns. They heal, but they hurt as bad as fall-ing asleep on the beach for the afternoon.

"Here. I bought extra for the front desk. For 'weather emer-gencies.'" Dawna held out a bright orange and blue tube. Like the makeup, it had the highest possible SPF.

A sigh slipped out of me. "You're the best, girlfriend. Sorry I've become such a pain in the butt."

She waved a hand at me with a "pshaw" expression. "You've *always* been a pain in the butt, girl. Just new and different kinds lately." Dottie chuckled but kept her eyes on the computer screen. "It keeps our relationship . . . spicy. Like my grammy al-ways says, spend your time with those who challenge you."

Dawna's grandmother is a tiny little Vietnamese woman who met and fell in love with an American soldier who pro-tected their village for a week against tough odds after his squad was killed. He married her and brought her back to his home because he said she made the best phở this side of heaven. I agreed. It was "grab your tongue and throw it to the floor" good. She said she married him because he was smarter than she was. I wasn't sure I agreed.

I squeezed a glop of white lotion into my palm, letting the coconut and other scents take me to a happier time, when all I had to worry about was off-center tan lines. "Did I ever thank her for the last batch of *phở*, by the way?"

Her brow furrowed and lips pursed. "Don't remember. But I'm sure I did for you. I should ask her to make another batch. That woman loves to cook and nothing in the world makes her happier than to be *asked* to do it."

I slathered the lotion on all bits of exposed skin, including my ears, before handing back the tube. "Thanks. All set now. Or have I forgotten anything?"

The two women looked at each other. "Nothing I can think of offhand," Dawna said. "What did Alex tell you about the sniper who tried to take off your head at the Will reading? I know they caught him, but did they ever find out why he was shooting at you or who he worked for? She wouldn't tell me squat."

I swore under my breath because it hadn't even occurred to me to ask. "No. But I'll ask her when I talk to her tomorrow." I glanced at the person in the waiting room, probably a client of Ron's, who raised his head at the mention of the word "sniper." I really didn't want to talk any more about it with people listening. "Thanks for the reminder." It's sad when a sniper who'd tried to put three bullets into your brain slips your mind. For most people, it would possess their every waking moment. For me, it was a humdrum daily event.

Sad, that. I need better days.

On the way to my car, I flipped through the messages using one hand and my lips because the other hand was holding the umbrella. Most were from existing clients asking if I was available for certain dates and times. I wouldn't know until I checked my calendar, so I tucked those in my pocket. As I unlocked the driver's door, one of the messages caught my eye and made me nearly drop the umbrella. I did drop the car keys.

The message was from John Creede:

> *You didn't have to return the fly, but the report gave me a lot of information. Thanks. But you're not off the hook for dinner.*

What the hell?

No wonder I couldn't find the fly. Someone had delivered it to Creede. And while it was nice the fly had found its way back home, that meant . . . crap!

I picked up my car keys and raced back into the building. Both women looked up and Dawna opened her mouth. I shook my head frantically, holding a finger over my lips. Dottie looked around as if she thought something was going to jump out of the shadows. I grabbed a pen and reached for the spiral-bound message book.

> *Call Justin. Have him come and do a FULL sweep for bugs. The roaches seem to have especially big ears upstairs.*

I turned the book so they both could see it. Dawna stared at the message, mouthing the words several times. On the surface, it seemed like I was asking them to call an exterminator because of an infestation. And I was. Except Justin didn't work for Orkin. He was our security consultant. The "bugs" I was worried about were of the electronic variety. Only Creede and I had been in the room when he'd handed me the fly and asked for a report, and I sure as hell hadn't mentioned that to Jones. Okay, it was *possible* that I'd talked while under the influence at the safe house. Possible, but unlikely. Former torturers would agree that I'm hard to break. Those who are still alive, anyway.

Then Dottie's face lit up and she wrote the words "listening devices" on her palm. Dawna's expression shifted from elation at understanding my message to fury at the implication. I didn't blame her. She nodded briskly and reached for the phone and I headed back to my car, feeling better. Jones is good, but Justin is better. He'd find whatever Jones had planted.

A perfect blue sky with fluffy clouds under a warm sun just didn't scream Christmas. It sucked that I had to drive my Miata convertible with the top up, but nowadays I can only put it down at night. The Salvation Army bell ringer on the corner near the building, in somber-colored long sleeves, was out of place in a sea of color and movement. But she reminded people of the season nonetheless and they opened wallets and purses to stuff coins and paper into the red plastic bucket.

About halfway to Birchwoods, I realized I'd forgotten to call my gran before heading out the previous night. I turned on the radio, then tucked my cell phone into the holster on the dash and attached the nifty device that lets the sound come through the radio speakers. I hit the speed dial and she answered on the first ring. "Hi, Gran. What's new?"

Instead of chipper or even calm, her voice was staccato with anger. "Celia Kalino Graves. Where in the world are you? I've been waiting for two hours!"

Crap! Waiting? For what? "Um . . . did we have plans to do something this morning?" It wasn't Sunday, so it couldn't be church. What had we talked about in our last call?

"It is December ninth, young lady. What do you *suppose* we were doing?"

Aw, man, twenty questions. I hate it when she does that. Let's see . . . December ninth. Not church, not a holiday, not . . . wait. It *was* a holiday and I'd completely forgotten. My voice probably conveyed my mingled embarrassment and frustration. "Mom's birthday."

"You forgot, didn't you? Did you at least buy a present?" There was reproach in her tone, and while part of me knew it was probably deserved, I can't help what I feel.

I let out a noise that wasn't precisely a word. "It's hard to get real enthused about gift giving when every year she throws the gift back in my face. Literally. Or tosses it in a trash can. Or sells it for booze money."

But as I expected, I got no sympathy. "That is no excuse and you know it. It's not what she does with it that matters. Now, you get to the mall and buy your mother something nice and then come pick me up so we can go visit her."

"Visit her? In jail? Can she have visitors yet?" Please, God, let me just go see the nice psychiatrist. I so didn't want to see my mother in an orange jumpsuit and handcuffs on her birthday. "We certainly can't take gifts *there*."

"Well, we can't leave them, that's true. And we can't wrap them. But I asked and they said we can give her a card and we can at least show her the gifts once they've passed inspection. She'll know we remembered." The last few words were soft and carried an edge that I recognized. I winced and rubbed my left temple to relieve the sudden tension.

"Please don't cry, Gran. It's not your fault Mom is a screwup." Actually, it was partly Gran's fault, but she didn't need to be reminded of it. I knew it had stung her hard when Mom got picked up. She'd let Mom drive the car without a license . . . while drunk. It was her third drunk-driving offense and I'd thought the judge had been really lenient by only giving her three months behind bars. And in the local jail, rather than the state prison.

"Lana has issues, Celia, and she's getting help for them. But she's *not* a screwup. Don't you think this is hard enough on her as it is? At least leave her a little dignity. She'd do the same for you."

I bit my tongue until it nearly bled. No, she wouldn't. She'd had the chance many times and the bottle was always more important to her than her own child. And while I'd like to say she was just weak, that's not fair, either. She'd actually been a terrific mother until Daddy left and Ivy died. Then she'd crawled into a bottle, and she hadn't come out since. I didn't think my visiting her would mean anything to her at all, but it would make Gran happy. That *was* important to me. I let out a sigh. "Okay, fine. But I have a lot of things going today, so we'll have to make it short."

"Half an hour. That's the longest we can stay this first time anyway."

I calculated in my head. "Okay. It'll be at least thirty minutes to get in and out of the mall and get back to your house. How about I come by at three?" It would be tight, but I could probably still fit it all in before Gwen left for the day. But if one single thing went wrong, the whole schedule would be blown.

Fingers crossed.

Gran's voice went back to her regular happy self. "That'll be fine, dear. I'll have a bite of lunch with the girls and see you then."

I said good-bye and pressed the off button. Honestly. It's days like these that I wonder if it might not have been better to have had all my memories erased by the vampire.

It was worse than I'd expected. Far worse. I hadn't anticipated that watching the video from the fly at the zoo would backlash on me in a regular jail. I'd been to jail before and it hadn't made my heart pound or my head hurt like this. The catcalls of women prisoners sounded like the screams of animals. The touch of the guards as they patted me down made me want to lash out with fangs bared.

What the hell?

I'd had two energy shakes at the mall and I'd been fine there. I'd resigned myself to trying to have a good time as I drove to Gran's new apartment at the assisted-living facility. It had been a surprise to see Pili there. I'd met her on the Isle of Serenity, the legendary home of the Pacific sirens. She was one of the primary prophets to the queen. I hadn't realized Pili had decided to retire and move to the mainland. I didn't know a siren *could* retire. But she and my gran were getting along great guns. They were bridge partners and fast friends already. Still, there was something serious in the way Pili looked at me when I said we were going to visit Mom that made me nervous. Pili's a powerful seer, and I recognized the look—I'd seen it on Vicki, and Emma, often enough. But Pili hadn't said anything, and I hadn't asked. Maybe she'd known what was coming. Because right now I wanted to run screaming out of this place. Or kill someone.

Desperation and panic began to cling to my skin like six weeks' worth of grime. I itched under my pretty yellow sweater as though lice were crawling on me. Even Gran noticed me clutching my hands and breathing fast and shallow. "Celia? What's wrong?" She touched me and I jumped. Now the guards started watching—noticing what seemed to be a person with guilt weighing on her.

"I don't know." My head shook as I looked around, searching for the source of the feeling. The visiting room was an open space with pale peach walls, furnished with tables and padded chairs. There wasn't anything in the room that should give me the feelings I was having.

Then Mom walked in the room, and I knew the source of my feelings. Her hair was in strings and she'd lost so much weight that her face was gaunt and pinched. But it was her eyes that dragged a horrified gasp from my throat. They were lifeless and distant—the thousand-yard stare of the abused. I know because I've seen them in my own mirror. "Mom?" I stood up and started to walk toward her. She didn't even look up. Before I reached her, another prisoner was escorted into the room, a tall mixed-race woman with unruly yellow dreadlocks. She pushed her way past Mom. Hard. The mother I'd grown up with wouldn't have hesitated to go toe-to-toe with someone who shoved her aside. But now Mom just stumbled and fell against a nearby table.

Two things happened simultaneously. I started toward Mom to help her up and the temperature in the room dropped by thirty degrees. Everyone in the room looked up as a familiar chill settled over the room, causing breath to be seen and windows to fog. The woman who'd pushed Mom was lifted from her feet and thrown a dozen feet across the room. She landed in a heap in the corner but came up fast, looking for someone to attack. No guard came to her aid and the one by the door who'd escorted her in looked rather satisfied as she dusted off her jumpsuit.

The woman wouldn't find anyone to retaliate with because you can't punch a ghost. I was surprised to realize it wasn't Vicki, despite the large amount of energy being expended. This ghost felt more petite.

Mom's eyes met mine, and . . . nothing. My own mother didn't recognize me and the look in her eyes chilled me even more than the effect of the ghost hovering overhead. It was almost as though Mom was trapped inside herself. I could feel her fear and the desperation beating at me like a cold wind, but none of it showed in her body language or face. "Ivy?" I whispered as I helped Mom to her feet.

The lights blinked once.

The other prisoner must have decided that Mom was the cause of her fall, because she was stomping toward us. I was all set to block her path when she was thrown backward again.

Once more nobody came to her aid, and this time she narrowed her eyes and stared at Mom, probably wondering if she was using telekinesis.

"Are you . . . *guarding* Mom?"

Another blink caused everyone to look up and around. Wow. I didn't know Ivy had it in her to expend this much energy in one session. But it would explain why Vicki couldn't give me a good answer on whether Ivy was okay. In a prison setting, she was likely draining herself to exhaustion at every turn. I was both happy that someone I trusted was staying with Mom to help and distressed that she so obviously *needed* help.

I led Mom to the table and got her seated. Gran was nodding sadly as she touched her daughter's hand. "This is what I wanted you to see, Celie. I don't know what's happened to her. They claim they're not using any medication on her and that nobody is hurting her. But look at her. What are they doing to my baby?"

Tears formed at the corners of Gran's eyes and I blinked back my own salty wetness. I had a feeling I knew what was wrong. But I was more afraid of that than if someone was hitting her. I touched her chin and turned her face toward mine. "Happy Birthday, Mom. It's Celia. Can you hear me?" I spoke the words both out loud and into her mind. But there was nobody home to answer.

Her eyes were unfocused, staring somewhere over my shoulder. I looked up to the sparkling formation near the ceiling. "Did someone hurt her before you got here? Is that why you came?"

The overhead fluorescent lights blinked . . . and then blinked again.

No? That made my brow furrow as a shout came from the other side of the room. "Fix the damn lights! I'm getting a headache!"

"Who are you talking to, Celie?" Gran's voice was nearly a whisper, as though she was afraid who would overhear.

"It's Ivy," I responded with a smile in a similar whisper. "She's here and has been watching over Mom."

I understood why Gran was whispering. We were getting way too much attention. The guard at the door was moving closer and two security cameras were spinning in our direction. The staff had already spent plenty of time on me at the entrance. The pale skin and fangs had bothered them no end, despite the fact that I'd walked in during broad daylight and passed through both the outer and inner magic perimeter. I'd even passed the holy-water test and had a cross shoved onto my wrist. But that didn't mean I didn't make them nervous. The more things that went wrong now, the more likely I would wind up in the cell next to my mother.

"Oh, honey, that's not good. Ivy's only a child. Things go on here she . . . shouldn't be exposed to."

"It's okay, Gran. She's *helping*. Really. She's keeping Mom safe from the other women. And I don't think you can stop her." I didn't add that there were quite a few things Ivy had seen in life that she probably shouldn't. After Dad left, Mom had spent most of our childhood drinking, drugging, and sleeping around.

Rather than say something I shouldn't, I stood and walked over to the guard near the door. "Excuse me. How would I go about talking to the doctor or nurse here? I think my mother is reacting badly to the medication they've given her." It seemed safer to say that than what I truly believed. I was afraid my turning more siren had kicked in my mother's abilities, too. Here in jail, she couldn't see the ocean. That was going to be a problem. But I didn't want to announce she had the same blood. Especially not after my rather public trial.

The woman was older, heavyset and dark skinned, with long hair worn in a bun at the back of her neck. She stood just about tall enough to stare at my neck, but I could tell immediately that she was all business and could probably teach me some new things about pain if I stepped out of line. She opened her mouth and I was transported out of California and straight south of the Mason-Dixon Line. "Honeychil', your mama started doin' that all on her own. I handle the medication calls on her block and I guarantee not a single pill has passed her lips. I'm worried about her, too. She's not made for this place. She's going downhill faster than anyone I've ever seen. It's like she's pining away, ready to join that pretty little girl of hers on the other side."

The guard's absolute acceptance and knowledge of Ivy spooked me even more. "You can see the ghost?"

"Oh, hell, yes. The women in my family are channelers from back before the War of Northern Aggression." I honestly could say I hadn't heard that term for the Civil War since . . . well, since high school. "You probably see a sparkly cloud, right?" I nodded. "I see a skinny little thing of about eight with long hair and a sad expression. Determined, though. Ain't nobody gonna hurt her mama." She made a motion with her chin toward the prisoner with the dreadlocks. "And I'm not inclined to stop her from trying. Nothing in the rule book says I have to stop a guardian angel from guardianing."

Despite the mangled language, I agreed. "She was a pretty heavy drinker, though. Could that be affecting her?"

The guard shrugged. "Body should have detoxed in the first week. I never say never, but I haven't seen it before."

"And you've been a guard for—?"

"Twenty-three years now. Two federal prisons, two state, and now here. I like it here best. Not many real badasses in this place, despite what Goldilocks over there believes she is." She gave me a small, evil smile. "She wouldn't know a badass until after one laid her flat. Frankly, makes me smile to see that tiny little girl whup her butt." Then she shook her head sadly. "Unfortunately, in that time I haven't seen whatever's wrong with your mama."

She shook her head and stared at Mom. I followed her gaze to take in the flaccid features and lifeless feel. She made tsking noises and let out a sigh. "This place is killing her and I don't know there's nothing anyone can do about it."

7

Lieutenant Rogers, the southern guard, promised to put our cards in Mom's cell for when Mom was "feeling better." Then I'd dropped off Gran after promising I'd speak to the administrator of the jail, who had already gone home. There had to be something we could do to get Mom back to normal. I might find her a royal pain in the ass when she was drunk, but even that was better than how she was now.

I was finally on my way to Birchwoods, only an hour late. I'd called Gwen and asked if she could stay. She'd agreed and hadn't even given me one of her veiled admonishments about time management or consideration for others. That meant it was pretty serious.

I was praying under my breath as I approached the guard station that the person handling the gate was anyone but Gerry.

No such luck.

He opened the door to the tiny shack and put out a hand for me to stop. I hadn't talked to him since the whole Eirene thing. I had no doubt it was going to be awkward at best. He'd been head of security until he went berserk on me after the trial. Then he'd been demoted back to gate jockey. But maybe if we both pretended it never happened, we could eventually heal. I was at least willing to give it a try.

I rolled down the window. The sun was low enough on the horizon that it stung. I leaned my head backward as casually as possible to stay in the shade. "Afternoon, Gerry. Dr. Talbert is expecting me."

There was a long enough pause that I was forced to look at his face. His lips were a tight line and I could swear I could hear him grinding his teeth. "Celia . . ." The way he said it made my discomfort rise.

"Look, Gerry. You don't have to apologize. I understand you were being manipulated. It wasn't—"

"*Apologize?*" The outrage in that one word made every nerve in my body stand at attention. "Apologize to *you?*" He lowered his voice to a hiss. "You're a damned vampire. You're undead evil and should have a stake driven through your heart right before your head gets chopped off." My jaw dropped just like Gran's had at the jail. "I wasn't being manipulated. I *volunteered* to help put you down. I'll do it again if I get the chance."

Excuse me? Did I actually hear that? "Did you just threaten to murder me? I could have you arrested for that. I'm *not* undead. Your own security footage will convict you."

He leered at me with a maniacal expression. "I turned off the tape."

I opened the car door in a rush and slammed him back against the guardhouse door. Keeping the pressure on his body with my admittedly supernatural strength, I stepped out into the full sun. It made me feel a little sweaty, but the sunscreen was still doing its thing. Gerry squirmed and swore to no avail. "Do I look dead to you?" I reached out and grabbed the massive silver cross he always wore over his blue tie and clutched it tight in my bare hand. No smoke, no smell of burning flesh. For me, no pain. Gerry's eyes went wide as I released the cross and held up my hand. "Either I'm still a human who just has a bad overbite or you're not a true believer. . . ."

He couldn't move his arms, so I reached through the guard shack's window and pushed the button for the gate. As it swung open I got back into my car. Gerry was still remembering how to breathe as I put the car in gear. "I suggest you spend a little more time reading the Bible. Follow the Golden Rule and do unto others as you would have them do unto you. Because believe me when I say that if you try to carry through on that threat, I'll be *doing unto* all over your ass."

I wanted to bare my fangs. The approaching sunset was making me twitchy. But I had better things to do with my time than give him the satisfaction of doing exactly what he expected me to do. Instead, I stepped on the gas and the Miata shot through the opening gates when they were open barely wide enough to avoid scratching the paint.

Gwen stepped out of the administration building just as I brought the car to a stop with a squeak of the tires. She was accompanied by someone I presumed was one of the security staff. It occurred to me that without sound the security footage would make it look like I'd attacked Gerry. I was surprised there weren't a dozen guards with rifles and crossbows leveled at my chest right now. Hell, maybe there were and I just couldn't see them.

I was still seething, but I'd slammed a nutrition shake on the way up the long, winding drive. Hopefully, with the edge off my hunger I'd just appear frustrated and not lethal. Gwen's arms were crossed over her chest and her brows were raised. "Would you care to explain yourself?"

I was not going to apologize. I wasn't the bad guy here. Even better, I recognized the man with her, Jesse Garcia. He was the facility's truthteller. He'd listen to my story—and Gerry's—using his magical intuition and then report to the security staff about what had really happened. He was a dozen times more powerful than any lie detector. He'd know which of us was telling the truth, or what combination of facts represented the truth. "I actually thought I handled that pretty well, considering the provocation. He ought to get fired for what he said to me, or at least reprimanded. He threatened my life. I could call the D.A."

"He *threatened* you?" Now Gwen's face showed confusion, and her body language changed.

I repeated the whole conversation for her as we walked into the building. Her whole body went rigid when I got to the part about doing it again. She looked at Jesse; his brows were raised, lips pursed as though tasting the truth of my story.

After a long moment, he nodded. "I'll be going down to the gate now, and I think there should be several armed officers with me, ma'am."

Gwen let out a sound that was as close to a growl as a refined professional woman in charge of a large facility could allow herself. Then she turned to me in full sight and hearing of Jesse. "Celia, on behalf of the administration and the owners of Birchwoods, please accept my apology for that . . . *serious* breach of protocol. I assure you that guard will be terminated."

The part of me that was insulted and hurt would be happy to have Gerry fired on the spot. But the other part of my brain made me let out a sigh. "You can't stop people from being prejudiced. All you can do is make it painful for them to say out loud what they really believe. If you fire him, it'll be all my fault and he'll never rest until he puts me in a grave. I never did a thing to hurt Gerry and it really bugs me that being attacked and nearly killed has somehow made me his enemy. It sucks, Gwen; it really does." That was an understatement. Gerry's reaction brought home every emotion I'd bottled up since I was attacked. I was a vampire now. Evil. Undead.

Damn it.

Maybe she saw that when she stared into my eyes. I looked away first. "Go ahead and discipline him. Dock his pay or give him a tail chewing. But don't fire him. Please. At least with a job he'll be busy most of the day and won't have as much free time to spend trying to shove a stake through my heart."

"Damn. You're nicer than me," Jesse said. "I'd have knocked him on his ass and *then* got him fired."

Gwen reached out and touched my shoulder. To my credit, I didn't flinch. "Celia Graves, you have turned into an amazing young woman. You've taken a difficult situation and, while I might suggest avoiding physical confrontation in the future, have handled it with grace. I'll take your advice and be *very* certain that Gerry knows it was only because of your plea for mercy that he still has a job." Her eyes sparkled. There was a

DEMON SONG ι 107

surprising amount of humor in her voice as she concluded, "That should keep him confused for quite a while."

Jesse snorted. It was obvious he was on my side; I hoped he'd stay that way after he talked to Gerry. Jesse headed for the security office, probably to assemble the team he'd take down to the gate.

As Gwen and I walked down the quiet, carpeted hallway toward her office, I let out a deep breath. "So, now that I'm here, what did you need to see me about?"

"Let's talk when we get to my office. For the moment, we'll let our thoughts drift."

Ah yes. I'd forgotten about the "thoughts drifting" thing. Gwen had always been big on the idea that solutions would come to us if we just allowed our minds to work, unhindered by emotion or intent. In a way, she was right. The twilight time between alertness and sleep was often when I got my best ideas or solved work problems that had confounded me for the whole day. There had been whole therapy sessions where we'd do nothing but stare at the walls, silent but touching hands or feet, to become "grounded and centered."

I remembered one particular breakthrough that had happened during such a time. I'd been staring at a painting in Gwen's office, a still life of a bottle next to a bowl of wax fruit. I'd blurted out a truth that still haunts me to this day: "Mom doesn't even realize she's hurting me, does she?"

Gwen's response had been, "No, she doesn't. How does that make you feel?"

I'd realized that just like Gran, I'd been enabling my mother's behavior. I'd never told her that her drinking bothered me. I'd just stayed silently annoyed and resentful.

So I'd decided it was time to tell her.

Bad move. That was the part that still haunted me. It had been another breakthrough . . . of sorts.

A small part of me had hoped that once she knew, she'd turn away from the booze. I'd expected her to pick me over the bottle. She hadn't. It had merely ramped up the tension, because we'd both been deluding ourselves about the other. She'd apparently thought I didn't mind her getting drunk. Once she knew otherwise, my disapproval became an embarrassment to her and she tried to hide her drinking from me. It put another wedge of distance between us that had yet to be removed.

Those were my happy thoughts as we reached Gwen's office. I was surprised at the changes to the place. The room's colors were the same—light sandy brown, plus muted blues and greens. But she'd moved the desk closer to the door and rearranged the furniture so it seemed more . . . relaxed. The pictures were different, too. Just as tasteful and expensive, but different.

She walked around to the other side of the desk and sat down in the chair that had once been Dr. Scott's. He was a big man, so when Gwen sat down she looked a little like a child playing in her parent's office. "Thank you for coming. I apologize once again for the way you were greeted."

I leaned back in my seat, tipped my head, and raised my shoulders slightly. "There's no need. I've heard worse and probably will again. I'd rather focus on which one of my friends is in trouble. You know I don't use that word lightly, so I presume you didn't, either."

"No, you're correct. I'm very careful with my words with you. I said a friend of yours and I meant it." She leaned forward and rested her arms on the desk with an expression of total earnestness. "I received a call a few days ago from a colleague who expressed a concern about his patient. He knew that I once treated you and he wanted some insight into what he perceived as a threat to her healing."

The only two friends I had in therapy were Dawna and Emma. A *threat to their healing* was a big deal. "Who is it?"

She grimaced slightly. Clearly she was reluctant to tell me.

"How can I help if I don't know who it is, Gwen?"

She closed her eyes and nodded. "You're right, of course. The patient is Dawna. According to her doctor, she's actually doing quite well. She's able to drive alone and walk to her car without an escort."

That made me happy. Lilith had grabbed Dawna on her way to her car, so no doubt that was a huge trigger to a panic attack. "Great! I'm so glad for her. But what's the problem?"

"Unfortunately, she was alone in her house when you killed Lilith. She was still bound to her and felt her die."

Oh, fuck a duck. "I knew she'd been tortured. You mean she'd become Lilith's *servant*?" My head started reeling when Gwen nodded. The master/servant relationship was a strong one. Breaking it by killing the master, rather than cleansing the servant, could have long-term repercussions. I couldn't even imagine what it might have been like for Dawna to go through that with no priests nearby and no one to comfort her.

Now I felt like a total heel. No wonder she'd been suicidal. It had never even occurred to me to ask if she'd been bitten. Of course, I hadn't even known Lilith had attacked her until after, but still, I could have *asked*.

"Crap. I don't know how to fix that. What does her doctor say?"

Gwen took a deep breath and let it out slow. Her French-manicured nails started lightly tapping on the desk. "He doesn't think she should live alone right now. It's when she's alone that the fear sets in. But she's still not trusting enough to even start looking for a roommate. He thinks she needs to live with someone she already trusts—and someone who is not a direct family member."

Yeah. I totally understood that. Dawna loves her family desperately, but they're major control freaks. They want to have input into every aspect of her life—from the clothing she buys to the food on her plate. Every decision should be a *family* decision. They had driven my very independent-minded best friend right out the door.

Gwen's voice cut into my thoughts: "Perhaps she needs to live with someone like . . . you."

Me? "You just told me I killed her master. How would that possibly make living with me a good choice?"

Gwen smiled softly. "You *freed* her from her master. There's a vast difference, Celia. Apparently, she told her therapist that you are the one person in the world she truly trusts; that's why she came back to work at the office before the doctor felt she was ready. Dr. Dewer was only concerned that moving in with her might harm your own therapy or, worse, lead to a codependent relationship where, in her mind, you would take the place of the master she lost."

Both were very valid concerns. "I honestly don't know what to say. I mean, sure, it would be fun to live with Dawna in the short term. But we get along well because we *don't* spend every waking moment together. I can't tell you what would happen if we did." I gave her a wry smile. "I don't have a very good track record of making relationships work, if you remember."

We both chuckled, though my laugh was a little nervous. It was true and she knew it. "Well, despite your family and love life, you have a solid group of friends. You're loyal, encouraging, and, from all reports, fun. Why don't you try a small experiment instead of leaping in with both feet? Go on a 'girls' retreat,' where you and Dawna stay in the same hotel room, maybe for a long weekend. You need a break yourself. Don't think I didn't notice you have surgical gauze on your shoulder."

Oops. "About that . . ."

She waved it away with a hand. "I don't need to know. If it was important, you would have mentioned it, and it obviously didn't affect your movements at the gate. But be honest, Celia, with me and with yourself. When is the last time you had an actual *vacation*? Not something for work or your family, just a regular vacation?"

One of the things I like best about being a bodyguard is the chance to visit new places and attend special events. Even though I'm working, guarding the client, I can listen to the music and meet interesting people. But when she put it like that— "Probably when Bruno took me home to meet his family.

We stayed in a hotel in Manhattan and spent two days seeing the sights."

Her face showed real surprise. "That was several years ago."

I shrugged. "I like to work."

She raised her brows at me. "Some time off would do you, as well as Dawna, a world of good." Then her head tilted and the last rays of sunlight caught me in the eyes.

I could feel the world slipping into shadows. My first sunset after I turned had been spent in this room and it hadn't been fun. Now I was more in control, but I could still feel my muscles preparing, gearing themselves up to chase down prey. But my human brain refused to obey. I realized then that her lips were moving, but I wasn't hearing any sound. "Give me that last sentence again please? The sunset got to me for a second." My voice had become more harsh, with a light growl on the ends of the words.

"I asked whether the sunset was bothering you and if you'd like to move to a different room."

Oh.

"No. It doesn't matter whether I can actually see the sun set. I feel it in my bones, in my blood. See, this is part of the problem, Gwen. There's no way to take a vacation when if I relax my guard for even a second I turn into a predator. And the last few weeks have just been one crisis after another." I didn't go into details. She wasn't my therapist. She'd made that clear. I respected that and refused to dump on her—to put her in a situation where she would have to either treat me or stress about *not* treating me.

She nodded, clearly not happy. But I think she understood.

"I hope you'll at least consider it, for Dawna's sake. Even if you can't let go totally, maybe you could indulge your friend. Give her a moment's respite. You're right that I didn't consider the vampire aspect of your life when I suggested this housing arrangement. But you do seem to have remarkable control. Even now, sitting there with your eyes and skin glowing, you're speaking with intelligence and concern." I looked down at my hands, only then realizing that she was right. I was glowing. When I looked at her again, she was glowing, too, but only for my eyes. The warm, rich energy was pulsing in time with her heart. I struggled to listen to her words and shut my eyes for good measure. "But you can't keep holding on to that control by your fingertips and toenails, Celia. Something will give and I fear it'll be catastrophic when it does. You need to find some way to give in to your new instincts in a non-destructive manner."

That made me laugh, but there was a sarcastic edge to it. I opened my eyes again and let her have the full effect. "My *new instincts* are telling me to chase you through the building until you're terrified and then pounce on you and drag you to the floor. Then I'd sink fangs into your neck and suck out your blood. Let me know if you can think of a way to spin that into *non-destructive.*"

She cleared her throat and swallowed hard. No surprise. Dr. Scott had had the same reaction. "Well. I can see where that could be . . . difficult."

I smiled and my fangs had already grown longer. "Only for you, Gwen." Now her pulse was starting to flutter. So was mine. A thin line of drool slid down my chin and that was it.

Without another word, I stood up and walked fast to the bathroom I knew was hidden behind a wall panel. I stepped inside and locked the door behind me. The mirror revealed the red-ringed eyes and fangs that had dropped down over my bottom lip. At least this time I wasn't covered with bloody juices. I turned on the spigot and splashed cold water on my face three times. The shock to my system was just what I needed. I bowed my head and gripped the edge of the marble sink until I felt the solid slab of stone crack. When I looked up again my hair was wet, but at least my eyes had stopped glowing and most of my fangs were back up inside my gums where they belonged. Patting my face dry took off a little makeup, but I could still fix it once I got back to my car.

I let out a slow breath, bracing myself for her reaction. Then I opened the door. She was still in her chair, looking a little haggard. I sat back down opposite her and met her gaze with unblinking eyes. "What you just saw is what I've been dealing with every single night for weeks. So you can see where my life has gone a little beyond a typical touristy R and R."

She nodded. "Yes. Yes, I can."

"The part nobody can tell me for sure is what will happen to me if I drink blood. It might do nothing or it might throw me over the edge. I might become a full vampire. Fingertips and toenails are all I have right now, Gwen. Yoga helps and so does exercise. But they're not the sort of relaxation you're thinking of, are they?"

"No. You're right that I was thinking of something a little less active than exercise or yoga. Have you considered a spa? A facial, sauna, maybe even a massage could help in the short term. If you were relaxed when sunset arrived, your reaction might be less . . . intense."

Okay, that was true. I knew I was reacting stronger to the sunset because I was still angry with Gerry. But her words resonated on another level, too—the human one. A spa. Wow. I couldn't remember ever going to a spa. I knew Dawna and Emma both swore by spas, but I'd never accompanied them. Maybe that would work, because if I was going to be honest, I *was* stressed. Swimming and bubble baths had even stopped working. Calgon was no longer taking me away.

The problem was that it was the busy season. I was booked every night. But why not a day trip? "Okay. Let me see what I can clear on my calendar. Work is busy, but if Dawna's health is at stake, I'll do my best." I stood up because I really needed to get something into my stomach or I was going to wind up doing something I'd regret. "Tell her doctor I'll make the suggestion. I know Dawna well enough that if *he* suggests it she'll get stubborn and claim she doesn't need to. And," I added with a sudden brilliant idea, "I hadn't come up with a single idea for a Christmas gift for her or Emma. We'll do a girls' day out somewhere down in the Napa Valley. Maybe take in a wine tasting."

Gwen was smiling now, most of her nervousness gone. Most, but not all. That made me sad. I'd been wrong. I'd thought Gwen being disappointed in me was second only to making Gran cry. But making Gwen afraid was worse, much worse. "Excellent. I'll let him know." I had my hand on the doorknob, desperate to leave before my stomach growled, when Gwen spoke: "By the way, Celia, I appreciate your candor here.

Most clients are unwilling to show their . . . true self to a therapist. I plan to do some reading on the subject of vampirism and I look forward to spending some session time with you as soon as my license is renewed."

That was good news. I couldn't look at her again, but it was good news. I nodded. "I'll look forward to that, Gwen."

I escaped before she could respond. The world was starting to shift again and I had to get out into the darkness and the safety of a locked car. It wasn't that Gwen was wrong. My control was going to give out someday. I just had to keep the odds in my favor and do the things I knew worked.

To give myself a chance to succeed.

8

burst from the water and took a huge gulp of air before diving into the surf once more. I used to swim every night, relieving the stresses of the day. Since Vicki died, I hadn't spent much time down here, in the water off Vicki's estate. Mostly because of the restraining order that Vicki's mom had put into place when she contested the Will. But one of my many phone messages over the past few days had been from my attorney, telling me the judge hadn't renewed the order. I was free to go back to the estate.

I'd parked at the guesthouse—my house, for years, until Vicki's death—and hurried to the beach, stopping just long enough to grab a couple of big towels from my linen cabinet, one to lie on and one to dry off with. The ocean was calling to me. Just hearing the waves, smelling the salt on the air, helped calm me.

I breaststroked out until the lights from Cooper Manor were just a small dot on the dark horizon. The water was cold, but I felt overheated, so it was perfect. I could feel the ocean like a living thing around me—each fish and plant made itself known without speech or effort. It had been like this my whole life, not just since I learned I was a siren. Maybe it should have occurred to me that my love of water was deeper than other beachgoers', but I'd trusted the grade-school aptitude test that told me I had no paranormal talent.

Flipping onto my back, I stared up at the twinkling stars and felt safe and secure for the first time in days. The bullet wound in my shoulder had healed and was now nothing more than another scar in a sea of them. I floated and kicked and let the tension seep out of my body with each rise and fall of the swells. Maybe I could sleep a full night for a change.

"I was going to suggest this, but you've found the answer on your own."

The female voice to my left startled me enough that I lost my buoyancy and dropped beneath the waves. I came up sputtering and blinking water out of my eyes.

Lopaka, high queen of the sirens, had watched me nearly drown with amusement. *You weren't drowning. Sirens can't drown. The oceans won't allow it.* She spoke into my mind and I tried to answer in kind.

Where her voice was the sweetest ringing of crystal wind chimes, my telepathy sounded like the harsh squawking of gulls: *I would appreciate it if you wouldn't startle me. I'm not like other sirens. I'd hate to prove your no-drowning theory wrong.*

She laughed and the water grew more alive around us. I could feel more fish come to investigate, and strands of seaweed, completely out of place this far from shore, drifted by. Lopaka plucked the narrow green fronds from the water and began to idly twist them. "I would hate that as well. Monarchs should never be proven wrong. But while I am no psychic, I am . . . connected to my people, in tune with my subjects. Which is why I'm here. What was causing you such distress? I felt as though your very soul was screaming in agony earlier today. But now you seem well."

Whoa. She could feel me in pain? I so didn't want to project my life onto anyone. "How *much* earlier? It's been a busy day. I got shot around two this morning and wanted to snack on my therapist about an hour ago."

She shook her head with mild confusion. "It wasn't physical. I've learned to tune such things out. This was psychic pain—panic and heartache and fear, all rolled into one. It was strong enough that I nearly fell, but I couldn't find the source for some time. It was as though I was being blocked when I searched." Her hands finally stopped fiddling beneath the water and came up bearing a crown fashioned of seaweed and tiny shells. She put it on her head while I wondered where in the world she'd found the shells. When I looked closer, I realized they weren't shells but living snails, mollusks, and tiny starfish, clinging to the stiff blades of sea grass.

We were drifting out to sea, and that was going to mean an exhausting swim back unless we started now. "First, the crown thing is a *very* cool talent. Second, we need to start back or I'm going to be too tired to make it to shore. Last, do you recall what time you had the panic attack?" I'd felt that kind of panic twice in the last twenty-four hours—first when Kevin was being shot at and again while at the prison. Both times I'd been behind magic barriers.

"It was late afternoon. Definitely not night."

I began to do the backstroke toward shore both so we could

continue to talk and because it's less tiring. The queen swam smoothly beside me. Her seaweed crown began to slip, but two tiny crabs crawled down and grabbed onto strands of her golden hair to stabilize it. "That wasn't me then. I know exactly what you were feeling because I was feeling it, too. It was my mom."

Lopaka turned her head and one storm gray eye dipped below the waves. The remaining pupil took on the color of the dark water and I could feel the strength of her will in its glittering depths. "Tell me."

So I did. I stared up at the stars and swam and talked. By the time we reached the shore, I was both mentally and physically exhausted. I wasn't sure exactly why I'd just told all my innermost secrets to Queen Lopaka, but I wasn't sorry I had.

As she climbed out of the water, she took off the crown of seaweed and let it float out on the tide. I watched all the animals scatter back into the water and marveled at the beauty of the ocean. She handed me one of the thick towels I'd left on the beach, a vivid blue one that reminded me of the sky above the Isle of Serenity, Lopaka's home. She took the red one that made her eyes turn silver. As I flipped my hair over to fluff it dry, I spotted a conch shell on the beach, one of the most beautiful I'd ever seen. I collect shells but only those I find myself. I tugged it out of the sand until it came free. I let the surf wash off the remaining dirt and held it up to look at it more closely.

Queen Lopaka stepped closer to see it in the dim light from the moon. "It is befitting a princess. The sea finds you worthy."

That pulled a laugh from me. "I've always considered finding shells luck, not design."

She smiled and it held a depth of knowledge that I didn't possess. "You're still young. Much of life, and death, is by design. Take your mother, for example. She is, by design, a siren. She carries our blood. There are many humans who carry siren blood, but not all are tied to the ocean. I believe she is, even if she doesn't exhibit any other symptoms."

I wrapped the towel around me and sat down on the sand. The queen sat down beside me, perfectly at ease. "What do you mean, *tied to the ocean*? I was afraid that was affecting her, but I don't really understand how it works."

The queen held out her hands to the water with a beatific smile. "You feel the ocean, as do I. It lives, moves inside us, touches our hearts. You feel it more strongly now that your talent has fully manifested, but you've always felt it. To be apart from the ebb and flow of the ocean is to be in pain. The psychic torture you felt was the tearing of the bond between a siren and her ocean. I've felt it before, which is why I came to you today. While I wasn't aware your mother had enough blood to be tied, it appears that she does. And now she's behind walls, far from the water, with spelled barriers that sever magical ties. In effect, she's starving to death . . . and she has no idea why."

Oh, crap. Mom wasn't only going through withdrawal from the bottle; she had been literally cut off from a vital organ. She was being tortured, though her jailers didn't know it. I felt a pain in my chest. "What can we do? Is there some way to prove this to a judge so she can get released?"

Lopaka shook her head. "I wouldn't suggest requesting her release. She's broken the law and, frankly, her drinking has to stop. She's endangering people and harming herself. Is it possible to simply add a saltwater fish tank to her cell? That would restore her connection, if only slightly."

I shook my head. "I doubt it. Even with spells to make it unbreakable, other prisoners would complain about the smell, or the lights, or something."

She nodded. "You may be correct. Perhaps there is a more elegant solution. We have a detention center on the island. I could petition the court to have her transferred to Serenity's jail for health reasons. I have no doubt that her state of mind is affecting everyone in her present facility. If there have been more fights or suicide attempts, the judge will surely see it's in the interest of all parties to move her. But if they refuse—" She touched my arm and her face looked truly stricken. "Then she will die. Not quickly and not kindly. And even if she is released when her condition becomes clear, the damage would be done and I don't know if she could be saved."

I looked out at the wide ocean and felt my eyes well. "I should have done something." I didn't know what I could have done, how I could have known, but I felt responsible.

"Celia, no. You have no part in this. You've already borne more burdens than most should have to suffer. I believe your mother can be helped, can be brought back into balance. I'd like to try, if you'll allow me."

Did I trust Lopaka to make my mother a whole person? Hell, yes!

She laughed because apparently I'd broadcast that thought.

I let out a slow breath. "Yes. I would be thrilled, and honored, if you could help her." Gran would be thrilled as well.

She might finally feel confident that Mom could get the help she needs, with people who understood why she'd turned to alcohol to mend herself.

"I'll contact the authorities in the morning. Now I must go. I've kept several people waiting on board my vessel." It made my eyes go wide. She'd interrupted a meeting to come see me? She stood easily from her near-yoga position and I realized once again that she looked really good for her age. Hell, for *any* age.

But she was more than beauty. She was mercy, too. I was completely sincere when I touched the glittering gold and pearl ring on her hand. "Thank you, Your Highness. I would never have expected the kindness you've shown me, and now my family. I don't know how I can ever repay you."

She smiled almost sadly and lifted my chin. "You have my brother Kalino's eyes. How could I see them in pain and *not* help?" Her hand pulled away from mine and she turned, walking into the sea. She dived into the water without so much as a splash.

I sat there, feeling both happy and sad, happy I had an answer to the question about my mother and sad because she was suffering. I stood up and realized my muscles had stiffened; fleetingly I wondered if Lopaka was feeling the burn, too.

I grabbed the clothes I'd left folded on the rocks and hobbled slowly back to the guesthouse that had been my home for the past few years, feeling muscles pull that I hadn't felt in months. I really needed to swim more often. I probably should drive back to Gran's house—it would always be Gran's house in my head, even though I now owned it and had been living

there since Gran had moved out—but I honestly wasn't positive I could work the clutch right now.

So I went into the house and checked the fridge. Nothing.
Nothing in the freezer or cupboards, either. Well, hell. I was
going to have to drive to town for an energy drink or walk up
to the main house and beg for kitchen privileges. David and
Inez certainly wouldn't mind. We'd always been close. But I'd
been working so much that I hadn't seen much of them lately.
Maybe I should call first?

Nobody answered. Well, I couldn't expect them to be home
every night of the week. They probably wouldn't mind if I
went up and used my key, but it felt . . . weird now that they
owned the place. Vicki's probate wasn't done yet, but her former employees had a valid lease.

I was just going to have to stop whining and suck it up to drive
back to town. At Birchwoods, I'd drunk the last of the shakes I
was keeping in the car. So, after a few minutes of stretching, I
forced my aching joints back into clothes, stowed my weapons,
and gingerly duckwalked out to the car. I'd left my cell phone in
its holster; it registered three missed calls, all from the same
number and all in the last few minutes.

Alex.

That was a call I definitely wanted to return. I started the
car and slowly pushed in the clutch to put it into gear. Ow.
Sharp little shooting pains coursed up my thigh, bringing
sparkles to my vision.

I was reaching for the phone when it rang. I answered immediately: "Celia. What's up, Alex?"

"Oh, thank God!" Her voice was low and panicked and all

of my senses went to high alert. The pain in my leg disappeared as if by magic. Adrenaline is a wonderful thing. "Celia, I did what I promised. I brought a priest out to the zoo. You're right; something weird is going on. There have been reports of people going missing for weeks, but nobody's followed up. I don't know if it's because of jurisdictional bullshit or if somebody's suppressing the reports inside the department. But . . . shit! There's screaming coming from inside now. They won't let me in to check on Father Joseph. I'm going to go back and get help, but in case they follow me I want you to get the photos I'm about to send you from my cell phone back to my lieutenant. He'll get the right people out there."

In case they follow, my ass! "Don't be a hero, Alex. I'm on my way."

Now her voice went hissing and harsh: "Don't *you* be an idiot, Celia. They'd be expecting you. I don't plan to play hero. I'm driving *away* from the facility right now. I don't like leaving the priest, but he's a warrior class two. He can handle himself. Hopefully. But if you don't hear from me by morning, get the files to Lieutenant Blanchard. He'll know what to do."

I didn't know her lieutenant all that well and the thought of having to talk to him made me uncomfortable. We'd met, like, once. I didn't like it. Not one bit. But Alex is as tough as I am, maybe more so. If she said "don't come," I had to respect that. "You call Vicki if bad things start to happen. Okay? Promise me you'll call on Vicki."

I didn't doubt for a second that no matter how exhausted Vicki was, she would help Alex. There was a sigh of relief in her voice when she responded: "I don't think I'll need to. I just passed through the farthest perimeter barrier. I should be home free. But we need to talk in the morning. I'm headed back to the station to turn all this in and file an official request for investigation. Get some sleep, girlfriend. I'll be okay."

"How about I stay on the phone with you until I *know* you're okay and back in the city? I've been ambushed out there before, and there's nobody around to hear you scream. Vicki would haunt me forever if I let anything happen to you."

There was a long pause; the only sounds were the crackling of static and the roar of wind past two cars. Finally she responded: "Okay. You're right. That makes sense. Let me plug in the car charger and put the phone on hands free."

So we talked. For the next twenty minutes we talked about the reports she'd discovered of guards going missing and escapes that had never made the news. "Then I dug deeper," she explained. "I wanted to see if there were any workers' compensation claims against the private corporation that runs the facility. If people were going missing, then getting hurt was the next step. There were almost a dozen claims in the last year. And though I couldn't find any record of a budget increase, there seem to be more guards on duty than are on the payroll. I saw dozens of guards, but the facility's website only shows a standard complement of fifteen for the overnight shift. If they're secretly hiring more staff, there are definitely problems there."

A hideous thought formed in my head. Did I dare tell her about the guard with the glowing eyes? He'd moved almost too . . . fluidly. Almost as though— "There may be another explanation, but you're not going to like it."

Her voice grew wary, with an edge of fear. "What?"

"When's the last time anyone did a head count of *prisoners?*" She didn't respond, so I kept going. The red light gave me a chance to flip over to the Internet on the cell. I typed in *demonic possession & werewolves.* Six pages of results came up, including three from the major churches. "What if . . . and this is only an *if* . . . demons were possessing the prisoners as well as the administrators, but *not* the guards?"

She began to follow my reasoning while I scrolled through websites. But the light turned green, so I couldn't spend much time reading. "There are too many guards and someone would raise a fuss if they all started acting weird," Alex mused. "But one or two administrators could order the release of prisoners. . . ."

"Who could then come back as 'new hires.' There would be no paperwork because they wouldn't be on the payroll. And nobody would be the wiser." It was a conspiracy theory of the highest order and no small feat. But the demon who had tried to claim me was both patient and smart, and since the disk with the spell to bring him forth had gone missing during the fight with Eirene, I couldn't guarantee that he wasn't already in this realm.

"Yeah. We've got to get someone in there. Immediately. Okay, I'm just coming up on the QualMart at Terrance Drive. I should be fine from here. Thanks, Celia. Really. This gave me a chance to think and I really do feel better talking to you."

We'd never been very close. It was more a matter of vying for Vicki's time than any actual animosity. I'd always hoped we could be friends. I figured if my best friend loved Alex, then I should try to like her or at least get to know her. But we'd never managed to get beyond the superficial.

Until now. "Me, too. Don't bother about sending me the photos. Give them to your lieutenant personally. Oh, and before I forget, what's the scoop on the sniper who tried to take off my head at the Will reading?" Alex had been there and had seen John Creede use damned impressive magic to stop the bullet before it reached me. He'd won a lot of points that day.

"Crap! That's right. I never told you about that. Guy's name was Selik Mahrain. He's a professional hit man and INTERPOL has been looking for him for a long time. They were more than happy to come collect him. Last I heard he was in a Turkish prison, awaiting trial for the murder of a Shiite leader. He'd been hired by the queen of a Grecian island to remove you before you met with the siren head queen."

"Ah yes. The lovely Stefania. Did I mention she was Eirene's mother and the one who'd put a death curse on me and Ivy when we were little kids?"

Alex let out a noise that was close to a raspberry. "Charming woman. Is that the one you killed?"

"No. I killed Eirene, the daughter. Mommy dearest was killed by Queen Lopaka, who didn't take kindly to Stefania trying to kill her brother's only remaining grandchild. Meaning me."

"Okay, the station is in sight. Go home. Get some rest and we'll talk tomorrow. I should know more after I make my report."

Conveniently enough, by the time I hung up I'd arrived at one of my favorite restaurants. La Cocina y Cantina is a little hole-in-the-wall Mexican place that was the favorite hangout of me, Vicki, Emma, and Dawna. We'd held Vicki's wake there. It served the best food in the world. As I pulled into the parking lot, the main lights flicked off. What time was it? I'd forgotten to put on my watch, so I checked my phone display: 10 P.M. Why was the restaurant closing? They normally stayed open until midnight or later.

I got out of the car and knocked on the front door. A woman's head poked out from the kitchen. Her face exploded into a smile and she rushed forward, rubbing her hands on the ever-present snow-white bar towel. She unlocked the door with a flourish. "Celia! What you doing here at this hour? Huh? Come in and sit down. Come. Come." Barbara was part owner of the restaurant. She ushered me in like there was a storm outside and locked the door again, being careful to pull down the blinds. "You want a late dinner? Pablo will make you a 'sunset smoothie.'"

Ooh. That did sound good. It was a concoction they'd come up with after my vampire attack. As long as I didn't think too much about the cow blood in it, it tasted wonderful. But at least the blood was cooked. So it was sort of a beef fajita shake, without the beef. "Sure. That sounds good. What's up, Barbara? Where is everyone? I was surprised the door was locked."

She looked around as though afraid. "Bats. A whole flock of them. One old vampire showed up about a week ago and turned three of the boys in the neighborhood. They were bad boys, always into something. Stealing, drugs. But they'd never hurt anybody until *he* found them. Now people are scared. They're not coming here after dark and I can't blame them. If we didn't have to clean up, we wouldn't be here after dark, either. But for you . . . we'll make an exception. Anytime. Day or night. You come and we'll make you dinner."

That was sweet, but I hated seeing nice people being terrorized. This business was all the family had. I felt my brow furrow and anger rise. "You fix me a shake. I'll be right back."

I stood up. She clutched at my sleeve. "Oh no, Celia. Don't go out there. They're not like you. They're bad, bad vampires. I don't want you hurt."

My smile probably had a dark edge. "Barbara, I was putting vampires in their place before I was turned. Now I'm a lot harder to hurt, and I'm a lot smarter than them. I got to keep my brain." I patted her arm. "I'll be fine."

Her face was wary, but she let me leave, then locked the door behind me. Every third streetlight was out. I'd heard some parts of the city were doing that to save money, but it made the sidewalks dark for long stretches.

I started walking, jingling my keys, anticipating that I'd soon be followed. It didn't take long. There were four of them hiding in the darkness. I could just make them out because of my vampire vision. Two of the boys were growling, which made the small hairs on my neck rise. Maybe this hadn't been such a good idea after all. It was one thing to take on one or two bats, but taking on four might be biting off more than I could chew. Maybe one of them would be willing to listen to reason.

Don't laugh. It could happen.

I hissed and let myself get all glowy. "Evening, gentlemen."

"Prey!" One of the boys leapt into the air and came down

on the other side of me. I'd done that leaping thing once. It was pretty amazing, but I didn't like being surrounded.

"I don't want to have to hurt your fledglings. But your flock has to leave. I'm protecting this block."

I wasn't sure which one I was talking to, but after a long pause one vampire floated forward. Yeah, I said *floated*. That's never good. Only the really old ones can do that. "This isn't anywhere close to your side of town, Celia. You don't make the rules here."

Oh, crap. I didn't know the voice, but he knew my name. He floated on power, gleaming with both internal and external light. He'd been killed early in life but long, long ago. The black eyes were ancient, pitiless and remorseless. The slope of the nose and high cheekbones reminded me of high-caste Spanish.

"Do I know you?"

He smiled, but it was really more a baring of fangs. "Lucien was right. You're just eye candy. You got lucky with Luther and Lilith. But Edgar's a fool for trusting you. That's why I decided to start my own flock. We don't trust anybody." He moved slowly forward and so did his fledglings, widening their group to flank me.

I guess that meant I wasn't going to get a name. I pulled my knives from the sheaths. He stopped abruptly and stared at the twin blades. "Are those the blades that killed Luther? They witched?"

"Better than you've ever seen. The black one killed Lilith, too. You willing to risk whether I'm faster than you?"

"She's not bluffing, Marco." The voice seemed to come from

far away and echoed between the buildings like it was everywhere.

Just as Edgar descended onto the scene, Marco hissed. He snarled, showing sharp teeth. "Nobody invited you to this party, Edgar. We'll all be better off if I just let the fledglings take her down. She's an abomination. My boys are still feral enough that she won't be able to handle them if they attack at once."

Unfortunately, he was probably right. Three against one is just plain bad odds. If I lost even one of the knives, I was probably a goner.

Edgar looked at me and there was something in his eyes that hadn't been there the previous night. Desire.

It wasn't sexual, but it was real. "Why kill her fully? She would be an amazing vampire. Tough, fierce, smart. A force to be reckoned with." He smiled and it made every hair on my body stand at attention.

Now Marco was smiling, too. Shit. "We could call her Lilith in honor of the one we lost. She'll never know the difference once her memories are gone."

Five against one, and I'd seen Edgar fight. "I helped you save Kevin." I was down to bargaining as I tried to find a wall to keep my back safe.

Edgar took another step forward. He wore chino pants, a gray dress shirt, and shining black dress shoes that were more suited to a boardroom than a slaughter on a deserted street. "True. And I'm certain he's grateful. But you don't realize just how safe it made you when I believed you were his Vaso. Now he doesn't have a clue where you are. If you were attacked by three feral new-turns and I *saved* you by bringing you over, there wouldn't be much he could do. Would there?"

Marco was licking his lips and drooling all over the ground. "I've heard siren blood is like nothing else. Never had the chance to test that rumor."

I took another step back and my heel caught the edge of a discarded bottle. I lost my balance for one brief moment and the air blurred as they descended. My arms were pulled nearly out of their sockets and my knives disappeared. Where Edgar smelled of expensive cologne and mouthwash, Marco smelled of sweat and leather. They were on either side of me, close enough that one strike would end it.

Edgar's face moved forward like lightning and I braced myself, waiting for the pain. But it didn't happen. Instead, I heard his voice in my ear like velvet over steel. "What will you give up for your life, Celia Graves? I can put a stop to this right now."

I didn't want to answer, but I heard my own voice, breathy with fear: "What do you want?"

"Kill her," Marco hissed. I ignored him. Edgar was the one with all the chips at the table.

"I want the artifact. If you swear you'll bring it to me, I'll end this and make your favorite café a nice place for tourists again. If not, then I bring you over and you'll *still* bring me the artifact. Except you'll be just like me—preying on friends, clients, and your saintly old grandmother for your next meal. And this time, I *will* be your master."

That set my blood boiling and I pulled away from the young vamps holding my arms. My muscles screamed in agony, but

I put the pain aside. Unfortunately, I hadn't a clue what Edgar was talking about. The only *artifact* I had in my possession was an ancient divination tool called a Wadjeti that had been given to me by . . . well, crap. It had been given to me by Eirene and Stefania. If Edgar wanted that, there had to be more to it than I'd thought.

Marco leapt backward when I crouched to fight, but Edgar held his ground and laughed. "You're definitely a fiery one. But you'll lose. You can't win with these odds."

"She can with a little help!" The male voice had a heavy Mexican accent and was followed by the sharp retort of a shotgun. One of the fledglings caught the blast full in the face. Whatever was in the rounds caused him to scream and race into the darkness before falling to lie still and silent at the edge of the next circle of light.

Pablo carried a double-barrel shotgun, but Marco floated into the air with confidence. "I'll take care of the little man. You handle the girl."

"Chicken!" I taunted him, not sure what I could do to help my friend. Then I realized he didn't need help. Barbara stepped out of the restaurant behind him, also carrying a shotgun, followed by Juan, their oldest son—who looked serious and competent as he jacked a round into the chamber of his pump-action weapon.

Nearby, two more shop doors opened and more shotguns appeared. A trigger was pulled. The young vamp to my right tried to dodge, but his chest exploded and he screamed as liquid fire burned through him. Then the one on my left was hit. I picked up one of the pellets that bounced on the ground and squished it between my fingers. I'll be damned. I didn't know they were putting holy water into pellets. It was like a high-powered paintball. Probably wouldn't kill a regular human, just bruise. But a vamp? Instant agony.

The third new-turn had enough sense to turn on his heel and run. Marco wasn't so easily dismissed. He descended on Pablo like an eagle, long duster flaring behind him like a cape, fangs as sharp as talons. Without even thinking, I pushed Edgar out of the way and raced forward, knocking Marco out of the air before he could collide with my friend. Juan and Barbara started taking potshots at Edgar. He must have realized he'd lost the upper hand, but he took a flying leap and landed on top of me. My face planted into the asphalt, chin first, as Edgar grabbed Marco with one hand and soared into the sky.

Edgar paused to give me a parting comment, just out of reach of the rounds of holy water blasting out of shotguns from nearly every window on the block: "This isn't over, Celia. My offer stands. You can't stay awake forever and I know where you live."

I was bleeding from nose and mouth as Barbara rushed over to help me up. People were collecting the bodies of the two boys who were from the neighborhood. The people's faces showed mingled pride and sorrow as they cut a branch from a nearby tree and sharpened the wood into a stake. The vamp with his face shot off was still alive enough to thrash under strong arms as the stake was driven into his heart. A wailing woman in the background was held back as three men struggled to put him down. Then he was still and the woman—probably his mother—was allowed forward to cry over the son she'd actually lost many nights before.

"Celia," Barbara admonished with both fear and cracking pride in her voice, "I told you he was a bad one. But did you listen?" She dusted off my clothes while handing me her dish towel to mop the blood from my face. I heard a sniffle and looked down to see her eyes wet with tears. "No, you didn't. And it was a very brave thing. It made everyone feel ashamed that we hadn't stood up to them earlier."

That hadn't been my intent, but I was glad it worked out. Damn, but my mouth hurt. I didn't think my nose was broken, but I definitely needed to see what my mouth looked like. "Bafrom?" I asked with a mouthful of cotton, and pointed to the open doorway. She let out a surprised sound and hurried me into the building. We were followed by a dozen other people, cheering and shouting my name like I was a conquering hero.

Except the hero isn't the one who's supposed to need *saving*. I felt like a complete idiot. I'd taken the enemy for granted and barely scraped out by the skin of my teeth.

Speaking of my teeth . . . I turned on the light in the ladies' room and worriedly held back my lips. My bottom lip was cut in two places where my fangs had dug in. That accounted for the blood. But my two front teeth and one fang were loose. I could wiggle them and it hurt when I did. I didn't know what would happen if I broke a fang. It was probably worth asking someone about. I was definitely going to have a fat lip in a few minutes. I hoped it wouldn't last too long.

When I exited the bathroom, cheers went up a second time.

Barbara and Pablo bustled forward and guided me to a chair. My knives were on the table and I gratefully put them back in their sheaths. I really didn't want Edgar to get his hands on them.

The sumptuous scent of cumin, chili powder, and onions rose in the steam from a shake glass. Yum. A sunset smoothie. Just like Mama never made. I put the straw between my lips and . . . ow! Okay, sucking was a bad plan. Who knew it required uninjured teeth? So, while everyone stared at me, I drank down the shake like it was a tall glass of milk. I'd lost blood, so I wasn't going to cringe about the contents.

It was good enough that I ordered a second. At least two adventurous people ordered one as well. Who knew? It might be the next hot thing in the restaurant if the surprised but delighted expressions of the others were any indication.

By the time I left an hour later, my purse still the same weight as when I arrived due to Pablo insisting my food was on the house, I was full but exhausted beyond all reason. Edgar and Marco were still out there, waiting for me to be alone. There was only one place where I'd feel safe, and it was the same place I'd woken up this morning.

After I changed all the alarm codes and locks, of course.

The night was about to get even longer.

9

I woke to the wailing of the front-door alarm. I'd like to say I leapt to my feet, ready for action. But in reality it was more a case of rolling off the couch to land in a heap on the floor while rubbing the crust of sleep from my eyes. Still, I made it to the door before more than a few seconds passed and bolted out into the hallway, my Colt steady in front of me, watching for threats.

"Enter the code!" Ron was shouting to be heard over the siren. I could hear Dawna punching in numbers until he pushed her aside. "Oh, for heaven's sake. Let *me* do it."

It was worth watching from the balcony for a moment to see him enter the old code once, then twice, before pressing random keys and then banging on the box.

"Jeez, Ron! Don't break the thing." I sprinted down the stairs and slid in front of him while holstering my gun. I entered the new code and the alarm shut off.

While Dawna shook her head back and forth to get the ringing to stop, I explained: "I got attacked by some vampires last night. Two of them got away and one knows where this building is. I wanted to make sure he couldn't get in without my knowing. Sorry about that. I'd expected to wake up before you got here."

Dawna let out a heaving sigh. "I'll call the police and the alarm company. Shit, Celia. You could have left me a voice mail or something. I'm not in a mood to deal with filling out reports and now I've got a headache."

She looked like she hadn't slept any longer than I had. "Sorry," I repeated. Ron left in a snit, muttering something about bringing up changing codes at the next tenant meeting.

"You okay?" I asked, noticing the dark shadows under her eyes that even the most skillful makeup couldn't hide anymore. "Really. Be honest."

She stared at the phone, receiver in hand. Her eyes closed and her lip trembled. "I just need a vacation. Life is just too . . . well, *too* right now."

Now I felt like a heel. She was right. I could have left her a voice mail. Vampires or not, demons or not, Dawna was my best friend. I should have been more considerate. So screw Edgar and Marco. Gwen was right. Dawna needed to get away and so did I.

But first things first. "Did Justin come by yesterday?"

She nodded. "You were right . . . as usual. He found two upstairs. One in the hallway right outside your office and one in the light fixture next to your desk. Oh, and he said he has an idea about what to do with your safe when *the baby's born.*" At least that made her smile.

"Well, just in case he missed any, let's go out for a quick bagel. I have news that I think you'll want to hear. Give me ten minutes to run a comb through my hair. I literally just woke up."

She grimaced. "Ron will be pissed. He has clients coming in, and you have a meeting in thirty."

I reached across the half wall and put my hand over hers. Then I looked firmly at her and squeezed her hand. "Screw Ron; screw his clients and mine, too. We need ten minutes out of here. It's important."

She'd just opened her mouth to respond when the first clients came in. She held up her hands helplessly and there was nothing I could do. I'd wanted to tell her about the spa thing early so she could plan to have the weekend off, but it'd have to wait.

On the plus side, I could get cleaned up for the day and maybe have time to go online before my first appointment arrived and find just the right spa. I decided to make three reservations. After the stress of Kevin being captured, I had no doubt Emma could use a break, too. I hoped I could convince Gwen of that. Emma was still in her first thirty days at Birchwoods. There weren't supposed to be *any* day passes and she'd already had one, for our shopping trip.

It took twenty minutes and many mouse clicks before I found just the right place. There would be facials, massages, and even a seaweed wrap. I'd never had one of those before, but for some reason it appealed to me.

"Celia," came Dawna's voice from the speakerphone. "Your . . . *client* is here. I think."

Well, that was an interesting way to phrase it. "Okay. Send them up." I took the final sip of my vanilla shake and dropped the can in the trash as I glanced at my calendar. Maria Busta-

mante was the client, but the handwriting wasn't mine or
Dawna's. It looked like . . . *Ron's.*

Huh?

One nice thing about our group is we freely send clients
back and forth. But while I've had several referrals from Bubba
pop up on my calendar, not one had ever come from Ron.

A tentative knock sounded, just a light tapping that I might
not have noticed if I hadn't been expecting it. "Come in."

I checked my outfit as I stood. Royal blue slacks, patterned
sky blue top, careful makeup, and just a little curl in my hair.
Putting on the blazer was hard after having my arms nearly
ripped out, but at least my teeth didn't hurt anymore. Still,
every time I looked in the mirror lately I saw chalk white skin
and dark, bruised-looking circles under my eyes. Add in the
fangs and if I didn't start to get some more sleep, even more
people were going to think I was trying out for a horror movie.

The door opened and the woman . . . actually, the *child*
who walked in had the gun-shy look of someone who was being threatened. She watched every corner, every shadow, in the
room. Her wide brown eyes moved constantly as she walked
forward. She didn't acknowledge the hand I held out but instead sat quickly in one of the big chairs and immediately curled
her legs up under her thighs.

Oookay.

"So. Maria?"

She nodded and finally focused on my face. Her eyes were
showing too much white and her breathing was fast and shallow. "Yes." The movement was tiny and frail, a baby bird who

knew the hawk was watching . . . waiting until she was in the open.

"Are you even fifteen yet?" I'd never been hired by someone younger than that. Most of my child clients were actors or singers who were being stalked by fans or needed guarding from their own family. But usually I was hired by a publicist, agent, or parent—someone who could legally sign the agreement.

Another movement, this time a shake. My firm voice startled her and actually calmed her down. "I'll be thirteen in March."

Twelve. Dear God. I'd been right when I thought child. I started envisioning an abusive parent or a sexual predator. Those weren't the sort of things a bodyguard could fix. But I was at least willing to listen. "Okay. So tell me what the problem is."

Somehow her eyes got even wider. "I need a bodyguard."

No, duh. "I presumed that. Why did you go to an attorney first and why did he refer you to me?" Ultimately, my mind kept going back there. What had she told Ron that he felt he couldn't help her with? Because as much of an ass as I thought he was, he was a hell of an attorney. Even if he couldn't have helped her, he would have referred her to one of his own. Why a bodyguard?

"He said you could keep me safe. I just want to be safe." *Really? Ron said that? Wow.* I hoped my dropped jaw wasn't too obvious.

"Who's trying to hurt you?"

Now the eyes went to the floor. *Uh-oh. Trouble.* "No one in particular."

That was such bullshit. No way would someone with that much fear in her face and body *not* know who was trying to hurt her. "Bullshit. Try again." My voice came out a little harsher than I'd planned. After all, she was just a kid.

But it snapped her out of it. The eyes went from frightened to angry. "Excuse me? You don't get to talk to me that way. I'm the one hiring *you*."

Reality check for the young miss. I held up one finger to stop the flashing eyes. She dropped her feet to the floor and held her body straight for the first time since she'd walked into the room. I could finally get a good look at her. She had long dark, shining hair and a little baby fat around her waist. But she was healthy and had good muscle tone, so she probably wasn't a runaway. "Let's make one thing perfectly clear, Ms. Bustamante. I put my *life* on the line for complete strangers. I walk into unknown dangers." I raised up my upper lip to reveal the fangs and watched her eyes go wide again, for a different reason. "I got these on a job. I plan for as much as I can, but I rely on my clients to be absolutely honest with me. If there are *known* dangers I need to prepare for, I need that knowledge."

"You're obviously in trouble. I can see it in your face. You're *twelve* and you need a professional bodyguard? What the hell did you do to someone or what did they do to you to require that?" Her fingers started moving in her lap, twining over each other. I caught a glimpse of pale pink polish on nails bitten nearly to the quick. Then one hand moved up to twist a lock of hair. She was holding my gaze but just barely. The tension in that small body . . . it was ready to explode and I didn't know which way the blast was going to go. I finally took pity and softened my voice. "Maria . . . one of the reasons people hire a bodyguard is to finally . . . *finally* be able to tell someone the truth. Someone who'll understand, will take it seriously, and will never, in a million years, tell a soul." I finished in a whisper that seemed loud in the silent room.

That was the straw. The coil unwound and she fell backward into the chair. The tough shell shattered into a million pieces and tears came to her eyes. "He's going to kill me, Miss Graves. He already killed my brother, Manuel, and then he'll kill me and there will be nobody to help Mama or Papa. Oh, God, please. I don't wanna die." The collapse was complete and she buried her face in her hands and sobbed.

"Who?"

"Jorge Encarcion."

Oh, dear God. Fuck a duck. Jorge "the Viper" Encarcion was the baddest of the bad drug dealers in this part of the state. He dealt mostly in flame and tame: magical drugs—enhanced versions of the typical coke or ecstasy that gave the user both a mental and physical high. With the temporary illusion charm, a user could do anything . . . *be* anything on flame. A model for a day? No problem. An actor at the top of his career was just a quick pop away. But the effects were devastating for people born without magic to draw on. The drug fed on the body itself, causing scars, muscle twitches, and paralysis. Tame was just the opposite. It was the Valium of the new millennium. A bad day at the office or major life tragedy was all better after a quick needle to the veins. But it was horribly addictive and could even make your heart or lungs stop cold.

Still, it wasn't the drugs that made the Viper a man to be

feared. It was his utter ruthlessness. It was one thing to be amoral or even immoral. Both were common in drug dealers. To rule that world required an ability to destroy anything and anyone who showed the least bit of weakness.

Including a twelve-year-old girl. "What did you do to him?"

She sniffed and reached for a tissue. I keep them on the client's side of the desk. I had to stretch if I needed one. "I was supposed to carry some product for him—take it to the mall and give it to the client. It was simple. Everyone said it was so simple, and the pay was good."

"But it wasn't simple. Was it? What went wrong?"

Her face blushed so hard I thought she'd catch on fire. "They were in balloons. You know, so they wouldn't show up on the sniff sensors at the mall entrances. I swallowed them the night before and was supposed to . . . pass them, clean them off, and deliver them."

Um. Eww. I'd never really thought about the realities of the balloon thing. But logically, they wouldn't decompose and could bend around the corners of the intestine. Still . . . double eww. "Okay. So you went to the mall, spotted the client, went to the bathroom, and . . ." I paused because a horrifying thought occurred to me. "*Which* mall?"

She nodded, knowing what I was asking. "Twin Palms."

My hand went to my mouth. I wasn't sure whether I was stifling a laugh or a scream. Her face contorted with the same blend of emotions. "They refurbished the bathrooms this spring."

Another nod and more tears sprang up. "I hadn't been there for a long time. My family, we can't afford stores like that. I'd never seen toilets that automatically flushed."

Crap. Literally. She'd passed the balloons and . . . swirlie city. No more drugs. "So you have no drugs, no money, and . . . what? You ran? Did you explain or just run?"

She had to blow her nose before responding. "I ran. Manuel, he went to see Jorge. He'd worked with him before. He'd convinced the Viper to give me a chance. He tried to explain, convince him we'd pay back the money. But the . . . *bastard* wouldn't listen." Her voice went harsh and was painful to hear. "He shot my brother and dumped the body in front of our house with a note pinned to his chest."

Somehow I knew she really meant *chest*.

I sighed. "And you're next." She nodded, her lower lip trembling.

The problem was, she really *was* going to die. The Viper was known for being relentless when pissed. I couldn't be with her every minute of every day. From what I'd read about him, right now he was targeting her personally. Unlike the Italian Mafia bosses, instead of trusting underlings with the dirty work, he liked to keep his hands bloody. But if he didn't get her himself in a few days, he'd likely get bored and simply put out a contract on her. Then there would be dozens, if not hundreds, of people after her. And she would die.

"When did this happen? When did your brother die?"

The heartbreak on her face was hard to watch. "Two days ago. That's when I came to see Mr. Ron. He'd helped my mama buy our house and I thought maybe—"

But Ron was a real estate attorney, not a criminal one. And even a criminal attorney couldn't do much except convince

Maria to do what was first on my mind, too. "Have you called the police? Told them what you know about the Viper?"

She shook her head, slowly at first and then quicker as if trying to shake the very idea out of her mind. Meaning she'd considered it. Maybe even to the point of dialing the phone. "No. I can't. The police are afraid of him. They never come to that side of town. He'll kill them, too, and they know it."

I tried never to think ill of the police in the city. They did an amazing job. But I had to admit that there were more reports of violence on Federal Boulevard than there were reports of arrests and convictions. Either Encarcion was really talented at concealing evidence of his crimes or the cops were afraid. I was betting it was talent over fear. Which could make my life very, very short if I took this job. "Is there anywhere you could stay for a while? Somewhere out of town?" It was not as much an admission of defeat as of reality.

She didn't argue, which said she wasn't too brave for her own good. "I have an aunt in Iowa. So you're saying there's no hope? What about Mama and Papa?"

"There's always hope." I believed that and tried to convince Maria with my face and body. "If you'd been more than just a mule, there would be *more* hope. If you knew something important that could be traded to the authorities for protection . . ." I let the sentence hang, praying she hadn't come completely clean.

She stared at my Rolodex and nibbled on her lower lip. I watched her anxiously. I wanted so much for her to have an out of this, to have a bright future that was worth her brother's sacrifice. "I know Jorge will be at Smallmouth Harbor on Saturday night to pick up a load of cocaine from South America. He plans to kill the captain and sink the boat so he doesn't have to pay for it."

Whoa. I'd expected maybe a tidbit I could beg for a favor on. But this . . . "Are you *certain*? How do you know?"

She shrugged and looked embarrassed again. "I had a hard time swallowing the balloons. I think he thought I'd left when he was telling his lieutenant. But his girlfriend was nice. She stayed in the bathroom with me for a long time to help me get them down. I kept gagging."

That was nothing to get embarrassed about. I was pretty sure I'd gag, too. But okay. This was big. It was in the future and it was actionable. But who to call?

I leaned back in my chair and steepled my fingers next to my lips. I could call Alex. But if she was still following up on my last tip, she was working to get a squad out to the prison. That was damned important, and I didn't want to interrupt her. Still, she was my only real contact in the local police. I knew more sheriff's deputies because that department allowed moonlighting, so I'd met a few guys off-duty, on bodyguard assignments. But a drug bust on the harbor wasn't a sheriff's department sort of assignment. Apparently, I needed to meet more people in the city police, and since the local cops couldn't take a second job, it would have to be the old-fashioned way—dropping in to talk. I filed the thought away for future action.

I saw Maria open her mouth out of the corner of my eye and held up a hand to stop her. "Give me a minute. I have to think."

A thought occurred to me and I moved forward so suddenly I scared poor Maria. "Got it!" I announced it so she didn't bolt right out of the chair with a scream. I spun the card index until I reached the "R" section and plucked out a business card that had been taped to one of the slotted ones. I was already reaching for the phone.

After two rings, my call was picked up. "Federal Bureau of Investigation. Special Agent Rizzoli's office."

Bummer. He'd answered personally the last time I called. "Is he in? I need to speak to him right away."

"I'm sorry." She wasn't. Her voice was bored and impatient. "He's out on assignment. Can I have him call?"

That could take ten minutes . . . or a week. Was it worth the risk? I sighed. "Yeah, I guess you might as well give him the message. Have him call Celia Graves. It's urgent. And I mean really, *really* urgent."

"Spell that for me."

How hard is "Celia Graves" to spell? Whatever. I spelled it, slowly and politely, just in case she was his boss or something and decided to pitch the message in the trash if I was rude. Just to be safe, I added, "Please tell him it's about Jorge Encarcion. Again, it's *urgent*."

There was a pause on the line and I was certain she'd hung up. "Hello? Did you get that?"

"Yes, ma'am." Her voice had changed. Now she sounded interested. "Let me read that number back." She did. It was right. "I'll have him call you as soon as possible."

Had I hit a nerve by mentioning Encarcion's name? God, I hoped so. I hung up and let out a slow breath. "Okay. We need to find a place where you can be safe for a few days until I hear back from the guy I just called." In normal circumstances, I would just escort her home and tell her to stay home sick from school for a few days. But Jorge knew where she lived, so that was out, and so was putting her with anyone I trusted to watch over her. The people I trust I also care about, and not everybody is suited to the life I live. What Maria really needed was a caretaker who could also take care of himself. Someone to keep her on the straight and narrow, to dissuade her from believing that the drug trade was a viable career choice. To protect her from herself as much as the outside menaces.

A warrior.

Or . . . a warrior *priest*. "What religious faith are you?"

She furrowed her brow, as though it were a stupid question. "Catholic."

"What would you think about staying at a seminary for a few days with your family? Specifically, with the local warrior priests?" It could be the answer to everything. A lot of the dealers from south of the border were Catholic. They'd think twice about shooting someone on holy ground. Maria could continue her schoolwork and her family would be protected. The warrior priests are kick-butt guys—skilled in both martial combat and demonic battling. Few messed with them. But the ones I'd met were all wonderful, caring men who would definitely be concerned for a young girl like her.

The fear was back in the girl's eyes, but there was something else there, too. I think it was hope. "I think Mama would be really excited. She's never met a warrior priest. But she doesn't know about this. I haven't told her Manuel died."

Hadn't told her? I didn't think anything else could shock me, but Maria had managed it. "You said he dumped Manuel's body in front of the house."

Now she'd clammed up. Crap. I was already in too deep. What the hell had she done with her brother's body?

Wait. That wasn't my job. Her brother was dead. I couldn't help him anymore. I could also understand her panicking when she found his body. Now I'd agreed to protect her. The best way to do that was to get her out of the line of fire. Yeah, she definitely needed some priests around her. If nothing else, for confession and helping her break the news to her folks. The police would have to get involved eventually. Maria had committed a crime by hiding a body someone else had killed, but they probably wouldn't prosecute if she could help them catch a bigger dog.

I pushed back my chair and stood. "Let's get you out to the seminary. I'll call them on the way and have one of the priests go to your house to collect your parents."

She seemed relieved I didn't ask anything more about Manuel's body and happy that I included her parents in my plans. I'd already put on my knife sheaths before she came in, but when I reached for my shoulder holster her eyes went wide. I shrugged. "We can't guarantee there isn't someone waiting outside. I want to be sure we make it to my car and to the seminary."

On the way out, I planned to tell Dawna to implement security level one. It was a literal switch at her desk that would turn on a special perimeter barrier that would sound an alert if anyone approaching was armed with something metal. The door would be locked so that each guest had to be buzzed in and a nitrates sniffer would activate as someone approached the door. We'd do it all the time except the sniffer caught too many things out of the air from the military base down the road. The random sirens had driven us nuts until we figured out why they were going off.

After putting on my blazer, I picked up my purse and motioned Maria to her feet. "We'll take the interstate. That'll give us more maneuvering room if—"

The intercom buzzer sounded and I looked at the phone as if it could see me. "Celia? I'm sorry to interrupt. Could you pick up?"

Dawna didn't interrupt a client meeting unless it was really important, so I reached across and picked up the receiver. "What's up?"

"Remember that FBI guy who came to the office a few months ago? He's on line two."

Rizzoli? Wow! I guess I had hit a nerve. "Got it. Thanks." I motioned Maria back to her seat and walked back around the desk, the phone's cord stretching to its limit as I did. I pressed the button and heard the characteristic static of a cell phone. "Rizzoli? Is that you?" For a moment I heard nothing but the sounds of a busy street.

"Make it fast, Graves. And it had better be fucking important to interrupt a deep-cover stakeout." Wow. I'd never heard him swear before.

"You've heard of Jorge Encarcion?"

"It's why I'm calling. Like I said, give me something useful or I hang up now and go back to looking like a drunk bum."

I might pay to see that. Rizzoli was very Italian and so very

cookie-cutter Fed that I couldn't imagine him in filthy
clothes, sucking on a bottle of cheap wine. "What would you
give me for a witness that could hand you Encarcion on a
silver platter?"

There was a long pause. "Don't tease, Graves. You're too
much of a lady."

Aww . . . that was almost sweet. But I could hear the drool
in his voice. "She's a minor. I want a guarantee that you'll protect her and her family before I hand her over. The Viper's already taken out her brother. And when I say 'guarantee,' I
mean paperwork with that lovely federal watermark on it."

There was muttered swearing that I couldn't quite make
out. But I could guess. Witnesses were nifty for court cases,
but paperwork that ties the Feds to the protection of those witnesses doesn't make for happy agents. Still, the word "minor"
was enough to make him sigh. "Done. I'll probably get an ass
chewing, but I'll do nearly anything to get a hot shower and a
good meal after a week out here." Was he implying he was on
a stakeout *about* Encarcion? No wonder he had called. "Call
my office. They'll arrange for someone to pick up the witness,
get the information they have, and get them to a safe house."

I made a noise that could be interpreted as rude in most
polite circles. "No offense. But I haven't had very good luck
with people in your office. I trust *you*. I'm going to take her to
the militant-priest seminary and I'm going to instruct them to
deliver her only to you. And I want her kept out of the operation until it's over."

Now there was a strangled scream of frustration and then
an angry hiss of words over the line. "You're killing me here.

154 I CAT ADAMS

I've got to have something to take to my superiors *before* I can protect her."

Oh. Well, yeah. I suppose that was an issue. Unfortunately, it was a chicken-and-egg thing. He didn't want responsibility without the information. I didn't want to give him the information without a guarantee of responsibility. "Tell me where you are. I don't want this broadcast. I'll hand you the information personally."

He paused for long enough that I would have thought he'd hung up if not for the traffic noise in the background. "Okay. I'm hanging out near the Sam's burger place on Federal. Find some place to visit around here that would be normal for you. A gun shop or something. You won't recognize me, so I'll find you. I'll start being more aggressive in my panhandling, so by the time you get here it'll look normal for me to approach you. Push me away and then hand me a twenty when I plead. Put the note inside the folded bill. I'll call you later after I've checked in and delivered the intel."

Wow. That was a lot of detail on real short notice. But it sounded like it would work. "I'll be there at—" I checked my watch. Already eleven? Damn it. Where had the time gone? I'd have to cancel my meeting with Shawn. If he wasn't already waiting downstairs. I looked over at the pretty young girl who was now looking at me with rapt attention and hope in her eyes. "At one or one thirty. How far do I need to walk in from so I still have wheels on my Miata when I get back to it?"

Rizzoli let out a sound I realized was a small chuckle. "Come in with fangs bared and I don't think anyone will mess with it.

Come in with fangs and those knives of yours and you'll have the street all to yourself."

I supposed an empty street was better than a faceful of holy water.

Or worse . . . a crossbow.

10

I t **was** twenty after one by the time I had Sam's in sight. This block of Federal wasn't one of the best. Litter was strewn haphazardly on the streets and sidewalks. Graffiti announced a gang's turf over the top of a previous announcement, and the obvious hookers and addicted vastly outnumbered the people just trying to live their lives in peace.

As expected, my car was creating quite a stir. I should have taken the bus. Normally I'd park right in front of the business I wanted to visit and get in and out quickly. But if I did that, then I couldn't "wander" past Sam's. My best bet was to drive around the block a few times, appear lost, and then ask for directions at a local business—one on the wrong side of the restaurant, so that I'd have no choice but to pass it on the way to the gun store. I'd looked the gun shop up on the Internet so I'd have some idea of what I wanted. There actually were some interesting items for sale, and I was always open to new places to buy gadgets.

The song on the radio ended and a news report interrupted even though it wasn't the top of the hour: "This is your KSML news center with a developing story. We've just learned that a warrior priest from Mission Viejo was found this morning buried in a shallow grave in the desert outside the city. According to police officials, Father Joseph Treer had been ministering to prisoners at the California State Paranormal Treatment Facility. Officials at the CSPTF haven't responded to requests for an interview, but an unidentified source in the Santa Maria de Luna police has revealed that a joint operation with federal officials is being planned to investigate allegations of mistreatment inside the state facility. The governor's office has indicated they're working closely with all parties to monitor the situation and will respond with National Guard troops if required. This has been a KSML special report. Stay tuned for more information as it becomes available."

So it was starting. Muscles I hadn't realized were loaded with tension relaxed just a bit and I could concentrate a little more at the task at hand. Maria was safe at the seminary and one of the priests was on his way to her parents' house to collect them.

Small groups of teens who should have been in school stared at me as I drove slowly by. Nearly everybody on the street was some shade darker than peanut brittle, which made my paleness all the more noticeable.

All of a sudden I realized I was slightly screwed. It was the middle of the day and I didn't dare walk around carrying my umbrella because I needed both hands free in case there was trouble. But my skin wasn't going to hold up for very long with only sunscreen to protect it.

It was a shame I couldn't call Rizzoli back to change the plan, but real bums don't normally have cell phones and I was

158 I CAT ADAMS

pretty sure he'd turned it off after we spoke. And despite my
best efforts as I'd driven by, staring at the various homeless
men hanging out on the block, I couldn't spot him.

Great. I was just going to have to tough it out. I parked the
car near a convenience store that was one of the few nearby
businesses with an awning. The shop was so crowded with
products that there was only a narrow lane between the racks
of items. Junk food and trinkets of all descriptions made for a
blur of color that was nearly blinding. The lone clerk was
stuffed into a tiny space behind a counter piled to the ceiling
with more things to buy. Talk about making the most of the
space available.

"Hi," I said with a smile that mostly hid my fangs. "I'm a
little lost. I'm trying to find Al's Gun Shop. Am I close?"

"No. Here there is no Al. You buy?" His eyes were bird
bright, his smile radiant, and his words heavily accented—
likely he was right off the boat from India.

"I know there's no Al *here*. I'm looking for his store. Is it on
this block?" I motioned with my hands and he watched them
carefully. I knew where the store was . . . and also knew I wasn't
going to get any information out of this clerk. But he'd probably
remember me if anyone asked, and that was the point.

"Ah! Al. Yes, yes." He reached out and handed me a pack
of chewing gum. How he'd pulled "Dentyne" out of "Al" was
beyond me. But I reached into my pocket and pulled out a
couple of dollars. He beamed, rang it up, and handed me some
change. I presumed I could still chew gum. I hadn't tried since
the fangs.

Armed with my pack of cinnamon-flavored "Al," I started to

walk out of the store. Then something caught my eye and I reached into my purse again. In a moment I was wearing an Angels baseball cap. It would protect my head and give my face a little shade. Standing there in the lone bit of shadow on the long, bright street reminded me of the time I hurt my knee while playing softball in school. The short distance across the diamond to the nurse's office seemed to stretch to the length of a dozen football fields, with my throbbing knee my whole focus. That's what the street looked like at this moment.

Suck it up, Graves.

I checked one more time to be sure the car was locked and started walking down the street. With each step I got hotter. The dim winter sun seemed to have the intensity of the desert in August on my fragile, exposed skin. There wasn't much showing, but my hands and the back of my neck felt like they were starting to blister. I needed to remember to wear the blazer with *pockets* next time. I tried to walk quickly but not so fast it was in the paranormal range. I readjusted my hair to cover as much of my neck as possible and brought my reddening hands up to where they were shaded by the hat visor.

I was sweating now and reaching the busy part of the street. People ignored me as I passed quickly by. The red and white sign of Al's Gun Shop at the far end of the block was my whole world.

"Can you spare some change, miss?" I heard the words, but they didn't register until I felt a hand on my arm. I turned and pushed his hand away, recoiling from the scent of urine and days of sweat.

"I haven't eaten in days, lady. Please?" The bum's wheedling voice didn't match the strength in that hand, which finally pulled my mind away from the stinging of my skin. The intensity in his hazel eyes bored through the grime and the three-day growth of beard. His body shape finally reminded me of the stocky Italian who'd sat in my office in a charcoal suit and muted tie. I looked up and sure enough . . . I was standing right under the Sam's sign. Rizzoli must have noticed something was wrong, because he frowned with concern. But I didn't want to get into my own issues, so I just looked down at my purse and reached inside.

My fingers found the folded twenty with the note paper-clipped inside. "Here. Skip the meal. Go buy yourself a bath." I tried to make my voice sound like a disgusted tourist and I sort of was, so I pulled it off.

A wry twitch of his mouth and a wink said I had the right man. "Thanks lady." He turned without another word and walked through the restaurant door. I nearly sprinted to the safety of the air-conditioned gun shop.

I needed to replace the boomers I'd used at the prison as well as pick up a few more mudders. Al's had the products and they were cheaper here than at Isaac Levy's store. Unfortunately, they were a brand I didn't recognize, so I had no idea whether they'd work as well. Normally, I'd insist on trying them out, the way I usually did in the gun range in Isaac's basement. Here at Al's—no gun rack, no demo. Plus, the guy who waited on me was the only person in the store—stupid, in my opinion. But not my business and I wanted to get back to my car while it was still there.

While he was writing up the paperwork for the ammo I'd

also bought, I stared out at the street through the window. The bars and grate over the glass fractured the view, but I could still see a trio of street performers across the way. There were two men, playing guitar and bongo drums, and a dancer, a very flamboyant African-American woman who was dressed in a bright yellow tribal robe and hat with geometric designs in black and orange. The group hadn't been there a moment before. A spirited Latin beat throbbed through the air. It was good music and good dancing and the performance was drawing a crowd. The woman twirled and stepped gracefully; the musicians gave it their all. A fourth man stepped forward, passing around a hat. Surprising to me, given the area, people were dropping money into it.

The store clerk let out a small laugh as his eyes followed my gaze. "I see Gwyneth and her crew are back. It must be two already. Every day, same time. I don't know what they spend their morning doing, but they make good money in the afternoon."

He handed me a bag with my purchases and I moved closer to the window to watch. My eyes were glued to her fluid movements. So much so that I nearly missed a familiar figure that darted by a few steps away.

What the hell?

I looked again, shifting my body and pressing my face to the dirty glass so I could see farther down the street. Was that El Jefe? What in the world would Kevin and Emma's father be doing down in this neck of town? I was curious, but I was torn. I was still furious with Warren for betraying me. When Eirene kidnapped Emma, Warren and Kevin had decided to use me as the ransom. They'd drugged me, trussed me up, and tossed me in the back of the car—and only then told me what was going on. I'd nearly been killed and so had Emma. I hadn't spoken to either of them since.

On the other hand, I had no idea how Kevin was doing since the prison break . . . and once he and I had been the best of friends. I opened the door and stuck out my head. Cupping my hand to my mouth, I shouted, "Warren! Hey, wait up!"

I wasn't sure he could hear me over the music, but he turned toward me. I saw his face shift from delighted to confused and then finally to guilt and fear. Without a word, he turned on his heel and started to *run*.

What the hell?

I didn't think it through; I just started to chase. What was he hiding down here in gangland? He knew full well I had vampire abilities now. I could overtake him in a heartbeat except that I didn't want to draw a crowd armed with stakes and garlic cloves. The garlic I wouldn't mind, but I'm starting to dislike pointy wooden things.

He was pulling out all the stops, probably fueled by adrenaline. What was he afraid of? It couldn't be me.

There's more than one way to skin a cat. I stared at the back of his head and thought hard at him: *Warren! Would you slow down, please? What the hell is wrong with you?*

The effect of my voice in his head was sharp and immediate. He stumbled and grabbed onto a light pole for balance as he turned openmouthed to stare at me. I caught up to him in a few steps. The amazement on his face confused me until he spoke: "Since when do you have telepathy?"

Oh. "Apparently it's a siren thing. It's new. I thought Kevin or Emma would have told you."

He shook his head. "It hasn't come up. We've been . . . busy."

That and the return of guilt to his face told me a lot. "So I presume you know about Amy and Kevin and the zoo?"

More surprise in Warren's widened eyes. But he was more than surprised. He was tired. There were lines in his ageless, tanned face that hadn't been there a few months before, and his silver hair was getting thinner. "How do *you* know?"

So Jones hadn't mentioned my involvement. Okay, I'd play along. "I just do. Are they okay?"

Instead of answering right away, he pointed to my hands. "You're getting burned. Let's get you out of this sun."

I crossed my arms over my chest to tuck my hands under my blazer and ease the stinging. The bag thumped against my hip when I did.

I motioned behind us with my head. "My car's back that—" But he turned away and put a firm hand on my elbow to guide me farther from my sheltered ride. We stepped up to the entrance of an old brick building that looked like it had once been a drugstore, judging by the faded red *Rx* painted on the wall. Warren unlocked the door and ushered me inside.

I heard muted voices, far below, like in a basement. "Who else is here?"

"Kevin and Amy. You said you wanted to know how they were." Warren's voice was harsh, and even in the dim light from the fly-specked windows I could see he was worried. He led me down a creaking wooden staircase that was probably original to the building. But if the upstairs was old, the downstairs was ultra-modern. It contained the latest and greatest in containment units. Two shining silver-steel cells had been installed and John Jones was seated at a control panel, monitoring twin screens that apparently kept watch inside the cells. There was a scent of chemicals in the air.

"Hello, Jones."

He turned his head in a flash at my voice and then shot an angry look at Warren, who shrugged with mingled annoyance and resignation. "She saw me on the street and chased me. What was I supposed to do? And why the hell didn't you tell me she was involved, John?"

Jones shook his head and let out a sound that was somewhere between annoyed and amused. "You have some kind of timing, Graves. That's all I'll say." There was a snideness to his tone that made me respond in kind.

"Well, if you hadn't been so obvious in letting me know you bugged my office, you might have heard I was headed this way. Or maybe I'm here because I bugged *you*."

He didn't turn his head, but I could see his frown, followed by a thoughtful expression, reflected in the monitor.

Rather than ramp up the tension any more, I stepped forward to look at the screens. Amy was lying on a bed in the corner of a room. It was an actual double bed with head- and footboard, rather than an examination table or hospital bed. She was curled under sheets and a comforter, auburn hair tousled in quiet sleep. As far as I could tell, there were no restraints holding her down. "So you finally exorcised her? She looks okay. Why the silver-steel alloy?" Few things had raised the price of precious metals around the world more than the demand for silver steel—a blending of high-tensile steel, titanium, and silver of such purity and strength that it would contain nearly anything demonic.

Warren leaned over the board and sighed. "Looks can be deceiving. She talks, acts, and moves like Amy. But she still sets off the demonic sensors. I don't know if we've got a doppelgänger on our hands or if she was just tainted deeply enough that she has residual energy that's setting off the detectors. We've got her sedated right now while we're waiting on some more experts."

"Speaking from experience, demons can dig way down, so you don't even know they're there." I hadn't known it when I'd been attached to one *and* I'd passed every sensor with flying colors. "Why not take her to the university lab?"

Warren shook his head. "She's still a werewolf. We don't need that kind of attention. A demon-possessed lycanthrope would make national news."

Should I tell them or not? Well, it hardly mattered anymore after the news report. But there was no reason they had to know it was my doing. "They probably already know. I take it you haven't been listening to the news."

Both men turned to me with concern, but it was Warren who spoke: "The news?"

I shrugged as though I was just repeating what the radio had told me. "I heard on KSML that a warrior priest was found dead near the zoo. The local police and the Feds are putting together a task force to go inside."

Jones pulled out his cell phone with lightning speed and clicked on the Internet icon. His home page had reports scattered all over it, so apparently it was national news now. "What the fuck?" He stood in a huff and bolted up the stairs, the phone to his ear.

I shrugged innocently. "Guess he hadn't heard." I sat down on the stool Jones had vacated and looked at the second monitor. Kevin was pacing the cell like an animal in a cage, reminding me so vividly of the people in the zoo that I felt a pang of revulsion, coupled with anger that I hadn't been able to help those inmates. "Is Kevin having the same problems? Did the demons possess him, too?"

"No," Warren said with frustration. "It's not demons. In fact, it's his own damned fault he's still in there. He needs his Vaso, but he won't tell us who he or she is."

I reared back and looked at El Jefe. "Why not? Is it some sort of secret that they're not supposed to tell?"

He let out a small growl and the hand that was nearest mine on the desk clenched into a fist. "No. There's nothing in the societal rules that says it has to be a secret. Normally the wolf tells his or her close family in case they need to contact the Vaso when there's an emergency. We thought it was you, but if it's not . . . well, I don't know why Kevin won't tell us. Or at least *me*."

Actually, I had a pretty good idea, based on what Edgar had said at the mall. He'd claimed I'd been protected by my status as Kevin's supposed Vaso, but I was betting it was also because I was usually armed. Whoever Kevin's Vaso was, he didn't want to put them in danger. I motioned toward the monitor. "Is there a speaker in there? Can I talk to him?"

Warren nodded and toggled a switch on the board before speaking: "Kevin? Celia's here. Do you want to talk to her?"

Kevin stopped in mid-stride and turned with unnatural slowness toward the camera set far up on the wall. "Celia?" His voice was low and gravelly, as though he was barely hanging on to his human form. "Get her. Send her here."

"Who? Your Vaso? I don't know who she is."

"At least we know it's a *she* now," Warren said under his breath. "That's more than we had ten minutes ago."

Kevin's eyes were like twin stars of energy, supernovas ready to explode. That couldn't be healthy. "You'll know if you think about it. She's the only logical person. Send her here right away and make sure nobody follows her. Lead them away. Do anything you have to do to keep her safe."

What? So once again I was bait? I was supposed to think out the solution and risk my neck. I could hear the sound of my own anger when I responded, "Why the hell should I? I don't even get a *thank-you* for getting your ass out of the prison and taking a bullet in my shoulder before you're sending me out again to die? Fuck you both."

That took some of the starch out of both of them. Kevin reared back in surprise and Warren's eyes went wide and panicky. "Celia," Warren began.

"No. Seriously. Who elected me the sacrificial lamb?" All my pent-up hurt and anger came roaring to the surface. Of course, it was getting closer to sunset, which probably didn't help. And

I hadn't eaten since I woke up. But the words were no less true because of all that. Sudden tears stung my eyes and my words were daggers laced with poison: "I *trusted* you. Respected you. Hell, I've idolized you since college, Warren." I pushed back the stool so I could stare at Warren's shocked face. "That night, you betrayed me and destroyed every single warm feeling I ever had for you. I've never gotten an 'I'm sorry,' a thank-you, or even an acknowledgment that you made a mistake. I don't know that I can ever forgive you and can't imagine why I should ever help you—either of you—again. Get yourselves out of this mess." I stood up and stormed toward the stairs just like Jones had.

Kevin's growling voice stopped me: "You would have done the same damned thing."

I turned and gawked at the screen even though he couldn't see me. "What? You really have gone insane."

His eyes were burning bright but with intensity rather than power. "If you'd known me back when your sister had been kidnapped, you would have taken the same chance. You would have known that I'd constantly beaten the odds and triumphed when everybody said I would fail. You'd know that I could take care of myself long enough to get everybody out alive. I'll admit that the sister I promised my dying mother I'd protect is more important than you. And if you can't admit that yours would have taken the same place in your mind, then you're just lying to yourself. I'll thank you, but I won't say I'm sorry, Celia, because it was the highest compliment I could have given you."

Bringing Ivy into this was a low blow. If his intent had been to throw a spear at my heart, he'd succeeded. But if I were going to be honest . . . If I'd known a skilled werewolf who could have skewed the odds enough that Ivy would still be alive today . . . what would I have done? Who would I have thrown, unknowing, into danger to save Vicki? Or Bob Johnson, who'd died in my arms the night I was nearly turned? The words came out of my mouth and they were so calm and soft that at first I didn't realize I'd spoken: "You're wrong."

Warren was standing back, letting Kevin and me have it out. I could see regret and pain in his eyes. I honestly don't believe he realized that he'd lost my trust that day and the consequence of that was just coming home to him.

Kevin just shook his head and snorted. "No. I'm not. You've thrown plenty of people into the line of fire for your own plans. Don't give me that holier-than-thou bullshit."

I walked back to the monitor but then decided instead to go to the door. There was a small bulletproof glass window set into the silver steel. I had to go up on tippy-toes to see inside, but I wanted him to see my eyes—so that he would believe what I was saying. I knocked on the glass and he turned to meet my eyes. I spoke loudly, in case the mic wasn't strong enough to reach across the room. "Yes. I've thrown competent people into danger. I freely admit that. But they *agreed* to help. That's the difference. I haven't hijacked them against their will. I haven't dismissed their intelligence. I wouldn't have done what you did and people wouldn't have died." His face showed sarcastic disbelief. "Okay, fine. They might still have died. You say you paid me a compliment by trusting my skills. But you decided my intelligence couldn't be trusted. That *hurts*. Face facts, Kevin.

Your *ego* is why that plan failed. You thought you had it all figured out, thought nobody could be smarter or better. You couldn't accept that a friend of your little sister, the sister who needed your protection, might come up with a useful strategy. That she—that *I*—might be just as smart and competent as you. So tell me, what makes me suddenly competent? The fact that you're stuck in there and can't do it yourself? You have to trust me because there's no other choice? Well, guess what? You may not have a choice. But I do. So. No."

I could see the final blow strike home as his eyes went from angry and self-righteous to shocked beyond words. I turned away. Warren couldn't even look me in the face. I was halfway up the stairs when I heard a quiet voice break the silence behind me: "I'm sorry." Warren's apology sounded sincere, but I wasn't ready to hear it.

"You should be."

Jones was at the top of the stairs when I got there. "Remind me never to piss you off," he said with raised brows. "But you do realize he'll go insane if we don't find his Vaso. The Company will put him down if that happens."

I hadn't known that. It didn't change things enough, because most of the problem was still due to his stubbornness and his ego. "Then he should probably tell you her name. It'll speed up finding her."

A wry smile turned up one side of Jones's mouth, but there was as much anger as humor in it. "He doesn't trust me."

I shrugged and adjusted my ball cap for the long walk back to my car. "Neither do I." My hand was on the doorknob when something occurred to me. Jones was staring at my back. I could see his reflection in the glass, and his face held both confusion and thoughtfulness. "But . . . I'm not heartless. I'm willing to find the Vaso." His brows rose until I added, "For a price," then lowered in suspicion and anger.

"You don't seem the mercenary type."

I turned and stared at him calmly. "I'm not. I'm the self-preservation type." I told him about my little run-in with Edgar the previous night. By the end of the story, Jones was openly growling and the flames of magic in his eyes were licking at his pupils. "So. You tell me what Edgar is trying to get from me and I'll find Kevin's Vaso. You refuse and so do I."

His lips pursed and I could see the wheels turning in his head. He was nothing if not a smooth negotiator. "What makes you think I know?"

I chuckled. "Call it a hunch. He didn't want my knives, even though they qualify as artifacts. The only other thing I have of any interest is the Wadjeti the sirens gave me. Is that what he wants?"

He shook his head. "Hardly. He must think you have a Millennium Horn. It does sort of make sense. We haven't been able to find it and you *are* part siren." The Millennium Horn? That sort of rang a bell, but I couldn't place the term right away. Jones must have noticed my confusion, because he let out a small sound of exasperation and continued. "Didn't you learn anything in college? The end of the first age of the sirens was marked by a battle with a greater demon of immense power."

Oh! Wait, it was coming back to me. "Right. I remember now. All of the siren queens banded together to seal the rift between our reality and the demon one. The Millennium Horn—"

"Horns. There were two. If they were blown simultaneously, the psychic and magical sound would shatter the barrier between the two dimensions. The sirens, as guardians of the oceans, decided after they defeated the demon that they could never again risk a demon finding the horns."

I was nodding now as the old folktale came back to me. "So they were hidden away and nobody ever saw them again."

He held up his palms and shrugged. "The Company has searched for them for years."

Why was I thinking it wasn't to destroy them? The very thought made me shudder. "But if Edgar left the Company—"

The frown was back on Jones's face. He put a hand on the banister. "Then he's working for someone else. Who I don't know. But I'd suggest that if you have an old horn hidden away somewhere, you keep it out of sight."

"Nobody's ever seen the Millennium Horns. There aren't any photos, drawings, or even descriptions of them. They purged the records so there was no trace. The only way someone would recognize one is if they were around to see them the first time they were used." And funny thing . . . I happened to know someone who *was* around. Queen Lopaka. It might be worth asking about it, especially if Edgar knew more than I did about them.

"So now I guess it's time for you to find a Vaso."

I sighed. I'd made the terms, and even though I had no idea how to accomplish it, I'd follow through. "I guess it is."

11

S ometimes the best way to think of something is to *not* think of it. This was not one of those times. My mind was working on two questions: who Kevin's Vaso might be and why Edgar was looking for the Millennium Horns. The problem was I didn't know which was more important. Night was almost here, which meant that Edgar would be out and looking for me. But how long could Kevin hold out with no way to drain his power? It had already been a full day that I knew of. How often did he need to give power to his Vaso? Did they have to do it in person? I could swear I remembered something about distance feeding from my lycanthropy classes. But maybe that just wasn't possible in this case, and Kevin obviously didn't want Jones or anyone else knowing his Vaso's identity. Her cover would definitely be blown if she went to him.

My hood ornament was missing when I got back to the car. Damn it. It was probably somebody's necklace by now, and I didn't have time to mess around searching. I'd just order a new one from the dealership or on the Internet and deal. Hey, I still had four tires and they weren't slashed. That was something.

The steering wheel was hard to hold with my burned hands, which were swollen and ached like I'd poured scalding water on them. I was betting they weren't healing as fast as usual because I hadn't eaten enough today. I hadn't had a chance to restock the car, and though I'd seen a thousand and one food items in the little Indian convenience store, I hadn't spotted even a single nutrition shake.

The bottom line was that by the time I got back to the office I was beyond twitchy. My pulse was throbbing in my head and every person on the street was glowing and looking tasty.

I parked the car in my reserved space and locked the door. I had to get a handle on my hunger before I walked into the office. I could feel the heat of the day sliding into cool darkness . . . as slow and delicious as easing your body into a pool. It was a sensual feeling that made my muscles come alive with the need to flex and chase. Hunt and feed.

My eyes snapped open when a tentative tap sounded on the window. Dawna was on the other side of the glass, but I couldn't see her face past the bright band of pulsing red energy that lit her up from the inside. She held something up to the window and it pulsed, too. "You're going vamp, Celia. Drink this."

Drinking was exactly what I wanted to do, but it wasn't the cup I wanted. Still, I held on to my sense of self long enough to lower the car window. I grabbed the Styrofoam container from her hand and raised it to my lips. Thankfully, I'd left my seat belt on.

She stepped back quickly, went into the building, and locked the door—I could hear the bolts snap home.

Smart woman.

The lid of the container defeated me for a moment, which told me just how badly off I was. I stabbed at the lid with my fangs until it finally gave way and wonderful warm bloody juices began to flow down my throat. It was a large container and I had no idea where she'd gotten it or how she'd known I needed it. But thank heavens she had. It was just what I needed. By the time I'd finished what must have been a quart or more I was feeling nearly normal. I'd even managed not to spill anything down the front of my shirt.

After I sat there long enough to see the sky edge to velvet, my hands felt like normal and I could see without a haze of red over everything. I didn't shake when I stood up, and when I went into the office Dawna looked like Dawna, not like dinner. She was working on bills, which was typical of this time of the month. While best intentions ruled and all of us tried to get bills out by the fifth, it was usually the tenth before they were approved and ready to mail. "All better now?" she asked as I walked up to her desk.

"Don't know where you got the au jus, but it was perfect. Right temperature, good spices. Yum."

She looked up at me and smiled. "Found a new source, that barbeque place down on Third. I stopped there for dinner the other night and they were pulling out this huge pan from under the grill, filled with juices that dripped down during cooking. Beef, chicken, and pork, and they were just pouring it down the drain, so it didn't take much effort to convince them to pour it into a bunch of containers for a few bucks. They're in the freezer, so all it takes is a few minutes in the microwave. But don't forget to do a shake chaser. Meat juice might feed what's still alive in there, but you need vitamins, too."

Good point. I went into the small kitchen and opened the fridge. Ooh! Chocolate caramel. That was new. I popped the top and took a sip as I walked back to her desk. "Sorry I flaked out on you earlier. It was sort of an emergency. And thanks for restocking the fridge."

She nodded but didn't look up from her data entry into the computer. "It's not the first time we've missed lunch," she said, and laughed. "The seminary called. They picked up Maria's folks and everyone's safe. What's going on?"

Dawna's a member of my team, so I didn't hesitate to fill her in about the girl and the balloons and the unexpected exit down the toilet.

"Omagawd! You're kidding!" She howled with laughter and I finally got to smile about it. "Oh, the poor thing. She must have been frantic. Is it all sorted out now?"

"Not by half, unfortunately. Fingers crossed, though." I held up my hand to show Dawna that I'd done just that. I didn't want to go into detail in case we hadn't gotten all the bugs out of the office. "Hey, you want to get out of here for the night? I really need someone to bounce some ideas off and I'm still a little nervous after Justin's visit."

A little snort escaped her. "You and everybody else. Ron wants to bring in someone for a second opinion. He's threatening to move out if the owner can't guarantee him some client confidentiality. Hard to blame him, y'know?"

I sighed. "Terrific. You know who the owner is, right?"

She furrowed her brow and cocked her head, sending dark hair spilling out of her tasteful bun to land on her shoulder. "C and S Corp. Do you know the contact there?"

I pointed a thumb at my chest. "Moi. C and S was Vicki, and I'm the new owner once the probate goes through. Haven't you received your letter from the attorney yet?"

"You're kidding! She left you a *building*? Wow. Yeah, I got a letter saying that Vick had left me something but that it was being held up in the lawsuit her mom filed. I figured it was a few bucks. I hope it's enough to pay off my credit cards."

I smiled. It really had been a while since Dawna and I had had a normal conversation. "It probably won't pay off your cards, but it'll free up your rent money." At her questioning look, I patted her hand. "She owned *your* building, too. That's your inheritance. In a year or so, you'll own an apartment building and will get all the headaches thereof. Just like me."

Her jaw was open so far a bird could have flown in without pulling in its wings. When she finally recovered, I'd nearly finished the shake. "There's like forty apartments in my building! How the hell am I going to take care of them all?"

"Join the club. At least Ron's not one of *your* tenants."

She rested her elbows on the desk and dropped her chin onto her hands just as the lights flashed twice and the temperature dropped enough that I could see my breath. I looked up at the sparkling formation near the ceiling. "Hey, Vick. Glad you're feeling better. Thanks for your help last night. Kevin's okay." I waggled my hand. "Mostly."

No prob. S'up? The words appeared on the front window in frost.

"I need to find his Vaso. He's in pretty bad shape. Needs to drain his energy. Any ideas?"

Nooo. But . . . I waited while she thought and then watched as white cursive letters appeared while the glass snapped and popped from the sudden temperature shift: *Work, sleep, eat. All he did.*

"True that," Dawna added with a nod. She'd noticed her undone hair and was putting it back into the bun by stabbing it repeatedly with the ornate chopsticks she used as hair ornaments. "We had to drag him out of the computer lab when we went out somewhere. Half of the time he wouldn't come because someone on campus had a broken computer. His Vaso must be someone he knew at school. He never went anywhere else."

"Makes sense to me. But it was a big university. Could be any of a hundred people."

No. Day or night? The words were hurried, like the ghost had an idea.

I knew so little about Vasos. I pointed to the computer screen. "Bring up the Internet. See if there's a time of day that a werewolf has to drain his energy. I'll bet Vicki's right. She usually is."

A few clicks later I was reading over Dawna's shoulder, feeling a chill on my neck as my dead best friend did the same thing. "Ooh, look at this. The best time is right before bed. But Kevin never went to bed until late. What's open on campus at night?"

"Infirmary," Dawna offered.

Security appeared on the window.

But I was the one who got it and we all knew it the minute

I wrote the word on the pad on Dawna's desk. *Library*. I wrote it to protect her identity from anyone listening or watching, just as Kevin had asked. The university library was open until midnight every day except Sunday.

The Vaso could be only one person. Anna, the metaphysics section librarian, had worked at the college for more than a decade. She was a smart, powerful witch who I didn't doubt could manage the excess energy. I'd seen them talking at least once a week but hadn't ever thought about it because everybody talked to her. She knew the library backward and forward.

Dawna let out a delighted guffaw and held up her hand—to slap cold air. "Girl, you know that's got to be right. Who else? Kevin was there *all* the time." The best part was that if Jones was somehow still listening in, he had nothing, and I'll bet he was seething.

So now I had to convince Anna to do whatever it was she needed to do. I just hoped she knew she was Kevin's Vaso. I'd hate to think he would do something like that without her permission, but then again, he'd done stupid stuff like that to me, so what did I know?

My cell phone rang. The screen didn't recognize the number, but it was an international call judging from the long string of digits. I pressed the receive button. "Celia Graves."

"My mother would speak with you." I recognized the voice. Princess Adriana was Queen Lopaka's daughter but was not her heir. Our relationship hadn't begun well—actually, Adriana had challenged me to a duel. I'd won and she had taken it pretty well. I wouldn't call us friends, but I didn't think she'd try to kill me again.

"Good evening, Adriana. How've you been? What's new?"

There was a pause, as though she'd never actually been asked that. "I'm engaged to be married. I suppose that's new."

Engaged? Wow! That *was* news. "Omagawd. That's fabulous! Where'd you meet him? Is he another siren or human or what? Are you ecstatic?"

There was another pause and her voice sounded confused by the question. "It's . . . um, complex. I believe I'll be happy. We have much in common. I will finally be a queen, even if it's not of my own people."

A queen? That would mean she's marrying a king. There weren't very many eligible world monarchs. Of course, there are a bunch of princes who might someday get the throne. "What country? Have I ever heard of it?"

Now she sounded amused: "I believe you have. It's Rusland."

She was marrying King Dahlmar? I felt my jaw drop. "But he's . . . well, he's *old*!" He was handsome, to be sure, but he was silver haired, elegant. A grandfather, not a husband.

Her laugh was the gentle tinkle of water over chimes. "He's younger than me, Celia. By a number of years. You forget how old *I* am. He's lost two sons and has no heirs. I have no hope to rule here but could be a queen there and gain an important ally for my mother. And he is quite attractive. We're both lonely and I've always . . . dreamed of having children." The admission seemed to startle her, and the tone of her voice changed from amazed wonder and joy to a more businesslike one. "Of course you will be invited to the wedding. But now my mother would speak with you. Thank you for asking after my . . . well, just thank you."

Wow. I'd never really thought about the realities of such a long life or the duties of a royal. To have to worry about strong allies and heirs just to find a mate. I hadn't heard the word "love" in her rambling, though her happiness was evident. But Dahlmar was a good man—strong, smart, and devoted to his people. He actually was quite a bit like Adriana. They'd make a good match . . . and maybe they'd wind up really falling for each other. It had happened before.

"Celia?" The queen's voice came over the wire. "You seem to have befuddled my daughter. She scurried out of my office with a red face and odd smile."

A small laugh escaped me. "I have that effect on people. I hope you have good news for me. Did your people talk with the judge?"

"I spoke with the judge personally." That made me wince a little and she must have realized it, because she hurried to add, "I swear there was no improper manipulation. I made certain he was protected from my psychic abilities before I walked into the room."

Oh! That reminded me of my talk with Alex. Lord, was it only yesterday? "By the way, before I forget, the police here have asked me to provide DNA to make charms for their officers. Would hair from me protect against *any* sirens, or just me?"

"Hmm. Well, likely with your weak bloodline, it would just be you. I understand why the authorities there would have reason to want protection. It's likely you'll be visited by other royals from time to time." Crap. That wasn't good news, because the other queens hated me. "I will have my security office coordinate with the police there to create suitable charms.

After that fiasco of a court case you were forced to endure, I will be certain the police do not treat you harshly because they fear you.

"As for your mother, she is on her way now to the Isle of Serenity to complete her sentence. While here, she will undergo treatment to heal her body and her spirit. Of course, to fully accomplish that there can be no early parole and she might even have to stay beyond that. Still, I hope she will return to the mainland as a whole person. I must tell you, Celia, it nearly made me cry to see what she'd been reduced to behind those dry stone walls. Just getting her on the boat did a great deal to bring her back to herself."

It was a day for sighs of relief. "My gran will be so pleased. *I'm* so pleased. And grateful. You can't even imagine. Thank you more than I can express, Your Highness."

"You are quite welcome, Celia. And you are welcome to call me Aunt Lopaka, if you prefer. It is fact and would go far to establish your credentials in the eyes of the others."

Wow. That was a big thing. Lineage is everything to the sirens. I'd had to defend my right to even exist, and when the queen had acknowledged me as a family member it had caused a lot of discontent with the other rulers.

But it might be too much too soon. "For the moment, Highness, I'll decline. I thank you, but there are already enough people who want to take off my head for overstepping myself."

She didn't offer a second time or insist or even try to convince me I was wrong. I liked that she respected my opinions even on our short acquaintance. "As you wish."

There were still a few items on my list of big issues and I

wondered if I might be able to scratch one more off tonight. "However, there is a history question you might be able to answer for me, if you will."

"The history of our people? Of course. If I can."

"What can you tell me about the Millennium Horns? Do they still exist?"

The pause on the other end of the phone was long enough that I thought about speaking. When Lopaka finally spoke, there was unexpected fury in her voice: "How *dare* you ask that! Family or no, this call is at an end."

There was a click without even a good-bye. My face must have shown my sudden shock and embarrassment, because Dawna reared back like I'd grown a second head. Crap. All that goodwill I'd built up with sweat and blood . . . gone because of asking one question? Shit, shit, *shit*! I felt sick to my stomach. "Oh, man. I think I just really messed up. And I don't even know what I said wrong."

"Why was that a bad question?" Dawna sounded honestly confused. "Even I've heard of *those*. The story's in the history books in school."

A sudden blast of cold air made me look toward the window. *Right story?*

My stomach squirmed even more. "Oh, I didn't think of that. What if the history books got it wrong? What if the real story is a huge scandal or something?" Well, there was nothing I could do about it now. I'd have to figure out some way to apologize for my faux pas.

"Well, I guess the best thing I can do now is find out everything I can about the horns."

Dawna smiled slyly. "I bet I know where you're going to go look."

I returned her smile. Kill two birds with one stone. "Want to come along?"

She shrugged and laid her hand on the mouse. "Sure. I've got nothing better to do and I have some stuff I want to tell you. Just let me shut down."

Yeah, I had stuff to tell her, too. I didn't know whether to bring up the idea of living together yet. So far she'd been a trooper with the vampire thing, but she was always careful to stay behind glass or concrete or such. The last thing I wanted was to be a source of trauma to her.

Actually, that wasn't true. The last thing I wanted was to be the source of her *death*.

12

I was a little worried about getting into the campus library. Though I'd graduated, I was still officially a student—I took a class or two every semester to maintain my health insurance. Right now I was getting a D in ornamental gardening because I hadn't been showing up for class and I'd missed the midterm exam. Well, my life had gotten just a *little* complicated. I think the only reason the instructor hadn't failed me outright was because he was giving the class for the same reason I was taking it, so he was somewhat loathe to make me lose my benefits. But he did warn that I was going to have to spend some time with the design books and a hedge clipper after the winter break or he wasn't going to be able to let me skate by anymore.

And while the vampire healing was holding up so far, I'd hate for something else to change in my life and leave me with no healing *and* no insurance.

But despite my status as a student, I might be kicked out of the library. I'd been eighty-sixed by Anna herself not long ago. She considered me a risk to the patrons. A normal vampire certainly would be, and she'd outed me as a bat the minute I was turned. That was one reason I'd brought Dawna along. She could get through the magical barriers to the basement level even if I couldn't and could give Anna the address where she could find Kevin. But I was hoping Anna hadn't increased the shielding.

Dawna obviously had had similar thoughts. As we drove toward the library she said, "Why don't I go in first? I can take her the note and see if you can come in. Just drop me off and drive around in case we're being followed. I'll call you in a couple of minutes."

While I didn't like the thought I could *never* go back to the library—because it was one of my all-time favorite places—the discretion made sense. Maybe hooking Anna back up with Kevin and making sure he was safe would get me back on her good side.

"Sounds good. And hey, if you manage it, I'll give you your Christmas present early. It's *really* nice." Actually, I had no choice but to give it to her early. The reservations were for the coming weekend.

She lifted her chin and looked coy. "Not as nice as the one I got you, I'll bet."

Oh-ho. A competition. "Think so? Can you top a luxury weekend at the Oceanview spa—including hair, nails, facials, and massages? You, me, and Emma and the pampering of our lives?"

She squealed in delight and bounced in her seat, looking the most excited she had in months. "Omigawd! That place is the *best*! It got five stars from *Resorts* magazine. When is it for?"

I smiled. "This weekend. You hadn't mentioned any plans."

Her sparkling eyes got even happier. "That's in the Napa Valley, isn't it?"

I nodded. "Right in the heart. Not sure why they called it *Oceanview*, but the pictures on the website are gorgeous."

She started bouncing again. "Omigawd! It's *perfect*. I think we're both psychic or something . . . because look at *your* present!"

Dawna reached into her purse just as we reached the library's parking lot. I found a spot under one of the big twin fluorescent lamps and light flooded the car. She passed me a gilt-edged envelope of heavy pressed linen. Pretty snazzy.

I opened it and removed three slips of cardboard with more gilt scrollwork and engraved lettering. I turned the shining letters into the light and . . . "Oh, no way! There is no fucking way I'm seeing this!" My jaw was well and truly dropped. Somehow she had managed the absolutely impossible. I was holding a *personalized* ticket to the event of the year. "How the hell did you get tickets to the release party?"

She smiled smugly and shook her head, refusing to answer.

California is wine country, so anytime a new wine shows up it's news. About two years ago, twin sisters with no grape-growing background came in and set up shop. They took over a little private winery and planted all new vines. It was very hush-hush and nobody really gave them a chance of success. Everyone expected them to do some big-time begging for press. Surprisingly, they didn't seek attention. They wouldn't even give interviews to the major wine magazines. There was a lot of buzz that they'd been in negotiations with the state growers' association and the EPA about whatever they were doing, and nearly every week some scandal sheet would claim to have the inside track on what sort of wine the sisters were making.

Then they started entering European wine competitions. The little California start-up took gold medals in both the red and white categories. But no one wrote or spoke about the wine itself—even the judges of the contests kept silent. A couple of French and Italian winemakers' groups protested, as did a consortium of Australian companies, and the courts got involved. The sisters' company insisted the court records be sealed because of trade secrets—and they were.

In the end the sisters gave up the medals, which ended the case with the nature of the wine still concealed. There was a full-blown riot in the press. Nobody in the public had tasted the wine. Nobody could find it. Nobody could beg, borrow, or steal it.

After all that, Saturday night was the big event—the official, very exclusive, public debut. The wine was named Witches' Brew and everybody who was *anybody* was going to be there. Connoisseurs from all over the world had been offering up to six figures for a single ticket, if Internet reports could be believed. But there were none to be had. And each and every one of the few legitimate tickets—like the one in my now-shaking hand—was engraved with the name of the guest.

"Oh, before I forget." Dawna took the ticket away from me, turned it over, and pulled a strip of cellophane from one corner. "You need to put your right thumb there and hold it for five seconds."

Okay, I was curious. I did as she asked. I felt an odd sensation on my skin, a sort of tickle. When I picked up my thumb after a count of five there was a perfect impression of my fingerprint on the gold foil, as though it was engraved. "Biometrics?"

"Of a magical variety," Dawna replied. "They *really* want to make sure nobody crashes the party. You can't scan or photocopy the ticket. It comes up blank."

Wow. This was just so . . . wow. "Who did you have to kill or screw to get your hands on these?"

"No killing, no screwing, and very sorry, but no telling." She stuck out her tongue and unlocked her seat belt. "I'm off to get you lots of books. Enjoy staring at the pretty gold letters and thinking of what you're going to wear."

"Uh-huh." I really couldn't take my eyes off the ticket. I liked wine and I'd been following the story for two full years, ever since I saw the first little page 10 blurb in the *Times*. I *had* to taste that wine. I already had an order in with my local store for a bottle when one became available. Now I had the chance to drink a glass before nearly everyone else in the world. Wow.

I only realized that Dawna had left the car when I saw her halfway across the parking lot, heading for the library entrance.

Well, either I could sit here and keep staring at the ticket until my eyes bled or I could do something constructive. First on the list was calling Gran.

Unfortunately, she wasn't home. She'd been home a lot less since she'd moved, but I was glad she was spending time with friends. I waited for the beep, then said, "Hi, Gran. Sorry I missed you. I've got great news. Queen Lopaka said that Mom's problem was being separated from the ocean. She convinced the judge to move Mom to the Isle of Serenity to finish her sentence. They're going to get her into alcohol treatment and give her counseling. Isn't that wonderful?" God, I hoped she thought so. "I'll be out of town this weekend with Dawna and Emma, but give me a call. My phone should be on."

I clicked off the call and heard the chime that told me someone had called while I was leaving the message. Typical. I expected it to be Gran because that usually happens. But the number was one I didn't recognize. It wasn't even a California area code.

I called my voice mail and heard a male voice: "Ms. Graves? This is Mick Murphy." He let out a frustrated sigh. "I know you've been working really hard on our behalf, but Molly and I have been talking and we're starting to think that . . . well, that maybe it would be better to just stop this whole thing. It's ruining our life. It really is. I don't know the laws in California, but I'd imagine there's a way to refuse a bequest in a probate. I know there is here in Arkansas. Anyway, I just wanted to call and let you know. We'll be calling the lawyer tomorrow to see how to get the paperwork started. Thanks again. We both appreciate it."

Oh, crap. I mean, I understood what he meant. My bequest was a major pain in the butt—just thinking about owning a building and being responsible for the grass cutting, the perpetually leaky roof, and all of the other things that I usually had handled by the owner. His bequest was just cash, but it was a *lot* of cash.

And none of us knew the reason Vicki had left the Murphys all that money. Even Vicki didn't know, though she insisted there was one.

I hit the calls-received list and dialed his number. He picked up on the first ring. "Hello?"

"Mick? It's Celia Graves."

He let out a small, embarrassed breath of laugh. "You know, I was actually relieved when I got your voice mail. I didn't want to have to defend our decision."

I wasn't going to pick on the guy. "Hey, it's hard. I understand. The whole idea of that kind of money messes with your head."

The sound he made was a sort of laugh but really closer to a donkey bray. "It isn't my head as much as everyone else's. The calls have been non-stop since it made the press here."

"Press? What press? Nobody was supposed to know about the probate while the court case was going on."

"This is a small town, Ms. Graves. Nothing, and I mean nothing, goes unnoticed in Fool's Rush. Someone like your investigator comes to town and everyone knows the story before lunch."

I winced. I knew all about bad press and people calling at all hours. "Everybody in town has probably called asking for loans, huh?"

"Or trying to sell me something I don't need or want. People started out happy for us, but now they're getting aggressive and pissy. I mean, yeah, it'd be nice to give my girls some security—a college education and a trust fund. Maybe buy a new house or expand the restaurant. But we get by okay. It'll get worse if we keep going. I know it—"

A noise started in the background on his phone, making it

hard to hear the last few words. "Sorry. I couldn't hear that last part. There's a really odd sound in the background, like a cat yowling on a fence."

He let out a burst of sound that was part laughter and part struggling *not* to laugh. "It's sad, but that really is what it sounds like. I'm at the school Christmas pageant. I didn't want to take the call in the auditorium, so I stepped into the hallway. You just heard my daughter Beverly singing a solo. I love my baby to pieces, but she can't carry a tune in a bucket. I know the choir director wants to be fair and give everyone a chance, but it's torture to listen to."

My face felt hot because that's just what Gran and Mom used to say about me. "I can't really comment because I have the same affliction and remember really well the music teacher wanting to *be fair* with me. I wished she would have been realistic, not fair. If anything, Beverly sounds better than I did. Does your younger daughter . . . Jody, was it? Does she sing any better?"

There was a creaking sound and the background music dimmed. He must have gone back into the hallway. "It's Julie and yeah, she has a better voice. She got most of the talent in the family, in fact. I love them both, but they're very different girls. Beverly's kind of standoffish and scored nearly zero on the standard paranormal tests. But Julie is outgoing, smart, can sing and dance, and has an affinity with ghosts."

I felt a cold chill crawl up my spine. "She's a necromancer?"

"Nah," he said, and I breathed a little sigh. "Does a little channeling. Remember I said at the Will reading that my granny's ghost stayed in the house after she died to show us where her Will was?" I did and said so. "Julie communicated with her to get the information. She was just a little thing back then, but it was pretty spooky to watch. It doesn't seem to bother her as much now that she's older."

I was getting an awful feeling there was a really good reason why Vicki picked this particular family. Two daughters, one twelve and one eight, one who was odd and couldn't sing, the other talented, with an affinity for the dead? That was just too close for comfort. "Mr. Murphy, could you give me a few days before you call the lawyer to refuse the bequest? Talking to you just now, I had an idea why Vicki might have left you the money. But I need to talk to a few people. I've got to go out of town this weekend, but I promise I'll call you on Monday. Can you wait until then to do anything? Please?"

There was a pause where the only sound was children singing "O Christmas Tree" in high, clear unison. The notes were pure and bright. Beverly must have been mouthing the words. Finally, Mick sighed. "I don't suppose it'll do any harm to give it a few more days. Okay. I'll talk to Molly and we'll hold off doing anything until Monday. But whether or not you call, we'll be contacting the lawyer then."

The door of the library opened and I saw two figures emerging. Anna was slinging her purse over her shoulder hurriedly, and Dawna was loaded down with a stack of books that reached her chin. "I understand. We'll talk more once I ask some questions of a friend of mine. Thank you and thank your wife as well. And I know it's none of my business, but I suggest you let Beverly complain about the music teacher on the way home. I'm betting she's fully aware of how bad she sounded and needs to get the frustration off her chest. I remember how much I hated seeing the pity in people's eyes when someone forced me to sing."

I remembered only too well Gran cautioning me to "be nice" and not to talk back or complain. My embarrassment had made me furious and I wished I could have just talked to them about how horrible it felt to be put on the spot like that.

His voice sounded thoughtful, with just a touch of worry: "Y'know? I remember her saying that once after another concert. Never thought much about it. But I saw pity in a man's eyes once when he looked at me, and I didn't much like it. I'll give it a shot, let her speak her mind, and tell Molly to hush about politeness. Never hurts to give a horse its head every once in a while. Thank you, Ms. Graves."

It made me smile to know he was thinking about Beverly's feelings. I wished I could have had a dad like him. "No problem. I hope it works out. We'll talk more next week."

I hung up just as Dawna reached the car. I leaned across the front seat, struggling against the seat belt to push open the door. She caught it with an elbow and swung it wide enough to hold it with her hip. She stuck out her tongue. "You could have helped, you know. It's a long way across the parking lot."

Oops. "Sorry. I was on the phone with Mr. Murphy, the mystery heir."

"S'okay. I didn't notice you were on the phone. But damn, these things are heavy!" She put down the front seat and started to stack the books on the floor of the backseat.

Anna had reached her car, a little silver sedan that suited

her personality—dependable and sturdy. She met my eyes for a brief moment and bowed her head once in what I assumed was a gesture of thanks.

Three things happened at once: Anna turned to get into her seat, Dawna finished stowing the books and sat down, and I noticed a shadow moving toward the silver sedan. The shadow was fast . . . too quick to be human. I had my seat belt unfastened and the door open before I even realized I was moving. My leg muscles tensed and I sprang forward. My hands planted on the roof of Anna's car hard enough to make dents and then my hips swiveled, spinning my legs around in a circle as my right arm rose to make way.

The kick caught the vampire who'd been about to grab Anna across the side of the head. He fell back and down. "Shut the door!" I yelled at Anna as I slid down onto the asphalt. "Lock yourself in!"

She did as commanded as the bat got to his feet. He'd been no more than twenty when he died. He had the awkwardness of the newly dead, so he should be no trouble. He bared fully extended fangs and hissed at me. I hissed right back and it startled him for a moment. I guess he'd expected me to be just a brave human.

"Leave now and you don't have to die." I pulled both of my knives in a cross draw as I spoke. "You're out of your league, kid."

"Or maybe you're out of yours . . . *Celia*."

Oh, fuck a duck.

Although I didn't recognize the face, I sure recognized that voice . . . and the evil chuckle straight out of hell that followed.

Note the word "hell" in there, because that's just what he was. While I'd never heard of a vampire hosting a greater demon, it's not that big of a jump. There's a reason why holy objects are a primary defense against both.

There's a time when bantering with the bad guys is a good idea—it gives you a chance to think and plan. But the demon had a voice that could make my body react sexually and make my mind turn off. I'd barely escaped with my life and soul the last time.

"Come to me, Celia." He turned on the voice and I felt it pulling at my stomach, right through my clothes and skin. But so no. Oh, I'd go forward all right, but not like he wanted.

I lunged forward, making sure to lower my head so he couldn't get those fangs anywhere near my neck. I had no idea what would happen if I got bit again, and I couldn't imagine that a demon inside the bat at the time would be a good thing.

I head-butted him in the stomach with every ounce of strength I could muster and simultaneously stabbed one knife toward his heart. He grabbed my arm and tried to pull the knife away. But I'd anticipated that. My goal was to put him off-balance and off-guard so that when he jerked away from my head butt he backed straight into the *second* knife waiting between his shoulder blades.

His eyes went wide and his mouth open in a soundless scream as the enchanted metal slid effortlessly into his heart. "Go back to hell, asshole." I threw myself away, making sure to yank my second knife with me. "And stay there this time."

The vamp slid bonelessly to the ground, unable to speak past the blue and gold flames that licked at him from the inside out. When Lilith had burned up from within, I'd thought it was a fluke. Apparently not, because this guy did the same. But while the vampire was burned to ash, it wouldn't kill the demon. You can't actually kill a greater demon. All I'd done was remove another link between him and this world. He'd have to find another portal. He'd made a mistake by choosing a new turn. I'd be watching now that I realized the demon was still trying to get to me. Especially for the next few days.

Because come hell, high water, or bats in the night . . . I was going to that wine debut.

13

The amazement in Dawna's voice could be heard over the music and road noise: "I cannot *believe* you slammed the door on Jeffy Benson. He's the hottest thing on the *Billboard* charts since Michael Jackson."

My eyes flicked sideways just long enough to see the shocked expression that matched the voice before returning them to the road. "I told you I was serious about our vacation. I canceled two other jobs. Why is Benson any more special?"

Even Emma's face became a study in amazement in the rearview mirror. "He's . . . *Jeffy Benson.*"

"He already had four other bodyguards and two of them were former Raiders starters. Marlon Braverton was a Pro Bowl linebacker. I was staring him in the belly button. What did Benson need me for?"

"All that press has been doing you proud, girlfriend. You're *the* bodyguard to have right now. Wait until you see all the appointments on your calendar when you get back."

I struggled against the sudden tension that appeared between my shoulder blades. "That's not exactly going to help me relax, Dawna."

"Oh. Yeah. Good point. So . . . what do you think about the flowers from Bruno?" There was both coyness and challenge in that question. She was digging for dirt.

I sighed, but a small part of me wanted to smile. As we were leaving for the resort, a deliveryman had arrived, holding a vase of what must have been two dozen red roses. They were beautiful. No, more than that—spectacular. But they also wouldn't fit in the rental SUV, what with all our bags and my work trunk. I was bringing along a selection of weapons, sturdy boots, and a change of clothes. Because despite the best of plans, my life often sucked. The trunk was heavy steel with three kinds of locks. It would take at least two strong men to move it—or one petite woman with vampire strength. Dawna had tried to insist I leave it home.

In turn, I insisted she leave behind at least one of her *three* makeup cases. Emma broke the deadlock by suggesting I take the flowers to Gran's to save them from the wear and tear of the long trip to the spa. It was a good solution except that now, as we drove to Gran's, Emma was spitting leaves, because the arrangement really did take up about half of the backseat.

The Glades retirement center on Parker Road wasn't a typical apartment complex. It was a combination of a high-rise nursing home and clustered groups of elegant assisted-living bungalows. There was the requisite golf course, site of an even higher-priced retirement community. There were pools, fountains, and gardens everywhere.

Gran was in the assisted-living cluster . . . not because she needed that much help but because she wanted to live among women she knew. Ahn Long, Dawna's *bá nôi*, or paternal grandmother, lived there, and so did several members of Gran's church group. Each of the connected single-story townhomes had two bedrooms and a small kitchen. Everything in the apartments could be easily navigated or reached by those using walkers or wheelchairs. Gran's unit was much smaller than the house she'd lived in for so long, but she seemed happy there. As we walked up the smooth concrete sidewalks that snaked among the greenery, she greeted us with a smile.

"Oh! What beautiful flowers, punkin. Who are they from?"

"Bruno. I think he's trying to make up."

Her brows rose and she appraised the flowers again. "As well he *should*. They're a start at least. But make sure you let him stew for a few days before you acknowledge them. He needs to know you can't be bought so easily."

My jaw dropped. It really did. That was so unlike any advice Gran had ever given me that I was frankly stunned. When boys had given me flowers in school, she'd coo and fuss about their beauty and insist I call immediately to thank the boy.

"That card still gives me tingles," Emma commented. And I couldn't disagree. She pulled the small white card from the tall plastic fork buried in the leaves and read it aloud with a dramatic flair, one hand held over her heart: " 'Celia, I'm so sorry for everything. I understand now why you were upset. You were right. I was wrong. Is there any way you can forgive me? I'm coming to California and want to see you. Please. Call me. Bruno.' " She sighed. "It's like the next-to-last scene of a romance movie. Yum."

Yes, there had been little flutters in my heart when I'd read the card and I'd immediately wanted to call him and scream, *Yes! Of course I want to see you!* Then reality had sunk in.

"It's not that easy, Em." I closed my eyes again, trying to ignore the butterflies in my stomach. Either it was time for another shake or I was just starting to realize the gravity of the problem.

Gran apparently knew what I was feeling. "Emma, honey, life isn't always like a romance movie. I watched Celia's whole relationship with that man, just like you. They were engaged, so I watched close. He said all the right things, but his actions spoke different too often. I want to believe that he's changed. I do, because I truly think he loves her. And this is a good first step. But how long do you honestly believe his *understanding* will last? That's what he still needs to prove. That he can accept Celie the way she is."

Emma's face crumbled. Dawna reached over and put a hand on mine. "I'm sorry, Celia. I know how much he hurt you."

That was the crux of the problem. It *did* hurt. I wanted it to work . . . desperately. But Bruno was who he was and I couldn't expect him to change. He was an old-fashioned Italian American who honestly believed in hearth and home. A woman was expected to fill a home with children, laughter, and love. To Bruno, that was a primal thing that was more important than anything else. It was the life he had grown up in and it was what he wanted for himself. I respected that, but that's not what I see as my role in life. At least not now.

Now I'm about keeping people safe. It's my business and, more, I'm *happy* throwing myself into danger. I'm willing to neglect home and hearth when necessary. Those two worldviews don't mix well. In truth, I wouldn't want him to change. I know he feels the same about me. Our relationship would always be based on an uneasy truce, no matter how reluctant either of us was to admit it.

"Anyone can change," Emma said after a long silence. "I truly believe that. If you try hard enough and want it bad enough, you can change." The words were quiet but impassioned and almost too personal to hear out loud.

She wasn't just talking about Bruno and we all knew it. The taint of the demonic isn't easy to escape, and I can't run from my fangs. The main reason we were going on this trip was as an escape from our own brushes with death and worse.

Gran stepped forward to pull Emma into a hug. "Of course people can change, honey. It just takes time and wanting it bad enough that nothing else is more important. And it takes people supporting you, keeping you on track." I knew she wasn't just talking about Bruno anymore, or even Emma. She was talking about all of us but, I suspected, mostly about Mom.

Lord, but we were a messed-up bunch.

"All right," I said after a long pause, "I'll call him. I promise. But next week, okay? This is our 'ladies only' weekend."

Emma pulled back from Gran's arms and beamed at me, while Gran offered me a sad half smile of solidarity. I knew she'd stand behind me, whatever happened. She was the one constant in my life . . . the only person I could really count on.

Dawna shook her arms, letting out the tension. "So, Emily, how are you liking the tai chi lessons? Bá Nôi says you're really doing well."

Huh? Dawna's grandmother was giving Gran tai chi lessons? She hadn't mentioned that.

Gran laughed and made a graceful movement of her arm, ending with a flattened palm held toward me. "Oh yes. For several weeks now. It's really improving my flexibility. Ahn is a wonderful teacher." She walked past me and started toward the entrance to her apartment. "But we should get those roses out of the sun. Please, come inside."

I was surprised to see Pili sitting on my grandmother's couch, holding a cup of tea. Gran didn't even *like* tea. There were colorful brochures with pictures of exotic locales scattered all over the table. Dawna clapped her hands in delight. "Oh! You *are* going away? I know you're going to have a wonderful time."

Huh? I didn't like the feeling that I was completely in the dark. I plastered on a smile and nudged Dawna's shoulder. "Could you come help me with the roses in the kitchen, please?" She turned, confused, so I gave her one of my patented *I need to talk with you. Now.* looks.

"Oh! Sure. Yeah, we should probably trim the ends, since they've been sitting so long." Dawna always had been quick on the uptake.

Gran sat down at the table and picked up her cup. "Do sit down, Emma, and have a cup of tea. Celia, the flower snips are in the drawer next to the stove and the trash can is under the sink."

"So what's up?" Dawna asked softly as we began to shorten the rose stems under cool running water. "Are you upset about something?"

I let out a little frustrated puff of air and whispered a reply: "I don't know. I'm trying to figure out what's going on. I didn't know about the tai chi and you did. And you seem to know all about the travel brochures. I guess I should be asking what's up."

She shrugged. "You've been really busy lately and she's been lonely. Sometimes she calls the office just to chat. I suggested the tai chi lessons to Bá Nôi. Emily needed something to do, since most of the events here aren't things she enjoys very much. Pili's been spending time with her and so has Bá Nôi. They've all gotten really close in just these few weeks. I think Pili's probably empathic as well as a seer. She's been encouraging Emily to plan for the future—not just live in the past."

I started arranging the trimmed flowers in the vase. "Why hasn't she told me any of this?"

Dawna sighed and turned around to lean on the counter. "Honestly? You should talk to Pili about it. She knows a lot more than I do. Let me get your gran to show me and Emma the gardens. I've actually already seen them, but it'll take a while."

Without giving me a chance to reply, she walked back into the living room. "Emily, could you show me and Emma the rose garden? I'm sure Celia and Pili would like a chance to catch up with things on the siren island."

And just like that, Pili and I were alone. I sat down on the floral tapestry couch cushion Gran had vacated and looked at the small ancient Polynesian woman. "So . . . Pili. How are you liking retirement?"

She smiled so calmly and gently that my muscles relaxed.

"We have no need for small talk, Celia. I know you're wondering about your grandmother, and that's understandable. She hasn't wanted to worry you because she knows you already carry such great burdens of your own. You speak so little of your problems that it makes others reluctant to speak of their troubles with you. Please don't take that as any sort of criticism. But you must remember that your grandmother has been affected by her minister's death, the revelation of the death curse, and everything that's happened to you and to her daughter. And now she's had to leave the only home she's known as an adult. She's needed time to adjust. Time to find a new way of living, just as you have."

My face felt hot and my stomach was roiling. I couldn't believe I hadn't put all that together before. My poor gran!

"I don't know what to say. Do you think I should cancel my trip and spend some time with her?"

Another soft smile as Pili touched my hand. "Not at all. You need time to heal as well, just as Emily does. I've become a bit concerned that she's attached to Ahn and me so completely in such a short time, which is why I suggested she explore *herself* a little more . . . meet new people, do things she's never done before. She's very healthy and may outlive many of her peers. To balance the continued loss of friends and family, she needs new friends and new experiences." A quick pat of her fingers didn't make me feel much better. "Please don't worry. I'm working very hard to get her to a place where she's not spending all her time worrying about you and Lana. To keep her heart light, we must make her mind and hands busy."

The continued loss of friends and family. Ouch.

14

Emma and Dawna laughed and the three of us simultaneously raised our margarita glasses. I felt a cool swirl brush around us in a ghostly hug. Dawna clinked her glass, first with mine and then with Emma's on her other side. "To the girls! No boys allowed. Although . . ." She paused and lowered her tortoiseshell sunglasses to the tip of her nose as one of the staff walked through carrying another tray of lime-topped refreshments. "*Pretty* boys are always allowed."

I leaned back with a sigh and stared up at the stained glass and carved wood above the heat lamp for a moment before raising myself on one elbow to look at my three friends lounging next to the shining turquoise pool.

Yeah, Vicki was here, and while we couldn't see her directly, there was a distinct body mark denting the thick white towel on the otherwise empty-seeming chaise. Emma and Dawna were bronzing under tanning lamps, but I was just as "allergic" to artificial sunlight as I was to the real thing. But a heat lamp is just heat without UV rays and such, and even if I wasn't particularly cold, I wanted to share in the luxury of the moment. The heat lamp, fourth lounge, and framed mirror for communication with our dead friend had thrown the staff into a little bit of a tizzy, but they'd recovered quickly.

I was done worrying, at least for a weekend. I'd promised Pili I'd do my best to relax while she helped Gran do the same. Then maybe Gran and I could go back to the warm, loving relationship we'd shared for so many years. I looked forward to getting to know Pili better, too. I not only trusted her; I liked her. Finding a new relative who was both wise and wonderful was one of the better side effects of the last few weeks.

The cabana boy saw Dawna flicking her eyes up and down the length of his body and responded in kind. His sly, confident smile was enough to make me roll my eyes and shake my head. If Dawna didn't get lucky this weekend it would be a miracle. Emma wasn't above gawking, too, but the last thing I needed was another man in my life. After all, I wasn't sure what I was going to do with the ones I already had.

After our drinks had been replaced—I'd sent the cabana boy back to get me an energy shake instead of another alcoholic margarita—I relaxed into the wave of warm air. "So what do you think about the mystery heir thing? Do you agree with me?"

Vicki had been noncommittal about my thought that she'd chosen Mick Murphy because his daughters were younger versions of me and Ivy—and because if Mom had had money to buy off the kidnappers Ivy might still be alive.

"I guess it's possible," Dawna said after a few seconds. "But it's not the sort of thing she normally saw in her visions, right, Vick? If she'd seen something, it would have been the actual kidnapping. Why see a happy family with no trauma?"

208 I CAT ADAMS

Dunno appeared on the mirror that was propped on an ea-
sel next to Vicki's lounge so she didn't have to get up to write.
It was interesting to me that after she'd first died she could
only write a word or two. Now she'd often do five or six with
ease. Could a ghost get stronger, or had she just learned the
trick to it?

"That makes sense, really," Emma said from the far end. "If
she remembered why, she wouldn't have asked you to investigate."

"True. But I really think we need to follow the money. That's
a *lot* of freaking cash. Why not a hundred thousand, or even a
million? Why give them a quarter of the estate?"

Yes. About the money showed on the mirror. It was the first
acknowledgment that I was on to something. *Needs to buy . . .*

"Needs to buy . . . what?" She'd disappeared. The room got
warmer and the heat lamp was abruptly almost too hot. I sat
up and looked around, searching for the sparkling cloud. But
she was gone. "What's up? Where'd she go?"

Dawna shrugged and sat up fully, setting her feet on the
floor. "Maybe she had an idea. She'll be back. Anyway, we need
to get to the salon. We have a haircut and style in fifteen minutes. Then facials and makeup. Ladies, we are going to *rock* that
debut tonight!"

So true. Who knew the spa would have such an amazing
boutique? Absolutely everything fit and looked good on me.
That was saying something. "Can you believe the dresses we
found? There'd better be cameras there, because I want a picture of us for my album."

Emma nodded. "Before you were attacked, I wouldn't have

picked silver and blue for you; they would have really washed
you out. But you looked amazing in the dressing room. I can't
wait to see you . . . and me and, well, Dawna, too. This is just
what I needed."

I tried to smile, wanted to because she looked so happy.
She used to be that way all the time. Well, not cheerful and
bouncy, but content in her own skin. We both were. Before.
Now she looked . . . haunted. And it was my fault. Worse, I
didn't know how to fix it. "I really want you to get what you
need, Em. You shouldn't have to be fighting this." It was a non
sequitur from dresses to a demon attack. I knew that I should
keep the tone light, but I couldn't seem to stop the seriousness
and pain that rolled out with the tears that filled my eyes. "It's
my fault that you're going through this and I hate it. I'd fix it
if I could. Eirene was trying to hurt *me*. You got caught in
the middle. That's not fair. . . ." I felt my lip trembling.

Her brow furrowed and she stood in a rush, knocking over
the small table that held her drink. It crashed to the floor, but
neither of us cared. "Oh, Celie! No! It's not your fault at all."
She raced the few feet between us and enveloped me in a hug.
There was a fierceness to her grip that took me by surprise. "I
took the job with Eirene. I could have said no. Dad *told* me to
say no—to not leave school." She pulled back to grab me by
the shoulders and stare into my eyes. "This is *not* yours. And
it's going to be okay. You'll see. They're really helping me at
Birchwoods."

Fortunately, Dr. Gwen had agreed with that sentiment. It
had taken more than a few minutes to convince her to release
Emma for this mini-break, but ultimately Dr. Gwen decided

that Em would be best served by doing some "normal" things. Normally, in the first month at Birchwoods it's lockdown city. Everybody is supposed to wear gray sweats to "level" everyone's class and status bars. After all, the alcoholic father of a middle-class family who is court-ordered to rehab isn't the same in the eyes of society as a top-money model with "alcohol dependency." But at Birchwoods they're treated the same . . . and they have to treat each other the same.

Birchwoods is exclusive and pricey and it gets results because of its strict standards and effective staff. It wasn't just a rehab center, and in fact Emma wasn't there because of any sort of addiction. She needed to get her head on straight and was undergoing frequent religious rites to remove her attachment to the demon who'd tried to claim her soul.

Dawna joined the group hug and we cried for long minutes until we finally laughed. Dawna wiped a long streak of mascara from her tawny cheek. "They're really going to have to *earn* their money to make us look good now."

I let out a choking laugh that was still a little bit soppy. "I'm all about value for my dollar. C'mon. Let's go let them make us look like movie stars."

"No, there's no flash photography allowed until the end of the event. Sorry." The heavyset guard at the gate before the long, winding path really did look apologetic. The burgundy red carpet and the fairy lights that followed the curves of the road were really impressive touches that made me eager to get inside. "The owners want this to be about the *wine*, not about who's attending."

I suppose it made sense, but it was sad. We looked *good*. Dawna's bronze and green sparkles had obviously stolen the guard's heart and Emma's blonde cheerleader beauty was only enhanced by the black and gold dress that hugged her every curve. And yeah, I really did look good in silver and blue, and the dress had a built-in bra that gave me more cleavage than nature had. The stylist had even put silvery white extensions in my hair that I thought would look cheap but were amazing.

Dawna batted those big brown eyes at the guard who couldn't keep his eyes off her long expanse of bare legs. She shifted to expose even more skin to hand him her ticket. "Could you take a picture of us . . . out here? That wouldn't break any rules, would it? We just want to remember looking this good."

It hadn't occurred to me to bring a camera, but it had to Dawna. Her glove-clad fingers pulled a little digital out of a purse that wasn't much bigger than the camera. "Please?"

There was no one waiting, so nobody would know. The press were a quarter of a mile down the road, waiting for the event to end. I don't know what kind of magic they'd done to keep the press at bay, but they literally *couldn't* come closer. We even saw one reporter try to pole-vault over the barrier. It had been entertaining in that *ouch, that must have hurt* sort of way.

We'd arrived a little late because Emma desperately needed highlights. The guard stared at Dawna and the camera with a frown. She tipped her head just a bit to show off her gorgeous neck. We all smiled winningly and he finally let out a sigh and held out a pudgy hand. She squealed and bounced and we got together in front of the winery's sign: *The Twins*. He snapped two pictures and let us see them on the screen before he pulled the camera away and tucked it in a jacket pocket. "You can pick it up on the way *out*. I'll be here until everybody is gone. But I'll lose my job if I let a camera inside, and I know you don't want that."

Dawna wasn't the only one who could work facial expressions. He gave such a sad puppy face pout that we had no choice but to let out little maternal noises and give him a peck on the cheek. Then he picked up his radio and said, "Three more to pick up and then we're ready to lock the gates, Dave. All invitations accounted for."

Wow, we really were late. Oops. It was only a moment before we heard the hum of an electric motor. A golf cart modified to look like a horse-drawn carriage—minus the horse—pulled up to the gate. The guard opened the massive silver gates and bowed us inside. I walked toward the cart and felt the moment the magic barrier pressed against me. It was an oddly familiar sensation, but I couldn't place why. I was through in moments, but it left the hair on my arms standing on end for nearly the whole trip up the path.

"Are you cold?" Emma leaned over as we rolled down the path. "You keep rubbing your arms."

"I just feel a little weird. Did the barrier make your skin tingle?"

They looked at each other and then shrugged with heads shaking. "No." Dawna looked at her arm. "Not really. It felt like a barrier. Maybe you're having a vamp reaction. I'll bet they stepped up the oomph on security for tonight."

That was probably it. Fortunately, I'd stashed a couple of shakes in my purse. There wasn't a doubt in my mind that wine was going to taste horrible with chocolate, so vanilla was all I'd brought. Not my favorite but definitely more Chablis friendly. I drank it quickly, then tossed the empty can into a tiny, almost-hidden trash can beside the golf cart's drop-off point.

We'd missed the early mixer, which was probably a good thing. I hadn't realized how many of my clients would be here. From movie stars to singers and a few politicians, it was old home week, and many eyes lit up with surprise as I walked in. No bodyguards were allowed at the premiere, and that meant I was, gasp, a *guest*.

Dawna likewise recognized a few people—mostly from dating them. She is so good at crashing high-end events that half of the beautiful people in L.A. probably think she's some reclusive heiress, rather than a receptionist who's still studying for a degree. Of course, now she really *was* an heiress, so it all worked out. Emma didn't see a single familiar face, judging by her brief look of disappointment.

I took it upon myself to grab her hand and pull her forward. When she tried to pull away, Dawna realized what the problem was and grabbed her other hand. "C'mon, Em. I know just the person to introduce you to."

I wondered who she was thinking of and started scanning the crowd. When I spotted him I smiled, because Dawna was right. He was perfect. Emma protested for just a moment until she saw the first frown from a guest. I leaned over and whispered in her ear, "We wouldn't ever embarrass you, Em. Just give us a chance."

Emma had always been the outgoing one in school, gorgeous and popular; I'd felt like the ugly duckling. To have the reverse happen was a bizarre feeling. But as my words sank home, she bucked up and stood straight and gave the frowning man a smile that was worthy of a homecoming queen. He let out a little chuckle and turned back to the group he was talking to.

A handsome man in the corner was our goal. He was tall and exotic looking, just the opposite of the so-American Emma. I'd guarded him on his way to a science award ceremony and Dawna had tried to date him because of his amazing looks. But she'd given up after one dinner, when he'd done nothing but talk about gene splicing.

Like I said . . . perfect.

"Remir? How are you?"

Emma's mouth went wide when he turned those sapphire blue eyes our way. I didn't blame her. It was like someone had set gemstones into a frame of aged honey pine. Gorgeous.

He reached out both hands for one of mine. "Celia Graves. What a wonderful surprise. I know so few people here." He rolled his eyes. "Too much time in the lab, I suppose."

"Remir, I'd like to introduce Emma Landingham. I think you two have a lot in common." He turned his head and smiled at her and tipped his head just a bit in a *how so?* expression.

As I expected, Emma's eyes had brightened. "Are you really Remir Sandrow? I loved your article in *Scientific American* last May. It's no wonder you were up for the Nobel." I hadn't

expected her to recognize Remir, but it should have occurred
to me. Every field has its rock stars, and Remir was definitely
one. They launched into a discussion about prokaryote cells
and DNA and both Dawna and I were lost in moments. They
never even saw us leave.

A gentle but piercing crystal bell caught our attention and I
turned before I'd reached the next person I wanted to say hi to.
I felt my heart rate speed up and let out a little internal cheer.
While there's nothing better than mingling with people in a
non-work environment to cement a future work relationship, I
wanted to get to the wine. The uniformed butler who had rung
the bell looked as if he could be moonlighting from Bucking-
ham Palace. "If I could have your attention, would everybody
please come into the next room? We're ready to begin."

I smiled at Dawna and we started to move forward with the
now-murmuring crowd. When I glanced back, I saw Emma
and Remir deep in discussion, completely oblivious to the sudden absence of people in the room. Would she hate me if I interrupted? He was really giving her his full attention. I'd
guarded him for nearly a week and I hadn't seen him look at
anyone like that. Or would she hate herself for missing the tasting? I asked Dawna, "What do you think? Should I tell them?"

Dawna looked back and took in the whole scene—from his
hand, not so casually on the wall next to Emma's shoulder, to
her bright eyes and animated expression. "Nah. She'll hate us.
Let someone else spoil their moment."

I agreed and went through the bejeweled curtain into the
tasting room. Yay! At the front of the room was a small stage
with a table covered by shimmering golden cloth. They were

really pulling out all the stops for drama, building the antici-
pation, and I was loving every second of it.

The lights dimmed and two women walked out onto the
stage and were hit by a spotlight. They were mirror images of
each other, though with different-colored hair. They smiled at
the crowd and picked up microphones. The blonde spoke:
"Welcome, everyone, to our home." She swept an arm gracefully to include the whole room. "I'm Pam."

The redhead brought her mic to her mouth. "And I'm Sam.
And we're—"

"The Darby Twins." They said the words together and everyone applauded. Pam lowered her mic and Sam kept talking.
"You've been invited here tonight to share our excitement as
we unveil a wine that's the first of its kind in the world. You're
the very sort of connoisseurs who will most appreciate Witches'
Brew."

What the—? First of its kind? Did they come up with a new
variety of grape? There aren't many different kinds of wine out
there. I heard others asking the same questions in quiet voices
that were barely audible. The scent of all of the expensive per-
fume and cologne was making me a little woozy in the closely
packed room, but I couldn't take my eyes off the sisters.

Pam picked up the story: "Sam and I come from a magical
background. Our mother is a witch; and our father, a mage.
The energy of the earth has filled our lives and we wanted to
share that magic with you. We tried to figure out some way to
make what we experienced available to others, and after long
experiments and tests we discovered that we could actually

DEMON SONG ∎ 217

infuse magic into the very soil where our vines grew . . . and that the grapes could absorb it."

The whispering stopped dead.

"Excuse me?" A slender man with snow-white hair in the front row raised a hand. "Did you say there's *magic* in the wine?" He looked around him, a bit blue around the gills. "Is that *legal*?"

Sam laughed easily, with no discomfort at all in her body language. "Oh, it's very legal, and we can assure you there has been *exhaustive* testing for both purity and safety over the past two years. Each bottle bears the seal of the EPA and the certified organic emblem, plus symbols from the FDA and the MPRC, the Magical Protection and Regulatory Commission. This is why we've taken so long to introduce the wine. We didn't want to risk any allergic reaction or other physical problems."

Wow. Just wow. A magic wine. I shared a look with Dawna. Like me, she was now more excited to taste the wine than ever.

Pam picked up the mic again. "And now we'd like to introduce the man behind the magic. We searched long and hard to find someone who exemplified the *spirit* we wanted our wine to have. Proud and confident but with a soft finish. He's world renowned for his skill and power and we've been beyond thrilled he's been part of our journey. Ladies and gentlemen, please welcome . . . John Creede!"

If I could have moved enough to faint, I would have. Wild applause filled the room until there was nothing but a roaring in my brain. I whipped around to stare at Dawna, and her sneaky smile told me exactly where our tickets came from. Creede stepped onto the stage and smiled and waved before hugging each sister. He was dressed in a traditional tux with a golden cummerbund that matched the decorations.

Not to mention the flame in his eyes. Wow.

Pam handed him her mic and he stepped over to the table. At his signal, Pam and Sam lifted the gold cloth and tossed it into the air. With a wave of Creede's hand that would do any stage magician proud, the cloth disappeared.

Another round of applause came from the crowd, me included.

I found myself smiling. When Creede turned to the room, his eyes found mine. For a moment he seemed confused and his jaw dropped. He recovered in seconds, smiled again, and began his speech. "Thank you all for joining us here. It's been really interesting, working with the Darby sisters in this venture. As many of you know, mages need to use their energy. We have to expend it somewhere. The more powerful the mage, the more there is to release." I knew that from being around Bruno. My knives were part of that release. "Like many other practitioners, in the past I've concentrated on creating weapons for my business and the charm disk trade." He spread his arms out with an expression of almost bliss. "But here at the vineyards, I've had the opportunity to give back to the very nature that provides my magic. It's infused in the land, in the vines, and in the grapes. A little part of the magic that makes the world work is everywhere you walk. Please come forward and help yourself." Another wave of his hand revealed long tables on each side of the room. I'd been wondering why everybody was squished together when the room seemed so much bigger. "We hope you enjoy the wine as much as the people who tasted it before you did." He winked at the crowd and said, as an aside, whispering, with his lips right next to the microphone, "You know, the ones who gave us the gold medals in Europe."

The tittering I heard around me said he had succeeded in ramping up the tension just a notch more. He'd never mentioned a word about this to me in all the time we'd spent together. It interested me that he would do something like wine making. I liked learning about unexpected talents in people I knew.

I tried to move forward toward the stage, but everybody else was heading for the tables and I wound up being forced in that direction. While I could have pulled on my supernatural strength and shoved my way through the crowd, it wasn't really worth it. He'd still be there in ten minutes. So I let myself be propelled to a glass of Chablis. Dawna wound up at the other side of the room, where the goblets held Burgundy.

Two years of waiting, of reading bits of news and searching online for more information, were about to pay off. I raised the glass and inhaled deeply with both nose and mouth. The taste hit my tongue first—vanilla, chocolate, and just a hint of strawberries. But my nose picked up roses and oranges. How weird.

The glass tipped nearly of its own accord and smooth, cool liquid filled my mouth. The taste burst across my tongue—everything I'd smelled and tasted as well as some cantaloupe and fresh green grapes.

Then I heard the woman next to me, holding a glass of the

very same wine, say, "Cherries with a woody overtone. It's heavier than I expected, with more tannin, which is perfect. I normally don't like white wines."

I stared at my glass with furrowed brow. Were we drinking the same wine? I tapped her on the shoulder and she turned. She didn't stare at my fangs, so I was being successful in hiding them. "I'm sorry to listen in, but I'm tasting chocolate and strawberries in mine." I held up my glass. "Could we switch? I'm wondering if we have different varieties."

Her elegantly painted brows rose slightly. "Interesting. I like strawberries. All right." We traded glasses and I took a sip from the side of hers without the lipstick print. Her brow furrowed and so did mine. "It still tastes like cherries and wood."

"No, like strawberries and chocolate."

Other people started doing the same thing, switching glasses, and pretty soon all of us were looking confused.

Then we heard Creede's voice over the growing noise of talking and everyone turned toward those glowing gold eyes. "And now you know what's special about Witches' Brew. It's like no other wine because it's tailored to the individual drinker. Every person will taste what he or she likes best. You can never serve a bad wine at a party again. The Pinot Noir will be perfect with shrimp or steak. The Chablis? Equally terrific with halibut or hamburgers. Always right . . . just like magic."

He snapped his fingers and he and the sisters disappeared. People wanted to applaud, which is hard to do while holding wine goblets, but they managed, tapping fingernails on the glass.

The sisters made a grand entrance through the far doors,

which burst open in a shower of glitter and fairy lights. They smiled and separated, moving into the room to do the meet and greet. But as much as I wanted to talk about the craft of making the wine, I wanted to do it with Creede. How had he managed the magic? I wasn't a witch, but I loved talking about crafting. Bruno had gotten me hooked on the technique of spellcasting.

And . . . yeah, I wanted to thank him for the tickets.

But I didn't see him. I looked around, through the sea of talking heads, and didn't see his familiar golden curls. I finally got up on the stage and looked out over the crowd. But the event had spread out into multiple rooms and it could be that I was just missing him. I did see Emma and Remir, clinking glasses of blush, while Dawna was snuggling up to Latino soap star Fernando Gomez.

"Miss? Can I help you with something?"

I looked down to see a young man with an earphone and clipboard. I realized that I must look like an idiot up on the stage. "Sorry. I was looking for John Creede. He's a . . ." A what, exactly? Associate? Friend? Colleague? Sort of all of the above and yet none of them. What the heck, I could embellish. "A friend. Have you seen him?"

He shook his dark hair with amusement. "Honey, *everybody* is Mr. Creede's friend tonight. Everybody wants a piece of him. But I know all of his friends and I don't know you."

Oh. Talk about putting me in my place. "I'm Celia Graves."

His eyes widened and his mouth actually dropped as he took in the dress and hair and, yes, he really did look for fangs. "Ohmigod! *You're* Celia? Wow. He didn't describe you quite like . . . um, well, let's say I had a little more down-to-earth girl in my head, not a model."

When I got back to the spa tonight, I was going to find my stylist and makeup person and hand each one a hundred-dollar tip. Because the look on this guy's face was worth the price.

I felt special for the first time in weeks. "So, have you seen him?"

His eyebrows dropped and he thought. "You know, I haven't seen him since the Darby sisters came back in. He *should* be around somewhere." I started to walk down the stairs and he immediately jumped to my side and offered a hand. I took it because there wasn't a banister and the risers weren't very stable with three-inch heels. Once I had my feet back on the thick Oriental rug, he tapped the receiver in his ear. "John? Can you hear me?"

I waited while he listened, then shrugged and shook his head. "Sorry. He's not answering." He held out his hand. "I'm Andrew, by the way . . . John's personal assistant. I've been with Miller and Creede since I was in college. He's an amazing practitioner. I'm learning so much about the trade."

I shook the hand. He had a good grip. Not too tight and there was a tingle of power there. But I could tell he'd never be at Creede's or Bruno's level. Maybe he was a level four. "Nice to meet you. I guess I'll just wander around and hope I run into him."

Andrew let out a frustrated noise. "I know he's going to want to see you." Then he snapped his fingers before giving his own forehead a little slap. "I bet I know where he is. He's probably taken some people down to see the grotto."

"The grotto? What's that?"

He flipped open the cover of his clipboard, pulled a pen from behind the ear without the phone, and started drawing. "Oh, you've got to see it. That's where all the magic happens. It's amazingly beautiful. Here. Just follow this map and you can't miss it."

The paper he tore off showed an *x* in a circle that I presumed represented where we were now. It wasn't much of a map—just a curvy line that ended shortly with another *x*. "Is it far?" I looked down at my slinky, strappy sandals. "These boots weren't made for walking, Andrew."

He put a hand on my shoulder. I raised my brows and lowered my chin. I don't like it when people touch me. He pulled away instantly. "Sorry. Too much, huh? John tells me all the time I need to learn *distance* to work in this business. I've got to work on not touching. But no, in answer to your question, it's not far. Probably not more than a hundred yards from where we are. Just follow the path to the right and it's all downhill on a paved path. You'll get to see some of the new vines, too. Very picturesque with all the paper lanterns."

Well, it was gorgeous weather and my friends were otherwise occupied. What the heck. "Okay, thanks." I took the paper and walked across the room to tap Dawna on the shoulder. "Be right back." She nodded and returned to talking to her new favorite leading man.

Andrew had been right. It wasn't a long walk and the path only went one place. The Japanese lanterns that had been strung along the pathways offset the twisted vines on waist-high poles and made them seem elegant. But when the string of lanterns ended, so did the paved path—as though people were supposed to stop when they reached the end of the lights. But there was a flickering light ahead in what looked like the mouth of a cave.

Oh. Duh. A *grotto*—as in cave.

There was enough light to see and the ground was hard-packed soil, so it was easy walking. As I approached, I could hear murmuring voices inside, so I stayed quiet, not wanting to interrupt. I expected the cave itself to be cooler than the outside, but it was actually warmer. The press of light magic flowed over me as I walked down the steep path into the earth. The barrier explained the dampening of sound. Now that I was inside, the voice was louder, but I couldn't make out what was being said.

Flowering vines covered the walls and ceilings, turning what would normally have been dark stone and soil into a burst of color and texture. The smell was amazing . . . soft and sweet but not cloying. Even though I didn't recognize any of the individual flowers, together they smelled like a butterfly garden in the warmest part of spring. "Hello?" I called out softly. There was no answer.

Finally I saw a brighter light ahead and heard a roaring sound that reminded me of a bath being run in a distant room. The air felt moister, cooler, and heavier with magic. The combination of sensation and scent was amazing. I stepped into the main grotto. The ceiling was high enough I couldn't actually see it, and the waterfall I'd heard was the height of a three-story building. I was so engrossed in looking around that I didn't notice the circle drawn in white in the very center of the room, where a hooded figure was kneeling.

Crap. I'd walked into a casting.

The candles on the points of the compass were the give-away and I should have recognized the muttering after hearing Bruno speaking in odd tongues all those years. I froze in place, remembering Bruno's stern lectures: *Never interrupt the caster, don't speak, don't break the circle, and don't freak out at anything you see.* He hadn't been kidding about the last part. I'd seen full-blown tornadoes spring up in a casting circle. Demons had appeared in chains, pulled out from inside the person they were possessing, spewing all the vile excrement and lava of hell itself until they were banished by the mage.

I looked around and spotted a bench carved out of the rock wall next to a massive taproot from one of the ancient white oaks I'd seen from the road when we arrived. I could be quiet and I was really curious to find out if I was going to see a sample of Creede's skill. I'd seen his power in battle and a hint of the finesse behind it. But to see a real casting was to see into the soul of a mage.

This seriously rocked.

I became a church mouse with a hungry cat nearby—utterly silent and watchful. Creede's hands began to move; it looked like he was holding an invisible volleyball in front of his chest. I could see his face peering out from the shadow of the hood. The spell got stronger and his voice louder. A ball of energy appeared between his cupped hands. It had no form or color, visible only as wavy air currents, like heat rising from hot asphalt.

He lifted his arms and the tiny candles became flares to reach his shoulders. Wow. "Removie il parse . . . et parse . . . en natur!" The ball of energy took on a life of its own. Power flowed out from Creede's skin to spin over his head until the ball of energy was bigger than a school globe and then bigger than a car.

Every muscle in my body jumped when he threw his hands forward. "Dispersei!" The energy exploded outward at his command, filling the whole circle until it seemed like it would burst. The candles tipped sideways, flames licking up the sides of the energy bubble until it was a full fledged ball of fire. I was a little afraid it was going to explode and stood up in case I needed to get out in a hurry.

That's when the ball blew.

Creede's hood was blown back by the force of the energy wave and his eyes were twin stars that were too large for his face. Concentric waves of energy began to flow out of the circle, ripples of magic that swept toward me with the speed and intensity of a tsunami.

I wasn't going to be able to get out of the way in time.

15

To hell with not interrupting the caster.

"Shit! Creeeede—" I backed toward the exit and then ran full out as the blast of power came my way.

He looked up then and saw me and raised his hands again. "Dispersei!" There was both panic and power in the word and I turned to see the white light in his eyes explode into the room. But it had gone too far, too fast.

Power caught me full in the chest and dropped me to my knees. It was icy cold yet hot enough to burn. Every muscle in my body came alive at the same moment and my eyes locked on his. There was a tether between us, a magic binding that encased me as solidly as if I were trapped in amber. I could see the room and Creede, but it was through a filter of golden light. Every hair stood on end and tried to pull out of my skin.

Then the cold and hot turned to a warm wave of . . . something . . . that made things low in my body tug deliciously. My skin started to feel swollen and my breathing became fast and shallow. It was the most erotic sensation I'd ever experienced and apparently it was for Creede, too, because he let out a moan of sheer pleasure and closed his eyes. I felt the power pull away from me and I could breathe. Then it was back and pleasure tore through me once more. We were trapped in a loop that was like a bouncing Super Ball. The harder the power hit me, the faster it came back after leaving, until there was nothing but heat and light and a thousand fingers on my skin, on my breasts, and inside me. It was pure torture and pure joy.

Finally the strain was too much and my body could take no more. I collapsed onto my hip and a cry was torn from my mouth as a powerful orgasm claimed me. It had admittedly been a long time since I'd been with a man, but this wasn't like anything I'd ever felt before. I tingled to the tips of my ears and the balls of my feet. I knew when it got the better of Creede. He didn't cry out, but I'd heard that kind of low moan before, followed by whispered swearing that spoke of a similar intensity to my own.

The magic dissipated slowly, leaving my body feeling both satisfied and utterly exhausted. It took more than a few moments before I could think or breathe normally, and when I opened my eyes I saw a pair of bare feet next to my leg.

Crap.

"Celia?" I looked up and Creede's eyes were normal again, even if his face was lightly flushed. "Are you okay?"

"I think so." I felt heat in my cheeks and turned my eyes from his. I did accept the hand up, because it's really hard to get up gracefully from the floor in a short skirt and heels. "What just happened?"

There was a trace of humor in his voice. "You need to learn how to knock."

Now my eyes rose to his face and the small hint of a smile that turned his mouth. "There's no door."

He acknowledged the truth of that with a soft, "Ah."

My hand was still holding his and I tried to pull away, but he wouldn't let go. He used his other hand to lift my chin. I was still struggling not to blush and kept my vision locked on the long line of bare chest that disappeared into the soft white magician's robe. It was impossible to ignore the musky scents that filled the air. "Creede—"

I knew I'd screwed up whatever spell he was casting and had no idea what the result would be. And what had just happened was too . . . personal, too intimate. And frankly, it had felt too good.

His finger pressed to my lips. "Don't overthink it, Celia. Just let it be." His voice was almost too soft to hear over the waterfall. I finally looked in his eyes. It was a mistake. He pulled me closer and I let him. When his mouth closed over mine I melted into his embrace and my arms slid around him of their own accord.

A first kiss is supposed to be soft, tentative—the barest taste of things that might later happen. But this was the sort of kiss that happens after lovemaking, a gentle joining while your body is still flush with pleasure. His tongue entered my mouth and his hands pulled me against him. I allowed the knowledgeable, languid caresses that didn't so much explore as acknowledge possession. My body wanted things my mind couldn't fully grasp and I found my hands were doing the same things as his, storing up in muscle memory the lay of his body and what touches brought an appreciative noise from his throat. He expertly navigated the twin fangs but explored them as well while his jaw worked slowly against mine.

It felt amazingly good and I relaxed against him fully, my muscles suddenly jelly and my brain fuzzy.

This was wrong. On so many levels. But I couldn't stop.

Creede pulled back from the kiss, then softly pressed his lips against my forehead. He ran his fingers through my hair and rested his cheek next to mine. "You terrify me, Celia Graves."

I let out a shaky laugh and moved my hands so they weren't resting right on his muscled backside. I wanted to bury myself in the warm power that pulsed from his skin and that terrified me. "Likewise."

He released me then, turning so quickly I nearly stumbled. "There's a bathroom down the hall on the left. I'll put my tools away if you want first shot at it."

A bathroom? In a cave? But I was more than happy to escape the room for a few moments. I closed the bathroom door behind me and turned on the light. It was a perfectly normal bathroom, including a bathtub with shower. I supposed if magic made the cave, why not make a bathroom? Heck, maybe there was a kitchen, too.

The mirror over the sink revealed the truth. I looked great. Damn it. There's no way to hide the flush of really good sex. Only time would do that, and friends like Dawna and Emma would spot it on me a week from now.

I cleaned up as best as possible, and when I turned to find a towel I almost ran into the tux Creede had been wearing at the event. That meant that he was *naked* under that robe. Well, hell. Yeah, I knew mages did that—the whole "get closer to nature" thing—and I'd seen the bare feet. I felt myself blushing again. Well, maybe he'd been wearing underwear. I could hope.

A light tap on the door made me let out a startled yip. "You about done in there? I need to get dressed."

"Sorry. Yeah. All yours." I unlocked and opened the door, keeping my eyes firmly on the floor as I tried to slide past him.

He let out a frustrated sigh and raised an arm to stop my progress. "Celia, would you please look at me?"

I'd faced vampires, assassins, and even demons with a steady eye. Now I was terrified to look a handsome mage in the face just because I liked him a little too much? I forced my shoulders to relax and raised my face to his.

There was a look in his eyes that told me that our relationship had shifted permanently, no matter how much I wanted to go back. The realization appeared on his face, too. We were suddenly *aware* of each other. I could sense his arm right next to my waist and didn't want to shove it away. If anything, I wanted it to curl around me. It was both a new kind of tension that wasn't there the last time I saw him and yet no tension at all. It felt natural, normal. When he spoke, it was with mingled confidence and worry: "It doesn't have to go further, you know. We can go back to the way it was."

A small laugh escaped me. "Please. You know better than that, Creede. There'll always be the wondering, the wanting to know whether this was the best or just a sample of something bigger."

He smiled and it wasn't forced. It was the smile I saw the first time I met him and it made him real, approachable, and frankly . . . datable. That wasn't a good thing, given the roses waiting for me at Gran's. "I don't know if I could handle anything bigger. You have no idea what that felt like."

Oh, but I did. I gave him a quick peck on the cheek and simultaneously pushed his hand away from the doorjamb. "Get dressed. I'll meet you back at the party."

"I'd rather you wait. Spend a few minutes looking at the grotto. I turned on the lights. It's some of my best work and you might never make it back here. I'll be quick. I promise."

My head nodded agreement even as I opened my mouth to gently refuse. It was at least a dozen steps before my legs were steady. As I walked back into the main chamber they went wobbly again, for a different reason. It was . . . amazing. The "lights" were a miniature sun, high overhead. Thankfully it was just light and didn't burn my skin.

He'd made paradise—a tropical rain forest in the middle of wine country. Birds chirped and called to each other from the branches of trees that were once merely underground roots. It smelled of fresh growth, of eucalyptus and flowers. "You like?" Creede's voice came from right behind me, meaning he'd snuck up on me while I'd been gawking. He was in the tux again and smelled of nothing but good cologne. If a tour really did walk in the door just then, they probably wouldn't notice anything unusual.

I smiled and nodded as I watched sparrows flitting around above me. "It's gorgeous. Was there even a cave here when you started?"

"It was a spring originally. This area had never been planted before, which is why one of the bigger vineyards hadn't bought the land. I knew if the girls' idea was going to work that I needed to be underground to push the magic *up* into the soil. Now the former spring is a waterfall and part of the water is piped up from the basin to storage tanks to water the vines while the rest keeps the grotto alive." The proud tone of his voice was justified.

"You did good. Really. I've never seen anything like it."

He smiled widely. "We should probably get back. My assistant is going to get grumpy if I'm gone much longer."

We turned and started to walk out, our heels making muted ticking noises that were tiny in comparison to the other sounds. "Andrew? He sent me down here. He *said* you were giving a tour."

Creede let out a sound that was close to a growl, but with amusement underlying it. "I don't know whether to give him a pink slip . . . or a raise. He knew damned well I don't give tours of the grotto. And he knew what I was down here doing."

"And that was? What kind of spell did I totally destroy?"

"It wasn't a spell. It was a purification ritual." He must have seen my furrowed brow, because he elaborated while we walked down the dim tunnel to the outside: "Despite what it may look like, I don't do well at public gatherings. There was a reason why George Miller was the front man of the company. I have horrible stage fright."

That surprised me. "You looked totally natural up there. Confident, charming. Really."

He put a hand low on my back to help me get my footing on the steep path up out of the cave. It tingled nicely and I had to struggle a little to keep my mind on the conversation. "Thanks, but it's all an act. That's what a purification ritual does. I did one right before I went onstage. It takes all the negative emotions—like fear, frustration, and aggression—and casts them off so I can function and appear calm. I've been dispersing those feelings into the soil for months now so the staff doesn't realize what a wreck I've been with George gone. The plants don't care whether energy is negative or positive, like a body doesn't care whether a sugar is honey or processed white granules or even fruits and vegetables. It's all broken down the same."

"And you had to do another one right after you spoke? Wow, you really *do* have stage fright."

Now he chuckled and there was a low, nervous, but satisfied edge to it that made me shiver. "Actually, this particular ritual was for a different kind of emotion. I saw you in that dress and suddenly couldn't concentrate for shit. Have I mentioned you look absolutely amazing?"

Um . . . oh. I was glad for the dark that enveloped us. It hid my blush.

"My speech was supposed to go on for another five minutes. Fortunately, I'd warned Pam and Sam that I might have to cut it short if my nerves got to me. They made it look natural."

"So you were getting rid of . . ." I couldn't finish.

He did it for me. "Lust. Yep. And when the object of a particular emotion steps inside the circle . . . well, you got to see the result. Good thing it wasn't anger. We might have leveled the place."

"But I *didn't* step inside the circle. I was really careful of that."

We were back at the main building and he held open the door for me. "The *grotto* is the circle. The smaller one is just the bull's-eye, because I don't feel like walking all the way around the whole chamber to light candles every time."

Oops. "Sorry."

The light caught his face and I could see that he was grinning. There was a teasing lilt in his voice. "Don't be. This way had a much more . . . satisfying effect."

I hit him in the bicep lightly because I couldn't think of anything else to do. We entered the house, expecting to find the party still going strong. We'd only been gone about fifteen minutes. But there was utter silence in the main entry, and the sound of sirens and shouting came from the next room. Adrenaline took over and we hurried to the tasting room.

People were crowded around a flat-screen television, staring at a news report. The camera moved from a broad scene of an explosion of some kind to the reporter on the scene. "The devastation is horrendous, Chet. The perimeter wall is gone, as are two of the inner walls. There are already five confirmed dead among the joint police and federal task force, but authorities believe that the number will go much higher once they get inside."

The words "joint police and federal task force" made my stomach lurch and I dug my fingers into Creede's arm as icy threads of panic raced up my spine. The news team cycled around to the top of the story. The camera switched to a serious woman in a yellow suit jacket. "For those just joining us, there's been a series of explosions at the State Paranormal Treatment Facility outside of Santa Maria de Luna. There are reports of escaped shape-shifters and vampires. Residents are being advised to lock their doors and move to non-windowed

rooms, and the governor has activated all EMTs, mages level
seven and above, and A and C card holders. Available warrior
priests are urged to check with their seminaries for instructions and all vacations or other non-medical leaves have been
canceled for National Guard and police agencies. News Twelve
has exclusive footage of the explosions due to an embedded
reporter who was accompanying the local police to the scene.
Bob, we're back to you. What can you tell us?"

Creede started to pull away from my grip. "I've got to go.
Stay here and be careful." He gave me a quick kiss on the
mouth and I saw Dawna's eyebrows rise with interest before
she looked back at the TV screen.

I followed Creede out of the room and grabbed his arm to
stop him. "Where do you have to go? What's wrong?"

"I've got an A and C card. I could lose my license to practice magic if I don't get my ass out there."

I didn't even know what an A&C card was. He must have
seen it in my face. "Mages level six and higher who want to
profit from their magic have to register with the state. Like
paramedics, if there's an emergency, we are required to 'assist
and control.' A and C. I'm an eight, nearly a nine. So I've got
to go."

"I'm going with you."

He sighed and dropped his head. "No, you're not. You don't
have a card and you have fangs. That's not a common attribute
of the good guys. There will be way too many trigger-happy
cops out there."

Every single thing he said made perfect sense. "I'm still going. Whether with you or behind you. Besides, do you *really*

want to take your Ferrari to the scene of a battle? We could take the rental. I bought the extra insurance on it."

He crooked his finger and turned. "Walk with me."

I fell in step beside him and we went out into the cool, still night. It was so lovely here and I hated that it was ending this way. But the adrenaline rush told me that I was looking forward to it, too. I'm just weird. "You know I'm right."

"No," he said with a sad sort of laugh. "I know you're too stubborn to play it safe. We can't take your rental because my car has special plates. I can speed and get an escort with the activation in effect. But you're right that I don't want to leave my car there for it to get destroyed. So, you'll come with me and then drive it back here. I can hitch a ride back with the police when the crisis is over."

If he knew how likely it was that I wasn't going to go through with that plan, he had the sense not to say it out loud. "Let me grab my stuff on the way. These shoes are killing me."

Creede's low-slung red chariot was in a cluttered garage next to the main building. I waited until he backed out before I got in. It might have been an emergency, but I could still appreciate the luxury and power of the car. He raced the engine and checked the fuel level, tapping his fingers on the steering wheel. "Remind me when we get closer to check the gauge. I might have to stop and fill up." I nodded as he put the Ferrari in gear.

Before he could step on the gas, the door of the winery opened and Dawna and Emma came racing out. "Where are you guys going?" Dawna sounded panicked, probably because she had already guessed where we were going.

I rolled down the window and shrugged. "Where else? Into the maw of disaster like normal."

Emma clutched my arm. "You *can't*, Celia. You didn't wait long enough to hear the whole story. It's not just a crime scene. The explosion opened a rift between the dimensions. Lesser demons are coming out of the rift."

Creede's jaw set and his eyes narrowed. "Then I'd better get moving. Get out, Celia. To hell with the car."

I turned my head and put a hand on his already tense and twitching arm. "John. With my knives and my strength, I'm more than a match for lesser demons now." He looked at me for a long moment and I could hear his teeth grinding. I felt the moment he accepted my statement as truth when his arm relaxed just a bit. I gently removed Emma's hand from my dress and handed her the spare key to the rental. I don't know why there were two on the ring, but I'd checked and, sure enough, they both opened the door and started the engine. "You should be safe at the spa. Call Warren and make sure Kevin's and Amy's cells have extra security. If either can still be called by the demon, they'll be in danger."

Dawna gently pulled Emma back. Her eyes were frightened, but she nodded firmly. "Go. Do what you have to and try to make it back safe."

I noticed the word "try" in there. It was all any of us could do. Emma's face was stricken as Creede and I roared off into the darkness, but I couldn't fix that. I could only hope that since she hadn't been *called* yet, the demons couldn't reach her. Yet. Everything depended on keeping the demons at the prison site and closing the rift.

We got to my rental, in the parking lot outside the main gate, in record time and I opened the trunk, where my weapons and clothes were. I tried to figure out how to change out of the dress with some discretion and then realized it didn't really matter. Creede had seen me nearly naked on the deck of a boat the last time we fought a lesser demon. I turned my back as I pulled the dress off over my head, but I knew his eyes were on me. I could see his face in the rearview mirror. There was more worry in his expression than lust. That was both a good and bad thing. It meant that my fear wasn't misplaced. Things had changed. Something bigger than simple attraction had grown between us, and I didn't know what to do about it.

When I turned back around, fully armed and wearing jeans, a black sweater, and socks and sneakers, he was on his knees on his seat, digging for something in the back compartment. As I slid into the passenger seat, he settled back in the driver's seat and tossed a small, gift-wrapped box into my lap. "Merry Christmas."

He'd bought me a Christmas gift? *Before* what had just happened? Crap. If we survived what we were about to do, I would have shopping to do.

"Thanks. I'll put it under my tree when we're done."

He shook his head and slammed the car into first gear; the tires spun briefly on the gravel before they caught the road and the Ferrari leapt forward. "Open it now. You might need them."

Them? Okay, that got my curiosity up. I had the package open before he reached fourth gear. Inside the small box were five ceramic disks on a bed of gauze. The letters *TBB* were stamped in tiny letters around the rim. Ooh, weapons. A man after my heart. "What are they?"

"You wanted a total body-binding spell, you got one. It was a hell of a complicated spell, so don't waste them. These aren't simple immobilization charms. I *mean* total body binding. A person could die of thirst if the spell isn't released in a day or two."

"Are there release disks somewhere?"

He pursed his lips and shook his head, which made me wince. "Nope, so be careful with these. I haven't had time to do a matching deactivation charm."

Well. That complicated things a little. "Thanks, John. Really." He let out that little tough-guy growl that said I wasn't supposed to thank him. "What's your favorite color?"

His brow furrowed as we zoomed onto the interstate. "Green. Why?"

"No reason."

But he knew. After all, he's a telepath, and while he didn't say anything, I saw the flash of his teeth by the light of the instrument panel.

"Shame we don't have the fly to give us some idea of what's happening inside the facility."

He twitched his thumb toward the rear seat. "It's back there. But I haven't had time to correct the problems you reported yet."

I unhooked my seat belt at just the wrong time—as he cranked the wheel hard to go around a slow-moving car—and I nearly fell into his lap. I threw up a hand to stabilize on the door and wound up doing a face plant on his chest. He brushed my hair out of his eyes without a word. If it weren't for the crisis, I'd swear he swerved intentionally.

It took a little digging among the accumulated junk in the backseat, including a number of candy bar wrappers, to find the familiar box with the fly. It was sort of nice that he wasn't a health fanatic. It's hard to go out to dinner with someone who's always criticizing the menu. And that might solve the gift issue. "Got it."

"Not a box of chocolates. Please. It would feel weird."

I raised my brows as I latched my seat belt again. "You know, it's considered rude to intrude in a person's thoughts."

He tipped his head to the side and shrugged one shoulder. "It's not like turning off the radio, you know. I have to concentrate *not* to hear. When I'm stressed, it's harder to shut off."

It was hard to argue with that. I remembered Ivy having more problems with ghosts and zombies when she was angry or afraid. "Then could you at least not comment on what you hear?"

"I'll try. Sometimes it just slips out."

That was likely the best I'd get. "By the way, what did the *report* say didn't work on the fly?"

He flicked his eyes my way and they were narrowed in suspicion. "You say that like you didn't write it."

I shook my head as I opened the box. Everything looked the same, but all of a sudden I didn't really trust myself to use it. "I didn't. Have you ever heard of the Company? They track down supernatural hard targets."

"Tough to be in this business for very long without hearing about them. Are you saying they got hold of my fly?" He didn't sound happy about that. "Shit. Well, there goes that patent."

242 I CAT ADAMS

Ouch. I hadn't even thought about that. "Sorry about that. There was a Company man on the job I was doing. Calls himself John Jones."

The harsh breath that came from Creede told me he knew Jones all too well. "Oh yeah. I know Jones. What sword did he hang over your head to get you to help? There's always at least one and usually two. I've been there."

"My friend Kevin Landingham was in danger. But I have to give Jones credit. He got us out of there pretty much intact. And, he did get someone to get the bullet out of my shoulder." I automatically touched the spot. It was still amazing to me it wasn't hurting.

Instead of growling as I expected, Creede reached across and squeezed my hand. There was real concern in his voice. "Try not to get shot tonight. Okay? Your luck is incredible, but it won't hold out forever."

He didn't have to tell me twice. I knew someday the other boot was going to drop, but the best I could do was not think about it. "So tell me about the report you got."

I've never actually tailgated a cop car with flashing lights in a speeding Ferrari and had the cop give way. About the only time that happens is in video games. But the bright orange glow on the horizon that had been making my stomach do flip-flops for miles was finally upon us. A trip that normally takes seven-plus hours on the interstate that most locals call the 5 only took four and a quarter. Wow. It was amazing just being in that car. According to Creede, his license plate was magically flashing with a green light that was tied to the A&C designation. The odd color behind drivers apparently makes them change lanes quickly. Nobody knows why.

As he pulled up next to a Highway Patrolman who was guiding traffic to the site, Creede glanced over at me. "You're not going to be sensible about this, are you?"

I was already unhooking my seat belt. "Pfft. What do you think?"

He rolled down the window and flashed his glowing green card when the cop turned the flashlight in our direction. "Who's the mage in charge?" Creede said, sounding like he'd asked that question before. I just kept my mouth shut.

"Special Agent Thomas Branch, sir. Take the main staked path and turn left." He motioned at me with the light and I stretched my upper lip down over my fang tips. "Where's your card?"

Creede started to speak: "She's with m—"

"Detective Heather Alexander asked me to report in." I flashed my state license after carefully putting a finger over the word "bodyguard." It was nearly an identical card to the ones the freelance consultants to the police used. I'd done that trick a few times, and if the patrolman had never been punked by it before this would be a valuable lesson. "Where is she?"

Creede didn't say a word, but there was humor on his face as he struggled not to smile.

"Down the main aisle and take the second right, ma'am." The officer moved the light away and I put the license back in my front pocket. I'd have to do that trick more than once before I reached Alex—if I could find her at all. I really did want to talk to her and find out what in the hell had gone wrong.

Because it was hell on earth. When we got out of the car, the true extent of the situation became dreadfully clear. The fervent chanting of priests in Latin couldn't quite block out the growls and unearthly screams that made my skin want to crawl off my bones. The ground was rumbling with an eerie intensity like the beginning of an earthquake but worse. I felt my muscles seize, and though I struggled to move, I couldn't. Creede took my arm and pulled me forward a few feet and I suddenly felt better. "Outer barrier to keep the curious away. You going to be okay? Sure you don't want to take the car back? I won't think any less of you."

I opened my mouth to reply when I heard a voice to my left: "Celia? What in the name of everything holy are you doing here?"

Creede and I both turned to see Father Matteo DeLuca, Bruno's younger brother, storming our way. "Good to see you, Father," Creede said with an outstretched hand.

Matty shook it absently, because his whole focus was on me. "It took me five *hours* to remove the taint of demon from your soul, Celia Graves. And this is how you repay me? By throwing yourself right back into the path of evil?"

If he thought guilt was going to work on me . . . well, he'd known me long enough to know better. "If I remember right, it took four hours to clean *your* soul after a certain vampire bite, Father. And yet here you are."

Creede was struggling not to smile. "As much as I'd love to see who wins this tug-of-war, I'd better report in."

He hadn't walked two feet before he nearly ran straight into Bruno. Oh no. I could fight vampires, I could battle demons, but I didn't want to face both Creede and Bruno in front of a priest.

My former fiancé's face lit up when he saw me and he broke into a run. He nearly tackled me and swept me into his arms. The scent of him, the power that flowed over my skin, felt good and right. He was as handsome as ever, and having him near me made my heart beat an extra thump. "Thank heavens you're safe, Celie! I've been worried sick. You didn't call and the house was empty."

He'd gone to my house? While I'd been off at the spa and . . . the winery? I couldn't help but flick my eyes over his shoulder to where a somber and serious John Creede was standing with arms crossed over his broad chest. He was watching every move I made. Was I going to have to decide between them right here and now?

No. First things first. "The flowers were gorgeous, Bruno. Really. They arrived just before I went out of town."

"Out of town? Working?" He was fishing, but I had no duty to check in with him and would not be bullied or guilted into being embarrassed.

"No, actually, I was at a spa in Napa Valley with Dawna and Emma. It was an early Christmas gift."

A tremendous howl of inhuman rage and pain filled the air. Bruno abruptly released me and I dropped nearly a foot to the ground. Matty turned and we all watched a flare of fire

246 I CAT ADAMS

shoot up nearly a hundred feet. Heat hit us in a wave, so strong that I was surprised my hair didn't catch on fire. I pushed Bruno away. "Do your job and I'll do mine. We'll deal with things later."

He nodded once sharply and gave me a fierce press of lips against mine that sent tingles all the way down my spine. He put a hand on my arm and we started down the path.

John gave way, but only slightly. I was both shocked and terrified when his arm went around my waist, pulling me away from Bruno. John's passionate magic-laden kiss added shivers to the tingles. He pressed his car keys into my hand. "Be careful. Get out if you need to." He didn't look at either Bruno or Matty, just stalked away with intense determination and quickly blended into the crowd of magicians and witches.

Matty's brows rose. Bruno was literally speechless, his face completely blank, and I took full advantage of his shock by running away, racing down the pathway past him toward the second right turn, where Alex would be. I needed an armed policeman close by right about now. I tucked the car keys into my back pocket as I went.

In a sea of black jackets lit with red flashing lights and the fires of hell, it wasn't too difficult to find one small blonde woman in the uniform of our local finest. "Alex!" I shouted, but she didn't hear me above the noise of chaos. I pushed my way past both uniformed officers and detectives I'd seen on the street and caught up with her before she disappeared underneath a line of yellow tape. The heat underfoot felt like it was going to melt my shoes any minute. I pulled on her sleeve and she turned.

"Jesus, Graves. It's about damned time you got here." Oh good. I had been hoping her response wasn't going to be, *Someone get her out of here.*

Alex is surprisingly strong for her size. She grabbed me by the arm and pulled me away. It was only when we were safely in a car with the doors locked and windows up that she spoke again, her forehead resting against the steering wheel: "I had no idea how bad this was going to go. They must have known we were coming and waited until we had all of our people positioned around the wall. Then they blew the place using car bombs on the other side of the wall. The press thinks we lost five people. It's probably closer to fifty. Then the rift opened and . . . heaven help us, Celia. I don't know how we're going to close this thing up."

"What have you tried so far?" It's not like I had any better answers than the experts they'd probably already consulted, but it couldn't hurt to try.

She lifted her head and shook it wearily. "We've got a ring of warrior priests around the facility, coordinating exorcism rituals. Mages are at work to create a spell that can be simultaneously cast to put a wall around the breech. That will at least keep the demons inside. A few imps have already wormed their way through gaps in the temporary barrier, but sharpshooters armed with silvered holy-water bullets are keeping anything from getting past the second perimeter. If they don't die of heat prostration first, that is."

Wow. I couldn't think of anything really useful to add. There were already more mages and witches here than I'd ever seen in one place. "What about escapees? Any idea how many got out?"

She grimaced. "A bunch. We don't really know how many yet. We might never know because of the blast and the lava. It'll be nine-eleven all over again, trying to identify fragments by DNA."

There was a tap on the driver's side window and Alex turned. A man I recognized, wearing an FBI jacket, was motioning for her to lower the window. She reached for the handle and started to crank it down. The problem was that I only knew one FBI guy—Rizzoli—and this wasn't him. It was one of the guards who had been inside the prison, and why he didn't recognize me I didn't know. Or maybe he did and was going to get to me through Alex. The police car must be magically spelled so that he couldn't get inside. But if she opened the window—

"Alex! Down!" I pulled her by the hair down to the bench seat just as the man reached into the car. I pulled one of my knives and lunged forward over Alex, effectively shielding her with my body. I thrust the knife into his stomach and he screamed. Heads turned at the sound and a dozen people headed our way. But it was too late. If he had been a normal human, he would have fallen to the ground with a horrible gut wound . . . which could have been treated by the EMTs. And I would have gone to jail.

But as it was, the lead policeman threw out his arms to stop those behind him when he saw flames lick out of the wound and eat the man alive, leaving only a few tatters of black nylon to float away on the breeze.

I crawled off Alex and she sat up, one hand to her nose. Blood was running between her fingers and she wiped it away with the back of her hand. She didn't look at me or thank me before she was out of the car. "Davis, go find one of the priests. I want everyone at this site to pass a holy-water test. Barnes, clean up this mess before it infects anyone. I want people in full magical armor from now on. We've got rogues among us. LaFuente, find the FBI SitCom and get him over here to see this before we bag it up." She turned to me and let out a sigh. "Graves, go . . . just go do whatever you're going to do. I don't even want to know how you did that."

"No creds," I said as I got out of the car and stopped, resting my hands on the roof. "I'll get hauled out of here by my teeth. I need to stick with you. At least you know me."

"I know you, too, and trouble isn't ever far away." I smiled at the familiar voice. Rizzoli was walking up behind the man Alex had called LaFuente. He stepped lightly over the pile of still-smoldering ash and handed me a piece of plastic over the hood. "Put this on and start ferreting out more of the bad guys. You've got talents we don't. Use them."

I looked at the tag he gave me. On one side it bore the seal of the FBI. On the other, underneath the plastic laminate, it said: *Celia Graves, Special Consultant.*

"How cool is this!?" I put the little clip on my shirt, unsure which side should show out. "Thanks, Rizzoli."

"No," he said very seriously. "Thank *you*. There's a boat

captain at Smallmouth Harbor who was very grateful we showed up last night."

My jaw dropped. I'd completely forgotten Maria's problem with the drug lord. "Did you get him?"

Rizzoli smiled and it had a satisfying dark edge. "Red-handed. He'll be behind bars for a very long time. The judge agreed he was a flight risk. No bail."

Awesome! "You rule, Rizzoli. So you got promoted to situation commander?"

Now his expression wasn't so pleased. The muscles in his cheeks and forehead tightened. "Field promotion . . . to replace the two guys above me who are in pieces. Now I'm the lucky guy in the line of fire."

Ouch. "Sorry. Anything I can do?"

"Yeah. There is." He stepped out of the way as a hazmat-suited team came up behind him with a body bag. "You have the strangest group of contacts I've ever seen. Call them. See them. Find out why this is happening. I don't want to know how to seal the rift. There are a thousand people behind me who can do that. I want to know why it's here—in this place, at this time. There's never been a problem before at this prison and the area got a seal of approval from the MPRC after a five-year white-paper study. I want to know that when we close the rift it won't show up somewhere else next week."

That was surprisingly forward thinking and I was flattered that he'd asked it of me. Of course, I might be one along with 999 *other* people whom he'd also asked. But it still felt nice. "You've got it. Do you want me to start right now? Because I'd have to leave." And I didn't know if I wanted to. There were people here I cared about. Alex and Rizzoli, Matty, Bruno, and, yes, John.

Wait. When had I started calling him *John*? I thought back and realized it was right after the grotto. No wonder he'd been smiling in the car. Shit. Still, there were demons afoot, plus vampires and werewolves who might well be lurking in the shadows, waiting to pick off stray cops who wandered off to take a leak.

Rizzoli nodded thoughtfully as the hazmat team used an ordinary-looking broom and dustpan to scoop up the bits of demon-infested guard and pour them carefully into a black zippered bag. "Stick around for a bit. Stay with the guys who are doing the holy-water tests. Anybody who doesn't pass goes to you."

"So you're sanctioning me to . . . kill people?"

"No," he said seriously. "I'm sanctioning you to keep the demons from getting out of this zone. If you know a better way to do that with every priest in Southern California already busy, I'm open to suggestions."

I touched my pocket and felt the press of hard ceramic. "Well, if there aren't more than five of them, I might have a solution." I walked around the car and whispered in Rizzoli's ear about the charm balls John had made. Damn it. *Creede. Creede had made.*

"I like it. Give them a try. We can put them in containment then and keep them from escaping until a priest is available."

All of a sudden a hum rose into the air. It was an airy, light sound, very much like the children's choir I'd heard on the call with Mr. Murphy. It caught everyone's attention and we all turned as one. A blue light rose into the sky like a beacon until it dwarfed the fountain of lava that was spewing from the earth. The air felt immediately cooler and I could finally take a deep breath that didn't scald my lungs. Everybody waited anxiously as the blue shield began to round over at the top. Some demons can fly, so it can't just go straight up. It has to close and lock.

"C'mon, guys," I willed the two mages I knew and the hundreds I didn't to give it everything they had. Slowly the shield began to close. A few imps threw themselves against the barrier nearby and bounced off before melting. Sweet. Someone must have added holy words to the spell to beef it up.

Sound faded and everybody took a collective breath. Lights flashed silently and the unearthly howls became quieter and farther away until, with a flash of light that was nearly blinding, the prison was contained inside the barrier.

A chorus of cheers rose into the air, but I heard two screams of pain. A female officer a few feet away started swearing and dropped to the ground to thrash. Everybody stepped back and a hundred guns were drawn from holsters. I didn't think twice. I grabbed one of the TBB charms and threw it hard. It hit her and exploded and she froze as solidly as if I'd thrown liquid nitrogen. Rizzoli held out his hand and I put two of the disks into it. He sprinted toward where the other screaming was coming from, and a moment later it stopped. I hadn't expected that the demons would start screaming when cut off from their own kind. Handy knowledge.

"Where'd you get those? How much are they?" The cop was young and eager and was staring at his paralyzed former colleague with unabashed admiration.

"Find a mage named John Creede. He's here, somewhere. He'll hook you up." I turned my head once he left and called, "Hey, Alex! C'mere."

She looked at me, put up a hand to stop the person who was speaking to her, and walked over. "What's up?"

"You might check with the priests to see if it's normal for a demon to scream and thrash when cut off from the rest of the pack. It might be an easy way to at least track down the escapees who were possessed."

She stuck out her bottom lip as she thought. "Might be a pain in the butt, but I can certainly call the nine-one-one dispatcher in the area to see if anyone's called in about someone with symptoms like that. And maybe the hospitals." She paused, then nodded. "Y'know, that might work." She turned abruptly, muttering to herself, and went back to her team and started to talk rapidly.

I grabbed two cops and had them carry the frozen, possessed cop while we looked for a priest. Matty was the first one I came across, and I explained the situation and how the officer came to be bound. He was impressed with the charm as well and grabbed his bag. "I don't know whether I can release the demon from a bound body. I've never tried. It would be safer if we could. Every seminary in the world would buy these things. But I'm afraid that the demon will be trapped and frozen just like the body."

"Will it hurt her to try it?" She looked like a nice person, and more than one of the cops had looked really stricken when they'd had to pull their weapon on her.

Matty pulled his cloth from inside the bag and put on a

larger silver cross. "Shouldn't. But we need to be prepared in case it does. Who did the casting on this? Bruno's tried for years but has never perfected one." He looked up at me and okay, I flinched first and turned my gaze to the ground. He let out a sigh. "Well, you'd better go get him. I might need him to take off the binding during the ritual and put up a fast circle." I started to walk away, then heard him clear his throat and call my name. "Celia!" I looked back; he was pointing in the other direction. "I'd suggest you go the other way. You'll run into my brother first if you take that route."

I took his suggestion and turned around. Just call me chicken girl. A week from now, I wouldn't care. But there was still a little bit of glow snuggling in my stomach and I just didn't want to have to explain it. I walked all the way around the blue perimeter, which took a while because the prison is actually damned big. But it gave me a chance to see the damage—and the rift—firsthand. I don't know how to describe what it looked like. It was an area of blackened sky that wasn't completely black. There were stars that were too low in the sky and a rainbow of shifting colors, like the aurora borealis. It looked the same from all directions, which was weird. Maybe a physicist could explain it, but I couldn't. I was concentrating on it so much I nearly tripped over Creede. He was sitting on the sand sucking down a bottle of water. He looked utterly exhausted. "Wow. You look rough."

He looked up and could barely smile. The light in his eyes was completely out—they were just regular hazel. If I didn't know him and someone had told me he was a mage, I wouldn't have believed them. "Thanks. I feel worse." Another long pull from the water bottle emptied it. I had something that would help a little; I keep a few in my vest for just such emergencies. I handed him a Hershey bar. He smiled for real as he took the candy bar from me. "Water and chocolate. The dinner of champions." He managed a chuckle.

I didn't tell him I'd been packing nutrition shakes earlier; I'd finished the last one off not long ago. I figured this wasn't a good time or place to suddenly start hunting for necks if I got too hungry.

I gave his calf a little kick. "Well, c'mon then, champion. I need you to take off one of the bindings. They worked great, but Matty doesn't know if he can do the exorcism with the person bound."

Creede collapsed onto his back, arms sprawled, and chewed. When he finally swallowed, he spoke: "Crap. I honestly don't know if I've got it in me, Ceil. Really. I'm toast." It was the first time he'd called me anything other than Celia or Graves and it came out sounding like "seal" rather than "cell."

"Well, can anyone remove it, or just you? We've got a couple of people bound and ready to get unpossessed."

Creede closed his eyes and I honestly thought he'd fallen asleep. But after long moments while I just stared at his slowly breathing body, he opened his eyes and pushed himself to a sitting position. "Okay. I guess I'm stuck. I think I have to be the one to release the bindings. I'm so used to doing my own workings that adding in the language for another mage to undo it didn't occur to me."

I offered him a hand up and he took it. He was as close to deadweight as I've ever seen and it took him a couple of tries to get his balance. Guess he wasn't faking. "You really put a lot of yourself into this barrier, didn't you?"

"Yeah. More than I should have. But we had a hard time closing it." I slowed my gait to stay even with him, because he was nearly shuffling. There wasn't any way he was going to make it around the long way. We'd have to go by Bruno.

I needed to be a big girl about this. It wasn't like I'd slept with John—not really. I hadn't dated him, and anyway, Bruno's the one who called it off with *me*, not the other way around.

But we didn't see Bruno until we reached Matty. My ex was muttering words and the frozen cop was lifting into the air and dropping back down in the center of a casting circle, stiff as ever. John stepped forward and pushed Bruno slightly to the side. "Here. Let me. You get the circle ready." John's hands made complex motions in the air with the grace of a pianist or maybe a painter. As he muttered words, a small glow finally came back into his eyes.

Bruno was likewise moving his hands and talking, but he was saying different words and the motions of his hands were tightly controlled and had military precision. Elegant in their own way. The moment the cop's body relaxed, she stood and started to scream. Bruno's circle sprang up around her and she was trapped. Matty started speaking in Latin and the woman went silent.

John took a deep breath and clapped a hand on Bruno's arm. My former fiancé responded by glaring, but Creede didn't seem to notice. "Guess we'd better finish up the other three so we can go home and get some rest. I'm sure we'll be needed here again tomorrow to recharge the barrier." He looked at me in an offhand way, but what he said next was clearly calculated for maximum effect on everyone in earshot. It sort of pissed me off. Yet Bruno sort of deserved it, too. "Ceil, go ahead and take the car back to Napa. I'll find a motel down here for a couple of days. You've still got the keys, right?"

I nodded, but I wasn't happy. There wasn't a win to this situation, and the best solution was probably to do just what he suggested. But I didn't want to leave Bruno with the wrong impression. "Okay. I'll take the car back to the *spa*, since that's where my clothes and my friends are. You can pick it up there. I'm sure the girls are wondering what's happened to me."

My response lightened Bruno's mood a little and darkened Creede's.

The perfect compromise leaves everyone unhappy.

Including me.

16

Y ou have *got* to be kidding!" My story had left both
Emma and Dawna with open mouths; Dawna was the
first to recover enough to speak.

My finger made a little *x* over my heart. "Hand to God."

It was three in the morning and my adrenaline rush was finally wearing off. Crises always made me sick to my stomach,
and about the only thing that had ever fixed it was orange sher-
bet. Luckily, the spa had some and didn't mind providing it at
such an early hour. Even better, it tasted just like I remembered
from childhood, and since I'd always let it melt in my mouth
before swallowing, it was one more treat I could still enjoy. Yay.

I took another spoonful and let out a sigh as the bright orange flavor exploded in my mouth.

"So," Emma finally asked, "was it good? I mean . . . better
than Bruno?"

I shook my head. When the last bit of liquid had vanished
down my throat, I responded: "Apples and oranges. It was pure
magic, not just regular sex."

They accepted the answer grudgingly. "What about the
kiss?" Dawna asked. "C'mon, dish."

Ooh. That was a tough one. "I'll have to make it a tie. Bruno for intensity, Creede for technique. The man is a *really* good kisser. And he has a nice car." There were knowing grins all around at that.

I finally returned to the topic I'd started with when I'd woken them both up from a sound sleep two hours before. "So now I've got to find someone who knows about dimensional rifts. That's your area, Emma. Whatcha got?"

She waved her hands in front of her. "Nope. Not me. Ask about ordinary multiple dimensions and I'm your girl. But this is metaphysical stuff. You'll find the best records in religious texts. But for history . . ." She leaned back into the stack of pillows she'd piled on the couch. "Your best bet would be Aaron Sloan. He's one of the top experts in demonology."

That perked me right up. "Is he the same Dr. Sloan your father knows?" When she nodded, I let out a sigh of relief. "I've met him. He does know his stuff and he's been looking into the death curse Stefania put on me."

One of the best things about voice mail was it didn't care what time it was. I left a long message and gave my cell phone number for him to call on Monday.

The girls left as I was checking my own voice mail. Dawna had been right. There were a *lot* of calls from people trying to hire me. It should have made me happy, but I was too tired to care. The morning was going to come far too soon, and I still had to make a list of things I had to do. I was yawning as I powered up my laptop.

It was the last thing I remembered doing.

I woke to a knock on my door and lifted my face from where it was resting on the laptop keys. Yuck! I'd drooled into the keyboard. God, I hoped it wasn't ruined. "Who is it?"

"Dawna. Are you packed yet? Weren't you supposed to be back in time to take your gran to church?"

My head was pounding like I was just coming off a three-day drunk, and there was a weird metallic taste in my mouth. I stumbled to my feet and caught sight of myself in the mirror above the dresser: pasty green-white skin, bloodshot eyes with dark bruising underneath, and a lovely checkerboard pattern of dents across my cheek. Terrific. I picked up my cell phone to see how many messages Gran had left, but the battery was completely dead.

I could already see this was going to be a very special morning. I decided I didn't want anyone to see me until I looked more . . . human. I went to the door and looked through the peephole at Dawna's annoyingly smiling face. I raised my voice enough to be heard through the door: "Could you call her? Please? Ask if she can take the bus. Otherwise, I can take her to evening services. I literally woke up when you knocked. I really need a shower before I can be semicoherent."

"Sure. Happy to." There was an edge to her voice that said she wasn't happy at all, but she'd do it because she was my friend.

The shower was heating and I was dumping out my whole makeup kit in a search for the concealer when I heard another knock. Yea dogs, what now?

I wrapped a fluffy white robe around me and went to the door. "Yes?"

"Aren't you moving yet, girlfriend? Am I just now hearing your shower running?" My brow furrowed, because it was Dawna. Again.

"Did you call Gran yet?"

"Why would I call your gran? Is something wrong?"

A buzzing started in my ears and my heart started pumping fast. "Did you knock on my door a few minutes ago and tell me to hurry up?"

"Hell, no. I've been downstairs with Emma, getting you something for breakfast." I looked out the peephole and saw her holding up a bottle of milk and a nutrition shake. "All they had was banana, but drink it anyway. You had a long night."

"Hang on just a second." I raced across the room and rummaged through my bags. When I walked back to the door, I used one hand to unlatch the security hook, flip the lock, and turn the knob. The other hand held a One Shot water pistol. "C'mon in."

She walked through the door and I fired. The water hit her right in the face and she sputtered and spit. "What is *wrong* with you, woman?"

My voice came out very quiet but very fast. "Dawna, you were just here—like two minutes ago. You told me we needed to go pick up Gran for church."

She frowned. "Was not."

"Yeah, you were." I nodded and raced to the nightstand. Screw the phone charges. I dialed Gran's number.

She answered on the first ring: "Hello?"

"Gran, this is Celia. Don't say a word. Did Dawna just call you?"

I held out the phone so the real Dawna could hear the response: "Yes, she did. You want me to take the bus to service this morning because you're running late. And I'd rather do that than wait until the evening service. I just don't like the choir selections at night. They're too . . . modern."

Dawna's mouth opened in shock and she raised a hand to cover her gasp as she realized the implications.

"Gran, get out of the house. Now. Go to the main office, call a cab, and go straight to church. You're in danger."

"Celia?" Her voice got very soft and worried. "What's wrong?"

"Dawna's standing right here with me and she didn't make that call. A demon is impersonating her . . . it probably escaped from the prison last night. Get to holy ground and stay there until I come for you. Okay? Promise me!"

Thankfully, my grandmother's nothing if not a pragmatist. She was there when Lilith tried to destroy Mom and when Reverend Al was killed by Eirene's minion. "There's a Catholic church right across the street. It's not *my* church, but I can walk there faster than a cab can get here."

"Good. Take your friends with you, in case the demon tries to coerce you."

"Pili's awake. She was going to go to services with me. We'll get Ahn, too. I'll hang up now. You stay safe, baby. Don't worry about me. It'll distract you."

Another knock sounded and Dawna rushed the few feet to the door. She peered through the peephole and mouthed, *Emma.*

I tossed her my last One Shot. Dawna opened the door slowly, and when Emma walked in Dawna squirted her in the face.

The thing that looked like Emma screamed and lashed out at Dawna, who ducked and did a diving roll while the demon was blinded. I hung up the phone and lunged for my weapons. The handgun was closest and was loaded with silver. I fired two shots at the entity's chest and it exploded into a million pieces. Wow. Never seen that before.

Viscous red gunk splattered across the walls and floor and even started dripping down from the ceiling. My credit card company was *not* going to be happy with me.

While Dawna curled into a near-fetal ball on the couch, I calmly sat down on the bed and picked up the phone again. I pressed zero twice and a chirpy voice answered, "Front desk."

"Hi. This is room eight-oh-nine. We need . . . oh, we need lots of things. Probably a detective and a priest to start with, and then Housekeeping will need a whole bunch of towels."

There's a point at which even the best spa is taxed to the limit. "Um . . . I'll see what I can do."

"Where's Emma?" Dawna's voice was soft and painted with fear.

"Did you go to her room or did she come to yours?"

Dawna's face brightened a little. "She came to mine. Do you think . . . ?"

It was worth a try. I dialed room-to-room and a sleepy voice sounded on the other end of extension eight fourteen. "'Lo?"

My whole body collapsed with relief. I felt almost numb. "Em? Are you okay? Tell me you're okay!"

264 | CAT ADAMS

Her voice sounded muffled, like it was under a pillow. "God, keep it down. I'm fine. I was asleep. My head is killing me from all that wine."

Dawna started crying with almost hysterical intensity and Emma heard. Her voice became more alert: "What's wrong? Celia, tell me what's going on."

I threw my head back against the wall and let out a long breath. "Keep the doors locked and turn on the magical barrier if you haven't already. And keep a One Shot handy. Something was impersonating you. It's dead now."

Her voice got suddenly shaky as my words hit home, and her sniffling gave way to crying. "I need to get back to Birchwoods. Tell me we're going back today."

One crying on the phone and the other crying on the couch. My relaxing weekend with the girls had backfired big-time.

Just then there was a knock on the door and the announcement, "House detective. Ms. Graves? Could you open the door?" Great. The local law had arrived and I was wearing nothing but a robe that was covered with blood.

Yep. This day was going to suck moss-covered swamp rocks.

17

'm sorry, but I really don't care what your corporate office said! *I'm* saying that your faulty barrier nearly got us killed." I slammed my hand down on the front desk and then threw what used to be a snow-white towel onto the elegant marble. It landed with a moist thud, thanks to the fact that it was covered with blood and visceral chunks of what used to be a demon. "This would be *me* if I wasn't a professional bodyguard who just happened to have the right tools on hand to kill this thing."

Yes, I'd made sure the towel had been blessed before I marched off with it. But I wanted to make it *crystal* clear to the management that I'd nearly died . . . in their spa. I wasn't a happy camper. Not only that, but my friends were suffering. Real therapeutic weekend.

The young desk clerk, whose name badge read *Cyndi*, turned white as a sheet and raced through the door into the office with a hand held over her mouth. The dark-skinned manager named Leonard made an expression of extreme distaste as his colleague noisily emptied her stomach behind the wall. He produced a trash can from behind the counter, grasped the towel's one relatively clean corner, and pulled the bloody mess into the wastebasket. "Ms. Graves—that was unnecessarily vulgar. There's no need to traumatize my staff."

I threw up my hands and pointed to the elevator. "Why not share the love? I've got two traumatized friends upstairs and I want to know what you're going to do about it. A demon should *not* have been able to get in this establishment. When did you really last have that barrier serviced?"

He looked down his nose at me and I didn't appreciate it. At least the detective had treated me like a victim. He'd let me get dressed before he sealed the room to do his investigation. "As I explained to you, we *regularly* attend to maintenance of our security shield. The police will be here momentarily to investigate and we'll let you know the result once we have the report."

"And as I explained right back, there are many different levels of *maintenance*. Was the shield renewed this month? This quarter? Was it even this year? That has nothing to do with the investigation. Surely there's an inspection certificate of some sort that I can look at. You have one in the elevator and in the kitchen. Isn't that public information? Or should I start calling the news media to see if they can find out?"

That did it. He tried hard to control his features, but the panicked look on his face said that either he didn't want any sort of bad press or he really didn't want me to see an inspection report of the barrier. "That won't be necessary, ma'am. The Oceanview Resort and Spa is always happy to satisfy our customers."

And so began the negotiations.

It was nearly fifteen minutes later by the time the rooms and spa treatments were comped, my credit card was refunded, and I had a guest pass to "give us another try."

I was shaking the hand of the nice manager, who by then was close to sweating bullets and not hiding it well, when Dawna came bolting out of the elevator. Panic preceded her like a cloud as she shouted, "Celia, you've got to come quick. Emma is totally freaking out!" Dawna held the elevator doors open, practically vibrating with anxiety.

Yay, she was talking again. But those weren't the words I was hoping for.

Oh, crap. "I told her to stay in her room." God, if she saw that mess . . . they were going to have to lock her in a rubber room. The buzzer started sounding and the doors were struggling to shut. The wide-eyed manager nearly shoved the gift certificate into my hand. I was betting he was planning to scoot out the door before anything else went wrong.

The elevator was a calm respite and I reveled for just a few moments in the soft music, dim lights, and elegant wood paneling. Dawna stood beside me with her eyes shut, probably trying to keep hold of her sanity.

Then the doors opened and sound and motion assaulted me. Two uniformed housekeepers were trying to hold Emma on the floor while the house detective was taking pictures of the "crime scene." The Unitarian minister had apparently already left.

Emma was screaming as fast as she could draw breath. The pretty young Latina maid looked up at me as she struggled to keep Emma's arms from thrashing enough to hurt herself. She had to shout to be heard over my friend's screams: "My manager went to call nine-one-one. Maybe the EMTs can give her a sedative or something. The poor thing was beating her head into the wall. We were afraid she was going to really hurt herself!"

I knelt down beside Emma and cradled her face, forcing her to look at me, while the other women tried to hold her body still. "Emma! C'mon, girlfriend. Look at me. It's Celia. You need to calm down." I tried to get her to focus on my face, but I could tell right away that she was beyond actually seeing anything. Maybe they were right. A sedative was what she needed. Mostly, though, she needed to get back to Birchwoods. Unfortunately, that was better than seven hours away and I was afraid if we didn't get her back there fast, she'd wind up in some hospital up here—and might never get out.

The detective let out a frustrated noise. "I wish we could put her somewhere soundproofed until the ambulance gets here. Or maybe just teleport her mouth somewhere." He and the maids let out a chuckle, but the word made me get to my feet so fast the maids probably thought I was about to start screaming, too.

There are few things faster than a phone call. One of them is a teleporter. Combine the two and I might know a way to help Emma.

I skirted around the detective with an apology and raced for the phone while Emma's screams made my ears ring. Complimentary room or not, I was betting they were going to stick this international call on my bill.

And probably the cost to clean up the blood that I'd just tracked farther into the room. Oops.

I turned on my nearly dead cell phone long enough to find the number of a recent call. I barely got the number written down before the phone died. The charger was somewhere in my bags, but I didn't want to waste time looking for it.

The phone rang once, twice, then, "Kanalai Palace," said the calm, unhurried voice on the other end, with a distinct accent I'd come to recognize. "How may I help you?"

"This is . . ." I paused, glancing at the detective who was taking in my conversation without seeming to. I didn't really want to identify myself as royalty, but it was probably the only way people on the siren island were going to listen. I turned away from him and lowered my voice. At least if he was going to listen in, he was going to have to work at it over the screaming. "Princess Celia. I have an emergency at my location and I need to know whether Okalani is available to transport someone to a physician."

"An ambulance has been called, Ms. Graves." The detective cocked his head and put a bloody bit of . . . something into an evidence bag. "There's no need to call a second one."

I raised my brows and put a hand over the speaker. "This is a little faster than an ambulance."

There was a pause on the line and I knew the receptionist was probably contacting someone telepathically. "Of course, Princess. She'll be right there. I have a caller ID on your location. Please don't leave that immediate area."

Okalani was a teenager from the Isle of Serenity—pretty,

insecure, troubled. She wanted nothing more than to visit the mainland. I'd have to keep watch over her pretty carefully to avoid angering Lopaka any more, assuming, of course, that was even possible.

Okalani managed to avoid not only every bit of furniture but me and the demon remains as well. And she wasn't alone. Adriana released the light grip she had on the teenager's arm and smiled thinly at me. Okalani didn't seem very happy, but I couldn't tell if it was because she had a chaperone, regular teen angst, or something more serious.

More serious would be a problem. I needed to be able to trust her with Emma. I smiled at the girl whom I'd first met on her back with a knife at her throat. She'd snuck into my room and I'd considered her . . . gee, an *intruder.* Go figure. I had to shout over the screaming: "Hi, Okalani. Thanks for coming so quick!"

She opened her mouth to respond, but Adriana spoke first, holding out her delicate hand like I was supposed to kiss her ring or something. Fat chance. "Good afternoon, Celia. May I ask what the crisis is?"

I looked around the room, wondering what dimension she was in that it wasn't completely obvious. "Can you not hear the screaming, Adriana?"

Okalani raised a tentative hand. "Princess, is that woman injured?"

Maybe I needed to just talk to Okalani. Adriana seemed really . . . *distracted.* The detective stepped over, his eyes a little wide at the sudden appearance of a dark-skinned teen in camo pants and a black tank top and a woman who would put pretty much every movie star to shame. "Ms. Graves, I can't let these people—"

I knew what he was going to say. He didn't want them to contaminate the crime scene. I understood that. I didn't want there to be *any* question I was the good guy. "They're only here to take my screaming friend to Birchwoods. Is that okay?"

He looked confused. "There'll be additional footprints." I could understand how he would think that.

"Okalani, could you and Adriana pop out to the hallway? My friend's name is Emma and she needs to go to the Birch-woods. Do you have any idea where that is?"

Now Adriana finally joined the conversation: "I will touch your friend's mind and see where the place is. Okalani will take us there."

Oh! That's right. They'd done that before. "Great. I appreciate this. Really. You won't be able to teleport her inside the barrier, but if you deliver her just outside the gates they'll bring her inside."

Adriana nodded once, sharply, and shifted her black shoulder bag in a way that made me realize she was carrying something significant. "Please remain nearby. We must talk. It's important."

They were gone before I could respond, and the screaming cut off abruptly before either I or the detective could move around the bed enough to see out the door.

Dawna was standing in the hall with shock written all over her exotic features. She was staring down at the two maids who were getting to their feet and likewise looking confused. "What the heck just happened?"

I dusted my hands together. You couldn't ask for a better resolution. "Emma's back at Birchwoods. I called in a favor."

Dawna looked confused. "What do you mean . . . back at Birchwoods? You mean, like . . . *now*?"

I nodded. "If you call the front gate right now, they're probably just letting her inside the shield." In fact, I probably did need to call Gwen to let her know what had happened.

I was betting it wasn't going to be a happy call.

"I know it wasn't intentional, Celia. I do. And the situation at the prison couldn't have been predicted by anyone." I could hear a big "but" in Gwen's voice. "But—"

Yep. There it was.

"It would have been better if you'd brought her down last night rather than having her go back to the spa."

I wasn't trying to argue. Truly. But that just didn't make sense to me. "I was accompanying Mr. Creede, who was driving a two-seater car at over a hundred miles an hour for four hours. Wouldn't that have been just a *bit* stressful by itself? Yes, I made the mistake of presuming the spa's security barrier matched the place's five-star rating. But I think anyone else would have done the same thing. If not for that, this wouldn't have happened."

There was a long pause and I could hear whispering in the background. "Emma is back in her room. She's calm now that she's been given a sedative. But we'll have to restrict her movements until we can evaluate her." Gwen let out a long sigh and I could imagine her eyes closing while she centered herself.

"This whole situation has been unfortunate, but I certainly can't find any reason to blame you for the events. We'll just have to chalk it up to bad luck."

I let out a sigh and shook my head. Dawna, sitting beside me with a sad expression on her face, reached over to touch my hand and then pat it, offering what little comfort she could. Yeah, I suppose a demonic death curse could qualify as *bad luck*. Damn demons were apparently drawn to me like honey.

"Celia, we must speak now." I looked up to where Adriana was now standing over the couch in the lobby. I held up a finger to shush her while I finished the call.

"Gwen, we're going to have to talk about this later if that's okay. They need me back upstairs."

"Of course. I understand. We'll discuss it after your therapy session with Dr. Hubbard next Thursday."

Crap. I'd forgotten about that. It was probably on my calendar, but I'd intentionally not looked at it except to cancel things for the weekend. "Fine. That'll work. Bye."

I pressed the end button and scooted over on the couch to make room for my cousin. Her elegantly arched brows rose just a fraction. "Might as well have a seat. I know teleporting always makes me dizzy. Where's Okalani?"

Adriana didn't sit. She stood there with obvious discomfort, clutching the black zippered bag for dear life. "I sent her back home. I'll call when I need her again."

Aww. Poor kid. Fifteen minutes on the mainland and she has to go home. "Couldn't you at least have taken her to a water park or a movie or something?"

But she wouldn't budge. "We're already having difficulty

274 • CAT ADAMS

keeping her from clandestine visits here. Having enjoyable experiences would only validate her behavior and make her want to disobey more."

"See, I have just the opposite opinion. If you let her have a taste now and again, she won't be as likely to disobey because she'll know there'll be a next time."

Adriana shrugged carelessly. "But you aren't her mother. Nor am I."

True. It wasn't my place to say how she was raised.

"Um . . . Celia?" Dawna's voice cut in. "Were you going to introduce us or something?"

Oh. Oops. "Dawna Long, this is Adriana, high princess of the Pacific siren clan." Then I looked at Adriana. "Adriana, Dawna Long. Although pretty soon it'll be *Queen* Adriana, huh?"

That raised Dawna's eyebrows. "Whoa. You're getting the throne? Sweet."

Adriana's face flushed just a bit and her tone took on an impatience tinged with panic: "There will be no wedding unless we speak. Now. And this is not the place for the discussion."

That wasn't good. "I'll have to check with the police to see if we can leave. If so, we can talk in the car on the way back home. It's a long trip. We'll have plenty of time and privacy."

Her eyes flicked toward Dawna. "Can your servant be trusted to hold her tongue?"

The look on Dawna's face was priceless—a classic *oh no, you didn't!* expression. Unfortunately, my phone was still dead, so I couldn't get a picture. Dawna opened her mouth to start spewing an offended response, but I interrupted with a laugh and a hand on her arm. We didn't need to escalate. Adriana had a pretty thin skin, too. "It's okay, Dawna. Remember that she's a *princess*. Servants and attendants are all she knows." Then I looked at my cousin. "Dawna is my best friend and an employee of my security company. She's not a servant in the sense you mean. But yes, she knows how to hold her tongue."

At least Adriana had the sense and courtesy to dip her head a fraction at Dawna after a second of consideration. "Apologies. I'm unaccustomed to princesses of the realm having . . . *employees*."

Or friends, I was betting. Dawna looked slightly mollified and her expression went through a few transformations before settling on *oh, well*. "Yeah . . . well, I'm not accustomed to Celia being a princess. We'll all have to adapt, I guess. How about I go check with the police to see if we can leave? I'll meet you two at the car."

I was going to suggest that, but it sounded less . . . princessy coming from her. "Thanks. If they still need me, just yell." I was actually surprised they hadn't come to get me already for a statement. I wasn't sure what was up.

I was still unlocking the car when Dawna came up behind me, a strange expression on her face. "No statements required. They said they didn't want to *inconvenience us any further*. We can go." She shook her head and reached for the backseat door handle. "They were acting really weird. All smiles and apologies. Not coplike at all."

That made me let out a little growl and look over the roof at the stunning redhead waiting for me to unlock the doors. "Did you manipulate them?" Because I sure as hell hadn't.

She shrugged. "As you know, I'm not capable of that level of psychic manipulation." Then she smiled. "But I am a princess, and soon to be a queen. They are not fools."

"I'm going back to give my statement. I want the facts behind my shooting of that demon on the record."

Now she looked petulant, as though I was being needlessly obstinate. "They won't take your statement, Celia. In their minds now, your actions were totally justified . . . which is absolutely true. You're being ridiculous. If it will make you use common sense, I assure you that I'm here for a crisis that's equally as dangerous as your earlier one. The world truly *is* about to end."

18

Okay, that got my attention. Dawna grabbed my elbow. "Um, Celia. Maybe she's right. Let's go while the getting's good and find a good place to hide and wait it out."

I turned my head and gave her a look. "I'm pretty sure *waiting it out* isn't an option during a world-ending crisis."

"Hardly." Adriana's tone was as dry as desert sand.

I slathered on a layer of sunscreen. I'd finally figured out about how strong the smell has to be for there to be enough. It's like sitting in a vat of coconut flakes—close to gag worthy. Still, it works.

Once we were in the car and on our way toward the 5, Adriana started to speak: "How much do you know of the first age of the sirens?"

"Not tons. That was the glory days of Atlantis, right? And when it sunk into the ocean after the battle between the sirens and demons, you all got relegated to a few small islands around the world."

Dawna spoke up from the backseat: "I always thought the legend of Atlantis was really interesting. I'll bet it was an

278 I CAT ADAMS

awesome place. It's so deep in the Atlantic trenches that nobody's ever found it." She moved forward slightly to catch
Adriana's eye. "Is it true they had electricity on Atlantis, even
back then?"

Adriana shook her head. "I can't speak to the question of
electricity, although it is quite possible they harnessed the sea
into batteries of a sort. But there's a very good reason why
Atlantis has never been found—it's *not* on the ocean floor."

That made me take my eyes off the road for a moment.
"Come again?"

Her face held both embarrassment and fear. "Atlantis was
the location of the *last* dimensional rift. Worse still, it was the
sirens who caused the rift."

Dawna's jaw dropped and she unhooked her seat belt so she
could lean forward. "Wait. I thought it was the sirens who
saved the world."

Adriana let out a sigh. "It was both. We had no choice but
to save the world. We'd nearly ended it. Or," she added with
another frown, "more precisely, certain contingents of the
sirens had."

"Like Stefania, you mean?"

Adriana nodded at the corner of my vision. I changed lanes
to get into the flow of traffic on the interstate. "Queen Eris
had bred badly and her daughters didn't hold the world's
children—the humans—in very high regard. Princesses Kraystal and Evana were of the opinion that the land would be
better off without the human race. But sirens were at that time
loathe to step too far inland, giving them no way to extermi-
nate humanity. So they sought . . . help."

"The demons." I was starting to get sick to my stomach. "And now it's started again, and I'm betting Stefania and Eirene had something to do with this new rift." Adriana's nod was answer enough. We drove for a moment in silence while I sorted out what I wanted to say. "So why change the history books? Why not just tell the world the sirens had a traitor, but you fixed it?"

Adriana shrugged. "Ego? Pride? I don't have an answer. But I do know that even now my mother is going to be *furious* I'm telling you this."

Oh! "So that's why she was so angry when I asked about the Millennium Horns. Because it's a reminder of the folly of the whole race."

Now a deep sigh issued from Adriana. "No. Her embarrassment is from the *second* folly of the sirens—we're not prepared for today's crisis because the queens refused to believe the past could repeat." I waited, and so did Dawna, until Adriana was ready to dish the details. After a long moment, she took a deep breath and continued, "When Queen Eris realized what her daughters had done, she sought the help of the greatest minds of the world. Human minds. To make the point to her daughters that sirens had to learn to coexist, she worked with members of what they considered a lesser race to come up with a plan to close the rift. It was a Greek philosopher and inventor, I believe, who first suggested the use of sound waves."

I knew there had been some great minds in the past—after all, we still use techniques developed by the Romans and Egyptians. "I didn't realize they'd experimented with that."

Adriana nodded. "Of course. The island nations have long

used conch shells as horns to signal over long distances. Humans were curious creatures. Where the sirens would choose any shell at hand to signal a boat or a friend across the island, the humans always tried to makes the tool better. This shape or that, the blowing hole larger or smaller to change the pitch. Queen Eris found people who showed promise and put them in the same room to offer ideas about what size and shape would work best. She then sent her best warriors out to find as many conch shells as she could and forced her daughters, as punishment, to find the one that would heal the wound in space."

Dawna's comment echoed my thought: "I'll bet she didn't give bathroom breaks, either."

Adriana's jaw set with either displeasure or concern for her own fate. "The warriors ensured they continued their task while the island was slowly eaten by the rift and the people were tormented by demons. The elder daughter, Kraystal, died of exhaustion after four days. It was Evana who found one that made the darkness waver and sparkle, after half of the island was gone. But it wasn't enough by itself to seal the breach."

Dear God. That must have been terrifying. For everyone. "So what happened? How did they seal the breach?"

Adriana raised her hands and frustration edged her voice: "I don't honestly know and I've scoured our libraries. We know there were two horns and that the rift *was* sealed. We know Atlantis was swallowed into the rift in an implosion of immense proportions. There's been no trace found because it doesn't exist in this dimension anymore. I found notes from one scribe that said the method was written down and hidden—as were the horns. After so many sirens were found to be involved in the scandal, the queens decided it was best if the memory was forgotten, so no future generations would ever be tempted."

My mouth opened and I spoke before I probably should have: "That is the stupidest damn thing I've ever heard in my life! Are they *idiots*?"

"Celia—" Adriana was tense, nearing anger. "You're talking about my *mother*. For better or worse, she was—they were—trying to protect humanity."

I let out a sigh. "I'm sorry, but if she was on the throne back then, what she and the others did was beyond foolish. Information is the only thing that keeps people safe. Diseases are cured by people sharing the clues from the dead; inventions are created from the ruins of failed experiments. Can we at least *ask* her what she knows?"

Adriana shook her head. "She doesn't know anything. I did ask. I wasn't joking when I said the memory was *forgotten*. They wiped their own memories of the event and left it to the scribes to keep the knowledge safe for the future. But either the scribes didn't do as ordered or the records disappeared. It seems that there are pages missing from some books. But they're very old texts. It could be that the sheets fell out and were thrown away by accident."

I pressed my foot down harder on the gas in pure frustration and the speedometer needle shot past 70. "So, we have no horns, no instructions, and a bunch of mages who are going to exhaust themselves soon to contain a rift that will never stop growing?"

Adriana nodded and Dawna let out a groan of near despair.

"Close. Very close. But only two of those are completely accurate." My cousin pulled the black canvas tote onto her lap and
extracted . . . a massive triton conch shell. "We have one of the
horns. Our troops found it in Stefania's palace after she died.
There's an engraving inside in old Atlantean cuneiform—
Eris, who mastered the dark. It's likely that she was the one to
blow the horn. She had the most formidable power."

I noticed the fuel gauge was getting dangerously low. "Let's
stop for gas. I want to look at that horn closer."

In a few minutes the digital numbers on the pump were
spinning upward and Dawna and I were admiring a shell that
had survived for over a thousand years. I collect shells, so I can
be a little jaded about them. But this was truly magnificent.
"Look at the *colors.* I've never seen a triton conch shell that
looked like this." Unlike king and queen conch shells, which
are a creamy apricot and have jagged points and spikes, a triton conch is long and smooth, with dark spots. This one had
not only dark dots and spots but also what looked like patterns
of gold flakes and burgundy sand. I ran a slow finger along the
etched figures that Adriana said were writing. They seemed
familiar, but I couldn't remember why. "It sort of makes sense
one of the horns is a triton. They have an amazing sound."

Dawna was likewise running almost reverent fingers along
the curves. "There are all sorts of carvings and paintings of
the sea god, whether you call him Triton or Poseidon, using
one of these to call his people to battle. And this particular
puppy can seal the rift, huh?"

I couldn't resist. I pulled it gently from Adriana's grip and put it to my lips. She shrugged. "I already tried that. No noise comes out. Even though they don't feel magical, there must be some sort of spell to make it work."

I took a slight breath and blew. A low, mournful sound erupted from the opening. I've always loved the sound a conch makes. But Dawna covered her ears like she was in pain and Adriana dropped her head into her hands. God, it wasn't *that* bad. But apparently I was wrong, because the car's windows started to vibrate. There was a loud *pop* and a crack appeared across the lower half of the windshield.

Oops.

Adriana pulled the horn away from me and stared alternately at me and it with mingled fear and amazement. Dawna was trying to recover her hearing by shaking each earlobe and opening her mouth wide.

"Um . . ."

The horn went to Adriana's lips. I saw her cheeks puff out, and then . . . nothing. No sound. And I mean *no* sound. "I have to admit that's a little odd."

"Let me try." Dawna held her hand over the seat confidently and Adriana passed the shell to her. I turned in my seat to watch, ready to throw my hands over my ears. But again, no sound issued from the horn. Dawna handed it back to me with an odd look on her face. "What are you, the chosen one or something?"

"God, I hope not. I can think of a thousand things I'd rather do than ever stand in front of that rift again." Adriana gestured, *Do it again.* Once more I blew, just a tiny bit—and the horn sounded. The volume didn't seem to be tied to the amount of air. That spoke of powerful magic. The windows shook again, but at least nothing shattered or cracked.

Fuck a duck. "Let me say for the record that there have *got* to be other people who can blow this horn, and if it takes the next three weeks, I'm going to find them."

There was a long pause in the car. It was quiet enough to hear the gas nozzle click off. I handed the shell back to Adriana and opened the door.

"We can do little with only one horn, so rest easy for now." I knew Adriana was trying, in her own way, to be thoughtful. But she could have left off the "for now" and I wouldn't have minded.

While I was paying for the gas, I checked on Gran. She told me the bus had come and gone while she was in the church across the street and she hadn't liked the look of the driver. She decided there was no reason why she couldn't stay where she was and just ignore the parts of the service she didn't believe. I couldn't find any fault with that logic and was happy to learn that the priest there was a former member of a militant sect. He promised to keep his sword behind the pulpit for the whole service . . . just in case. I didn't tell her about the horn. She'd only worry.

We spent the next hour driving quietly with the radio playing bubblegum rock. I wish I could say I was thinking lofty thoughts, but all I was really doing was trying to figure out some way out of this.

When we were about an hour from home, something occurred to me. I clicked off the radio and glanced at Adriana. I could feel the furrows in my forehead. "Do you think the other horn is the same way?"

She got a confused look on her face. "I don't understand. What same way?"

But Dawna got it and I could see in the mirror the moment she realized what I was asking. "Omagawd. That one in your collection!" At Adriana's look of puzzlement, she explained, "Celia collects seashells and has a bunch of conch shells. But there's this one, a king conch—"

I interrupted, "That has never made a sound. Not for anyone. My grandpa gave it to me as my very first shell when I was about five and I've always been disappointed it's silent."

"Do you mean that it doesn't blow a good tone or it's silent—"

"It's silent like *this one*," Dawna said with significance. "I never could figure out why you couldn't even hear air come out."

My voice sounded very small and scared, because I had just remembered why the inscription had seemed familiar: "There are carvings inside it, too. They looked like the kind of scratchings a kid might make. I've never had them checked out because I figured my grandpa had done it. He said he'd had the shell all his life." And we both knew that *his* father had been Queen Lopaka's brother—who probably had also been around during the fall of Atlantis.

My cousin's voice was thoughtful: "In the first age, the Isle of Serenity was the home of only the female sirens. Hearty seafaring men were lured to the island for breeding and then were sent away. Male children either were given to the father or . . . well, only girls remained."

Well, the sirens certainly weren't the first society to favor a particular gender, and even though I didn't like it, I couldn't change the past. "So why would a male have one of the Millennium Horns?"

"That's what I'm wondering. It was a long time before we realized what had happened at Atlantis. The queens knew because Eris sent them word of the crisis, but the general populace didn't. It wasn't until the sailors started to arrive with tales of destruction and great floods caused by tsunamis that we knew for certain that the rumors had been fact. Could it be that a sailor found the horn and took it to a male siren?"

"Were you born yet? What stories did you hear?"

Adriana shook her head. "I was born many hundreds of years later." But that still made her several hundred years old. Yowzer.

"Maybe we need to not worry about how they got where they are and concentrate on why they're still here *at all*. If Atlantis disappeared into the rift, shouldn't the horns have gone with it?"

Adriana's head was moving up and down like a bobblehead doll created by Tiffany and Max Factor. "I've asked that since this one was brought to me. Of course we already knew Stefania was trafficking with demons, so I wondered if perhaps it was a gift from them. I've also been concerned that the horns were a double-edged sword of a kind."

"Ooh," Dawna said from the backseat. "You mean that

maybe the horn can *open* the rift instead of close it and maybe that's why the wicked queen of the west had it?"

Oh, that would be bad.

"Indeed." Adriana's perfect nails were tapping a staccato on the tote. I flicked on the right turn signal and eased into the exit lane. We were getting nearer to finding the answers to a lot of questions. "There is every chance that the records I've found are wrong—changed *after* the memories of the queens were altered. I fear using the horn unless we have some authority."

I pulled my cell phone from the dashboard charger and tossed it backward over the seat. "Dawna, check my voice mail and see if Dr. Sloan has called back. I only called him yesterday, so he might not have, but if he has, I want to talk with him while we're all together and nothing's trying to kill us."

There was silence in the car other than the clicking of keys. I could hear my own voice far in the distance, and then Dawna was writing on her hand while nodding absently—just like she did at the office. "Yep," she said after a few minutes. "He called you back, and left a number. Want me to call him and set something up?"

"It's illegal, so yeah, I don't like to, and I hate the way calls sound on those Bluetooths. Or is that Blueteeth?"

She smiled and even Adriana let out a small amused sound. Dawna paused and then her smile turned to a grin. "Two other calls, by the way." Her voice went singsong. "John and Bruno both wanna see you. Celia's got two boyfriends."

I looked over to catch Adriana's reaction, but it didn't really mean anything to her. Why would it? She's probably completely used to men falling over her. Dawna must have noticed Adriana's lack of reaction, because she leaned over and whispered, "Her first triangle."

I swatted at Dawna and she ducked. But Adriana let out a *real* laugh. "My first was amazing, but it's also the most difficult, Celia—especially if you find them both attractive in return."

"Oh, she does. Both are mages and both are completely *hot*."

That grabbed Adriana's attention. "Mages. Are they skilled?"

I nodded, fighting off the blush that was probably making my white skin a vivid pink. "Very. Bruno is more powerful, but John has an amazing talent."

Adriana touched the tote as I came to a stop at the light heading toward the beach. "Would they be able to feel the magic in the horn? Perhaps even know what spell was cast on it?"

That was such a logical question that I kicked myself for not thinking of it. "It's sure worth asking, but I don't know if we can reach them. Were they still down at the prison, Dawna?"

She glanced at the time display on the face of my cell. "The messages were both about an hour ago and they were just leaving for the night. Again, want me to call?"

What the hell. "Sure. Call all three. Have the whole bunch meet me at the guesthouse. That's where the other shell is. But I have got to have something to eat first, so tell them to make it in an hour or so and if they get there before us they should wait."

I figured if they were early and we were late, we could focus on the shell and not on . . . well, less comfortable subjects. I glanced in the mirror to see how Dawna took my instructions while I turned away from my house. Her brows were raised and there was a small smile on her face, but she didn't say a word.

That was best, because I had suddenly become a bundle of nerves. I didn't want to have "the talk" with Bruno and I certainly didn't want him to see the effect Creede's magic had on me. Nor did I want John to see the pain in my eyes when I looked at Bruno. Damn it. I could really use one of those cleansing rituals right now, because I wanted to throw up and was brushing back tears. If Adriana noticed my slightly green expression, she didn't mention it, but I was betting she didn't notice.

Apparently I was wrong, because moments later she spoke with absolute seriousness: "This is something you must learn to live with, Celia. None of us *chose* to be a siren. If you spend all your time worrying about what effect your beauty and natural attraction will have on the hearts of the men who love you, you'll curl up in a corner and die." She stared at me so intently that I couldn't help but turn to meet her gaze. "I mean that literally. Others have."

"If that's supposed to be encouraging, it's . . . well, your delivery needs a little work." I turned back to concentrate on my driving. I was glad of the ocean breeze coming through the open windows; it helped me calm down. "Let's find somewhere to get some food before I start chomping on necks."

19

There were three cars parked at the guesthouse, but no people were visible. As I pulled in, I spotted Inez slowly climbing the stairs back to the main house.

Oh, shit. She'd let them in. Great. They were probably pawing through my stuff right now.

Nah. They wouldn't do that. Would they?

At least the house was still standing and the walls weren't melting . . . yet. That was a plus. I wasn't as emotional anymore, either. Apparently aggression isn't the only thing that happens when I get hungry. The people at the Italian restaurant had probably never seen a weepy vampire before. Interestingly, spaghetti with marinara sauce isn't half-bad in a blender. Definitely on the keeper list.

But my emotions weren't in perfect order, because my stomach did flip-flops when I saw two men watching me arrive from my own living-room window. So when I parked the SUV next to a rental Mustang that was as red as a certain Ferrari but not as fast, it wasn't much of a struggle to answer the cell phone when it rang. Dawna let out a clucking noise and leaned next to my ear to whisper as she was getting out, "Chicken."

I shooed her away. Adriana had an amused look that said she agreed with Dawna. Just what I needed—two amoral compasses. I pressed the green button as both doors shut and they walked toward the house. "Celia Graves."

"Afternoon, Ms. Graves. It's Mick Murphy."

It wasn't Monday. "I'm sorry, Mr. Murphy, but I haven't had a chance to talk to those people yet. Didn't we say we'd talk tomorrow?"

"We did. Yes, ma'am. But something interesting came up and I thought you'd want to know about it."

Okay, that got me curious. I got out of the car and started to walk toward the stairs . . . not to climb them to the door but to stand under them where there was shade. It was December, but I was suddenly dying in the car. It hadn't really hit me until the breeze stopped moving and I started sweating. But out in the open air a cool wind took away the heat and the sounds of gulls and of waves crashing against the rocks calmed me. "Tell me about it." *And please take a long time doing it.*

"Well, I got a call today from an older gentleman named Nathan Fulbright. His family has been in the county for generations, but I'd never really talked to him before. Called me right out of the blue and offered to sell me his ranch. The interesting part is he's asking the exact amount of money Ms. Cooper is leaving me."

Really. I let my sneakers sink into the soft sand and rested my tail against one of the stair treads while I thought. "Did the amount you're getting appear in the local papers or make the rumor mills?"

"No, ma'am. That's why I thought it was significant. Gave

me a shiver right up my spine. Most of the people around town think I'm getting a million or so. Mind you, that's still a *lot* of money down here."

It was just about anywhere except Hollywood. "Is that a normal price for land down there?"

The choking laugh that burst from him was the answer without him even saying the words. "No. Nowhere close. It's nice land and there's always been a rumor he's got a little diamond mine there, but other than that, it's just ordinary ground. Not even very good grazing. Might be good for crops once all the undergrowth is gone. It's about two sections—so a little over twelve hundred acres. But land's only about three thousand an acre hereabouts."

"Diamond mine? There are diamonds in Arkansas?"

"Yes'm, in a few places. A couple of the mines are real steady producers. A lot of them are industrial-grade veins, but there are a few that are jewelry quality. I talked to my boss, the judge, and he thinks the reason Nathan's offering the land to me is to keep his two moneygrubbing sons away from it. That I do understand. His sons are real no-accounts. Nobody likes or trusts them and their names have passed by my desk in the court more than once."

Sort of like Vicki's situation but in reverse. "I guess the big question is, are you interested?"

He let out a deep breath. "I haven't had much of a chance to think about it, to be honest. I just barely got off the phone with him and we immediately thought to call you to find out your thoughts. I mean, it's nice land—overlooks the river and parts are real pretty. But for that price there'd better be something really special about it. I just don't know what that might be. And I don't think he'd tell me if I asked 'lessen we were under contract."

"And by then, it's a little late to be disappointed."

His voice said he'd already thought out the problems: "Yes, ma'am. He even offered to carry a loan if our bequest wasn't enough. So I guess that sort of puts the skids on our plans to cancel the bequest . . . at least until we know what this is about. Molly agrees with me that it's too coincidental to ignore. I told him I'd call him back next week, after I'd talked with the attorneys and my family. I didn't mention telling you, but you're sort of part of the attorneys, in my mind."

"I appreciate you calling. Let me see what I can find out and why don't you do the same there. Don't tell anyone about it, but do some discreet work to find out his background."

He chuckled. "Molly has already started her quilting circle finding things out. By morning, we'll know everything there is to know about his family. I'll let you know what we find out, but it might not be until Tuesday. He asked if he could come over and talk with us tomorrow. He'd like to meet Molly and the girls, but he made it clear it had to be in the daylight. The only way to do that is to have him over at the diner at noontime. We all meet there and eat together every day."

This was all happening really fast, but that's the way it is with visions sometime. Hit just the right trigger and the whole thing unreels. Movement caught my eye and I looked toward the vehicles to see a dust devil forming. The wind picked up sand and spun it. The sand sparkled in the afternoon sun. Or was it not the *sand* that was sparkling? "Mr.

Murphy, I think Vicki's here. Let me talk to her about it and see what she thinks."

He let out a light laugh. "Please call me Mick. My dad's Mr. Murphy. I find it funny you say you think Miss Vicki's there like she's walking up the road. You seem to handle ghosts pretty well. Sure you're not a channeler, too?"

I asked that of myself for a long time. But it's only select ghosts. "Thankfully no. But they do seem to like me."

He chuckled again and said his good-byes while I stared at the sparkling whirlwind that was bouncing off the car roofs. I walked out into the warm sun and felt an immediate sting in spots on my nose that said I'd sweated too much and some of the sunscreen had rubbed off. I addressed the circle of dust: "So, did you hear? What do you think?"

Of course there wasn't any way for her to respond in writing—no windows. But once again I was wrong, because she shot up into the sky and my eyes followed. Words appeared on my picture window in frosted letters two feet high. *Yes! Find out . . . urgent!*

Urgent? Why was it now urgent rather than a mildly frustrating curiosity on her part? But she seemed really agitated. So much so that the people in the house came to the window to stare at the hovering tornado of sand. "It's okay. I'll be talking to him again on Tuesday."

She wrote again, right over the tops of the other words. That was really unlike her. It took me a second to make them out: *No! Go there. Hurry.*

Go there? To Arkansas? "Sweetie, land sales take months to

complete even if they signed the deal today. We've got a pretty big crisis right here to deal with first."

Once again, letters appeared over the top of the others without her waiting for the sun to warm the previous words away: *Same crisis . . . I know it!*

Oh, crap. Was there a second rift opening in Arkansas? Why now, and why *there*? Or was it more simple than that? I needed to talk to people who would know, and fortunately, they happened to be just upstairs. "You're too upset, Vick. You need to relax and regroup. I'll talk to the others and then we'll talk again. Okay?"

'Kay.

Then she was gone, leaving the sand to drop to the ground with the force of a dump truck spreading its load. I sighed, grabbed the broom I keep near the stairs, and scattered the pile before my bushes broke under the weight.

As I climbed the steps to the front door, my mind was racing. How could the owner of a diamond mine in Arkansas have anything to do with a demonic rift in California? Why would the Murphys need to *own* the land?

A dozen more half questions and random thoughts were racing through my mind as I opened my front door. "What was *that* all about?" Bruno asked, and I looked up from contemplating my sneakers to see his concerned face. He was standing near the window, trying to make out the words Vicki had written. Being backward and on top of each other didn't make it easy.

"Long story," I admitted. "You want it first, or you want to tell me what you've been talking about?"

"We should definitely proceed with all available information. It might answer questions we've been asking each other," Dr. Sloan said, and, as usual, he made sense. The dessicated little man's freckled brown skin seemed pale, as though he'd received a shock. His watery eyes told me the same.

So I told them about the call and Vicki's reaction. There was silence all around for a long moment. I took the opportunity to look around the room for somewhere to sit. I don't generally give parties, and having this many people in my living room filled every chair. Creede was installed in my favorite recliner, a big brute of a chair that enveloped me in cushiony softness. A wooden chair from the kitchen would have to do, because I wasn't about to kick a guest out of his seat, especially when he looked so damned comfortable.

As I headed for the kitchen, he stood and stepped in front of me. "You sit down. I'll get one."

Okay, having a telepath in the house wasn't always a bad thing. I smiled and gratefully sat in my chair, made all warm and tingly by his residual magic. Bruno noticed the interaction and didn't like it much, but how could he say anything about John being a courteous guest that wouldn't make him sound like a troll?

Thankfully, Creede decided to be a gentleman and brought not one but two chairs. He put one on either side of my chair and sat down in one—offering the other to Bruno with his eyes and a tip of his head. Okay, he was trying to play fair. That won him a few points. Bruno sat and touched my hand. I smiled at him, too. I was happily lulled by magic beating on me from both sides like a shiatsu massager.

"Ms. Graves," said Dr. Sloan after a few seconds, "could we hear a demonstration of the horn's tone?"

Yeah, that would be a good idea. Adriana held it out toward me. When I went over to get it, she didn't let go for a moment. Her eyes were sparkling with amusement when she whispered, "If you ever have cause to wonder whether you come from our line, don't. I became a garden statue in their eyes when you walked into the room."

My blush was immediate. Next to Adriana, Dawna smiled like the Mona Lisa. I didn't dare turn around and let the boys see my reaction, so I picked up the horn and put it to my lips. Like in the car, a low, clean note filled the room. I heard glass shattering somewhere in the distance and immediately stopped blowing. The sound didn't dissipate for long moments after I'd put down the horn. I felt a hand on my elbow and turned to find Bruno holding my arm. "Come over here and do that again."

Creede was drawing symbols between two circles of chalk . . . on my polished wooden floor.

"Aw, man. You'd better clean that off when we're done. It'll ruin the wax."

He looked up at me with bemusement before looking down again to complete the last symbol. "You'll thank me later when you're cleaning up only a *few* pieces of shattered glassware in your hutch instead of all of them."

Touché.

Bruno held me back for a moment while he studied the circle. "You laid down two identification spells. What else are we looking for?"

Creede shrugged. "The spell might be on the shell or it might be on Celia. No sense doing a second circle to find out."

Bruno grunted and nodded. Then he positioned me in the middle of the circle. His brow furrowed and he knelt down to add another precise, complex symbol in a very different hand-writing than Creede's smooth, flowing loops. Creede noticed and crossed arms over his chest with raised brows. "Interest-ing. Hadn't considered a trip wire to pull away the horn if it goes south. Good thinking."

"Unique circumstance," was Bruno's reply, but I could tell he was pleased. The sad part was they could probably be really close friends . . . if not for me. He touched my leg to get my attention and then stood. "Okay, here's the plan. Put the horn to your lips and take a breath. But don't blow until we have the circle up."

"Why not put the circle up first?"

Creede answered, "There's a chance that whatever the spell is will have safeguards that prevent it from being identified. Neither of us could find any overt spell or residual magic in the shell. So it must be in the sounding. I felt . . . something when you blew it. Something that wasn't there before."

Bruno nodded. "So did I. But with a circle around you, you might be unable to lift the horn or take a breath. You shouldn't be prevented from releasing a breath, but if you are, raise your hand or stomp a foot or something and we'll pull the whole works down."

"Gee, you guys are making this sound like so much fun." I looked down at the circle, now mildly nervous. "Damned good thing I trust you *both* to keep me safe." I stared from one to the other, bringing home the point.

Creede winked. "Damned good thing you're hard to kill."

Bruno's smile made me feel better. "That vampire did make it a lot easier to protect you."

Okay. One more time for the cameras. I lifted the horn to my lips and took a deep breath. I raised one finger to let them know I was ready. Golden and dark eyes began to blaze with power. They stood on either side of the circle and began to whisper words and sounds that seemed better suited to a dark night with cool sheets.

If I hadn't already inhaled, the feel of the magic would have stolen my breath away. Power crackled across my skin and pressed against me with claustrophobic closeness. They gave no signal, but I could tell the circle was complete by the way my every hair was standing on end. I blew the horn, this time not tentatively. I gave it all I was worth. The sound filled the circle and pushed at the edges, wanting to go farther. It vibrated in my chest but didn't seem to bother my ears. The sound was a pleasant, low hum, like a distant interstate. I risked a glance at the mages and found they'd had to step back several feet. The circle wasn't straight up and down anymore. It was cone shaped and it apparently was all they could do to keep it intact. Their hands were blurs in the air; and their eyes, pairs of twin stars. I didn't start to worry until Bruno turned his head and yelled something to the other people in the room. I couldn't hear him past the deep, dark wall of sound from the ancient horn, but the panic on my friends' faces made me pull

300 | CAT ADAMS

the horn from my lips. Everybody either ducked behind furniture or bolted out of the room.

Not good.

Creede and Bruno started talking to each other across the void of hazy air, but I still couldn't hear them and I suck at reading lips. Whatever they decided made Creede call out. Dawna came running and after listening to him raced to the front door and opened it.

Creede's fingers moved lazily and gracefully. He reached out as though to pull a rope. I felt the magic surrounding me follow. It was as though someone had turned on a vacuum and applied the hose to my skin. I started to take a step toward the door, because it seemed like he was going to move the circle. But Bruno waved his arms in wide, frantic gestures and I could see the word *No!* in his mouth movements. I put my foot back down and he put a hand to his chest and let out a heaving breath like I'd nearly given him a heart attack.

The pulling, tugging sensation moved from mere pressure to actual pain as Creede backed slowly toward the door. Bruno saw me wince and gave me a look filled with sympathy but made it clear I shouldn't move. My skin was now stinging like tiny ants were biting me. The air was like honey thickened to a near solid and full of sharp crystals that cut when I moved. I had to struggle to do anything except breathe.

When Creede finally reached the door, he shouted something to Bruno, who raised his arms and steadied his stance. With an apparent massive effort, he threw power forward, and I nearly fell over under the assault of energy. I dropped to my knees, trickier than it sounds while staying carefully in the circle. I sat on my heels and put my palms flat on the floor to stay steady.

I closed my eyes and tried not to think about the smell of burning wood and hair that surrounded me, or the intense pressure and pain all along one side of my body. All I could think was, *Please don't destroy my house.*

When the release came it was like slamming a door against a hurricane. The sudden silence and absence of wind topples you. I fell backward, and although I tried desperately to correct myself, I was going to break the circle. Shit!

But then strong arms grabbed me and I found myself in Bruno's lap, looking up at his relieved face. His lips moved, but like in a B-grade kung fu movie the sounds reached my brain a few seconds after they left his mouth: "That was a close one."

Full sound returned with a pop, and I could hear the wind whistling through the doorway and the hum-tick of my Kit-Cat Klock on the wall. "What happened?" My voice was breathy, which was pretty much how I felt—weightless, breathless. My heart was beating out a healthy dose of panic. "Is everyone okay?"

He gave my arm a gentle squeeze. "You gave me a scare, woman. If you'd broken that circle we'd be picking up pieces of your house in downtown L.A."

I looked around. The house looked fine, but Creede looked a little crisp around the edges. He was on his knees at the doorway, hands on his thighs, relearning how to breathe. He looked past me in Bruno's arms to the other man's eyes. "We're going to have to find some way to shore up that barrier. We didn't craft it to handle anything like this. This circle just barely held it until I could get an edge out the door to release it, and I don't think she was really trying. Do the identification spells give any hint of what we're dealing with?"

I didn't have to ask *what* barrier. They'd apparently decided it was a foregone conclusion I'd be sounding the horn to close the rift. Bruno nodded and reluctantly eased me off his lap until I was sitting on the floor. He spun on his butt and looked at the circle, no longer chalk but a charred mess that was still smoking. Aww, man—my hardwood!

He stared at the symbols as if reading a report. "The spell's definitely on the horn. Never seen anything quite like it. See what you think, John."

Wow . . . working together. Creede got slowly to his feet, pushing off the doorjamb with that same deep weariness he'd shown at the prison. He shook his head repeatedly and blinked as though dazed. When he got close, he squatted down and stared where Bruno was pointing. I took a second to tug on both of their pant legs. "Thanks, guys. I think it might have been ugly if anyone with less skill had been casting. Sorry I keep being so much trouble."

Bruno reached out to squeeze my hand with a smile and Creede gently ruffled my hair with a wink and said, "You're like skydiving with only a backup chute, Celia. Once you survive, the rush makes you want to go back and try again."

I heard Dawna's voice from the kitchen door: "Is everyone alive out there?"

Bruno laughed. "Barely. But yeah—the coast is clear. C'mon back and we can talk this out."

Dr. Sloan was the first one out and swept past me to kneel
on the floor next to the circle. The horn was still in the middle
of the ring and he picked it up with absolute awe on his face.
"Amazing. And yet neither of you found any indication of
power when you examined it. What about now?" He handed it
to the closest mage, which happened to be Creede. "Did blowing it activate anything?"

Creede held it in one hand and waved his other over the
shell. He shook his head. "Not a damned thing. I'd swear on
my grandmother's grave this is *not* an artifact."

Sloan sprang to his feet with more grace than I would have
given him credit for. "What about the other one? The king
conch?"

It was still on the mantel in its usual place of honor. I pointed
and Sloan brought it and almost shoved it into my hands; his
eyes were bright and excited. "Try to blow it. Does it make any
sound now that the other one is close?"

I pointed to the still-smoking circle in my floor. "How about
we move this outside? I still have to live here when this is
over." And it was my fault, since I knew full well it had cracked
the windshield. I handed the king conch back to Sloan. As he
took it, he grabbed my other hand and pulled me toward him.
Sloan and propriety have *issues*.

"Fascinating! Have you noticed the death mark darkens after a near-fatal event?"

It does? I stared at my bare palm and realized he was right.
After the exorcism, the mark had faded into the background. I
barely knew it was there anymore. But now it was like a fresh
scar, the pink after a scab is removed.

Soon my palm was lifted awkwardly so everyone could see. Creede was the first to speak: "Was that the hand you were holding the horn with?"

I thought and then shook my head. "Nope. This one was just loose at my side." I tipped my head in amendment. "At least until I had to catch my balance on the floor. Then it was on the floor."

Bruno said, *"That's* when the floor started to smoke!"

Oh, great. That was just what I needed to hear. I knew the death mark couldn't be removed without killing me, but if the mark itself could be used to burn down a house around me . . . that was bad.

But Creede shook his head. "Yeah, but the circle was already going wrong. We've got two different events going on."

"Those are Atlantean." Adriana was standing over all of us squatting and sitting people. She was staring at the four new marks that had appeared on the floor inside the twin circles. "They spell *Eris.* Just like in the horns."

Dr. Sloan turned my conch into the light and his bushy gray brows rose until they looked like caterpillars crawling across his forehead. "You're right! But did the spell identify the horn Ms. Graves was blowing or the name of the spell caster . . . or was Eris the caster?"

Adriana shook her head. "Eris was queen of Atlantis. Siren queens can never be mages. They can have no other gifts." The pain in Adriana's face was sudden but very real. But her pride was too much for me to offer sympathy. Maybe someday, in private. But not here in a crowd. "She would have had priests, though, and many of them would be mages."

Creede pointed at the new marks. "My spell was to learn the name of the spell, not the caster or owner of the horn. So I have to presume the name of the spell *is* Eris. Likely something crafted for a single event—which, of course, this was. The problem is—"

Bruno completed the thought. "There's no such spell on the books. So there's no way to re-create it or counter it. The spell could do anything. It could close the rift, open it, or destroy the world. We just don't know without activating it and letting it run its course."

I pointed to the smoking circle. "We *didn't* just let it run its course?"

They both shook their heads and Bruno said, "No. When you pulled the horn away from your lips, the spell stopped. We channeled the power, but I have no idea what might have happened next."

"How would the person blowing it know when the spell is done?" I was careful in my choice of words. I was still hoping someone else could do the deed.

Creede raised his hands with a shrug. "Honest opinion? The horn would probably stop blowing. It's likely only sounding now because it senses the rift—that's probably what has activated the spell."

I didn't buy it. "That's a lot of guessing. So far I'm the only person who can make the triton blow. But that doesn't mean I'm *the* only one. It might well be that there's a hundred people who can do that. I don't know whether it would have sounded a year ago because I'd never seen it before Adriana brought it to me." Which raised another question I'd been meaning to

ask. I turned my head to catch her eye. "Why *did* you bring
it to me, anyway? Why not have Okalani take you straight to
the rift?"

She shrugged gracefully in that special way that only danc-
ers can pull off. "I foresaw myself giving it to you. And frankly,
you're the only person I know on the mainland. I could trust
no one else with something of this value."

Hard to argue with that logic. Creede rose to his feet and
offered me a hand. I took it and he pulled. In fact, he sort of
overpulled and I wound up pressed against him for a brief
moment before I could back away. He didn't seem to mind
and neither did my body.

Just to play it safe, I offered my hand to Bruno and repeated
the exercise. Strange, but for all my former fiancé's superior
power, I didn't react the same way to him. There was just something about Creede's magic that made my body sing. But oh,
the eyes and smile on that big Italian lug made my stomach
flutter with nearly the same intensity. Yum.

Dr. Sloan hadn't noticed our little song and dance, but the
two women did. Dawna was looking amused and I'll bet she
couldn't wait until she had me alone and could grill me about
every minute detail. But Dr. Sloan's voice pulled my eyes away
from her, back to the shell in his hand: "I see your point about
the reason and scope of the spell. But we really need to test the
king conch—see if you can also make it sound. We need to go
out to the beach." He stood and proceeded to do just that, a
horn in each hand. I shrugged and motioned that we might as
well go with him. I didn't want anyone or any*thing* to swoop
down and take them away.

———

Twenty minutes later, we were no closer to an answer than when we'd started. No, I couldn't blow the king conch. Nor could anyone else. The triton sounded only for me and with the barest of breath.

Once they started doing testing circles on the shells alone, I relegated myself to the shadow of the biggest palm I could find, because the sun was getting low on the horizon and was becoming painful to be out in it. I needed another liberal application of sunscreen—which I didn't have handy. I'd apparently left the bottle I'd used in the hotel back there somewhere, because I couldn't find it in the SUV. There was another bottle in my luggage, but we'd packed in such a rush that I had no idea where it might be.

I also needed another shake even though it hadn't been four hours yet. The people on the beach were starting to glow and pulse, and it wasn't helping that there was magic flying all over the place.

As I sat hunched in a tiny pool of darkness, it occurred to me that for too long I'd been letting situations rule me. The break I'd sought at the spa hadn't turned out to be what I'd hoped for. Well . . . certain parts of my body had gotten nicely relaxed. I supposed it was good to find out everything down there still worked after the bat bite—before I started doing any serious dating again.

But there were too many disconnects between body, mind, and spirit. And I knew just the cure. Fortunately, there was just enough room in shade, if I sat right next to the tree trunk, to assume a lotus position. I'd done yoga for years, but lately, with all the things that had been happening, I hadn't stolen back the time it takes. Now, with everyone otherwise occupied, I figured I had at least ten minutes of good, solid meditation time available.

I took a deep, centering breath and crossed my legs. My thighs reminded me I hadn't done this in some time. Ow. But getting past the pain is part of the process, so I cupped my fingers and rested them on my knees. Closing my eyes made the world disappear, and soon the only sounds I could hear were the crashing of the waves, the calling of the gulls, and the wind in the palm fronds overhead. I imagined the water around me and soon I was floating on the waves, letting the ocean take me where it would.

I'd taken a dozen slow breaths when I heard Bruno's voice near my ear: "Celie? Hon? Um . . . not to interrupt, but we sort of need the beach back."

I blinked my eyes and tried to focus on his face. The waves sounded louder and I felt sort of . . . damp. I looked down to find that the tide had come in . . . but farther inland than I'd ever seen it. Water was lapping around the tree's shadow but not actually touching me. Seriously weird. I looked up and there were at least a dozen gulls perched in the tree overhead, staring down at me with curious black eyes.

What the hell? "What's happening?"

Bruno shrugged. "Your cousin said it's your doing, but I have no idea how to fix it."

I raised a hand and motioned toward said cousin, inviting her over. Adriana gave an exaggerated sigh and splashed her way toward me, pants rolled to her knees and tan boat shoes in her hands. She started speaking before I could ask the question: "The water responds to you as it does to the other sirens. It seeks you out when you call—as it did when sirens of old would call the ocean onto the rocks to wreck ships and strand sailors. Unfortunately, I don't have the ability to send it back. I don't know if this will help, but Mother simply motions it back like a puppy who's strayed from the yard."

A puppy. The ocean is not a puppy. Still, who was I to argue? I made shooing motions with the backs of my hands. "Go on. Get back in the yard."

Bruno laughed and I shook my head with bemusement for thinking it would work. At first, I thought I was imagining it. But damned if the waves didn't start to lap farther from the tree with each inward flow. Maybe it would work with the gulls, too. I looked up and made the same motions. "Go on. Shoo. Go find some fish to eat."

With flaps of massive wings, the birds took to the air and soared into the distance. "Oh. Wow." I looked up at Adriana. "I probably need to tell the queen about this, huh?"

She tipped her head with wide eyes and nodded. "I would. You need training to control what appear to be growing abilities. They're completely natural to our kind but can be a nuisance when the waters come at unexpected moments." She gave me a significant look before turning and walking back along the sodden beach to where the others were waiting.

Yeah. Unexpected would be bad. I needed to make sure that in future meditations I visualized grass or wildflowers. Or maybe flatland prairie or a nice sandy desert.

Anything but water. I wouldn't want to find the waves scratching at my front door because I'd finally relaxed into a true meditation. The door's on the second floor. My car is on the first.

"Maybe this is a hint it's time to wrap things up for today. I need to fee—*eat*, and I think all of us need some rest. Tomorrow's going to come too quick already."

Bruno nodded. "John and I will set up temporary barriers for the horns—one for each, so they don't touch or . . . go off."

I took a deep breath. "Thank you for being willing to work with him. It's not really what it looks like between us."

Bruno sighed and there was pain in those brown eyes that I would erase if I could. "Yes. It is. It's exactly what it looks like. But he reminded me rather strongly that I was the one who threw you away and that I didn't have any right to blame him for catching you." He shook his head in frustration. "I just wished he wasn't so damned *talented*. It would be easier to hate him if I didn't respect him so much."

I didn't know what to say to that. We looked at each other, feeling lost. I took his hand and gave it a gentle squeeze. "Creede's been very kind and I can't deny he's awfully hard to resist. But we haven't gone to where you and I have. If that helps any."

His smile and chuckle weren't up to his normal standards. "A little. But I can't ignore how you look at each other and I honestly can't say he wouldn't be better for you. I've got . . . a lot of thinking to do." He raised my hand to his lips and gave it a gentle kiss. "I do love you, Celie. You know that."

My laugh was a little teary around the edges. "You did last time, too. And the time before."

He nodded and tucked my arm under his as we walked back across the beach. John stood watching, leaning on the Mustang with arms crossed.

I had the feeling it was going to be a long, restless night for both of us.

Maybe for all three of us.

20

Night turned to morning and I watched every freaking second unfold. My brain had run at full tilt the whole night. I even tried sleeping medicine. Note to self: Drugs that should be taken with food, even if crushed and dissolved in a shake, don't sit well when there's only liquid in your stomach. No matter how nutritious the liquid is. The medication insisted on coming back out the way it had gone in, and then I had to drink another shake after scrubbing the taste of bile from my tongue.

But even the unmistakable sounds of vomiting didn't wake Adriana. I'd offered her a room after we'd stayed up late reading library books. She'd stayed because she hadn't wanted to incur a mother's wrath by calling Okalani to transport her past curfew. After meeting the girl's mother, I didn't blame my cousin.

I yawned loudly around the house until a second cup of coffee finally got me to a semblance of alertness. I'd discovered that pouring one of the chocolate shakes into the coffee adds the sugar and cream I like, plus a little chocolaty goodness. Strolling down the hall with cup in hand, I rapped on Adriana's bedroom door for the third time. "C'mon, Adriana.

Daylight's burning. We need to get moving." I still had to return the rental car. She was going to follow me in my car and
then we were going to take back the books we'd finished and
see if there were any Dawna had missed.

I'd learned during our late-night reading session that Adriana had been asked to meet with my friend Bubba and find
him a new boat. Of course, that was before the rift appeared,
but Adriana was a "duty first" sort of person, so I was betting
she'd try to fit it in.

Adriana didn't respond to my knock, but there were . . .
noises behind the door. Either she'd snuck someone into the
room and was having really intense sex or something was very,
very wrong. I tried the knob, but the door was locked.

Damn it. I really hated the thought of kicking down one of
my own doors, but it wasn't the kind of lock set that used a key.
Sigh.

I put the coffee cup on the floor, far enough from the door
that it might not spill during a fight, and put my shoulder to
the door. Maybe I could pop the lock without tearing off the
whole doorjamb. Supernatural strength is occasionally a good
thing. The wood was solid against me and I pushed in tiny
increments, feeling the door bow under the pressure. They're
solid-core doors—Vicki built the guesthouse to withstand a
Category Three hurricane—so I didn't have to worry about a
thin layer of veneer cracking. By pushing in the exact center,
I was hoping the hardware would give way first.

It did.

It was a good thing I had one hand braced on the wall or
when the door yielded I would have landed on the floor. There

were no intruders or secret lovers in the room, but I ran in because Adriana was on the floor, tangled in bedsheets and thrashing. Her eyes were rolled back in her head and she was making odd grunts and hand motions. I'd seen the same thing before more than once . . . with Vicki. Okalani's mother had told me that Adriana was a prophet, the sirens' term for a clairvoyant. It was one reason she would never be queen. She was apparently a pretty powerful one, too.

I did for her the same things I always did for Vicki. I got Adriana into a sitting position with her back against the side of the bed, propped up by the nightstand. Vicki had once almost choked to death on her own tongue while thrashing on the floor. Then I put a cold, damp washcloth on the back of Adriana's neck. Vicki always swore it helped her climb back out of the vision to reality.

Then I sat down to wait. Clairvoyants are always the most vulnerable when in a vision. They need to be guarded from danger. It was one reason Vicki had chosen to live at Birchwoods. There were empaths there who would know she was having a vision because they could sense the changes in her emotions and would send an attendant to watch over her.

I'd barely grabbed my coffee and taken up residence in the comfy corner chair when Adriana came to with a start. I didn't say a word until she reached back and grabbed the washcloth from her neck and stared at it with an odd expression.

"My friend who was a prophet always said it helped her get back to the real world."

Adriana finally focused on me after long moments of staring. Then she nodded. "It did. Thank you. I'd never considered that such a simple thing could work. It was as though you threw down a rope ladder for me to grab."

I took a sip of coffee. "You're welcome. You had a vision?" I'd also learned not to ask Vicki what the vision was *about*. Frequently she wouldn't tell me because she either didn't trust the images or couldn't interpret them so soon after they had happened. Or the vision might involve me and she didn't want me to know. Sometimes she'd simply say yes. Only occasionally would she give details. It was often frustrating to be the friend of a clairvoyant, but they desperately needed friends who would simply ignore the visions and give them space. Emma, on the other hand, wanted to be asked about the details. She didn't get many visions, so she needed help to interpret them. It was often frustrating to be the friend of a clairvoyant, but they desperately needed friends who could give them what they needed—ignoring the visions and giving them space or prodding them to recall everything.

Adriana nodded. "Yes. And now I understand your spirit prophet's urgency yesterday. It truly is critical that we visit the gentleman in Arkansas. Today."

Really? "Care to tell me why? What are we looking for?"

She shook her head and dropped her gaze to the floor, her frustration clear. "It's complicated. There were so many images. But I believe there's a chance the missing instructions for the horns are there."

In Arkansas? "That's a long way from Atlantis. And Serenity."

She pulled herself to her feet using the bed and nightstand. "Indeed it is. But I'm quite certain. We're going to need help, though. There's strong magic involved. I saw multiple threads where we found the instructions but other images of us failing and dying."

Nifty. "I guess I'll get on the phone and see who's available to jump on a plane today."

Her smile was brilliant as she started to make up her bed. What a nice guest. I stood and walked over to help. "No need. I also saw a certain dark-skinned teenager at our side. But I will need to make a call to the island—if I may use your telephone."

I sighed as I tucked the burgundy wedding-ring quilt Gran had given me a few years back up under the pillows. "I'm going to need to get a different phone plan. I've never had to make this many international calls before. But sure. Go ahead. I'll get dressed in something more appropriate. Do you have any idea where we're going? Specifically?"

"That will be a little bit of a problem. It was clear to me that we need to show up unexpectedly or the person who will take us to the instructions won't show up. He both fears and craves sirens, but his fear is stronger."

That made me frown. I didn't like the idea of descending on someone and forcing him to take us somewhere. "That plan borders on kidnapping, you know."

She shook her head. "Not at all. It's merely a case of cold feet. Once we're there, he won't object." Then she tipped her head with a little uncertainty in her face. "At least as far as I could see."

And there's the problem with visions in a nutshell. "Just so you know, if he *does* object, it stops there. I won't be a party to manipulation again. I told you that."

Her shoulders moved gracefully up a fraction, but she didn't respond. "I'll need to get dressed so we can leave soon." Her eyes flicked to the wall clock shaped like a seagull. "We need to be there in an hour. I'd suggest you find a mage to accompany us."

With that, she turned and walked into the bathroom and shut the door behind her. I heard the shower turn on seconds later.

It took most of the hour for her to get ready, while I was making calls and getting my schedule at the office changed . . . again. This was going to be the worst December for income I'd had in years. Normally I make enough to take a good part of January off, but now I was going to be scrambling. Provided I had any clients left after this many cancellations.

Adriana came out of the bedroom just as Bruno arrived. I hadn't bothered to call Creede because before he'd left last night he'd said he wouldn't be available today because of meetings. But Bruno could handle anything that might come our way. He gave her a brief nod as he entered. Her delicate features struggled between amusement and offense. I could understand why—she really did look good. I don't know if she had dressed to impress Bruno or the man we were going to see, but the turquoise bodysuit I'd loaned her hugged every curve while the hip-huggers with the distressed panels on the thighs fit her to a T. It had actually been kind of fun to go through my clothes with her last night. Neither Vicki nor Dawna wore my size, so we hadn't done much closet swapping. Adriana, on the other hand, was my identical size and while her coloring was different, everything she tried on from my old color palette not only fit but looked better on her than on me now.

"Good morning." I stood as he came in and gave him a quick peck on the cheek. "Thanks for doing this. I know it's short notice." Then I whispered in his ear, "You should at least say hi and tell Adriana she looks nice. She's used to people fawning over her."

He got a startled look on his face and then turned to where she was about to sit down on the couch. "Oh. Good morning, Princess. I'm sorry. I'm a little distracted this morning. You look lovely today." He paused and then looked *me* up and down. "You always look gorgeous, Celie. Sometimes I forget to mention it. Sorry."

I hadn't actually been fishing for a compliment, but I'd take it. "Thanks."

Adriana had likewise brightened and dipped her head regally. "Good morning, Mage DeLuca." She didn't thank him for the compliment because, as I said, she expects them.

Bruno squatted down by the two shells and carefully ran his hands over the small casting circles that still vibrated around them. "Honestly, I was going to call you back and cancel because I thought you were overreacting . . . until the news report. Now I'm glad I rented a fast car."

He must have seen my brow furrow, because he motioned toward the television with his chin. "You should probably take a look while I get these shells ready to travel."

I hadn't realized we were taking the shells with us, but I reached for the remote. Adriana turned in her seat with raised brows. A click of the remote made sirens blare and filled the room with flashes of red and green lights. The camera was trained on the rift, which had tripled in size and was pressing against one edge of the barrier.

Oh, fuck a duck.

"That's the scene at the prison this morning, Tamara. Federal, state, and private mages from all over the world have begun to arrive to shore up the hastily crafted barrier around the rift."

Bruno let out a little grumble. "It was *not* hastily crafted. He makes it sound like we threw a plastic tarp over it."

"We spoke with the FBI situation commander earlier today."

Rizzoli appeared on the screen.

"Agent Rizzoli, can you explain what we're seeing?"

I could tell he thought it was a stupid question. I mean, one look and it was pretty obvious what we were seeing. But his facial expression remained calm and blank.

"David, the situation is getting critical. We're working on solutions to close the rift, but right now our goal is to keep the public safe. The governor has activated the National Guard to keep the curious away and I've been informed the vice president is on her way to be briefed by the mages and warrior priests. We're doing all we can and we would continue to ask the public to stay clear of the area so our people can work without distraction."

The microphone was pressed closer and Rizzoli backed up slightly. "Are any evacuations planned for nearby cities?"

Crap. That was just what we *didn't* need. There'd be no way to get anywhere on the freeways. I clicked the mute button on the remote. "Did you get hold of Okalani? Can she transport us?"

Adriana dipped her head but kept her eyes on the screen. I wondered if she was seeing the fall of Atlantis again as the details from the scrolls she'd read started coming to life. "Yes. Fortunately, once I explained my vision to Mother, she agreed it was best for everyone involved for Okalani to aid us. She'll be here shortly." Hmm. Adriana had had to appeal to the queen for Okalani's services? I wondered if Okalani's mother had petitioned the queen to stop using her daughter as a royal taxi service. Couldn't really blame her, but teleportation is a damned handy ability. I bet Adriana had spent a good part of the hour before Bruno arrived talking to Lopaka.

I turned my head back to the television, realizing I had missed whatever Rizzoli had said about the cities. "What did he say about evacuations?"

"None planned at this time." Bruno had lowered the circles around the shells and was putting them into a thin nylon duffel bag he must have pulled out of a pocket, because he hadn't walked in carrying it. "But they're keeping their options open and asked people to keep the radio on for further announcements." He stood up. "So who's Okalani? Helicopter pilot? That's probably the only way we're going to get to Arkansas in time."

Adriana and I both smiled, but I answered, "Of a sort."

And that was the cue. There was a knock on the door and I got up to answer it. I was surprised to see both Okalani and her mother standing outside. Normally, Okalani pops directly into the room. I opened the door and waved them inside. "Good

morning, Okalani. Good morning—" I realized I didn't know
her mother's name. Well, crap.

My cousin came to the rescue. She stood and walked over
to touch the woman's hand. "Thank you for allowing us to
utilize your daughter's time, Laka."

Laka didn't seem happy about it. "The queen explained we
have little choice. Is it true what they say about another demonic rift?"

I pointed toward the television. Both newcomers' eyes went
wide and they were drawn into the living room to stare at the
black, star-filled gash against the bright blue morning sky.
Creatures with wings and horns and various colors of scales
and fur were prowling inside the barrier—occasionally throwing themselves against the magical border only to be thrown
back or burned up by the holy magic. "Merciful waters . . . ,"
Laka whispered with both terror and awe in her voice. "Is there
no stopping it?"

Adriana was standing beside her, likewise staring at the
screen. "We have found what we believe are the Millennium
Horns and our hope is our trip today will uncover the instructions on how to use them. You can see why speed is critical."

Laka's awed face turned slack jawed. Her voice trembled
when she spoke: "You've found the horns? May I see them? My
grandmother twice removed was born on Atlantis and lived
there for a few years before her family moved to Serenity. We
have stories handed down of Queen Eris the Just."

The way she said it was like "King Richard the Lionhearted"—a
description so strong, so revered, it became part of the actual
name.

Bruno unslung the duffel from his shoulder. "Don't see why not. In fact, it might not be a bad idea for you both to try blowing them. Especially if you come from an Atlantean line."

That was a really good point and Adriana's eyes lit up. "Your mind is sharp, mage. I should call my mother and have her put out the call for those of Atlantean lineage. It may be that one of such birth is required to sound the king conch."

I raised a finger. "How about we go onto the porch for that?"

Bruno looked a little chagrined as he headed toward the door with us right behind. "Really, we had no idea that would happen, Celie."

"It was as much my fault as yours, but I don't see any reason to repeat the mistake. It's going to be a bad enough day without burning down the house."

It turned out to be overreaction, because not a sound was produced. I could tell that frustrated Laka. I think she would have liked to be *the one* who could blow the horn. Since I wouldn't wish that fate on anyone, it was a little frightening to me to know that someone *wanted* to stand at the maw of hell in the hope that she could be a hero. Especially with a daughter to raise.

"It is time," Adriana announced as Bruno was putting the shells back in the bag. "We must go. Now."

"Except we still have no idea *where* we're going. Or have you got that worked out?"

She walked the few steps until she was next to Okalani and touched her arm. The girl's eyes looked vacant for a long moment and then she nodded. "I think so. At least, I can get us close."

Bruno said, "Okay. I'll drive. Where are we go—" My stomach lurched violently and I felt woozy. "—ing?"

The scenery had changed. We were standing on a narrow sidewalk several feet off the ground. On my right a chipped and worn staircase led down to a paved road, and on my left I saw a row of turn-of-the-century brick buildings. I turned to Adriana. "Fool's Rush, Arkansas?"

She nodded. "I used the computer in your room to look at world satellite images. I couldn't see the precise building, but there weren't many restaurants in town. This seemed the most likely."

The sign painted on a wide, pale blue wood panel read: *Come On Inn. Breakfast served all day—'cause we know what time you got to bed last night.*

Cute. And probably true in a town this small.

Bruno sounded seriously impressed when he looked down at the pretty teen: "That's a serious talent you have, young lady. There aren't many people who can teleport groups. Every agency in the world will want to snap you up when you're old enough."

Okalani beamed, but Laka lowered her chin and raised her brows. "*After* she completes her schooling."

Bruno rushed to mollify the older woman: "Of course. She's too young right now. But I do hope you'll find someone to help her develop that ability. I could give you a few names of instructors."

Okalani touched her mother's arm with excitement. "Could

I, Mom? I'd love to know more about how my gift works. I *do* it, but I don't really understand how it happens."

Laka looked from her daughter's hopeful face to Bruno's calm one. "I'll think about it. But right now, she's getting Ds in math. That would have to be corrected before I'd consider any . . . distractions."

Bruno was nothing if not a great male role model. He stepped closer to Okalani and put a firm hand on her shoulder. "There'll be no chance of a teleportation instructor taking you on without above-average grades in math and science. I know enough about the process to know that higher-math skills, like geometry and string theory, are critical."

Her eyes got wide and her lips pursed into a small *o*. "I didn't know that. It's not that math is hard; it's just boring. So I don't do my homework like I should. My test scores are fine."

Bruno nodded and then addressed Laka, his hand still on the girl's shoulder: "She's probably bored because she has an instinctive understanding. You might move her to a higher class that'll challenge her and see if it helps."

Laka considered his words, her nod thoughtful. "She always could add things in her mind, even when she was little. Once she counted roof tiles on houses and then multiplied them to find out how many there were in the whole town. She was two."

Oh yeah. That girl was a serious math geek. I nodded at Laka. "Get her into higher classes. Definitely. She's going to wind up a math professor or in the space program, even if she doesn't use her gift."

Laka opened her mouth to speak, but Adriana beat her to it:

"We must go in *now*. This is the scene I saw." She'd been looking into the restaurant through a small opening in the gingham
drapes over the window. "Please, no one go into broad explanations of anything. But Celia . . . you'll need to introduce me
properly. This must be handled carefully."

And then she was through the door, leaving us all to catch
up and wonder what the hell she meant by "carefully." Sigh.

The small bell on top of the door made a pleasant jingling
sound and the people at the nearest table looked up. The inside of the diner was clean and simple, with wooden tables
bearing blue and white gingham tablecloths that matched
the curtains. The walls displayed amateur paintings by locals
that were for sale, if the price tags were any indication. Laka
held her daughter back in case they needed to get to safety. I
doubted it. The only people in the restaurant were Mick Murphy, three females I'd bet were his family, and an older gentleman who must be Mr. Fulbright.

Adriana stood in front of the group silently, looking every
inch a princess and future queen. There's something about the
bearing of certain people that screams royalty, no matter how
they're dressed. She dipped her head and shoulders ever so
slightly. Fulbright's eyes went wide and panicked. He looked
for somewhere to go, but there was no back exit. If she hadn't
said it was simple cold feet, I'd swear we needed to get the
police to dig up his yard looking for bodies.

A pretty chestnut-haired woman with a scattering of freckles similar to Mick's was sitting at a table with two young girls.
They all stared at Adriana with undisclosed awe. Mick pushed
back his chair and stood up. He walked toward us with hand

out. "Ms. Graves. It's a pleasure to see you again. A surprise, but a pleasure."

I held out my hand to shake his. "It's a surprise to me as well. This trip was sort of sudden. But let me introduce the people with me." I thought I knew what Adriana was up to and hoped I wouldn't get it backward. "Back by the door are my friend Laka and her daughter, Okalani." It wasn't quite accurate, but what else could I say except *friend*?

Mick took the two extra steps and shook their hands, playing the good host. I was betting in normal circumstances his wife would have, too. But she couldn't take her eyes off my cousin.

I touched Bruno's sleeve. "This is Bruno DeLuca. He's been a friend of mine for years and is a very talented mage."

Bruno offered his hand, keeping absolutely silent, and Mick shook it. I touched my own chest. "Of course, I'm Celia Graves. I met Mick Murphy at the Will signing of my best friend, Vicki Cooper."

Now his wife's eyes turned to me. "Oh!" Her shock turned to a friendly smile. "Finally we meet, Ms. Graves. I'm Molly Murphy." She motioned at a redheaded girl of about twelve with pigtails. "This is our daughter Beverly and this little scamp"— she reached across and affectionately ruffled the blonde curls of the younger child—"is Julie."

"Mom—" Beverly had the look that screamed, *Please don't embarrass me!* I've worn it many times myself, so I took a moment to smile directly at her.

"Whoa," she said with a suddenly shocked expression. "You really *do* have fangs!"

Mick turned and gave her a furious look. "Beverly! That is quite enough."

"It's okay. Really. I know it's a curiosity." I stepped away and held out a hand toward Adriana, who was starting to get a little antsy. "And this glorious vision is my cousin. May I present Adriana, crown princess of the Pacific siren clan, prime minister of the Isle of Serenity, and future queen of Rusland." I was hoping I got all that right. I hadn't a freaking clue what her full title was, but at least what I'd said was all true and hopefully sounded impressive enough. I'd seen the prime minister part on a document in her mother's office. It made sense, I suppose. The queen couldn't do everything.

The blonde girl stood and walked forward as though hypnotized until her father caught her by the hand to stop her from actually touching Adriana. "Are you *really* a princess?" Julie's voice was a bare whisper.

Adriana gave her a smile that was both kind and loving—just the sort of expression you want to see on a queen on her throne. She must practice to have it down that well. She touched the girl's hair. "Yes, child. And I believe there's a chance you are as well."

Whoa. Come again? I bent forward until I caught Adriana's eye. "Excuse me?"

Instead of answering me or responding to the shocked looks on the faces of father and daughter, Adriana turned to the old man in the corner, who'd stopped looking frightened but was, instead, staring at the interaction with interest. "Would you care to explain, Mr. Fulbright? There's a reason you offered your land to the Murphy family, isn't there? My siren blood can feel yours . . . and the children's."

There was silence all around the restaurant because . . . well, frankly, she'd managed to stun us all. Fulbright narrowed his eyes and let out a harrumphing sound. When he spoke it was with such a thick southern accent that I could barely make out the words: "So, you've found me out, heve you? A royal of the blood, come to finally look for us? Well, y'all are a thousand years too late and I ain't hepping you. Go tell your mother I said the earth could just eat ya up. You and your bloodsucking cousin, too."

Adriana's eyes narrowed dangerously and so did the old man's. Thin skin all around. Sheesh.

"Okay, hold it. Everybody's talking in circles here and I'm getting lost." Adriana opened her mouth to shush me, but I wasn't going to shut up. I didn't care that the situation needed to be handled "just right." I wanted explanations and we didn't have time for a song and dance.

I stepped away from them all to address the old man: "Look, I'm just a poor California bodyguard who discovered about a month ago I had siren blood." I lifted my upper lip to show him the full fang view. "I got attacked by a vampire but didn't die. After that, I discovered that my blood wasn't only siren with a touch of vampire, but it's also royal." I held up my hands like a revival preacher, but my words were sarcastic: "Woo! Lucky me! But guess what? I don't *care*. Whatever old score you feel you need to settle with the whole of the siren race, Mr. Fulbright, isn't my fight. I only want to find out how to stop a demonic rift from eating up my hometown and the people I love.

Because if we can't close it, eventually it'll be your hometown and the people you love that will disappear. My cousin believes you can help us. The only question is whether you *will*."

Fulbright stared at me for a long time and then stood slowly. He was hunched by arthritis and leaned heavily on a plain wood cane. There was nothing fancy about him, from his faded jeans and beat-up boots to his stained straw hat. "Mr. Murphy, I believe you and I should discuss this matter . . . away from the wimmin folk."

Wimmin folk? Excuse me? Maybe my face gave away my anger, because I felt Bruno's hand on my arm. He squeezed like he used to when his mother would talk past me like I didn't exist. It asked me to please let him handle it. He put the straps of the duffel bag in my hand. I narrowed my eyes and let him have the full force of my outrage. He shrugged.

Fulbright walked out the door and Mick followed after releasing his daughter's hand. Bruno was the last and closed the door after him.

Molly's eyes went to the floor and Beverly's expression was outraged. Poor Julie bolted back to her mother, crawled into her lap, and buried her small face against her mother's chest. I was betting Julie was picking up either thoughts or emotions from the "men folk" and didn't much like them. Mick had said she had all the talent in the family.

I gave the others in the room a Pollyanna smile. Brilliant but empty. "Well, that went well." I snorted. Molly offered a shy smile. Then I touched Adriana's arm. "Was this the part of your vision where we got killed? Does he come back in here with a shotgun and mow down us *wimmin folk?*"

One corner of Adriana's mouth curved up. "Actually, this is the scenario that went well. In the other scenario, I spoke first and he ran out of the restaurant screaming in fear and we never found the cave. I was hoping he'd manage to offend you. You can be quite . . . forceful when angered."

"Gee. Thanks." My smile was more a baring of teeth. Then I turned to the outraged redheaded girl who was stabbing her sandwich with a fork like she wished it was a certain elderly gentleman. She looked humiliated and hurt. "Beverly, I know you'll still have to live here after we're gone and will have to deal with people like him every day. You'll be forced to ignore it for now to keep the peace. But please know most of the rest of the world takes offense at what that man just did. It's not okay for people to treat you like you're a second-class citizen just because of your gender."

Laka finally spoke up from near the window, and there was fury and pride in her beautiful face with its strong African influence: "Or your race."

"Or your . . . disability." Adriana's voice was as strong as I'd ever heard it. "Let no person tell you you cannot do something. You are siren. And you are human. Be proud of both."

Molly was shaking her head. "I've done our whole family tree—right back to the Magna Carta. I'm sorry, ladies, but we don't have any siren blood in our family. I know it. Both of our families came from Ireland and England."

That didn't matter. Blood spoke to blood, and our words had sunk home with Beverly. Her face was intense, thoughtful, and just a little bit offended by Fulbright's words and her mother's response. I didn't want to get involved in a battle between mother and daughter, so I nodded, grabbed a chair, and sat down. "Atlantis was supposedly due south of England before it was destroyed."

It took a moment to sink in, but when it did Molly's face turned stark white. "But why has nobody ever known until now? Surely someone would have said something, put a clue in the records."

A door jingled and Bruno stepped in the door, speaking as he walked toward us. "Because it came down the paternal line, just like Celia's."

Mick followed right on Bruno's heels. "You said it yourself just a few weeks ago, Mol—how the girls were such a blessing because there'd never been a single girl born on my side of the family that didn't die in infancy, for as far back as you could find."

It all made sense now. I took in the scattering of pimples on Beverly's face and the near-constant tugging at the side of her shirt like she was wearing her first bra. The girl had hit puberty. "Beverly's gotten old enough that it made Mr. Fulbright notice. I'll bet he saw you in a store or something and realized you had the blood."

Adriana looked behind Mick. Her voice wasn't quite panicked, but her concern was clear: "Where is Mr. Fulbright?"

Bruno tipped his head toward the door. "Let's go outside and talk." His eyes flicked past me to the children. Ah. Not for the ears of kids. I hadn't really liked that about adults when I was a kid. But now I understood the reasoning.

Mick pointed toward the girls. "You two finish up your dinner. Your mom needs to get you back to school. We'll have to write a late slip as it is." He walked out of the diner and I watched through the sheer lace curtain as he sprinted across the narrow street ahead of a slow-moving semi filled with bawling cattle.

Molly lifted Julie off her lap and set her in the chair where there was a plate with a sandwich still untouched. "Go on. You heard your father. Finish up." Molly tipped her head toward Okalani—who admittedly looked younger than her fifteen years. "Would you like something, too, while everyone talks? I have turkey and roast beef or I could make a hamburger on the grill."

Okalani turned her face toward her mother, asking with her eyes. Yeah, it wouldn't surprise me if she was hungry. I was constantly ravenous at her age. Laka nodded and Okalani looked back at Molly. "I'd love a hamburger if it's not too much trouble."

Then she moved forward into the room and offered her hand toward the other girls. "Hi, I'm Okalani."

Beverly smiled. "That's an awesome name. Is it Hawaiian?"

Okalani shook her head and reached for a french fry from a big plate in the center of the table. "Siren. Mom and I live on Serenity Isle."

Bruno was holding the door for me. As I went out, I set the duffel down on the floor next to the door. I was tired of carrying it. I'd just have to remember to pick it up again before we went . . . wherever we were going. "Okay, so what's up with the men folk that us little wimmen couldn't hear?" I whispered to Bruno in an exaggerated southern accent as I walked past him, and he let out a snort that matched the twinkle in his brown eyes.

God, I missed the laughter in those eyes. I used to stare at them for hours when he didn't know I was watching.

He put an arm around me and pulled me against him until my head was on his shoulder and we were walking down the sidewalk toward where the others were waiting. "You actually impressed Nathan Fulbright. Said you reminded him of his deceased wife. You have *spunk*."

It was my turn to snort. "Yeah, but note the 'deceased' part. He kill her for talking out of turn?"

Bruno kissed my temple. "They were married for fifty-two years. Mick said she just died last spring." Everybody was on a first-name basis already? Apparently there'd been a lot of male bonding out here in a really short time.

But wow. Fifty-two years. That was just impressive. My first thought was, *How sweet.* My second thought was, *Oh, that poor woman.* "So did impressing him help us or hurt?"

We'd reached Mick and Fulbright, who were now sitting in a pretty gazebo on the expansive lawn surrounding an old stone courthouse. Adriana took a seat next to Mick. "It helped us. A lot." Bruno kept his arm tight around my shoulder. It probably looked loosely draped, but there was a tension in it that I hadn't expected. Bruno nodded to Fulbright. "Okay, what have you already told them, Nathan?"

Nathan deferred to Bruno with a wave of a hand. "You know more about the history, so I figured I'd leave it to you."

"Well, I lived on the East Coast my whole life, so I grew up

334 • CAT ADAMS

hearing legends of the lost city of Atlantis. There was always one expedition or another taking off with some new plan or a new invention to get into the trenches where everyone swore it was. When I went to college, I first wanted to study metaphysical biology. I had a theory that the island had simply collided with a continent and evolution had taken over."

Meaning, were the Atlanteans just plain folk who lived everywhere now or did they have a unique biology that could be traced—like sirens? Now I remembered this about Bruno's studies, and I remembered some of our old conversations. I picked up on his idea: "There are, after all, continents with odd angles. France looks like it was slapped on as an afterthought and so do the northwestern tips of Africa and Florida. They've all been speculated to be the 'lost' island." I made quotes in the air with my fingers. Raising my arm moved his hand, which slid down to my waist.

Possessive thing today. But that wasn't surprising, considering yesterday.

Adriana shook her head. "No. Atlantis was most definitely part of the siren empire. Eris the Just was the queen of queens for many centuries. The location has never been a secret from our own people, and I assure you it was nowhere near the supposed locations stated in books. Atlantis was no myth; it didn't collide, and didn't sink. It's not in this dimension. That's why nobody can find it."

Bruno nodded. "The dimensional rift is a brand-new concept I've never seen anywhere. But I did find evidence that more than a few Atlanteans survived the cataclysm and moved to integrate with other populations."

Adriana didn't look happy to admit it, but she tipped her head with a grim face. "Refugees wouldn't have been accepted on the other siren homelands. They were all deemed to be traitors who nearly destroyed the world. They would have been killed on sight. Living among the humans was the only hope they might have to survive."

Mick picked up the story. "Then enters a young sea captain named Henry Fulbright. He was master of his own ship at only twenty-two when he came upon an area of horrible devastation. Debris and the decaying bodies of humans and fish made a whole region of the ocean stink of death. Other ship captains warned him against entering the waters for fear of disease, but he needed to get his cargo to harbor before it spoiled. He found a raft of people floating among the dead. His crew nearly mutinied when he insisted on picking up those survivors."

"Atlanteans?" I asked, and Mick nodded.

"Only six survived the trip back to England. He married one of the women and they settled down to have a family. The men went to work in the town and eventually became landowners with new names, borrowed from the hosts who took them in."

"Murphy." My voice was as positive as I felt. "And Fulbright. So you're both descended from the original Atlanteans?"

Mick nodded. "And, if Nathan's source can be trusted, he says my multi-great-grandfather was actually the son of Kraystal, the older daughter of Queen Eris. Although she'd sent him away to be killed upon birth, as was the custom, the nanny took the child to a family on the shore to raise as their own."

Wow. Shades of Moses. Adriana raised her eyebrows, then

nodded. "I did find evidence of some family units around the cities on Atlantis. Craftsmen with human wives, mostly, who built the palace. The carving of stone was usually left to the men before they were . . ." She grimaced slightly. "Discarded." Nobody likes admitting their ancestors did horrible things. It changes how you remember them. At least she was suitably disgusted. That spoke well of the future of Rusland, where she would rule. "But it would be quite easy to learn the truth on Serenity. We have geneticists who specialize in identifying—"

At that moment, a bright, sharp tone split the air. It was similar to the high-pitched whine of a radio weather alert. It seemed to come from everywhere at once. The other four people in the gazebo dropped to their knees almost simultaneously, with their hands on their ears and pain etched on their features. I turned when I heard glass shatter and that the window of the restaurant had fractured. I raced forward before all of the glass hit the ground and leapt onto the sidewalk just as the tone stopped.

The three girls were sitting at the same table where we'd left them. If you opened the dictionary to the phrase "the cat who ate the canary," their pictures would be there. My hands were on my hips instantly, but I couldn't get out a word before Molly Murphy was in the room. "What in the name of heaven is going on out here? A whole tray of glasses just out of the dishwasher shattered right in the tray."

I fibbed just a bit: "I'm a vampire, girls. I can smell who's got something to hide." In a manner of speaking, that was true. Beverly certainly smelled more musky than she had when I'd left, and her pulse was racing a mile a minute under pale, sweating skin.

Molly and I both stared at them until they were literally squirming. Julie broke first: "It was Beverly. I told her not to touch it. I did, Mom." Now she started rubbing her earlobe and I saw that there was blood dripping down her neck. "That sound really hurt my ears."

Her mother raced forward the moment she saw the smear of red. "Oh my lord, sweetie!" I very intentionally *didn't* step forward.

But I wanted to. This was twice now that I'd gotten twitchy longer before four hours had passed after a meal. I wasn't liking the trend.

It took a moment for all the pieces to fall into place. Shattered glass, pain in people's ears, and one person whom it didn't bother at all. I looked at Okalani. "Did the sound hurt your ears?"

She nodded and I pointed toward the door. "Go see your mother right now and get checked out. Watch out for the glass."

Okalani nearly sprinted for the door—probably to get out of the line of fire. I looked at Beverly. "That sound didn't bother you at all, did it?"

My eyes were locked on hers and she finally shook her head just a fraction.

"Was it one of the shells in the bag?"

She opened her mouth and I could tell from her shifting, panicked eyes that she was about to say something to protect herself. I wanted none of it. I held up a hand to stop her and said, "You won't get in trouble. Just please tell me. It's important."

Part of me knew what she was going to say, but every fiber of my being wanted her to deny it. I felt actual pain in my stomach when she nodded with her eyes fixed firmly on my shoes. "Yes'm. It was the orange one. Okalani said nobody could make it blow."

Bruno and the others came in as I was staring at the ceiling, fighting back tears with my arms wrapped tightly around my body. He took one look at me and pulled me into an embrace. "What's wrong, Celie? What's happened?" I gratefully accepted the comfort and dug my fingers into his strong back muscles. He looked around, trying to find the source of my pain. I could see Beverly out of the corner of my eye, doing her best to look small and insignificant—just a girl trying to finish her sandwich. Molly had taken Julie into the other room to check out the bleeding. I knew Beverly was also wondering what was wrong with me.

It was hard to put words to, and I found I was weeping as I spoke: "She's only *twelve*, Bruno. It's not fair. I can't do that to her—to her family . . . and her sister. But if I don't, how could I live with myself? What if there's nobody else?"

Bruno tensed abruptly, holding his breath as he got it. He always was one of the smartest people I knew. He looked at Beverly over the top of my shoulder. "Was that sound one of the shells? Was it the orange one?"

She nodded, now with more ease but also more fear. She understood that something significant was happening but had no idea what. Likely Okalani hadn't had time to explain the whole story.

"Holy Mother of God," Bruno swore forcefully. I looked

over to see Adriana likewise stricken, which surprised me a little.

Mick was just looking confused. He crouched down beside his daughter. "Hon, you can't touch other people's things. That's a very valuable artifact, and magical. You could have hurt it. You could have *been* hurt."

She nodded. "I know it was stupid, Dad. I shouldn't have touched it. But nothing happened."

"Yet—" The word just slipped out, but it made Mick stare at me with renewed worry. He stood in a rush and put a protective hand on his daughter's shoulder.

"What's wrong? Do I need to get her to a doctor?"

It was Adriana who put things in perspective and made his face go pale and trembling: "A priest might be more appropriate, for last rites."

21

It took two hours at a table with Mick and Molly to answer all their questions. And then there was nothing left but the fear.

"No," Molly said simply and with force. "I won't allow it."

There was a television in the corner of the restaurant, on a shelf mounted near the ceiling. Bruno reached far up to turn on the set. As expected, my little town was on every national channel. The rift now was the equivalent of a dozen city blocks across. Bruno looked back at the Murphys with a serious expression. "When we arrived here, the rift was only a quarter the size of what you see here. It's increasing exponentially. Soon it'll breach the barrier. I don't see how it *can't*. There aren't enough magic practitioners in the world to keep up a barrier this size. It's pulling at me right now. The mages like me who put up that shield are being drained, minute by minute. If some of the people I crafted this with aren't already dead, I'll be surprised."

I looked at him with abrupt fear. I hadn't known it was a continual drain—that he was somehow *tied* to the shield. "Bruno . . ."

He waved it off, but now that I knew I saw the weariness around his eyes. The laugh lines were deeper, as were the creases of his brow. "I'm one of the most powerful mages in the country, Celia. It'll be a week or better before it starts to pull on my life force. The shield won't last that long." Then he turned back to the Murphys, who were holding white-knuckled hands and staring at the screen. "When it fails, we all die. The priests, the *Pope* . . . they've tried everything in the Vatican vault. Things hidden from the public eye for centuries. Yesterday I heard from some friends back east that black-arts sorcerers are volunteering to help, knowing even they're at risk from this. We have no choice but to ask this of you."

"But she's only a child." Mick's voice was soft and frightened and it was hard to blame him. "She doesn't understand what—"

"Yes, Dad. I do." We turned to see Beverly standing in the doorway to the kitchen. Her words were calm, but there was a fierceness in the set of her jaw and cold clarity in her eyes. I'd seen that face before in the mirror, and at that age. Was I a different person now than the child I'd been when I'd looked like that?

I knew. I wasn't.

She walked forward a few steps and then stopped again to take us all in. "I do understand what this means. If I can stop that, then there's no choice. I'll blow the horn or do whatever the instructions say I have to."

I stood and walked over to her and put both hands on her slim shoulders. She'd taken out the pigtails so that her bright red hair flowed like waves around her face. She looked like an adult suddenly, trapped in a body that didn't match the strength inside those green eyes. "You could die, Beverly."

She reached up to touch my hand and there was a hint of something in her eyes, another expression familiar from my mirror. Was it cynicism, so early? But then, I had no idea what trauma she'd had in her life. Perhaps this was just one more piece of a terrible pie that she shouldn't have had to eat. Like me . . . so very like me.

She curved one side of her mouth into an ironic smile. "So could you. But us tone-deaf people have to stick together."

That was the real key, according to Bruno. Beverly and I were old-fashioned tone-deaf. It was why the horns didn't bother us like other people. Why we could sound them without our eardrums breaking. Yes, there might be a hundred thousand clinically tone-deaf people out there and yes, it was possible we could find others who had siren heritage and could blow the horns. But could we do it in *time*?

Adriana motioned from the window. "Mr. Fulbright is back. Are we ready?"

"No," I said honestly, still staring into those bright green eyes. "But that doesn't really matter."

"Are you sure you want to do this, Nathan?" Standing in the small courthouse, Mick was staring at a piece of paper with a fine trembling in his hands. "I'm not positive it's legal."

The old man nodded once, firmly. "It gives the terms in writing, it's signed, and Joe's signed as notary. Once you hand me a ten-dollar bill, it's a deed. You'll own this land and there's not a thing anyone can do to take it from you provided you eventually pay off the twenty-four-million-dollar note." He shrugged. "And the first payment isn't due for two years. If you don't have the money by then . . . and we're not dead, I or my heirs will just take back the land."

Mick looked truly torn. Being in law, no doubt he knew how many things could go wrong. I shrugged. "Couldn't you add in a sentence that nullifies the deal if you don't get the bequest? In case the challenge to the Will succeeds?"

Fulbright nodded his head. "I'd agree to that. Seems fair." He pulled the paper out of Mick's hands and proceeded to carefully print the words and initial them. He handed it to the other man—Joe, who was acting as notary. "You need to initial it, too?"

The man nodded and did. "For a situation like this, I'd suggest the Buyer also sign." He pushed the pen across the desk toward Mick, who was nearly as pale as me. "Then there's no questions." When Mick didn't move, Joe half-stood from his chair. "Mick. Look at me." The terrified man did. "Would I ever suggest anything that could ruin your name or family or stand you in front of me?"

There was something about the way he said it that caused me to look around the room. Ah. A brass plaque was screwed to the door behind the swinging wooden gate that separated the room. *Judge Joseph Robertson.* I could tell the old stone courthouse had recently gotten a face-lift to return it to its original glory. The dark wood gleamed and pale blue paint the color of robin eggs on the walls was edged with white woodwork all the way up to a hammered-tin ceiling that was nearly identical

in design to the one in my office. Must have been a common
pattern back in the day.

Mick picked up the pen and initialed, then handed the
paper back to the judge. "I'll trust you to get this recorded, if
you don't mind." He pulled out his wallet and took a deep
breath before opening the double fold. "May my wife forgive
me if this goes badly." He gave a nervous chuckle. "I'd ask the
Good Lord's forgiveness instead, but I'm more afraid of Molly."

"It'll be okay, Dad. You'll see." Beverly came up behind him
and gave him a bear hug while he handed over the money. His
eyes shut and his arm snaked around to pull her tight against
him for a long moment.

He snuffled hard once. "Damned allergies. Well, we'd better
get going before your mother changes her mind about me keeping you out of school for the da—"

Nausea hit my stomach hard enough to raise bile into my
throat and mouth. I wasn't the only one feeling that way, either.
Bruno was heaving whatever he'd had for breakfast into a patch
of cactus and Beverly was on her knees in a wide expanse of
knee-high dry grass that had abruptly replaced the courthouse.
She vomited noisily and even Okalani looked a little unstable.
"I'm sorry, Highnesses. I tried to teleport us to the cave the princess saw in Mr. Fulbright's mind, but we were pushed away."

I didn't get a chance to answer before Fulbright was spitting
fire: "Damned fool know-it-all mind readers!" He was the picture of backcountry fury, shaking his walking stick at us and
spewing spit with each word. "If you'd waited five minutes I
woulda explained why it was so important we had to finish the
deed *first!*"

Bruno had recovered and was waving his hand in the air in slow arcs. As I watched, symbols appeared and disappeared as though he were shining a black-light bulb past fluorescent stone. "Wow, this is *very* old magic. And Nathan's right. It's pagan . . . land based. Mick, see if you can walk across this line." He picked up a wide stick and pulled it hard across the ground, creating a rough line in the grass.

Mick approached Bruno tentatively, hands stretched out like he was reaching for a wall in a dark room. Nothing stopped him and he walked forward. He shrugged and looked backward. But Bruno still couldn't enter and I could feel the pressure of the barrier even from where I was standing, a dozen feet away.

Fulbright stepped right across, which confused Mick. The old man pointed a shaking finger at him with a self-satisfied smile. "Yep. You're the owner, but now you know why I hold the mortgage. Till it's paid, I still own rights in the land." He walked forward pretty quick, a snarky laugh wheezing out of him. "C'mon then. I'll show you what you own."

"Sorry. I didn't know he was going to do this." Mick had no choice but to shrug at us and chase Fulbright. Then Mick turned in mid-jog and called back, "I'll take pictures if I can— there's a camera in my phone!"

I threw up my hands in frustration and looked at Bruno. "Isn't there anything you can do to get through this barrier?"

He squatted down and then sat in the grass, patting the dirt beside him in invitation. "The only thing anyone can do at this point is pull up a rock and wait. I guess you've never heard of a fee-simple barrier?"

I thought back to my college classes and even my recent library acquisitions but finally shook my head. "Does that term mean something?"

"Well, it's a big thing in real estate law, but it's also what puts pagan magic in priority over any ritual or innate magic." He must have seen my confusion, because he twitched his finger for me to step forward and then patted the ground again with an expression of impatience. Okalani and her mother sat on the dirt, as did Beverly, but Adriana found a relatively flat boulder to perch on.

What the hell. I sat where his hand was patting.

"Pagan magic is tied to the physical world. Father Sun, Mother Earth, Sister Moon, et cetera. Land used to belong to anyone at large . . . until people began to allow others to rule over them. Then the Crown became the owner by mutual consent of all. The Crown granted fee estates to people— giving them a freehold interest."

"Wonderful history lesson on land. But does this have anything to do with the barrier?"

He dipped his head once, bemused as usual at my impatience. He always found my frustration at his calm amusing. "It does. When the Crown granted the 'fee-simple' freehold, it decreed that the ownership was"—and he raised fingers into the air to make quotation marks—" 'from the heavens above to the center of the earth.' Magic that's tied to the land to prevent entry follows those same markers. There is no way—and I mean *no way*—to cross a pagan fee-simple barrier while the owner is present. You can't dig under it or fly over it. It's a solid mountain of magic that passes beyond our reach."

I shook my head. He was wrong. "But that makes no sense. If that was true, then any Pagan priest would be completely safe at home just by casting a simple spell on the ground. And we know that's not true."

One finger rose into the air with a peaceful, patient expression on his face. "Ahh . . . grasshopper. You need to listen closer. I said *pagan magic*. I don't mean magic created by the Pagans, the religion with a capital *P*, but old pagan, with a lowercase *p*. It's the land itself that's casting us out, not a mage or witch who's raised a circle. This barrier has been here for a very long time. It could have been cast by the original Captain Fulbright or his wife—if she was a siren witch—or even by an older group of humans or protohumans. It's part of the land, like oil or gas or even fossils. This is a really unique thing. I hope I survive this mess so I can get Mick's and Nathan's permission to study it. A person could make a doctoral thesis about just this one piece of ground."

"Interesting," was Adriana's only comment while the others just nodded.

But I saw a pretty big downside. "So, basically, if they can't find any instructions, we can't go look. Nobody can. You're saying we're screwed if they don't come back."

Another small twitch of his lips. "Not at all. It's quite possibly the best thing that could ever have happened. Whatever's inside the cave Adriana saw is completely protected from anything—including demons. The magic's all-inclusive and keeps this one small bit of the world safe from even the rift. It has all the strength of every heavenly body in space and the molten core of the Earth. It means the world can never be fully destroyed and with careful planning mankind can survive, because this place will always be. So long as there's an owner who truly believes the magic's real, that is." He smiled brilliantly, with the exuberance of a child. "It's a *very* cool thing."

I guessed if he was happy about it, I should be, too. He was a true student of magic. Just then his face contorted into a small grimace and he reached up to press on his torso near his diaphragm.

"You okay?'

He shook his head in tiny movements. "Probably pulled something when the magic knocked us back. I need to walk it off. Wanna go with?" He pushed off and got his knees under him. I did, too. We might as well walk around. It sure beat sitting and staring at the lack of scenery.

He reached out his hand to me and I took it. I said to the others, "We'll be back in a minute."

We started down what looked like it was once a wagon path—two narrow lines of hard-packed dirt tracing through the weeds and grass. When we were mostly out of sight, I quietly asked, "So, what did you want to say that you couldn't say in front of the others?" The *I've got a stitch in my side* ploy was one we'd used before.

"Actually, I really did need to walk." He pointed to the first place he'd touched. "It's starting to bug me."

We stopped and I looked at him with concern. "Did you maybe get a spider bite or something? Lift up your shirt." He rolled his eyes, but I twirled my finger in the air. "C'mon, Bruno. Don't be such a tough guy that you wind up with something really wrong."

It was hard to fault that logic. He sighed and pulled the pale blue cotton shirt out of his pants. It would have been fun to watch him lift it up to expose bare skin, but what I saw when he did made me suck in a harsh breath. He noticed the look on my face and turned his eyes down. "What . . . ? Oh, crap."

There were three raised red marks in a long diagonal line across his chest. That was no spider bite. It looked like something had clawed him. "Is that from the barrier? Are you sure it's a friendly one?"

He turned his head fast and stared at the seemingly empty air. "I don't sense anything hostile. Nothing at all."

Then, while I watched, a fourth line ripped across his stomach muscles. This one was deeper and caused him to let out a pained sound. "What the hell!" He put a hand on the new scratch, and when I crouched down in front of him and pulled it away I saw blood on his palm. But more important, there was also an odor I recognized—brimstone.

"Definitely what the *hell*. We need to get you to a priest. Now. These are demonic. They're identical to the ones I got when I fought the greater demon at the ballpark."

His breath stilled and he looked down at me with wide, suddenly frightened eyes. "Oh, God. The barrier. It's figured out how to attack us through our magic." He winced again and his head rocked to the side like he'd been slapped. A red mark appeared near his temple. An inch to the left and he would have lost the eye. "I've got to get back to California. Now. If it's doing this to me, the other casters could be dead by now."

Fuck a duck.

He held out his hand to help me to my feet. I took it and we started to run back across the landscape. I didn't know if the demon could somehow sense Bruno's location or what he was doing, but it was a pretty weird coincidence that the next strike was to his right leg. It buckled and I grabbed him to keep him from tumbling into a cactus patch. He started muttering swearwords in a blue streak and put a hand to his thigh. He took a tentative step and let out a low growl. When he tried to put weight on the leg, it held. Barely. "Just do the best you can, Bruno. It's only a few more feet." The others were in sight now. Okalani, watching, noticed that something was wrong and disappeared from sight to appear right next to us.

"What's wrong?" Then she saw another claw mark tear down the side of Bruno's face and she knew. Her mouth opened wide. "It's a demon, isn't it? Like the one that attacked you at Pili's house."

I nodded. "He needs to get back to California. The mages who put up the shield are being attacked and need to be blessed by priests. Can you take him? Come right back. We may need to make multiple trips."

She nodded and took my place at Bruno's side, holding his weight on her slender shoulders. For once he didn't argue, but he did hold out a hand to me with a concerned look. "Be careful, Celie. This could just be another ploy by the demon to get to you."

I leaned in and gave him a gentle kiss on the lips that had more emotion than heat. "I don't think I have anything to do with it at this point."

I hoped and prayed I was right.

They disappeared and I ran the short distance to the others. "We've got a problem. Bruno was attacked by a demon. Okalani took him back to the rift barrier. As soon as she gets back we need to start moving people around, fast." I pointed at the young redhead. "Beverly, can you cross the barrier?" I was hoping pagan magic recognized the family connection— giving ownership to her as an heir of Mick's. "Concentrate on the need to tell your dad what's happening. Think really hard about him, because this is important."

She took a deep breath, set her jaw, closed her eyes, and started walking. Her forward progress stopped, but she pushed against the invisible barrier like a street mime, using her whole body weight. Panic showed on her face. There was a shimmering of the air around her, a sparking of magic that flowed over her skin and raised her hair in a cloud. Then she was inside, so suddenly that she fell to her knees.

I let out the breath I hadn't realized I was holding. "Okay, good. Go find your dad. Scream; yell; do whatever you have to do to get his attention. When you find him, bring him back here and wait for us if we're not here. Most important, stay behind the barrier."

"But you need me to blow the horn."

I was frankly hoping neither of us were needed. "If we need you, I'll send Okalani to get you. But we may be beyond that now. I won't know until I get there."

She nodded and then sprinted into the distance, yelling at the top of her lungs, "Dad! Come quick!"

Adriana was alert but hadn't moved from her comfortable

seat. "I'll remain here. It's quite possible the instructions will be written in Atlantean. Someone will have to translate them and bring them to you."

Good point. If the spell needed to be spoken, a faulty translation would be bad.

"Okay, I'm back. What's next?" Okalani had appeared right next to me.

"What's going on at the rift? Is that where you took Bruno?"

She nodded and let out a heaving breath like she had been running. "Yeah. He also had me transport his brother and another man in robes to him and the other mages. I would have been back sooner if not for that."

In *robes*? "Was he an older white man with an accent? Were his robes all white?" Had she actually transported the Pope to the rift? I wasn't sure if that was good or bad.

"No. He had tan skin and black hair and the robes were red and black."

Ah! Archbishop Fuentes. He was a friend of Matty's and a damned tough former warrior priest. "Okay. Good job. Now, here's what I want you to do."

I arrived to a scene of pure chaos. I looked around, searching for Bruno or Matty or anyone else I knew, with no luck. "Ma'am, you can't be here." I turned my head to see a uniformed Highway Patrolman with his hand on the butt of his service revolver.

I still had the FBI badge Rizzoli had given me and now I hung it so the cop could see it. His stance immediately relaxed. "Sorry. Ma'am. But your friend will have to leave. No kids allowed."

"What friend?" I didn't even turn my head. Okalani should already be on the way to her next task. When he looked around for her, she was gone. Just like we'd planned. "Sorry, Officer. The heat must be getting to you."

He shook his head and wandered off, muttering to himself. I pulled a little on the hair I'd put into a ponytail to keep it out of my eyes, loosening some strands to cover the tops of my ears. Sunscreen can only do so much good.

"Ceil! Where have you been?" I turned to see Creede headed my way. There was a stitched gash across his forehead and a patch of gauze covering half his neck. I felt a pang at the sight. He pulled me into a hug so hard my backpack fell off my shoulder. "I've been worried sick about you. Why haven't you returned my calls? DeLuca said you were right behind him when he got here. That was an hour ago."

I opened my mouth to answer, but he put his lips over mine and the speed and pure energy behind the kiss left me breathless when he finally pulled away. "Um. Wow. I've been . . ." Where *had* I been? I looked down at my forearms and held them up. "Weapons. I had to get my stuff together. Where are Bruno and Matty? Are they okay?"

Creede nodded as he put me back on my feet. Oh yeah—he definitely noticed that the kiss had gotten to me and I was trying to change the subject. "DeLuca got here just in time. All of us got beat up pretty bad in that first attack. As you can see." He motioned to his forehead and then stared at the black gash of space with undisguised anger. "We might still lose Panna and Bordan. They were the first two hit, before we could get a secondary circle up." He grabbed my hand. "C'mon. I'll take you to our staging area."

We race-walked through the crowd and it was a good thing Creede had hold of my hand, because there were even more people here than last time, if that was possible, and I never could have made my way through the crowd without his help. Matty was sitting on top of a steel drum, in serious discussions with three other priests and Archbishop Fuentes. I didn't know Fuentes personally, but I'd seen him on the news plenty of times.

Bruno was painfully putting his shirt back on. A wide surgical patch of gauze was covering his chest and another strip of white covered the side of his face.

I didn't even have to pull away from Creede. He just released my hand when he noticed my reaction to Bruno. That simple act made me turn to look at him. I couldn't tell what emotion was swimming behind the fire in his eyes. He was a solid blank wall. I touched his hand with my fingers and gave him a wink. That earned me a small smile before he turned away to head toward Matty and the others.

"Bruno!" I rushed forward just as he looked my way. Relief made his whole body slump. He opened his arms and smiled. I didn't throw myself at him because I imagined that would hurt. Instead, I stopped just before we touched and put a hand on either side of his neck. "I was worried about you."

"You and me both, Celie." I put my lips against his and he pressed forward, opening my jaw with his. He reached for my waist and pulled me in tight. If it hurt, he didn't give any sign.

I hadn't kissed him like this in a long time and wasn't sure what it would feel like—especially considering how Creede had just turned me into butter.

But Bruno had a whole different kissing style than Creede. It made me feel warm and safe and left me wanting more without feeling frantic or out of control. If Dawna asked me which I liked better, I'd have to struggle and probably wouldn't give an answer.

"I knew you'd come, Celia. I've been waiting." The words boomed through the air, silencing all conversation around us. Bruno abruptly released me and we all stared at the figure of a man, at least eight feet tall and completely naked, watching me from the other side of the barrier. He was . . . excited, too, which made me turn my eyes away.

You'd expect a greater demon to be hideous—uglier than the lesser ones. But no. He was gorgeous. A beauty so perfect that statues should be carved of his likeness and paintings hung down from the ceilings of cathedrals. He had wings of luminous pearlescent feathers like every cheesy Halloween costume ever made. Except real and perfect and . . . beautiful.

But it was all for show and I'd seen it once already. "Why don't you drop the act and show everyone what you *really* look like. Nobody here buys the fallen-angel story."

I saw a man in a charcoal suit speak into his hand: "It's made contact. Get the vice president."

The demon chuckled low and I hated that the sound pulled at things deep inside me. He definitely had my number. "Perhaps this form would be more pleasing to you?"

I flicked my eyes up and then down again because now he

looked like Bruno, down to the gauze, in all his naked glory. The demon looked just the way Bruno did just before really good sex. It was . . . impressive. "Sorry. Try again. No sale." Bruno was likewise watching the ground uncomfortably, because that's not really the sort of thing you want displayed to a few thousand people. Nobody was jeering, though; it was too scary. But a week from now, after we'd all survived? It would be all over the tabloids. "I can't believe you're going to all this trouble just to try to get me here to kill me."

He made a clucking sound with a long tapered tongue that seemed really freaky coming out of Bruno's mouth. "Celia. I didn't do this for you." The form changed again. I could tell from the feet. This time it was even worse and I had to throw up my hands and turn around with a blush. Now he looked like Creede. And wow, if his representation of Creede's body was as accurate as his version of Bruno had been . . . just wow. "But you *will* be my first stop when the barrier's down. Though . . . maybe you'd prefer even fresher meat."

"Who the hell?" Bruno's anger was immediate, so yeah, I had to look. But oh, jeez!

I looked at Bruno and now Creede, who were both staring at the vision of Gaetano's war-scarred, heavily muscled body. They both looked at me with raised brows. I had one arm across my stomach and the other hand was shielding my gaze from the heat in burning eyes. Finally I threw up my hands. "Fine. He asked me out! But I don't even know his first name."

"Christopher!" a woman yelled from the crowd, and a few people tittered. Yay. My humiliation was complete.

Then both Creede and Bruno let out sharp, simultaneous

gasps and blood splattered across my arm and face. The demon was back in his demonic form, complete with red skin and tail. He was clawing a long line through the magic barrier while the men I cared about cried out in pain. I didn't dare look at them to see what had been damaged. It would only make me crazy.

"Stop it!" I shouted, and finally stared right at the demon, stepping closer to the barrier and drawing a blackened knife. "Leave them out of this. If you want me dead, bring the fight to me."

His smile was a leer of razor-sharp teeth. "This *is* bringing the fight to you, Celia. They're the two most powerful mages here. If I kill them, the shield will fall and then I'll have you. What could be simpler?"

Put that way, he was right. Damn it. "You're starting to bore me." I channeled my old drama teacher to give him the look of a snippy head cheerleader being asked to the prom by a nervous freshman. "When you get new material, have someone find me."

It was the hardest thing I'd ever done to turn and flounce away from that barrier, the demon, Bruno, and John. Matty stared at me with undisguised anger until I shot him a *c'mon, let's get out of here, we need to talk* look and stabbed my thumb toward a battered canvas tent that I'd noticed was housing the triage for the priests.

As I walked past, he leapt off the barrel and tried to grab my arm. I shook it off and turned the knife on him. With his eyes locked on mine I spoke directly into his mind: *We need to get the horns ready to blow. Call my cell phone and tell Okalani, "Now!"*

He should recognize her name. A single nod and he pulled his hands off me in a mock surrender that made it seem like he was afraid. In reality, Matty could probably kick my ass to town and back. Nobody else stopped me until I reached the tent. In fact, a few people cleared a path. The demon let out a howl of rage that I would dare walk away from him. My heart was pounding like a trip-hammer, fearing he would simply make an all-out effort to break the shield.

Instead, he quieted down, so by the time I was enclosed in the cool white cotton shelter I could breathe and take a moment to close my eyes and regroup.

"Celia." When I opened my eyes, I was facing the third naked man depicted by the demon. Of course. Why wouldn't I expect to see a medic in a triage tent?

"Gaetano."

He let out a small smile before turning to an IV unit to adjust the amount of fluid dripping into the arm of a priest. "Might as well call me Chris."

I was saved from responding when Matty walked into the tent. There wasn't any way he couldn't notice my blush, along with the cause for it a dozen paces away. Matty patted my arm with actual sympathy and handed me the handkerchief from his pocket to clean up the blood that had spattered on me before speaking: "If you survive the day, we probably need to talk."

My weary sigh sort of said it all. "That would be nice."

"Ms. Graves?" I looked up to see Vice President Marion Lovell briskly walking toward me as I spit on my arm and rubbed it with the now-pink hankie. "Could we speak?"

Can you actually refuse to talk to the vice president of the United States? I wasn't sure, considering all the Secret Service agents at her sides. "Sure. Why not? What else can go wrong today?"

22

I felt amazingly vulnerable in the wide circle. The whole area had been deserted. Troops and police had pulled back fifty yards to a newly constructed outer barrier. There was no question that the one a mere twenty yards from me was going to fall. Everybody knew it, so it made sense to create a new one, tied to hundreds of mages, rather than just a few—so no one man could be hurt as badly as Bruno and Creede and the others had been. I'd never seen that much magical firepower in one location before. Just the residual bleed from it made my teeth feel like they'd been chewing on live wires.

The demons all knew something was up. They were standing all along the flickering casting circle, just waiting. I was going to be between the barrier that was about to drop and the new one that had to be raised—with the horn.

Matty was with me in the circle. He'd volunteered once the archbishop said I'd probably only survive if someone was constantly praying for my salvation.

"I feel like I want to throw up."

"You ate, right?"

I hate night? Huh? I pulled the noise-canceling headphone

from my ear. "Sorry. What was that? I can't hear a thing with these on."

He looked appropriately chagrined. "Sorry. You're not supposed to hear. I asked if you ate."

Oh. "Yeah. Dawna gave Okalani a couple of bowls of that awesome broth from the barbeque place. I should be good until this finishes, but if not, there's a spare in the backpack." I motioned to said backpack with my toe. "How about you?"

"Filet mignon and fresh asparagus," he said appreciatively. "The Feds are really good about last meals."

"It's *not.*" I had to believe that and stared at him hard, willing him to believe it, too. While Matty and I hadn't really ever gotten along during my engagement to Bruno, we'd seemed to have come to an understanding in recent weeks. Matty was thinking of me less like a really annoying person and more like a person really annoying things happen to. "You want to go over the plan again?"

He pursed his lips and whispered, "Seems pretty clear to me. The first barrier goes down and all the bad guys race toward you, me, and the other priests—the fresh meat."

I nodded and replied in a similar way: "Then you raise the first trip wire and the circles go up around and everyone starts praying the same prayer."

He glanced at his watch. Just seconds left. "That'll be the tricky part. I haven't tried to raise four separate circles before. I know it's the magic from the others that will keep them up, but it would have been easier just with the two of us. We have enough firepower to hold off an army."

I touched one of the dozen protection charms and major

holy items strewn around my neck and waist. The Archbishop of Canterbury had donated one of the crosses from the Tower collection. Supposedly it had been used during the Crusades. Matty was carrying a shield with a white rose barely visible on the old iron; it vibrated with energy, even after hundreds of years. They were our "just in case" backups.

"True. But they'd overwhelm us before I could get a note out. This causes more confusion. Once they're all flying around and attacking the circles, the archbishop sets the second trip wire and Okalani brings in Beverly and the second horn." Who knew the archbishop was a minor mage? That turned out to be the final stroke of luck in the vice president's plan. She was a very smart lady.

"And then we all pray." Matty sighed. "And I don't mean just novenas. Here we go. Seven, six . . . get those earphones back on." I did as he said and all the other priests did the same in their separate painted circles.

Like on a movie set, the last three numbers were silent, demonstrated only by Matty's lowering fingers. The last was a fist, and all the other priests mirrored him and raised glowing swords. My stomach lurched as the blue barrier in front of us began to flicker and fail. I knew Bruno and Creede were working their tails off to be sure that everything went smoothly. It had broken my heart to see the slash marks across their handsome faces. When this was all over, they'd need health charms to help them heal up.

The lesser demons began to collectively smash into the barrier and finally it gave way. All manner of creatures from the worst nightmares of the worst horror movies ever written

flowed toward us in a wave that made me want to run screaming backward. It took every ounce of my willpower to stand
still. I saw Matty's mouth and hands move and suddenly there
was blue everywhere once more. It looked like all the other
circles went up just fine, because demons were bouncing off
and burning up left and right. But nothing approached our
circle and in moments I discovered why.

There was a *Reserved* sign on our table.

The greater demon was walking forward and every*thing* in
his path crawled or skittered aside. He looked at the barriers
around us and the holy items and ... smiled. His mouth
moved and that made me smile in return, because I couldn't
hear a word he said. I raised my shoulders in a shrug and
pointed at the headphones before pulling my knives and waiting. Matty prayed and counted beads on his rosary while the
demon became frustrated, striking out at a barrier that seemed
to be holding just fine.

Then pain erupted in my head and it suddenly occurred to
me that I should have had someone do a mental-attacks casting on me. Damn it! *I'm not so easily defeated, Celia.*

I mouthed the words slowly, so there was no question:
"Go ... back ... to ... hell!" It wasn't time to raise the horn
yet, unfortunately. We needed as many demons outside the
rift as possible, or so claimed Adriana. She'd returned with a
translation of most of the instructions just in time. Unfortunately, there was one passage she hadn't been able to work out.
Okalani had taken her to the library to talk to Anna, who spoke
a number of dead languages. I ignored the pain in my brain
and looked right past the demon at the pretty stars in the night

sky. It actually was pretty. Lots of shooting stars and weirdly colored planets.

You said I needed new material. I think this will do nicely. The words sounded like my own voice on my phone-mail message. I shouldn't have looked up. One of the priests—I think his name was Father Ignacious—was suspended from the demon's hand and was thrashing in pain. The demon now looked like . . . me.

Fuck a duck.

The sheer horror of the vision kept me from closing my eyes. I saw myself, fangs extended and skin glowing. The demonic me grabbed the priest's hair and pulled his neck to my waiting mouth.

No. Please. Not that.

I did close my eyes, but the demon's connection with me forced the images straight into my mind. Forced me to feel my teeth penetrate the skin, taste the thick, coppery blood splashing down my throat. The priest's screams made my skin twitch and my stomach ache. *I'll share, Celia. Come feed. So sweet and warm.*

There was a sharp slap on my hand that burned and I opened my eyes to see that Matty had smacked me with the flat of his sword. I'd nearly crossed the circle threshold. Shit. But why had the sword burned where it touched me?

I hoped and prayed that it had because the demon was touching my mind. I refused to watch the priest's body twitch as the demon finished feeding. Instead, I lowered myself to a squat and picked up the black duffel.

The demon watched with interest as I unzipped the bag.

When I pulled out the narrow triton conch, the demon's face went from mildly amused to very much *not* amused. I stood and watched as Matty adjusted his headphones to be sure he had a solid fit.

If you put your lips to that, I will make sure you suffer when I kill you.

I raised the horn to my lips and stared into the demon's yellow eyes with their slits of red down the center. The first note was long and low and I could feel it resonate through my body like a warm wave. Demons began to scream and thrash and throw themselves against the barrier. I blew until my breath gave out, and while the sound made the darkness waver, it wasn't anywhere near strong enough to seal the rift.

Then I felt the answering tone—a high-pitched clarion call that made the greater demon scream. He looked around for the source of the agonizing sound, but the archbishop had done his magic well. He'd used illusion to hide the circle where he and Beverly stood. So the sound seemed to come from nowhere and everywhere. I blew again and so did she. The twin horns made the very air vibrate. Tears of blood were streaming down Matty's face and I realized that I was crying as well. It was a pretty good bet that if I reached up, my hand would come away red.

The demon began to stalk around us, hitting and kicking and throwing things—searching for the hidden circle. He would eventually find it, but hopefully not in time.

Celia? The voice in my mind was one I recognized, but I couldn't trust anything I heard. I couldn't think of any reason why Pili would be inside the circle. But what the voice was saying sounded just like something Pili would say: *You must not look at what is to come. There is never a good time to say good-bye, but this is the only way; I swear. There must be a sacrifice, and it must be a siren with demon taint. I am the only other, and she is the only one who can guard my path.*

I should have listened, because when I opened my eyes there was a tornado a few paces away. It sparkled and raised sand and threw demons in ever-widening arcs. Vicki?

Inside the area of spinning sand was a single figure, walking slowly toward the waiting demons. I recognized her, too. What the hell?

Sound the horn, Celia. Let nothing break your concentration. A sacrifice is the only way.

Sacrifice? No! Not Vicki! Not Pili! *There has to be another way. We'll find another way.* My face felt hot and I couldn't concentrate. Both of them? What would happen to Gran now? What would happen to me?

Pili's voice was stern: *There is no other way. You must. The tainted must be sacrificed to give life back to life and death back to death. So it was written.*

Matty saw me make a break for it and pulled me back before I could cross the barrier. He literally threw himself on top of me and pinned me down by stabbing the sword through my shirt into the ground. Pili took a hit from one of the demons but got up and kept walking. Vicki spun the demon and threw him back into the black gash. "Damn it, Matty! Let me go!"

In a last-ditch effort, the warrior priest pulled away my headphones.

Shrieks and unearthly sounds that no person should hear assaulted my brain. But I could hear Matty's desperate voice clearly: "If you break that circle, Celia, we're *all* dead! Pili, Vicki, you, me, and an innocent child whose soul will become a *toy* to those things."

My hands were clawing at the dirt, mere inches from the barrier. I could feel the heat from the blue flame lick at my skin. I looked across to where I knew Beverly's circle was and it was now visible. The circle was broken. The greater demon was towering over the cowering child while the archbishop held him off with a cross that glowed like a star, inside a makeshift circle made from a Bible and sword crossed. I'd heard of that sort of circle before. It's not big, but supposedly it's pretty powerful. But it wouldn't hold forever.

I picked up the triton conch and fought back the sobs that wracked my body as I watched two people I loved walk to their death. It was hard to catch a deep enough breath to blow the horn, but I managed.

The sound reverberated through the circle and spread out like waves. Beverly looked up from where she was huddled on the ground, her green eyes wide and panicked.

I wanted to stand, to give my friends the dignity they deserved. Matty must have realized what I was doing, because he got off me and helped me to my feet. The young redhead stood as well, her head high—taking strength from me.

The greater demon abandoned her circle to fly toward mine at breakneck speed. He hit my circle and made the ground shake hard enough to knock Matty and me to the ground. The blue fire flickered and nearly went out. Before the demon could hit us again, I picked myself up and blew the horn once more.

That's when I noticed four bright points of light in the distance. They glowed with the strength of halogen flashlights. Two were golden and two were white. Matty noticed, too. He didn't abandon his prayer, just spread his arms wide to become a channel for John and Bruno. I could feel their energy flow into him and be made pure by the touch of his faith. The casting circle became white-hot light with golden edges that made the demon scream in pain.

To my extraordinary relief, I *didn't* scream in pain.

I blew for all I was worth and so did Beverly. I wanted to close my eyes so I didn't have to see Pili and Vicki, but they deserved to have me witness their courage. I watched the rift shift and shudder as the sound attacked it from both sides. The demon flew back and forth, hitting the barriers. Another priest fell and I tried not to listen as he died horribly but honorably—doing what he had sworn to do.

The ground began to shudder beneath us. I was nearly out of breath. It was taking everything I had to keep the sound going without pause. Finally a full-blown quake, a big, deep one, began to move through the earth and Matty and I were forced to kneel down to avoid falling over. The tornado that was Vicki waited for a long moment at the edge of the abyss, waiting for just the right moment. When it came, she threw herself forward, carrying Pili with her.

An explosion of sound and light made me reach for my headphones. But they weren't enough protection. The casting circles blew apart like so much sand. Even the outer barrier strained and bulged and finally collapsed as the entire world seemed to shudder. I tried to see past the light, but the brightness burned my skin, my face, my eyes.

My head couldn't take any more and everything went dark.

23

The doorbell rang. Or at least I thought it did. It was hard to hear over the bedlam in the living room. You couldn't ask for a more picture-perfect morning for the party. The rift had messed with the weather—maybe the only positive result of the whole disaster. The jet stream had shifted and there was a white Christmas in California. It would likely be gone by midday, but for now it wasn't an irony to play Bing Crosby on the stereo.

I made my way through the crowd only to get stopped by Mick and Molly Murphy before I'd made it two feet. They were smiling at each other in an excited way and turned that same energy to me. "Well, we talked it over. We're going to take it."

That brought a smile to my face. "Really? You're sure? I don't want to pressure you or anything. But Gran's got her place and I have mine, so I thought I'd at least offer."

Molly got a little teary and waved a hand in front of her face before answering: "It's perfect. Really. I already love this house. Just hearing the stories from your grandmother was enough to sell me, and the girls have already claimed rooms upstairs. There's a yard and it's in a good school district."

"And it's near the ocean," Mick added. "That never used to be an issue, but now . . . well—" He looked at Beverly, who was poking around under the tree with her sister, looking for what I might have bought them. And how could I *not* buy them something? "I presume she'll have to have some training on Serenity. We've already been invited to attend some seminars to teach us what she'll need to survive."

I nodded and put a hand on his arm as the bell sounded again. "Okay, we'll work out the details soon. Don't worry about the price. We'll come up with something fair."

As I left them to dissolve into the crowd, I felt another weight lift from my chest. Gran had really taken a liking to the Murphys, and she and I both felt that her house deserved to be enjoyed by a family again.

I only wish Vicki could have been here to see the snow. She'd always wondered what it would look like to see palm fronds covered in white. When I realized she was really, truly gone, I'd spent a day in bed, crying. Yes, I was happy she finally found her way to her just rewards. But I was going to miss her so very much.

Gran and I hadn't really talked yet about Pili's sacrifice, but I knew she needed to. I just wasn't sure I was the right person to help her through it. I got the impression from Dawna that Ahn and Pili had gotten together to tag-team Gran once Pili knew what needed to be done. Dawna suggested I not bring up Pili's death for a few weeks to see if the lessons they'd been trying to teach Gran had taken. She wasn't exactly sure what those lessons were, but she'd gotten the impression they were metaphysical rather than simple counseling. But it was hard to look at my grandmother and know she was in pain and be unable to help her.

My little piece of melancholy was dispelled when I opened the front door and discovered Bruno standing there with a smile and a gift. The scars on his face were nearly healed, which was amazing considering how bad he'd looked when the rift was sealed. I threw myself at him and planted a big kiss on his lips. "You came! I thought you were flying back to New York this morning."

He motioned back with his thumb toward a waiting Yellow Cab. "On my way to the airport. But I had to drop your gift by. You're sure you're okay with me going back?"

"What would a DeLuca Christmas be without fifty people in a house meant for ten? Of course you need to go. Please give Matty my best. How's his arm doing?"

"The doctor says the rotator cuff is torn. He'll have to have surgery, but they're confident of a successful repair. But you can ask him yourself pretty soon."

I gave Bruno a questioning look and he smiled. "He's been asked to take over as head of the seminary here as *Bishop* Matteo DeLuca. Mama is beside herself."

"Whoa. That's a big deal. I'd heard that Archbishop Fuentes was going to get bumped to cardinal, but a field promotion to bishop is sort of out of the ordinary, isn't it?"

Bruno nodded. "Very. But the Vatican felt if there was going to be another demonic event it would probably be here— sort of like aftershocks to a big quake. And they still haven't found all the inmates who might have been infested. Besides, he'll need a desk job until the arm's better anyway."

Too true. I looked at Bruno's gift again. "I don't have yours. I already shipped it to New York so you could open it at your mom's." Then I realized I was wrong. "Wait. I *do* have something." I reached into my pocket, where I'd thrust the item when Alex had given it to me. "It's not wrapped, but I want you to have it because you said you wanted to think."

I put the soft leather bag into his gloved hand, coiling the thin silver chain atop it. "What's this?" he asked, looking at me curiously.

"Siren charm. Then you'll know for sure that whatever you decide is just you." I touched his other hand. "And just me. The charm is specific to me. I asked the forensic witch where Alex works to make it up and the queen's mage approved it."

Bruno looked uncomfortable, but I didn't give him the chance to refuse. I put the chain around his neck and leaned in to give him a slow, soft kiss that gave me more shivers than the icy north wind. "I don't want you to have to question yourself. It'll take a few days to kick in and then we'll talk." I took the wrapped present from his hands and backed up a bit with a warm smile.

He picked up the small bag, which was trimmed with silver wire, and stared at it with more than a little worry in his face. Then I heard a familiar voice from behind him: "Hey, I recognize that charm. Got one just like it. Pity it doesn't work against kick-ass leggy blondes."

Creede was walking up the sidewalk, likewise carrying a gift.

"C'mon, you guys. You tell me to mail my gifts and then bring yours so I'm stuck looking like a cheapskate."

374 • CAT ADAMS

"Merry Christmas, Ceil. Guess DeLuca and I had the same idea, 'cause I'm on my way to the airport, too." He leaned in and pressed lips against mine warmly, causing Bruno to let out a small, possessive growl.

"I'll be back in a couple of weeks. Don't get too cozy with her."

Creede turned to look at him with eyes full of sparkling challenge. "It's a marathon, not a sprint. I'm in no hurry. Of course," he amended with a sly smile and a wink, "that doesn't mean I'm not willing to take advantage if you fall down on the job." He checked his watch and let out a small swear. "And speaking of jobs, how about we ride together to the airport? I've got something I want to discuss with you and I'm going to miss my flight if I don't get moving."

Bruno also looked at his wrist. "Shit! Is that the time? Sorry, Celie. Really gotta go. Tell your gran Merry Christmas for me. Be safe." He gave me a quick peck and so did Creede. As I watched them walk away together and start to move luggage from one cab to the other, I realized I didn't want to lose either one of them. But there wasn't any way to keep them both and have it be fair to any of us.

I opened the door slowly, letting the smells of roasting turkey and apple pie fill my nose. Before I went inside I heard another vehicle and turned to see a familiar car pulling up, one I'd been afraid wasn't going to make it. Sheesh. My place was turning into Grand Central Station.

Just how I like it.

Dawna got out of the car and let out a squeal of pleasure before running up the snowy sidewalk to give me a big hug, being careful to avoid the packages in my hands. "Merry Christmas!" The passenger door opened and Emma climbed out carrying an armload of packages.

Dawna pranced into the living room to give Gran a big holiday hug. She'd been spending the holiday with me and Gran for years because most of her family is Buddhist . . . which is why Ahn wasn't here. As Emma came up to me, I hugged her gently and quietly asked, "How are Kevin and Amy holding up?"

I could see the worry in her eyes as she answered, "Kevin's back at work at the university, but he's got a bunch of post-traumatic stress that we don't know how to help him with. He gets weird panic attacks from seemingly no cause. Someone at work suggested an assistance dog—one of the breeds sensitive to the demonic, like a hellhound." She sighed. "Amy is still pretty withdrawn. I think the taint is mostly gone, but I know what she's going through. It'll take time for her to feel normal again." She smiled then with genuine pleasure. "Thank you for inviting them to come today. I know you still haven't gotten over what they did to you, and I know they really appreciated the gesture. Father might stop by later."

"Christmas is a time for forgiveness. At least that's what they tell me." I forced myself to smile. I might never completely get over the betrayal by Warren and Kevin, but I'd try. For Emma. And for the past we'd all shared.

"Wow. A lot of people showed up!" Her smile grew broader as Gran gave her a peck on the cheek.

Finally Emma reached the couch and sat down. "I wish I didn't get tired so fast." She sighed. "It's the meds. They keep me calm, but they make me sleepy."

Dawna patted her hand. "You're getting around. That's what counts. We're in no hurry today, girlfriend. It's a day to take it easy." She looked at the tree and then dropped to her knees in front of it. I took in her red and white velour pantsuit and wondered if Dottie was having a bad influence on her. But I had to admit the pantsuit was stunning. It made Dawna look like a very tanned and fit Mrs. Claus.

"Wow. You must have had more presents delivered. I didn't see these yesterday." She picked the one out of my hand before I could stop her and opened the card. "Ooh! 'Merry Christmas, Ceil. *Love, John.*'"

I raised my brows at her teasing. "You can see full well that all he wrote was 'Ceil' and 'John.' The other words are pre-printed."

She refused to be denied and gave me her pretty pout. "He picked out the card."

I shook my head. "Doubtful. It's wrapped too well. Does that look like a guy wrapped it? That's a mall wrapping."

She started to shake it and I winced, leaping forward to take it away from her and put it carefully under the tree. "He gives things that explode, Dawna. I don't want Santa to find you up on the roof."

The girl must have some sort of radar, because next she pulled Bruno's. "They were *both* here and I missed them? That would have been something to watch." She eyed the box critically. "Now, I know Bruno wrapped this himself. Why do men use eight times more tape than necessary?"

I took that box away as well and moved it far from her. He had also been known to give things that go boom.

Bless 'em both.

"Ooh!" Dawna said when she spotted the one I thought I'd hidden behind the bookcase. Damn, she's got a good eye. It was a small bag filled with fluff. "'MC, Gaetano.' New player, ladies!" She looked at me and then skeptically at the bag. "Also kablooie?"

I shrugged, because I honestly didn't know. "He's a doctor—or at least a medic. I'm thinking not. But he's also a soldier."

She handed it to me and leaned forward to whisper, "Go on, then. Open it. First one is always the guest's pick." Well . . . I was sort of curious and I could always put it right back in the bag.

I was frankly a little nervous about opening Gaetano's gift. Surely he wouldn't make it too personal. Would he? We still hadn't even gone out on a date. The last I'd seen him was when he was pulling chunks of melted artifacts from my legs and chest.

I dug to the bottom of the bag and extracted a small, unwrapped box. I let out a little sigh of relief and actually brightened. "Cool!" I held up the box of emergency first-aid charm disks. "Look—two for broken legs and three for cuts up to an inch deep."

Dawna and Emma wisely didn't say a word at my exuberance. Only Gran was willing to comment: "That was very . . . thoughtful. Try not to need them, dear."

I put the box back in the bag and the bag back under the tree. As much as I wanted to open them and read the instructions, that would be rude. Gran patted my hand. "I need to get back to cooking. When you have a minute, maybe you could make up some ranch dressing for the salad?"

I nodded. "In a second, Gran. I promise." I leaned back against the chair and let the white noise settle over me. The cop contingent had gathered into a group around Alex and were talking shop. The Murphys were chatting with Adriana, Okalani, and Laka—who had apparently just popped in, because they hadn't been here moments ago. Dawna touched my hand and I looked over at her wearily.

"So . . . while everybody's busy, tell us about the boys. Is Bruno moving back?"

I nodded and smiled. "It'll be a few months, I think. He doesn't have a job yet, but I get the impression Creede wants to talk to him. They decided to ride to the airport together. I don't know what I think of that." Granted, they had worked together really well at the rift, but I could see a lot of potential problems, given their personalities.

"Speaking of Creede, how did the big lunch date go last week?"

I rolled my eyes. "He showed up at ten o'clock."

Emma let out a disgusted sound. "I *hate* it when guys do that. Your hair's in curlers and you probably just stepped out of the shower, huh?"

"Ten p.m.," I corrected.

Now their jaws dropped, which was exactly what mine had done. "Yeah. For a lunch date." I'd been beyond livid. "It was the third time in a row, and frankly, I let him have it."

"Damn straight, girl. Although, really . . . it was only the second. You canceled once."

Okay, fair point. But I raised a finger. "I did text him to let him know the client's game had gone into overtime. He didn't even go that far."

Both girls rolled their eyes and let out an exasperated breath on my behalf. "So what was the excuse?"

I shrugged. "Same as last time. He got busy. But I will admit he made up for it." I paused and glanced up to make sure Gran was still in the kitchen. Then I lowered my voice and leaned in toward them. "Moonlight cruise on his sailboat to San Diego and a four-course dinner in a private room at the Silver House Restaurant." I blew on my hand and then made polishing movements on the front of my sweater. They reacted like I thought they would.

"Damn. There's like a yearlong waiting list for even a regular reservation there." Dawna let out a slow breath. "It wins points, but does it win *ten hours late* of points?"

"No. But the back rub on the boat did." Oh my, had it won points because my back wasn't the only thing he'd rubbed. "But we're taking it slow. I think both of us are a little wary of each other right just now."

Dawna started to respond, but my head turned at the sound of a loud knock on the door. Had I missed another bell? I touched her hand. "Hold that thought."

I waved at Adriana, who was motioning me over. I pointed at the door and held up a hand. I did need to talk to her about some stuff, but I was still playing hostess.

"Merry Christm—" I swung open the door and my voice died in my throat. I recovered after a few seconds, but it was awkward. "Rizzoli? Um . . . Merry Christmas."

He wasn't on my invite list, and frankly, he looked like he'd just woken up. His voice was flat and without inflection: "Merry Christmas, Graves. Grab your badge. We have to go."

Badge? Go? Um . . . Maybe if I tried again, this time with a smile. I put on my best client smile and cocked my head a little. "Let's try that again. Merry Christmas, Rizzoli. Do you want to come in for a leisurely cup of coffee and a chat? Lots of cops here to talk shop with."

He let out a frustrated sound and slammed his fists down in the pockets of his trench coat. "No, what I *want* to do is to go back home and sit in the living room with my family, opening gifts. I was up until midnight assembling my son's first two-wheeler and had sort of hoped to see whether he liked it. But instead, I'm here and my wife is pissed beyond belief. So, if you'll just get your badge we can get this over with and both get back to our respective celebrations." He finally looked me up and down, as though assessing me. "What you have on is fine for this." He said it like it wouldn't be fine for other things.

What the hell?

"In case nobody gave you the memo, Rizzoli, I don't work for you."

One hand came out of the pocket and he leaned heavily on the side of my house. He looked inside, noticed all the local cops—some in and some out of uniform—and lowered his voice to a dangerous whisper: "Let me explain something, Graves. The notoriety you got for saving the world was both a good thing and a bad one—for *you*. You're seen as a threat to certain elements in the government. I've been keeping the heat off you and you haven't even known about it. But I'm getting

ridden like a pony at a kiddie party. Now, I can either *stop* doing it or keep doing it. Which would you prefer?"

Oh. I was liking the no media and no investigations. I'd
been sort of wondering why things had been so quiet. "It's that
important? To call you out on a holiday?"

"If they're not lying to me, you'll want to save snapshots
of the rift in your scrapbook as your last happy memory."
He paused. "Did I mention it's at double your regular rate? It
should only take a half hour or so."

Well, the month wasn't over and I did have bills to pay. The
party probably wouldn't miss me for a few minutes. I held
open the door. "C'mon in for a second. My badge is upstairs."
He came in but stayed carefully on the tiled entry. I bolted up
the stairs as Dawna called out behind me, "What's going on,
Celia?"

I grabbed the badge from the top of my jewelry box and
picked up my duffel. No sense going anywhere unarmed. I
headed down the stairs but made a sharp right turn before I
reached the door. "We don't have time for good-byes, Celia,"
Rizzoli snapped as I moved away from him.

Dawna's expression was somewhere between surprised and
angry. "Where are you going?"

I shrugged. "The usual. Bad people want to hurt good people
and Rizzoli wants me to throw myself into the line of fire."

She got up and walked to the door, putting her face right into
his. "It's *Christmas*, Mr. Federal Agent. See all the people?
We're having good cheer and high spirits."

"Yes, ma'am. I can see that. And if you'd like to see another
Christmas, I have to borrow Graves."

I was pretty sure he wasn't kidding. Just to be safe, I picked up the bag with the first-aid charm disks, then grabbed Bruno's and Creede's presents.

I was stuffing the boxes into my duffel as I joined Rizzoli, leaving my now-silent guests staring after me. He motioned toward the gifts. "What are those?"

"With any luck, they're things that'll keep me alive long enough to eat dried-out turkey later."

We could but hope.